"IT'S GREAT TO HAVE SYDNEY SLOANE, P.I., WITH HER GRITTY NEW YORK PIZZAZZ AND HUMOR, BACK ON A NEW CASE!"

Annette Meyers, author of *Murder: The Musical*

"CSI, c…

"Syd…

"S…

"Bang, ba…

I heard a scream, unc… me. The explosion felt like it lasted for minutes, but the truth is, just as quickly as it had occurred, it was over. When I peered out from behind the desk I saw that one of the arched windows facing Broadway was gone and the frame around it looked as if it had been chewed up by King Kong.

"Call the police," I told Kerry with a calm I didn't feel. I slowly neared the window, glass shards crunching under my boots, and looked down to see if anyone had been hurt. On the street below, about three dozen people had gathered and were stupidly peering up. Just a bunch of bewildered onlookers, their curiosity overwhelming the fact that they might be in danger.

I reached down, picked a tulip petal out of the debris and rolled it tightly between my thumb and index finger until it was nothing.

"THE WORLD NEEDS MORE HEROES LIKE SYDNEY SLOANE—AND MORE MYSTERY WRITERS LIKE RANDYE LORDON."

Tom Savage, author of *Precipice*

FATHER FORGIVE ME

RANDYE LORDON

AVON BOOKS NEW YORK

This is a work of fiction. Names, characters, places, and incidents either are the product of the author's imagination or are used fictitiously. Any resemblance to actual events, locales, organizations, or persons, living or dead, is entirely coincidental and beyond the intent of either the author or the publisher.

AVON BOOKS
A division of
The Hearst Corporation
1350 Avenue of the Americas
New York, New York 10019

Published by arrangement with the author
Visit our website at **http://AvonBooks.com**
Library of Congress Catalog Card Number: 96-95176
ISBN: 0-380-79165-X

First Avon Books Printing: May 1997

Printed in the U.S.A.

WCD 10 9 8 7 6 5 4 3 2 1

This book is dedicated to my three M's:

Maude, who taught me how to play with the truth,
Marla, who taught me how to play with words,
and
Mac, who taught me how to play.

FATHER FORGIVE ME

One

When I was five my mother's sister Sophie would pull me up on her lap and tell me in her rich, deep baritone, "It's not easy being a woman, Sinda. You'll understand when you get older, believe me." Thirty-five years later I can still remember the scent of her Crepe de Chine, the way her woolen suit scratched against my bare legs, the faint smell of tobacco on her breath. I can hear her voice as if it were yesterday, "It's not easy being a woman."

Sophie would then slide me off her lap, place a fifty-cent piece in my hand, and say, "The only advice I can give you, darling, is to save your pennies, be true to yourself, and trust as few people as possible."

Aunt Sophie's fifty-cent piece would go right into my rose-colored glass piggy bank, but her advice—to trust as few people as possible—was tucked away in the back of my mind. It's come in handy in my line of work. My name is Sydney Sloane, and I'm a private investigator.

Sophie's gone now, but every now and then her words come back to me in waves. Especially during the times when it's hard to be a woman, hard to be a person—times like this past winter. It's finally spring, and, like everything else in sight, I am beginning to thaw after a long hard winter.

It all started on December 9. It was a gray and cold Monday, and I was finishing up the paperwork for our most recent job; tracking down a fifteen-year-old runaway who had made it cross-country to San Francisco. I was pecking out on my computer the last depressing details of why she had bolted when my office door opened without warning.

Kerry Norman, our secretary, whose career as an actress is beginning to take root, came and planted herself in front of my desk.

"What do you want?" I asked as I reread the last of what I had written. *Debi Cullerson's father began sexually abusing her when she was three years old.* I pushed away from the computer and peered over my glasses. My head was still in the Mission district with a frightened, angry, and pregnant fifteen-year-old.

"I know you didn't want to be disturbed, but there's someone here to see you."

"I'm not in today," I said, without taking my eyes off the monitor. Kerry knew that a week earlier I had brought home the body of a child who ended her life because her life had been unbearable. I hadn't been able to make a difference. Hell, I couldn't even stop her from killing herself.

"What about Max?" I asked, motioning to my partner's office. "I really have to finish this." I turned back to the computer and pushed my glasses back up to the bridge of my nose. My glasses are a new addition in my life, and my girlfriend, Leslie, has observed that I often use them as a signal to state, "this conversation has come to a close." As a whole I see them as one of life's signs that I am getting old. My eyes burned as I stared at the computer screen.

Kerry cleared her throat. "I don't think so. Mrs. *Cullerson's* out there, and she wants to talk to you."

I took a deep breath and nodded. I then activated the screen saver to my computer so Joyce Cullerson wouldn't be able to read it, and followed Kerry back out to the outer office.

When I saw her pacing the reception area, Joyce lowered her eyes and gave the impression that she wanted to be invisible.

Oddly enough, so did I.

However, wishing didn't make it so. I ushered her into my office and closed the door.

"I'm sorry to come by without calling." Joyce Cullerson was a plain woman with straight, light brown hair, flat, almost colorless eyes, and a wide mouth. She stood in the center of the room looking as if she didn't know what to do next.

"Have a seat," I suggested, as I moved behind my desk.

"Thank you." Instead of sitting, though, she dropped her coat on the sofa, walked stiffly to the windows that face Broadway, and looked out onto the street.

I waited for Joyce to tell me why she was there.

It was several seconds before she finally mumbled, "I came to warn you about Tom." When she said her husband's name, her shoulders seemed to rise. She turned to face me and I could see her pain as clearly as the navy blue sweater, white oxford shirt, and blue jeans that she was wearing.

I arched a brow but said nothing.

"Ever since you brought Debi back, he's been in a rage. When he gets like this, there's no telling what he's likely to do." She winced as she sat carefully on the windowsill. It was clear that she needed to keep a distance between us.

"Are you all right?" I asked, more concerned about her than her message.

She let out a sarcastic laugh, like a sigh, and shook her head. "Oh, I'm great." She then buried her face in her hands and started crying.

Mrs. Cullerson had good reason to cry. When I finally found her daughter, Debi was living in the back of an abandoned building with two other runaways. I liked her right away. She knew her parents had hired me to find her, but I promised her I wouldn't bring her back if she didn't want to go. There were other options, I had assured her, other ways to make things right. After two days I'd convinced her to stay with me at the Fairmount. The day after she moved in, her father called, though we had all agreed that until Debi was ready, there would be no contact between her and her parents. I don't know what they said to one another, but by the time I realized what was happening, Debi had withdrawn into a thick silence. The only thing she would say was, "He'll never let go. Never." I had tried to get her to talk to me, to tell me what her father had said, but she was mute. Finally she told me that she needed some air, needed to go for a walk. I wanted to follow her, but knew I had to respect her privacy because no one else ever had. The air she took was on the roof of the hotel. She left a simple note before she sailed off the edge of the building: "It's not your fault, Sydney."

It struck me, as I watched Joyce sniffling across the room, that I didn't like her very much. I didn't like her, and I was angry at both of us for the miserable way in which we had failed Debi. Joyce had to know that Tom had been sexually abusing Debi for years, yet she chose not to take action against him, a decision that directly resulted in her daughter's death. As far as my own role in Debi's death? It is a blunder I will have to live with for the rest of my life.

"I'm sorry," she whispered.

I grabbed a few tissues from the box on my desk, crossed the room, and held them out to her.

"What for?" I asked.

"Coming here like this." She waved her hand in a helpless gesture. "Crying."

"Crying is probably the healthiest thing you can do at this point."

"I didn't think I had so many tears." She blew her nose gently and cleared her throat.

"There's a lot of ugliness in your life, Joyce. How come you never stopped it?" I surprised myself with how abrasively harsh the question sounded, but is there a delicate way to ask something like that? I turned and went back to my desk.

She looked frightened. "Stopped what?" she asked in a small voice.

"Tom. What he was doing to Debi."

Her eyes flashed with the hesitation that reads loud and clear: DENY. DENY. DENY. But there was no denial when Joyce shook her head, and asked, "Aside from killing him, how do you fight a man like Tom?"

"There are ways. She was your daughter," I said, well aware of the futile attempts people make daily to protect themselves from bullies and paranoid paramours.

"Do you think for one minute I don't feel as if I personally pushed her off that building?" Her voice cracked.

"I don't know what you feel," I answered honestly. "But you didn't come here for my opinions or my approval, did you?"

"No. I came here to warn you. Tom is convinced that you're the reason Debi killed herself. He wants revenge." Her eyes seemed to sparkle before she looked away and added, "I don't hold you responsible, Sydney. You have to know that. I blame Tom and myself, and that's it."

I wished I could share her take on it, but I didn't. I said nothing.

"Anyway, ever since last Wednesday, Tom's been swearing that he's going to even the score with you."

"And you think I should be worried about that?" I asked.

She gently pushed off from the windowsill and carefully walked to the desk, where she slowly alighted on the visitor's chair. "Oh yes. When Tom gets started on something he just won't let go of it. His mother was Sicilian. I always thought people were just being prejudiced when they said if a Sicilian's mad, they won't let go and it can make them crazy, but it's true. Believe me, Tom can be vindictive and mean." She crossed her right leg over her left with great difficulty.

"Did Tom do that to you?" I asked, feeling certain she was sporting some ugly bruises under her Banana Republic attire.

"He has a bad temper."

"I can give you the name of a place where they can help you."

She shook her head and looked remarkably peaceful. "I tried that before Debi was born. There's really nothing anyone can do. Except . . ." She raised her eyes to meet mine and seemed to be trying to tell me something telepathically.

"What?" I asked.

"Nothing." She sighed.

Being the youngest of three I long ago learned how not to play the *Have-I-got-something-to-tell-you-oh-never-mind* game that older siblings use to torment kid sisters and brothers. I shrugged as if to say, "Okey-dokey," which naturally brought her to the point.

"There's only one way to stop Tom."

"And that is . . ." I prompted her.

"To kill him."

I returned her gaze, never once taking my eyes off her. Neither of us spoke for what seemed to be an eternity.

"Why are you telling me this?" I finally asked.

"Tom plans to hurt you." She twisted the tissue in her hands.

"And do you know *how* he plans to hurt me?"

"No. But I honestly think the only way to stop him is to stop him." It was clear that Joyce Cullerson was serious and way out of her league.

"Are you telling me, Joyce, that you want me to kill your husband?" There. It was on the table.

She looked like a mouse caught in a maze surrounded with the scent of cheese. "I thought maybe if you knew someone . . ."

"To kill your husband," I enunciated clearly.

"Well, yes." She shifted her gaze to her lap, where her fingers were furiously shredding the tissue into bits.

I took a deep breath. "Do you realize that you could go to jail just for trying to hire someone to do that?"

"I can't live like this anymore." The color had long since faded from her face, and her features all seemed to blend into one another, but at that moment I was struck with how much she looked like her daughter. And I was reminded of a conversation identical to this in an abandoned house in San Francisco where a mattress on the floor had served as the sum total of home furnishings and a fifteen-year-old had insisted there was no future for her as long as her father was sharing the same planet.

"Murder is never a solution," I said feeling a little like Jack Webb on *Dragnet*.

"I think maybe sometimes it's the only solution," she whispered. "Tom and I have been married for seventeen years. For sixteen and a half years I have been afraid. Do you have any idea what that's like?"

"No. But I'm a private investigator, not a gun for hire. If you thought by being sympathetic to your situation that I would agree to kill Tom, you were wrong."

I was suddenly exhausted. I was also angry that she had thought I would agree to murder anyone. I considered asking her to leave the office, but I couldn't.

"Here." I scribbled down the name of an organization that helps women in her position. "These people can help you. Things are different now than they were fifteen years ago. Tom doesn't have to know where you are. You don't have to spend the rest of your life in jail because you couldn't think of another solution."

She balled the tattered tissue into her fist and nodded. "Yes, of course, you're right." She spoke to her lap. "This is my problem. I don't know why I brought it to you. I'm sorry."

"Don't be sorry. Just don't throw your life away because you're afraid of him."

She raised her thin eyebrows. "Well, at least now you know to watch out for him." She grabbed the arms of the chair and steadied herself as she rose painfully.

I stood and handed her the name and number of the women's crisis center. "Please call them. If you like, I can take you over there right now."

She looked at the paper, shoved it into her jeans pocket, and shook her head.

"You need help, Joyce. But you have to understand, I can't do what you ask."

"Maybe I'll go to this place later. I just need time to think." She held out her hand. "Thanks for taking the time. I appreciate it."

"Don't do anything foolish." I opened the office door.

She nodded. "Be careful. You don't know him. He really is crazy."

Two

"That is one sad lady," Kerry said when the front door closed behind Joyce Cullerson.

"She has good reason to be," I observed from my office doorway. "Max here?" I asked.

"Yeah, but he won't be for long. He has a lunch appointment with Beverly Tiari."

I groaned. "You've got to be joking." Beverly Tiari is a regular client of Max's whose paranoia has kept us afloat when things were slow. Everyone is out to get the moleish Miss Tiari, and she has the money to prove it. So far Max has investigated everyone on her co-op board, her last three boyfriends, and every single "servant" she's ever employed.

I knocked once and entered Max's office. Unlike my office which is airy and open, his is cozy, more like a library or a den. He was standing at his desk tossing darts at the picture of the month on his dart board: Oliver North.

"Busy as ever, I see." I waited for him to toss his final dart, then crossed the room and settled on his sofa.

"I'm thinking," he said as he retrieved the three darts he was tossing at Ollie.

"What about? Beverly Tiari?" I rolled my eyes as I stretched out on his blue-and-white-striped sofa.

"Why, now that you mention it, yes. She's convinced that her accountant is embezzling from her. This could be interesting.'' He shook his finger in the air as he took his place to shoot more darts.

''Oh God, Max. The woman's a nutcase.''

''That may be, but you have to consider cases like Ms. Tiari more of an afternoon's entertainment than a job. And yet, we get paid.'' Max squinted his left eye, aimed, and tossed a dart. Bull's-eye, right in the old nose.

''Think about it, every single person you've checked for her has been clean.''

''Thank God. Could you imagine what would happen if I ever got something on one of them?'' He pretended to shudder and tossed another dart. ''So how are you coming along with your report?''

''Oddly enough, I just had a visit from Debi Cullerson's mother.''

''No. Really?''

''Really. She wanted to hire me again.'' I kicked off my ankle-high cowboy boots and tucked my feet under me.

''To . . . ?'' Max asked as he threw the last dart. He didn't even look to see where it had landed. He stepped over the coffee table and took a seat at the other end of the sofa, his eyes never leaving my face.

''Kill her husband,'' I said almost casually.

He smiled in disbelief. ''Are you serious?''

''Unfortunately, yes. Apparently he blames me for Debi's death and wants to even the score. Ostensibly she was here to warn me to be careful, but then she finally got to the point.''

''Did you tell anyone?'' He meant the police.

''She just left two seconds ago.''

''*Are* you going to tell anyone?'' He pushed back his broad shoulders as if he was expecting an argument.

I shrugged. ''I'm hoping she'll drop the idea and take my suggestion to call a women's crisis center.''

''You think she will?''

''I don't know.'' I paused. ''You know, Max, I'm usually a sympathetic person, but I just don't like her.''

''Christ, Sydney, she let her daughter get pregnant by her husband.'' Though Max had never met the Cullersons, his contempt for them was unqualified.

I looked at my friend, but all I could see was Debi Cullerson lying on the pavement, broken and bloodied.

"How could she do it?" I asked, not knowing if I was talking about Debi or Joyce.

"I don't know. People dig themselves deeper and deeper into these situations until they feel immobile. My charitable guess is Mama Cullerson didn't think she *could* do anything. However, that's not the point now. Now the problem is twofold. First"—he linked an index finger around his pinkie to keep count—"do you think he really does have it out for you, and, if so, would he act on it? And secondly"—he added his ring finger to the link—"do you think she'll follow through with her plan to kill him?"

I shook my head. "I don't know. He looks harmless enough, but so did Gacy and Bundy and that little guy in New Jersey who murdered his entire family. So who the hell knows? I mean when I first met him I didn't think, 'Why this man looks like a pedophile and a wife beater.' " I held up my hands in bewilderment. "They are a normal-looking, average, middle-income, ordinary, flag-flying, American family. He could be crazy enough to try and hurt me, but he may not. He may have the ability to do something, but I don't know. As for her, she might actually seek assistance in killing him or—for all I know—this could be a scenario the two of them play out over and over again. I don't have a clue." I stopped and stared at my hands, which had fallen still in my lap.

"What?" Max asked softly.

"That's the problem. I just don't know." I looked up and was touched by the concern on Max's handsome face.

Max probably knows me better than anyone, expect maybe Caryn, an old love who now lives in Ireland. I could have used Caryn when I came back from California. She wouldn't have tried to make me feel better or less guilty. She wouldn't have coddled me or taken it personally when I couldn't respond to what was being offered. She would have simply packed a suitcase and taken us both out to the beach, a place where healing seems to come easier for me.

Max rubbed his stubble chin. It sounded like sandpaper. "You okay?" He asked, knowing that the answer would be negative.

"I used to be good at this, Max."

"You still are. Debi's death wasn't your fault."

"Tell that to my heart."

"I'm trying to." He moved next to me on the sofa and wrapped his big old arms around me. "You're a good person, Sydney. And a damned good investigator. I know how much this hurts, but now is the time you have to be as kind to yourself as you would be to me if I were in your shoes." His arms were warm and comforting.

"If you were in my shoes, it probably wouldn't have happened."

"Bullshit. Listen to me, Debi made a choice. She decided that it was better to end her life than to continue. It had nothing to do with you, except that you were there."

"Right." I pulled away from his embrace, slipped back into my boots, and stood up.

"No, no, no you don't. There was nothing you could have done—"

I cut him off loudly. "I should have been able to protect her. That's it. Period."

"Sydney, if it didn't happen then, it would have happened later. Sooner or later she would have found a way."

"I know," I shouted. And I did know. From the moment I met her, it was clear that this sad, pretty girl had no more desire to live than I had the desire to jump out of an airplane. "I know." I sighed. "But knowing doesn't seem to be making a bit of difference."

I went to the door that separates our offices. I was determined to finish the Cullerson report that day, if only for my own files. I turned back to Max and said, "I don't think I have anything to worry about with Cullerson. As far as Joyce is concerned, I'll call Gil." Gilbert Jackson is an old family friend and a hotshot on the police force. I figured I could pass this headache on to him and let him decide what to do about it.

"I'll be back after my meeting with Beverly. You want me to bring you some lunch?" he asked, still sitting on the couch.

"No, thanks. I'm not hungry."

"Sydney," he said, as I crossed the threshold into my office, "I won't let you blame yourself for this one."

"Okay," I replied as I gently closed the door between us and returned to my Macintosh computer. I suppose I was hoping that putting Debi Cullerson's last week of life on paper would give me a sense of clarity and order. Maybe, if I could see it on a piece of paper, then I would be able to let it go. Or maybe, what I really wanted was to hold on to it forever, to somehow keep her alive.

I spent the rest of the afternoon inputting every single detail I could recall regarding the Cullerson case—every note I had taken, all phone calls I had logged, all conversations I could remember.

Max had brought Kerry and me falafels after his meeting with Beverly Tiari, and though I hadn't thought I was hungry, I savored it. Is there anything more comforting than food? I don't think so.

At around three, Max left for Brooklyn. A new client, an Englishwoman, had given her car, a 1968 Volvo two-seater, to a mechanic to fix, and now both the car and the mechanic had disappeared. Max was headed out to find the two.

By four I was exhausted, but finished with the Cullersons. Getting it out of my head and into the computer, however, didn't make me feel any better. I walked to the windows and studied Broadway. On the street below a wiry little man stood bare-chested in the cold, begging for money from passersby. Each time someone gave him change, he bowed with gratitude. Directly across from our office is a sixplex movie house. I stood there trying to decide between vegging out for two hours at the movies or schlepping in the snow either downtown to Tina's Gym or uptown to the health club where I swim. Decisions, decisions. At Tina's I'd get a real workout and a chance to spend time with good, caring friends. At the health club I was anonymous and, during the winter months, the pool always seemed to have a free lane. The movies had absolutely no fitness benefit. It was just a dark place where I could eat popcorn and avoid thinking about my life for two hours. Over a tee shirt and thin black sweater, I slipped on a handmade sweater Caryn had sent from Ireland. During the winter months I like to layer my clothes and slowly peel them away as needed.

As I was getting into my leather jacket, Kerry came in. "What are you doing?" she asked.

"Leaving," I responded.

"You can't." She closed the door behind her.

"Sure I can. I'm going to the movies." I decided as I spoke. I liked the idea of sitting in a darkened movie house with a bag of popcorn and a box of Junior Mints. I remembered being ten years old and going to the Saturday matinees with my sister and her *friends*. The fact is, there were no friends. Nora would buy my silence with a box of Junior Mints and a large buttered popcorn and leave me alone in the first row of the balcony while she made out in the back row with Dickie Pontrelli.

Kerry neared me like a coconspirator. "You'll never guess what's out there." She jerked her thumb to the outer office.

"A space alien?"

"No, but close. A client."

It's true, we don't get many walk-in customers at CSI (Cabe-Sloane Investigations). It's not that kind of business. Most people call first and often prefer to meet us anywhere but here. Maybe there's an unwritten stigma attached to visiting a private investigator, or perhaps they like the cloak-and-dagger concept, but whatever the reason, most of our clients have us meet them outside these finely appointed walls.

"Well, don't look so surprised. Who is it?"

"A woman. She said she got your name through Leslie."

"Leslie?" I asked, with minor irritation, as I slid out of my jacket.

''Right, Leslie. Remember her? Your girlfriend? Tall, dark hair, blue eyes? I'm sure you remember her, she's a very nice girl.'' Kerry arched her perfectly tweezed eyebrows. ''This one's name is Vanessa Stephens, and, boy, is she a looker.''

''Looker?'' I glanced at her as if she had two heads. ''Let me guess, you're Velda and I'm Mike Hammer.''

''Wait till you see her. You'll know what I mean.'' With that Kerry slipped out of the office, leaving the door opened behind her.

''Ms. Sloane?'' Vanessa Stephens strode into the office with utter confidence. ''Thank you for taking the time to see me.'' She moved easily across the room and extended her hand. Her grasp was firm and the faint scent of her perfume was like a breath of spring.

''My pleasure. Why don't we sit down?'' I motioned to my desk and offered her one of the canvased chairs. I was tempted to have her take a seat on the sofa, but when I talk business, I prefer to keep a desk between me and my clients. In an odd way, distance is essential in this business. Someone hires a detective to get information they need about someone else, but it usually ends with the detective discovering their client's most profound secrets. And yet, distance is one of the most important tools of the trade. As with Impressionist art, the farther you move away from it, the clearer it becomes.

Vanessa Stephens took the seat closest to the door and crossed her legs. Kerry was right, our prospective client looked like a model. She was thirtyish, slender, with auburn hair, light brown eyes, and the most perfectly bow-shaped lips I have ever seen.

''What can I do for you, Ms. Stephens?''

She took a folded copy of the *Times* from her bag and placed it in front of me. A story had been circled with red ink. The headline read: Boy Found Dead at Pier.

''That's my brother,'' she said.

I read the brief story and thought of Debi. Two young kids who had both taken their own lives. When I looked up she was studying me. I took off my glasses and gave her an inquiring glance.

"He didn't kill himself. I want you to find out who did."

Knowing how badly I'd just botched my last investigation, I felt like stone. I sat there, with a million thoughts racing through my mind simultaneously, and finally said, "Why don't you tell me everything."

Three

Vanessa Stephens's story took close to an hour to tell. Having been raised in Texas, she *escaped* when she was seventeen and never looked back. ''My father was a difficult man.'' By the tone of her voice and the arch of her brow, it was clear she meant to convey that he was far more than just difficult. But still, I asked, ''How difficult?''

''He was what most people would call tyrannical. Dad runs his family the same way he runs his business. He expects total submission and deference.''

''Does he get it?''

''Yes. At least from his wife and employees. Certainly not from me, or my brother, Peter, which is probably why he hated us. The day they dropped me off at college was the last time I saw them.''

''Why was that?''

''Aside from the fact that we hated each other? Wallace would never have let me live my own life. By the time I was fifteen I knew the only way to survive was going to be on my own. I mean, I loved my mom, but I didn't want to wind up like her. So I did the only thing I could think of—I skipped out as soon as I had the chance'' She loosened the silk scarf around her neck and shifted in her seat.

Vanessa Stephens didn't look like she had been a runaway. I always think of these kids turning to drugs and prostitution, hard times fueled by loneliness, fear, and rage. Vanessa had come to New York with her meager life savings, found an apartment, enrolled in school and waited on tables to pay the rent. Now she sat across from me wearing designer clothes, expensive perfume, and an air of confidence to which I was immediately drawn.

I, on the other hand, was a walking advertisement for the Gap: faded jeans, white tee shirt, black sweater, black boots. My sister Nora says that I don't dress like a real adult, but her concept of adult apparel is polyester-blend monogrammed jogging suits—the thought of which makes me cringe.

As Vanessa talked about Peter, there was no mistaking the love she had for her baby brother. It reminded me of my dad and his sister, my aunt Minnie. The two of them had been the best of friends throughout their adulthood.

I reread the article. Peter had been found on the pier the day before. Evidence of a drug overdose was pointedly clear, from the needle still sticking into his vein to a fresh packet of heroin in his pocket. The paper reported that the Coroner's Office had listed the death accidental—which is standard in such cases—but the article went on to list three previous suicides of teenagers during the last few months, implying that this last death was also a suicide.

"Did your brother live here?" I asked.

"No. He lived with our parents. They were here on a business trip. My father is Wallace Long, have you heard of him?"

Wallace Long was LongTec, one of the biggest computer companies in the industry. He had been in the papers recently not because of his business, but because of his bid to enter the political arena. He was being presented to the public as the new hope for the future, a down-to-earth self-made man who had his finger on the pulse of Middle America. I told her I knew of him.

"Well, they're here fund-raising. Wallace thinks that he can change the world. My guess is, he just wants to control it." Her face clouded over.

"Just like any politician, I suppose." I toss politicians

and real estate brokers into the same basket: people who know how to stretch the truth to get their way.

"Believe me, Mario Cuomo he ain't." She said this with more than a hint of contempt.

"Tell me about Peter. Did you see him on this trip?"

She shook her head. "No. We were going to get together Sunday."

"But you didn't?"

"No."

"Why?"

"He died Saturday night, early Sunday morning."

"I see. Do you know if he ever took drugs?" I asked.

"No, never." She answered before the question was out of my mouth.

"You seem pretty certain of that."

"I am."

"So you and your brother were close?"

"Very."

I wondered how that was possible, given that she had left when he was so young. "You spent a lot of time together?" I asked.

She paused. "Not exactly."

"What does that mean?"

"After I left home, I made certain that my folks wouldn't find me. But Pete and I kept in touch. We each had a post-office box where we would write to each other every day."

I shifted in my chair and picked up a pencil. I began to doodle musical notes. "Peter was nineteen, right?" I asked as I swirled a treble clef onto the page.

"Twenty. He just turned twenty last month."

"And you were seventeen when you left home?"

"That's right."

"So, that means Peter was how old when you left?"

She stared at me for a long time before answering.

"I'm twenty-eight. He was nine."

"And you both had a post-office box? Was that recent?"

"No." She popped the knuckles on her right hand, and explained, "My mother's sister and I have always been close. She knows what it was like growing up with

Wallace. She used to tell me what Mom was like before she married him, before she just gave up and started drinking. Sarah, that's my aunt, has always been supportive of both Pete and me, but she knew she couldn't interfere on the home front.

"Anyway, before I left home I confided in Sarah. I told her what I planned to do, and she offered to help me. She knew how worried I was about Pete. She promised me that I would be able to keep in touch with him: swore that we wouldn't lose contact with one another. Sarah always keeps her word. She never told Mom, but she was the one who arranged for the post-office box for Pete."

"And Peter never told your parents about this arrangement?" I drew the face of a man with a mustache from whose opened mouth a series of musical notes flew.

"Never." She shook her head.

"Even when he was nine?"

"Sydney, our parents are not the sort of people you confide in; we both learned that at a very young age."

"So tell me about your communications with Peter."

She stared at my desk top before getting up and crossing to the windows that face the street rather than the avenue. Spider plants, coleus, poinsettias, and cyclamen lined the windowsill. She gently rubbed a cyclamen petal between her fingers and looked down onto the block between West End and Broadway. My eyes went past Vanessa to the buildings across the street. On winter days like these, when it's gray, and dingy snow still covers window ledges, those old buildings remind me of Jack Finney's book, *Time and Again*, the ultimate New York time travelogue. I was brought swiftly back to the twentieth century when Vanessa continued, keeping her back to me.

"I have boxes of Pete's letters. I haven't thrown out a single one. I'd be happy to show them to you. I was, essentially, his journal, his diary. He knew he couldn't keep one in the house because Wallace would find it and use it against him—that's his style. Everything's about him, everyone's out to betray him. It was especially hard for Pete after I left.'' She turned back to me, her face sad and hard. ''I knew it would be. I almost didn't leave because I knew how hard it would be on him, but I had to. The only way I could help Pete was if I established myself somewhere far away from them, someplace he could go when he was old enough.''

''But he didn't,'' I said.

''Well not yet, but he planned on it.'' She sighed. ''You see, he and Wallace had an agreement. Pete felt as if he sold his soul to the devil, but he'd agreed to see it through college there, and that's what he planned to do.''

''Sold his soul?'' I asked.

''Basically, Wallace bribed Pete to finish his education there and give him some time at LongTec,'' she noted with disdain, but it seemed to me a fairly common trade-off between parents and children. I'll pay for college, you work for the family business.

''So this bothered your brother?'' I asked.

''Yes it did. But he was, as I said, resigned to the agreement he'd made.''

''Forgive me,'' I said as gently as I could, ''but everything you've said so far points to a situation where a kid like your brother just might take his own life.'' A broken body sprawled on the pavement flashed in my mind's eye. ''There was a sense of helplessness, self-doubt, resentment.'' I paused, knowing I was describing Debi Cullerson as well as Peter Long. ''Kids faced with that often choose to end it rather than resist it. You said yourself that he felt as if he'd sold his soul to the devil.''

She put her hands in her pants pockets and moved closer to the desk. ''My brother didn't kill himself. You have to trust me on that.''

I did. There was no question for me that this woman truly believed her brother had nothing to do with the ending of his life. I wasn't as certain as she that that was so, but she was asking me to find the answers, which is what I do for a living.

''Can you think of anyone who would want your brother dead?''

Her eyes were remarkable: I could actually see her

thought process through them. After a moment or two she shook her head, and said, "I don't know. I hate Wallace, but I can't imagine he would want to see Pete dead. Then again, I just don't know."

"Can you think of a *reason* why Wallace would want Peter dead?"

She exhaled a sad laugh. "Well, let's see." She returned to where she had been sitting and eased herself back down on the chair. She linked her fingers together and took a deep breath. "Pete wasn't the macho guy Wallace expected a son of his should be. Apparently this caused a lot of friction between them. My brother liked to read and paint, he loved museums and sailing. He wasn't a jock."

"Was he gay?"

She held her hands out, palms up. "He was dating a woman, but I don't think he knew what he was. He was only twenty." Her voice sounded both pleading and compassionate. "I don't think most of us know who we are at twenty."

"That's true enough," I agreed. At twenty I had just left college to join the police academy. I knew I wanted to be a cop, but I didn't have a clue as to who I was as a sexual being. I was dating a guy named Bud who was studying engineering at Columbia University, where we met.

"Well, Ms. Stephens—"

"Call me Vanessa."

"Vanessa. I'll see what I can do to help you, but you have to understand, you may not like what we find."

She nodded.

"Well then," I said pulling out a fresh piece of paper, "let's get to work."

And so, as the sky darkened outside on an early-winter evening, Vanessa Stephens and I began the journey that would take us places we couldn't have ever predicted.

Four

It didn't take long to get enough information to start the investigation. Vanessa didn't know where her parents—whom she annoyingly kept referring to as the Longs—were staying, but that information would be easy enough to get. Peter's best friend, Brendan Mayer, lived in New York and had seen Peter on Friday, the day before he died. Vanessa had Brendan's phone number and address as well as their aunt Sarah's number, and Peter's girlfriend's name and number. That, along with a detailed description of who Peter was, as Vanessa knew him, gave me a solid springboard.

By the time she left, there were hordes of moviegoers waiting in the cold to see one of the four movies being offered in the six theaters, so I decided to skip it and head home.

After close to a year together, Leslie and I had established a routine during the last few months where we spent at least five nights a week together, usually at my apartment. But that had recently changed. As I shut down the office, I tried not to think where Leslie was at that very moment. She was, I knew, on a date. Where and with whom was a mystery, and one I didn't feel much like solving.

My apartment is ten blocks, or half a mile, from the office. As I walked against the wind, my face tucked into a scarf, I kept replaying my last conversation with

Leslie. My line of work has always been a problem for her, but this last go-round with Debi Cullerson had done her in. When I returned from California, Leslie thought she could provide the balm that would heal my wounds, but the psyche doesn't necessarily work in such a neat little package. When I came home from the West Coast, I needed time to lick my own wounds, but she didn't understand that. When I couldn't respond to her nurturing, she took it as a personal affront. Unable to determine my own needs, I could hardly answer hers, and we found ourselves, once again, battling over what I do for a living.

"You should know I'm going out tomorrow night." She had said this with her arms crossed protectively over her chest while leaning against the doorframe to my bathroom.

I had looked at her reflection in the bathroom mirror. "Okay." I dried my face with a forest green towel and asked the reflection, "Are you telling me you're going out with a friend or on a date?"

At this point she pushed off from the doorframe and wandered into the bedroom. When she answered her back was to me, and the words were lost in a mumble.

"I'm sorry, I missed that," I said, tightening the belt to my robe around my waist.

"A date." She swung around defiantly and tucked her fingers into the back pockets of her jeans.

I loosened the belt and pulled the collar up around my neck. We stared at one another for the longest time without saying a word, then I nodded. What could I say? If this was her way of dealing with our relationship, then I supposed we both had a lot to think about.

"I'm tired. I'm going to bed," I said.

"That's it?" she said, stunned.

"What did you want, Leslie? For me to rant and rave? I can't do that right now. I just don't have it in me. The last week has knocked the wind out of me and—"

"Which is why your work—" She tried to cut me off, but I kept talking above her.

"And I'm sorry if I haven't been able to give you what you need, but if you feel you have to start dating either to get even or move on with your life, then go right ahead. But let's get one thing really clear: this is *not* about my work.'' By now I was angry. I was also tired of her hating what I do for a living. ''This is about how *you* choose to work in a relationship. Now I'm tired, I'm angry, I'm hurt, and I'm not about to cater to your need to be coddled and cooed. You want to date? Date. But I suggest you get your beauty rest for it in your own bed.''

I replayed the scene in my head as I passed fellow upper west–siders en route to dinner dates and Christmas shopping, cappuccino at Starbucks and shopping for supper at the host of Korean markets along the way. The wind was bitter, and the thought of home was comforting.

Unlike most of my friends who have been transplanted to New York from other places, I was born and raised not only in the city but in the same apartment in which I now live. The laws in New York are such that with rent-controlled apartments the apartment can stay in the family for as long as there is a family. Mom and Dad moved into this West End Avenue apartment when my brother David was born, back in 1949 and we've held the lease ever since. When my father died in 1980 I renovated and moved back into the apartment with my then lover, Caryn.

Most of my life has been played out between these walls. I had thought when I moved back into the apartment that I would dispel the memories of my past by changing the configuration of the apartment, but it doesn't work that way. And, after close to a dozen years, I've discovered that that's okay. There were a lot of good memories created here.

After having been asked to kill a man in cold blood, it was good to return home, to a safe place. I'm like a big old oak tree when it comes to home and hearth, no matter where home has been; I set my roots down deep and get nurturing from the place in which I live. On a cold winter night, when the world beyond my windows is black and uninviting, I feel embraced by my home. Tonight was no exception.

I ran a tub of hot water with juniperberry oil, slipped into a big terry robe, and opened a bottle of Coltibuono Chianti.

I brought a glass of wine with me to the bathroom and settled into the tub with Ursula Hegi's *Floating in My Mother's Palm*, a book about growing up in postwar Germany. As I soaked in the warm water I read the section where she describes learning how to swim, actually floating in her mother's palms, and I was transported back to the time when my father taught me how to swim. There was a lake in upstate New York. It was summer. I couldn't have been more than three. I was frightened, but knew that because I was with my dad nothing bad could happen to me. By the end of the day I was showing off shouting, "Watch me! Watch me!" as I jumped off the dock and dog-paddled around and around in circles.

I put the book on the floor and shut my eyes, trying to recall if there had ever been a time when I was afraid, truly afraid, as a child. Debi Cullerson had told me what it was like when she was not yet four and her father would tuck her in at night. "I hated nighttime," she had told me. "It meant I had to do things to Dad that were gross. He'd tell Mom that he wanted to put me to bed, and then he'd start touching me. He kept telling me how much he loved me and that I was his little girl and then he'd lie down next to me and start rubbing his thing against my leg until he got hard. I didn't know what the hell was going on, but I was so scared. Then one night he stood next to my bed and told me that he had a present for me." Debi had bitten her nails as she confided to me how her father had told her he had a new candy for her and she'd like it once she got used to the different flavor. "He said, 'It's a lollipop. It tastes different at first, but you'll like it, I promise.' Motherfucker always lied to me. God I hate that son of a bitch. I wish he was dead."

But Tom Cullerson wasn't dead. Instead his beautiful fifteen-year-old daughter was beginning the rotting process in a grave in New Jersey.

My dad, Nathan, was the antithesis of men like Cullerson; he was a good, strong, honest, generous man who knew the fine art of loving without placing expectations on those he loved. He gave of himself without hesitation, which ultimately caused his death. It was spring, and he was representing a woman in a divorce/custody battle. The woman's husband had come to court with the intention of killing his wife. Instead the bullet shattered my father's chest and ripped his heart apart. He was dead before he hit the floor. Dad had seen the gun and thrown himself between the man and his wife. I know he did this without a thought; it was his natural instinct to protect.

I was angry at him for months after his death. But his legacy lingers on inside me, for which I have been alternately grateful and chagrined. The older I get, the more comfortable I am with the lessons I learned as his daughter, but there was a time when I struggled with his concept of how things ought to be. After all, it killed him and left me without my best friend. I still feel the gap created by his death and wonder what if, what if Dad had ducked instead? At sixty he was too young to be taken from me. There was still so much to learn.

I don't know when the water turned cold, but I was suddenly aware that I was chilled and my wineglass was empty. I needed to be indulged and warmed, so I covered my body with Neutrogena sesame oil, wrapped myself back into my robe, draped a towel around my neck, and brought another towel to wrap around my feet. I went to the den, where I lit a fire in the small fireplace, lay on the sofa with a fresh glass of wine, tucked the towel around my feet, and pulled the phone onto my lap. I dialed the number Vanessa had given me for Peter's girlfriend, Nancy Albus. There was no answer. There was no answering machine. I wondered how a young woman in the twentieth century could live without a tool that most New Yorkers (at least) find as essential as a refrigerator or television.

Television. The idea of blocking out the corporeal world was inviting. I unplugged the phone and, with the remote control, clicked on the television. After a good twenty minutes of channel changing I found *It's a Won-*

derful Life with Jimmy Stewart and Donna Reed. I must have seen the movie eight dozen times before, but I needed fantasy right then. I needed to remember that not all men are sick like Tom Cullerson or controlling like Wallace Long. I needed a movie about a good man who loves his children and wants to make this world a safe place for them. Ah, Jimmy.

Partway through the film the doorbell rang. I had half a mind not to answer it, thinking that it might be Leslie, but she has a key and could have let herself in without my help.

To my surprise it was Max.

"What are you doing here?" I asked as he stood in the doorway with a filled grocery bag and rosy red cheeks.

"It's freezing out there," he said as he stepped inside. "I've been trying to call you guys for over an hour. Something's wrong with your phone."

"I unplugged it," I said as I followed him through the hallway and into the kitchen.

He stopped short and looked hesitant. "Am I interrupting anything?"

"No. *It's a Wonderful Life* was on TV." I watched as he started to unpack his bag of groceries. "What are you doing?"

"What does it look like I'm doing? I'm making dinner." He took off his big down jacket, draped it over a kitchen chair, and nodded at me. "You forgot, right? Or is this how you dress for all your dinner guests?"

"I must have forgotten, because I don't know what the hell you're doing here." The wooden floor was cold against my bare feet.

"Last week Leslie and I made a date for me to make dinner tonight. Didn't she tell you? Where is she?" He started past me into the living room.

I turned, and said, "She's not here."

"Not here?" He stopped halfway into the room and came back. "Where is she? I made chicken pot pie. And endive salad with walnuts and pears; I even bought a tart from Bontè." He was back at the kitchen counter removing the items from his bag of goodies.

"She's out on a date."

"Oh right, that's a good one." He laughed. "You're joking, right?" He held a pear in his hand and looked at me. Clearly, I wasn't joking. "Why didn't you tell me?"

"What's to tell? She doesn't like my line of work. She thinks it's too dangerous."

"Christ, driving a taxi's more dangerous."

"Don't think I haven't told her that." I looked down at my hands. On my right hand I was wearing a silver-and-sapphire ring she had given me for my birthday.

"Jeez, you've been through the mill lately, haven't you?" He put the pear on the counter and caught it before it rolled off onto the floor.

"Well you know what they say about mills."

"What?"

I stumped myself. *Mills*, I thought. *Donna Mills, the Mills Brothers, gin mill, one in a million*... I finally shrugged. "I don't know, something about all the shit being mist for the grill."

"Seriously, Syd, why didn't you tell me?" Max didn't try to hide the hurt in his voice.

"I couldn't. Between Debi and Leslie, it's all just gotten crammed down inside me. I'm afraid if I let it out, I'll just explode."

"There's nothing wrong with a good explosion every now and then." He took a deep breath, and, with renewed vigor, said, "Well, I'm here and I'm hungry. Did you eat yet?"

"No."

"Then go put on some clothes and by the time you get back, dinner will be served." He cocked his head to the side like a puppy and asked, "Okay?"

"Good. I'm starving. There's some nice wine on the counter," I called out as I went to change.

By the time I came back, wearing sweats and warm slippers, Max had the pie in the oven, another bottle of wine breathing, and a fresh glass poured for me. He motioned for me to take a seat at the kitchen counter while he tended to dinner.

"Good wine," he observed, wiping his hands on a

dishcloth tucked into the waistband of his slacks. "So, you wanna talk about it?"

"No, not especially." I leaned onto the counter and said, "You know how you felt after the Miller kid drowned?"

"Yeah." He cut off the end of the endive and separated the leaves.

"Well that's how I feel about Debi, only maybe more so, because I feel responsible for what happened to her. Anyway, when I came home I just wanted to keep my own counsel for a while, you know what I mean?"

"Sure. As I recall after Miller I left town for a week."

"That's right, you did. Well, Leslie doesn't get it. She thinks I'm rejecting her because I can't take what she wants to give me. That's all. And she's never liked what I do." I shrugged. "Now, I may not be any *good* at what I do—"

"Stop the bullshit," he warned me.

"But it's *what* I do, and I'm not going to stop just to satisfy her. Which is why"—I waved Vanessa Stephen's deposit check in the air—"we have a new client as of four this afternoon. A client who—oddly enough—came to us through Leslie."

"Ah-ha," Max said, rinsing off the endive and drying it with paper towels. "Tell me about it."

"Well her name is Vanessa Stephens, and her brother, Peter, was the kid who was found at the pier yesterday. Did you read about that?"

"No."

"Wait a minute." I got up and went into the living room, where I had left that day's *Times* untouched. I opened the Metro section, found the story, and gave it to Max to read.

As he read the article, I set the table. The chicken potpie smelled like heaven, and I realized that all I'd eaten that day was the falafel he'd brought in for lunch.

"How do you know this was her brother? All it says is a body was found." He put the paper down and rummaged through the refrigerator for salad dressing. "This good?" He held up a jam jar and shook the contents.

"Red wine vinaigrette. It's fine." I took the bread he'd brought and put it on the table.

"So how do you know it's her brother?"

"She says it is." It was as unprofessional a response as I could have given, and we both knew it. Max had the good grace to let it pass without comment, and I hurried on, not wanting to pause too long on my growing list of mistakes, but the list, I knew, was growing. "I figure tomorrow we'll start checking everything. First we'll get a positive ID, both on Peter and Vanessa. Also, she gave me a few names and numbers to start with."

"Okay." He sprinkled dressing on the salad and passed the bowl to me. "So, go on."

"So she doesn't think he killed himself." I put the salad on the table and lit the candles.

"Why?"

"She said he wasn't that kind of kid."

He gave me a doubtful look as he took the potpie out of the oven.

"I know, but the fact is she doesn't think he did, and I believe she's sincere." I inhaled and practically drooled. I took the wine off the counter and brought it to the table.

"So she thinks someone killed her brother." Max set the pot pie on a trivet and took his seat.

I nodded and waited for the chef to serve up the grub.

"Does she have an idea as to who would want him dead?"

"Well, their daddy—who just happens to be Wallace Long—heads the list of not-nice guys. She can't imagine that he would want to see his own son dead, but that's the only one she even alluded to."

"Long of LongTec, computer king who's running for governor of his fine state?"

"That's right."

"I see." He spooned out a heaping helping for each of us and held up his glass in toast. "Well, to friendship, love, and good food."

"I'll drink to that." Which I did. And then I tasted his famous chicken pot pie. It practically melted in my mouth. I moaned with pleasure as I let the world's finest comfort food do its trick. Within mouthfuls I was feeling warmed and cozy from inside. A sense that all was right with the world may have been fleeting, but it was lovely.

After several moments of silence while we both pigged out, I finally said, "You know, I was thinking before, everywhere I look lately I'm seeing miserable kids. I mean, truly, deeply unhappy children. Every time you pick up a paper there's another story about some innocent kid who by the age of four has suffered such abuse that their death seems to be a blessing. Or you have kids like Debi Cullerson or this Peter, who have decided to take their own lives. Christ, Max, they haven't even begun to live."

"I know." He nodded and wiped his mouth. "Listen, I don't want you to take this wrong, but I know you, and I worry that you might confuse what happened to Debi with other issues." He checked me out to see if I was closing off. I wasn't. He was right. It would be a natural reaction for me to try and right an old wrong by making up for it in the next similar situation.

I speared a big chunk of chicken with a parsnip and nodded. "The fact is, I've accepted her as a client so I guess any discussion about my working off guilt is academic at this point."

"I fear for this. So." He broke off the heel of the bread and dunked it in the cream sauce. "Tell me everything you know."

And I did. It wasn't much, but it took us through dinner. By the time we were ready for coffee and apple tart in the den by the fire, we agreed that I would start the Long case and keep him apprised, as we had three other things we were working on at the time.

"What happened in Brooklyn?" I asked, regarding the Englishwoman's missing mechanic and car.

"Well," he said, putting his feet up on the coffee table, "this guy Carlos, he's the mechanic? He's garbage. And he's slick. When I got to his place in Brooklyn, it was shut down. So then I went to see Marcy and had her run a check on him." Marcy, Max's number one girlfriend—and my personal favorite—is a police officer who often helps us gather information. "This

Carlos hasn't been licensed once, not once. He sets up a business and as soon as his customers get wise and start complaining, he closes up shop, moves and starts all over somewhere else. The DMV has a list of complaints against him like you wouldn't believe."

"So?" The coffee—a present from Kerry from one of the new bumper crop of coffeehouses—was delicious. I handed Max some, along with a large helping of the tart.

"So it's going to take longer than I thought." He balanced the coffee on the arm of the sofa and started in on the tart.

I sank back into the pillows of the sofa and stared at the fire. "I keep thinking about this Tom Cullerson."

"You worried?"

"No. It's not that. I don't understand how a man could do that to his daughter. I'm not naive, I know it goes on all the time, but it makes me sick. Naturally I keep thinking about my dad and how good he was. I mean he was my hero."

"Your dad was a rare and wonderful man."

"You know, I still cry sometimes because I miss him."

"Me, too." He finished his dessert, put the plate on the cushion between us, and took my hand. "I had a hero when I was growing up." He took a sip of coffee.

"You did? Who?"

"Gene Autry. God, I loved him."

"Speaking of which, when are you going to Montana?" Every year Max and his friend, Jed, take a week to play cowboys. They fly out to Montana, rent a couple of horses, and spend a week roughing it in the woods with nothing but each other and their four-legged pals.

"In May. I've already made arrangements." His smile revealed the little boy inside the man, which is one of the things I like best about Max; he's not afraid to be a kid.

When Max left, a light snow had started to fall. There's nothing quite so magical as New York City under a blanket of fresh snow. All the dirt and litter is hidden under pristine white flakes and the illusion of order and cleanliness lulls most of us into forgetting, if only for a moment, that under the beauty there still lies the garbage.

Five

That night my dreams were infused with images of Leslie and Vanessa Stephens making love, Debi Cullerson lying bloodied on the bed beside them, and dead children hanging from rafters. All in all not a pleasant night's sleep.

I was up early and after twenty minutes of yoga and forty-five minutes in the pool at the nearby health club, I dragged myself to CSI feeling leadened, both physically and emotionally.

I arrived at the office at eight-thirty, before either Max or Kerry, which meant I would have at least an hour of solitude.

I took out the three names Vanessa Stephens had given me. Peter's best friend, Brendan Mayer, had moved to New York as soon as they were graduated from high school. He now lived in Manhattan, in the thirties on the east side. I called the number Vanessa had given me, but there was no answer, so I left a message on his machine asking him to call me regarding Peter.

Next was Aunt Sarah. I put her name and number off to the side to call at a later date, should I need it. Again I tried Peter's girlfriend, Nancy Albus, and again there was no answer. I checked my watch. It was almost nine o'clock in New York, which meant it was seven in Texas. Busy lady.

Last on my list to call was Gil Jackson. I had forgotten

to call him the day before regarding the Cullersons. Now, needing information on Peter Long's death, I could kill two birds with one stone—or boulder—considering it was Gil I was calling.

"Jackson." He snapped into the phone with his usual finesse.

"Hi, Gil. Sydney. You busy?"

"Me busy? Naah," he said sarcastically. "I'm just working on a watercolor until they find something for me to do here." There was a heated conversation going on in his office. He told me to hang on, put his hand over the mouthpiece, and yelled at the combatants to "Get the hell outta my office. I got an important call here. Go on, move it."

I could just picture my dad's best friend shooing everyone out of his office so he could take a call from me; his hound-dog face etched with impatience, but his brown eyes soft.

"Now what the hell do you want?" he asked roughly.

"Know anything about this kid who was found on the pier?" I asked casually.

"The suicide?"

"Yeah, that one. You got an ID on him?"

"Why?" he asked warily.

"I've been hired to find out how he *really* died."

"By whom?"

"Un-un, first you tell me if you have a positive ID on him, then I'll tell you who my client is." I could hear Gil unwrap a piece of gum and noisily start to chew it in the mouthpiece. "Jesus, Gil, you sound like a cow." Ever since he gave up smoking, Gil chews—and swallows—three packs of Juicy Fruit a day.

"Sorry." He continued chewing. "Kid's name is Peter something. I forget exactly."

"Really?" I asked, knowing perfectly well that he was holding back. "Does the name Long ring a bell?" I prompted him.

He sighed. "How did you know?"

"His sister hired me. She's convinced he didn't kill himself."

"I don't know, kid. I didn't see the body, but the

word is he had enough shit inside him to kill a horse. No sign of a struggle, nothing. Apparently he went to the pier, sat down at the end of it facing the water, shot up, and died before he could even remove the needle. Must have been cold. The wind whips off there like a son of a bitch."

"Is he Wallace Long's son?"

Gil paused. "Yeah," he exhaled, sounding a little like his old sheepdog, Waldo. "The family wants to try and keep this as quiet as possible."

"Isn't one of Long's pet causes to be stricter with crime?"

"Yeah, but the family doesn't want the media ramming cameras into their faces. Apparently they're broken up over this. Hell, who wouldn't be? It was their son . . ." He trailed off, thinking, I knew, about his daughter Bonnie's recent miscarriage, which had hit him so hard. More than anything, Gil wanted to be a grandfather.

"His sister doesn't think it was suicide. She's hired us to find out what really happened. Can you help?"

"The case is closed," he said formally.

"Excuse me?" I wasn't sure what he meant by that.

"Officially the case is closed. Given that it was Long's son, the higher-ups rushed their investigation, the autopsy verified the cause of death was overdose, the manner, accidental. Case closed. They've already sent the body home."

"*Sent* it home? They didn't escort him back to Texas?"

"That's right." I could practically see Gil shaking his head sadly. Despite his tough-cop exterior, Gil is a softhearted family man first and foremost. "Imagine that? Not even taking their own son home? Breaks your heart."

The Longs' not taking Peter home didn't break my heart. I wasn't sure how it made me feel, only that it made me question the motive behind their decision.

"How come?" I asked as I reached for my coffee.

"Guess they still have business here. Who knows?" He did a verbal shoulder shrug. "I don't know."

I could tell that Gil didn't have any great affection for the Longs, which meant that it would be easier to get information from him. When Gil gets on one of his moral bandwagons, he's always more amenable to helping me out.

"Got a lunch date?" I asked.

He paused. "No," he said cautiously, "but I know what you're up to, kiddo, and I don't think I want to get involved."

"Gil, if the boy was murdered, like his sister thinks, then we owe it to him to find out the truth, don't you agree?"

I waited patiently while he decided. Finally he said, "I have an appointment in the Village at noon. Should take me about an hour. Why don't you meet me at the Waverly coffee shop at one?"

"I'll be there." I hung up before I could tell him about Joyce Cullerson's attempt to hire me to kill her husband. One more thing to chat about at lunch.

I was antsy to start the ball rolling on the Long case, but until I had a little more information, my hands were tied. I turned on the computer and input what little I had. As I typed in Vanessa Stephens's vital information, it started to really bother me that I didn't know how she knew it was her brother, Peter, on the pier. As it turned out it was Peter Long—but how did she know that, as there was no mention of his name in the article? And how could I know for certain that he was, in fact, her brother? Not even thinking to question it the night before had been bothering me throughout my morning workout. I had blown it with Debi Cullerson, and, without so much as a second thought, I had just blithely walked into another case.

I was angry at myself when I placed a call to her work number. When the receptionist answered "Newcomb Levinson" in a melodious voice, I knew that Vanessa was somehow involved in commercial real estate. Vanessa wasn't yet in, but I left a message on her voice mail for her to call me.

As soon as I hung up, the phone rang.

"CSI, can I help you?"

"Sydney?" Leslie's voice sounded far away.

"Leslie?"

"Yeah." She paused. "How are you?"

"Dandy, and you?" I could feel anger starting to spread from the pit of my stomach.

She sighed. "I'm miserable. Are you free today?"

It seemed sad that the woman with whom I had been practically living was now asking me if I was free to see her.

I took a deep breath. "Leslie, I need time to sort through things."

"What do you mean?"

"Last night hurt me. I understand that you may want someone who's better suited to you, but I don't want to enter into a relationship knowing that my partner will keep hoping that I'll change."

"*Enter* into a relationship?" she asked, obviously wounded. "We *have* a relationship, Sydney. We've been lovers for close to a year."

"I know. But Leslie, if I'm committed to a relationship, I don't start dating other people when the going gets rough. I think right now we both might need some time apart, just to see what it is we really want."

"Do you want me to move my things out?" she asked softly.

The question took me by surprise. I didn't know what I wanted. Did I want Leslie to move her things out or did I want to work through things with her?

"What do you want?" I finally asked.

"I love you, Sydney," was her response. I didn't know what that really meant, so I said nothing. When I was silent, she added, "Just for the record, I had a lousy time last night."

"I'm sorry to hear that."

"No, you're not."

"You're right, I'm not. I'm glad you had a lousy time."

"I want to see you."

"Let's just give it a few days. I have a new case, and I'm not sure where it's going to go."

"Sydney?"

"Yeah."

"I'm sorry it hurts."

"Me too."

When we ended the call I felt like smashing my coffee cup against the wall. Instead, I turned on the answering machine, left a note for Kerry that we had a new client and for her to start collecting data on Wallace Long. I also told her that I was expecting a call from Brendan Mayer and she should make an appointment for me to meet with him ASAP. Then I closed up the office and headed out to Tina's Gym where, if I was lucky, I would find my friend Zuri and go a few rounds in the boxing ring before meeting Gil.

I jumped on the number 3 train to get to Tina's in midtown, a hole in the wall that's become my home away from home. I crowded onto the subway along with eight thousand other New Yorkers, most of whom were headed in late to their nine-to-five jobs (a concept I have never been able to grasp).

At Tina's someone had made an attempt to brighten up the place with holiday decorations. An electric menorah sat atop the front desk, a three-foot fake tree with blinking lights, tinsel, and red ornaments was almost lost in a corner by the front door, and a festive cardboard streamer reading *Happy Holidays* had been hung over the desk.

Tina Levitt, the owner of the gym, and Zuri were standing in the doorway of Tina's office when I arrived.

"Hey, girlfriend, I was going to call you today. I'm throwing a party next week, and I want you and Leslie to come." Zuri was wearing sweats, a cap, and gloves with the fingers cut out.

"What kind of party?" I asked.

"Christmas. Remember that holiday?" She smiled, exposing the most perfectly white teeth I've ever seen.

"Oh humbug. What happened, Tina, you forget to pay the rent again? It's freezing in here."

Tina shook her head and rearranged the scarf around her neck. "It's this building. What can I tell you? I haven't had heat since day before yesterday, can you believe it? I should have closed, but there are the few mental cases who don't mind freezing their pupkies off for the sake of exercise. Go figure. I think it's sick."

"What's a pupkie?" I asked, wondering if I would mind freezing mine off.

"It's like a *pupick* only different," she said with the hint of a smile.

"What's a *pupick*?' Zuri asked. "I been here two days, girl, and if mine's gone, I wanna know."

Tina paused and looked mischievously at me. "It's a gizzard. A *pupick*'s a gizzard."

"What is a gizzard?" I asked Zuri, who had two teenage sons, so she had to know about gizzards.

"I dunno. Some nasty part of a chicken. It's related to the giblet." We paused, looked at one another, and cracked up.

"Think of it as the bellybutton." Tina laughed. With that she turned and went into her office.

"Why, such festive holiday decorations," I said to Zuri as we moved into the main room, where there were two boxing rings and half a dozen workout areas. There were only two people in the place, which made it feel emptier than if there had been none. A guy in shorts and a tee shirt was jumping rope to a Walkman, and in the far side of the room by the windows a woman in sweats was doing sit-ups.

"Tina and I stayed late the other night, shared a bottle of red, and decided to pull the decorations out from a locker and do it ourselves. Not bad, if I do say so."

"I'm not ready for Christmas this year," I remarked, watching my breath as I spoke. "Besides, fluorescent lighting always seems to obscure potential ambience, don't you think?"

"I think you're cranky. What's up?"

"I need a workout. You up for a round?" I asked as I blew warm air into my cupped hands.

"So you wanna freeze you pupkies off, is that it?" Zuri gave a little shake but nodded. "I need *something* to get the blood moving. I've been freezing my ass off for two days."

After a half hour warm-up, Zuri and I donned bulletproof vests for protection and climbed into the ring. It was just what I needed. As we sparred in the ring I could feel the energy inside me start to focus. Instead of a free-floating electrical charge feeling as though it was surging through my body, I began to feel grounded and directed. By the time we were done, three more people had started their workouts and the place felt warmer. We'd even managed to work up a sweat.

"Tell me there's hot water," I said as we unlaced gloves and shed our gear.

"There's hot water," Zuri said flatly.

"Is there?" I asked as I headed to the locker room.

"Nope, but it's what you wanted to hear, right?"

"Hey, Zuri?" I called out as she headed to the far side of the room to put away the gear.

"Yeah?"

"I think you lost a pupkie in the ring." With that I decided to brave the shower, which was, thankfully, at least tepid. I left Tina and Zuri as the radiators started clanking away, noisy proof that heat might soon follow. I wished them warm and headed to my one o'clock with Gil.

Six

The subway was crowded with wet shoppers toting bags of Christmas presents. Christmas. I hadn't even begun my holiday shopping. Normally by this time I would have my sister, Nora, her husband, Byron, and their daughter, Vickie's, presents already mailed off to Baltimore. Her present to me was sitting in my living room, still in the brown box in which it had been shipped. There was no tree, no mistletoe, no sign in my apartment that the holidays were upon us.

I took the A train to Fourth Street, where I was slightly more than an hour early for my meeting with Gil. First I stopped at a bagel store, where I got a cup of coffee and could use an indoor phone. I called the office and found all was well. No, Brendan Mayer hadn't called. Yes, she had started the search on Wallace Long. No, Max wasn't there, but there were four messages for me: Vanessa Stephens returned my call; my dentist called to remind me that I needed a cleaning; my aunt Minnie called and needed to talk, "very important," and another woman called who didn't leave a name, but Kerry felt certain was Joyce Cullerson. I jotted all the messages into a notebook I carry expressly for that purpose, told her I'd be back at the office by three, and hung up. I then rummaged through my pocket for another quarter and found three: a virtual gold mine.

I called Peter's friend Brendan Mayer for the second time and had to leave another message.

With the second quarter I called Minnie, my father's sister and my favorite relation. She wasn't in, so I left a message telling her I'd be out all day and call her later that night. With my third quarter I dialed Vanessa Stephens, who, I was told, was in a meeting.

Three strikes, and I was out of quarters.

I still had close to an hour to kill before hooking up with Gil, so I went to a bookstore intent on starting my Christmas shopping. As I wandered through the aisles of Dalton's I could feel the holiday spirit seeping out of my every pore. Christmas music was being piped in to subliminally urge shoppers to be generous with their gift-giving. The more I meandered, the crankier I got. During the half hour that I was there I picked up three books with Aunt Minnie in mind and realized that she would hate each and every one I'd chosen; the last thing my gourmet chef aunt would want is another cookbook. I put them back and hurried out of the store.

With half an hour left, I decided to walk along Eighth Street, a street too narrow to be comfortable on most days and with the NYU students, holiday tourists, and shoppers, was almost impassable that day. I got a block and a half before turning back. Unless I planned on buying someone a pair of Doc Martens or motorcycle boots, Eighth Street didn't have much by way of Christmas browsing. Back to Sixth Avenue. Maybe music was a good idea.

I popped into the store next to Dalton's and stood helpless in the middle of the vocalist section. *I have nothing to give*, I thought as I flipped through the Jimmy Durante collection. It seemed like everyone around me was in high spirits, which only pointed out my own bah-humbug mood. It felt like my shoulders were carrying the weight of eighteen anvils. I bagged the shopping and went across the street, where Gil was already waiting for me. He had a newspaper in front of him and a half-filled cup of coffee.

"I'm not late, am I?" I asked as I slid into the booth across from him.

"Nah. I was early." He folded the paper, looked at me, and winked. "You look as gorgeous as ever."

"Really?" I said without enthusiasm. "I feel like Ebenezer Scrooge."

"Well, you don't look anything like him," he said as if the line were rote.

"Un-huh. Which only proves how deceptive looks can be." I shrugged out of my jacket and felt a chill go through me.

"What you need, my friend, is a little holiday cheer."

"I knew I needed something." I tapped my temple with the heel of my hand. "You wouldn't happen to have any of that lying around, would you?"

Gil patted his torso and shook his head. "Must have left it at home." He looked around and waved to the waiter. "I'm starving. If I don't eat, *I'll* become Scrooge. Know what you want?" Gil's face had changed a lot during the last year. My dad's old friend was finally showing signs of aging, and I wondered if in his eyes I was going through the same process of slow, steady deterioration. Oh yes, happy thoughts, indeed.

"Mr. Gil, the usual?" The waiter asked, rocking back on his heels, not bothering to take out a checkbook.

"That's right, Paul. Cheeseburger deluxe, well done. Burn the fries."

"Miss?" The waiter bowed slightly to me and clasped his hands behind his back. "For you?"

"A grilled cheese and tomato on rye, please."

"American? Swiss? Muenster?"

"American."

When the waiter left I took a deep breath and sighed. "So, thanks for meeting me."

He shrugged and pushed the corners of his mouth down. "I don't know what help I can be. I've told you everything I know."

"What about Long?"

"What about him? You probably know as much as I do. The guy's a zillionaire who wants to run for office." Gil picked up the coffee cup in his fist, practically dwarfing the thing.

"What's he doing here?"

"What else? Fund-raising," he said, before polishing off his coffee. I waited for more talk, which I knew would come if I kept my mouth shut. "You understand this is a concept that doesn't make any sense to me. There should be a law; if you've got billions of dollars, pay for your own friggin' campaign, don't ask Joe Blow Willow to support your run for ego. And if you have to ask the public, ask your own public, stay the hell outta someone else's state. Don't get me started here." Gil shook his head as he continued. "Probably 80 percent of these gasheads buy the offices they run for anyway, so why even make the pretense that they were voted in fair and square by the populace. It's enough to make me sick."

"Long," I reminded him.

"They got to town four days ago, him and his entourage. Wife, son, and a couple of security people."

"Security?" I asked as I stirred a packet of sugar into my coffee.

"Yeah. Two guys on twenty-four hours a day, I think."

"Why?" It didn't make sense that he would need twenty-four-hour-a-day protection.

Gil motioned to the busboy for a refill of his coffee, and said, "Apparently Mr. Long has made an enemy. Before they got to town they made a formal request for additional protection, but, as you know we had a visit from the First Lady *and* that thing at the UN, so our plates have been pretty full. Obviously we didn't have the extra manpower, so we suggested they get private security while they're here—at least for the first part of their visit. You and Max were the first ones on the list. To tell you the truth, I was a little surprised that they didn't call you."

"Who did they call?"

"No one. He brought his own security, I'm telling you." He pushed his cup and saucer to the end of the table for the refill. "Thanks."

"So tell me about this enemy he's made."

"You know how it is when you're in the public eye;

mental cases crawl out of the woodwork and want to marry you or kill you. He's gotten threatening letters, death threats, I believe. Naturally as soon as we had the manpower, he was offered extra security, but instead of taking us up on our offer, he got on his high horse and played the martyr to the hilt.'' He tore open two packets of artificial sweetener and added it to his coffee. He didn't bother to stir it before taking a sip.

''Did you offer the protection before or after his son died?''

''After.'' Gill rolled the pink sweetener packets into a little ball and flicked it into the ashtray. ''Why?''

I shrugged. ''I just thought if protection was offered after his son died, maybe someone thought it wasn't a suicide.''

Gill shook his head. ''You're barking up the wrong tree, kiddo. But you wanna hear the bizarre thing? Long's a big supporter of capital punishment and his campaign line is 'Wallace Long. It's a matter of life and death.' Have you heard that?''

''I doubt it. That sounds like something I'd remember.''

''Ironic, don't you think? His whole campaign based on that one line, and his son takes his own life. Anyway . . .'' Gil sipped his coffee, taking in the whole restaurant with a quick glance. He set the cup back on the saucer, and said, ''Long's ultraconservative and my guess is that'll make him very appealing to the public. He supports the NRA, he's a bulldog for tougher sentencing for criminals, insists that the death penalty is necessary for our survival, and he's taken a definite antiabortion stance.''

''How do you know all this?'' I asked, mesmerized by Gil's political acumen. I read two papers every day and couldn't remember any of this stuff.''

''The *Clifford Bartholomew Show*. You know who I'm talking about?''

''I know the talk show.'' Clifford Bartholomew is a radio talk show host who has slowly over the last twenty years reached star status by appealing to the ultraconservative sector. Two years ago his show really took off, which was a sign of the changing times regarding conservative politics in the United States.

"Well, Bartholomew and Long are close friends. As a matter of fact, Bartholomew's been real instrumental in helping raise money for Long. Now—and listen up here because this should be interesting to you—initially Long told us he wanted to keep this thing with his son as quiet as possible. Naturally we respected that. That kid's death was closed up faster and tighter than anything I've ever seen before. The press was kept completely in the dark, nobody knew who the kid in the morgue was, but—now get this—Bartholomew blabbed it all over the air this afternoon. I heard it on the ride up here to meet you."

"Jesus. Long must be pissed," I said, moving my coffee to make room for my sandwich.

"I don't think so!" Gil laughed. "The son of a bitch was on the show with him. Imagine that? He's actually getting mileage out of his own kid's death."

"But you said he didn't want publicity."

"That's right, that's what he told us when it first happened. I don't know, maybe his good friend Bart caught him off guard and placed him in a rough spot, who the hell knows? All I know is they take this kid's *suicide* and turn it around to be the New York Police Department's fault. Burned my ass, I can tell you that."

"I don't get it." I salted my sandwich.

"What are you doing?" Gil asked as he held his ketchup bottle over his burger.

"What?"

"You're salting grilled cheese? That's disgusting. Salt'll kill you."

In response I added a touch more salt and a little pepper.

"Fine, go ahead, kill yourself." He poured enough ketchup on the burger to disguise what it was and slathered a blob of mayo on the bun top for good measure.

"You should talk," I mumbled. "So, wait, I don't get why they blamed you guys."

"Ostensibly because we didn't give him the additional security they'd asked for. You want my opinion?

He's a politician, and politicians don't give a shit about anything but getting elected. This tragedy gets him the public's sympathy, plain and simple.'' With that Gil bit into his burger, leaving a streak of ketchup on his chin.

''I don't understand how they could blame the cops for what happened to Peter.''

''Bartholomew says that if we were doing our jobs right, the streets would be clean of all dealers.''

''That's ridiculous.''

''I know that, and you know that, and a couple of their call-ins tried to point that out, but this Bartholomew is real good at twisting things around. And sarcastic? The man makes Howard Stern look genteel.''

''What else?'' I asked the man who insisted he had already told me everything he knew. Oh these divas.

''The Longs—or at least Wallace—is in town for another three days. They were originally supposed to go to Washington after this, but now they'll be going straight back to Texas.''

''Any way you can arrange for me to meet him?''

Gil wiped his chin and smiled knowingly. ''You're a piece of work, you know that? What do you think?''

''I think if I don't ask, I won't know.'' I mirrored his smile. ''So where are they staying?''

''You know, you're gonna cost me my job one of these days.''

''You're getting ready to retire, anyway.''

''Now you sound like Jane.''

Gil's wife, Jane, has been waiting for him to retire for the last fifteen years. We're all resigned to the fact that retiring isn't something Gil will do with grace when the time comes. Every year he promises Jane, and every year she tells us she isn't holding her breath.

''So where are they staying?''

He told me the name of a fancy-schmantz midtown hotel where the rooms cost more a night than I spend on rent in a month. He also gave me the room number for the Longs, knowing that hotel security would at least keep press and people like me at an arm's distance.

''What about his security?'' I asked.

''I haven't met them. Like I told you, two guys. I

think one of them is an ex-cop. Capable enough, I guess. Nothing's happened to Long, so I suppose they're doing something right.''

''Has there been any trouble since he's been here?''

''Aside from the fact that his son killed himself?'' Gil's pointed sarcasm wasn't lost.

''Yeah, aside from that.''

''No.'' Gil finished his burger and started on his fries, sans salt. Yuck.

''You have anything on Peter?''

Gil stopped chewing. His brown eyes darkened. ''No. But the kid shot up enough heroin to kill a horse. When they found him his body was nearly frozen. The pictures are haunting.'' He shook his head and moved the plate away. ''I can't stop thinking about it.''

''His sister's convinced he was murdered.''

''You know, after we talked this morning, I checked, and there's no record in the files that he even has a sister.''

''She's estranged from the family. Has been for a long time.'' I salted his last few fries and helped myself to the remains.

''Where does she live?''

''Here.''

''Do the Longs know that?''

''Well now, you'd think with his connections he'd have had tabs on her for a long time.'' We shared a glance. ''I asked her during our initial meeting, but she seems confident that he doesn't know where she lives.''

''And you think that's bunk.''

''Who knows? Yeah, maybe.'' I yawned, feeling the lack of sleep creeping up on me.

''So.'' He unwrapped a pack of Juicy Fruit and offered me a stick.

I took a piece and slid off the bright yellow wrapper. ''So, I need all the information I can get. An autopsy report would be key. Speaking of which, who did the autopsy?''

''Pearlman,'' Gil said, referring to Margot Pearlman, one of the best medical examiners in the city. I knew of Margot's reputation, but we'd never met.

"Can you get it for me?"

"No. But—" He held up his hands before I could lace into him. "But I'll take a look at it myself and tell you if there's anything useful in it. Okay?"

I chewed the gum slowly. "You know, if I saw it myself, I might see something that—"

"Take it or leave it, kid. That's my final offer. I could get in a load of trouble as it is, and you know it."

"Okay," I said with a sigh. "How about the police report?"

"That doesn't have anything. The kid was found at about one in the morning. The syringe was still in his arm. Pearlman determined the time of death to be between eleven and twelve that night."

"Who found him?"

"Two guys."

"You have their names?"

"Yes, dear." He shoved his hand into his breast pocket and pulled out a torn scrap of paper from a legal pad. "Here." He checked his watch and motioned for a check. "I don't think they'll be able to tell you anything. They just found him, that's it. They went out to the pier for a quickie, found him instead, and called the police."

"They went out on the pier for a quickie when there was a snowstorm?" On the paper was scribbled two names, under each a phone number and address.

He looked embarrassed. "It wasn't a *storm*, but yes, that's basically what the report says." He took the check and waved my hand away as I offered him money. "This one's on me, kid." He peeled a ten and three singles out from his money clip.

"Why would two guys go out to the pier, to the coldest point in the whole city, just to get laid?"

"Maybe they're into some sicko stuff, who the hell knows? They just said they were out for some air. Who the hell *cares*?" He shifted uncomfortably like he had ants in his pants.

"I do, and you should. It doesn't make sense. As a matter of fact, there's a lot here that doesn't make any sense."

"Yeah, well, I'm sure you'll do your best to figure it

all out. But if you want my opinion, the kid was unhappy and killed himself. That's it. Simple. Straightforward."

Before Gil could get up, I put my hand on his.

"Wait. There's one more thing."

He swallowed his gum, and said, "I'm telling you, kiddo, that's it."

"No, this is completely unrelated." I quickly updated him on what had happened in California, deftly dodging most of his questions. "The point is, the girl's mother wanted to hire me to kill her husband."

"No." He sat back into the booth.

"Yes."

"You think she was serious?"

"Who knows? The thing is, obviously both of these people have problems, so I think we have to assume she is."

"Shit."

"My sentiments exactly."

"Okay." He sighed. "Give me the information."

Anticipating this, I had already printed out the data Gil would need. I handed him the paper. I didn't know how I felt about setting Joyce Cullerson up for a sting, but as far as I knew, she might be better off in jail than living with Tom.

"Too bad we can't get *this* son of a bitch." Gil said, meaning Tom Cullerson.

"Please." I could practically taste my hatred for Tom Cullerson.

"How do you know the call to his daughter in San Francisco was from him?"

"I spoke with him." I bit down on the gum and nailed my tongue instead.

"That must have hurt." I didn't know if Gil meant Debi Cullerson's death or my tongue. I simply nodded.

"You think, what's her name?" He held the paper I'd given him at an arm's length and read it. "This Joyce Cullerson was on the level when she said her husband had it in for you?"

"I don't think so," I said, knowing that whether I felt it or not, the possibility still existed.

Gil was up and into the same down jacket I'd seen him in for the last ten years.

I let him help me into my equally old leather jacket. "So, should I go with you now and get the autopsy information?"

"Not unless you want to go Christmas shopping with me for Jane's present because that's where I'm headed."

"I'm thinking about skipping Christmas this year." We started toward the door.

"That's not like you." He slapped my back gently. "What's up? You becoming the Grinch in your old age?"

"It's a thought."

"Grinch or not, we're still expecting you for Christmas dinner. Minnie already said she'd be there, and of course, we expect you to bring Leslie. Nice girl. I'm glad you have someone in your life. Lord knows it took you long enough."

"I was only alone for two years, Gil." It didn't seem like the right time to tell him about Leslie. Besides, I didn't know what to tell him.

"Two *long* years as I recall." He reached in front of me and pushed open the door. The cold blast took us both by surprise. "Christ, can you believe how friggin' cold it's been?"

"I like it."

"You would."

"When will I hear from you?" I asked, trying not to get knocked over by a sudden wind gust.

"This afternoon. I'll be back in the office by three-thirty." He leaned down and gave me a bear hug. "It's good to see you, Sydney. You be careful, you hear?"

"I'm always careful," I reminded him.

"Yeah, sure." He pointed to an old bullet hole in my jacket and laughed. "So long."

I stood on the corner with the wind whipping through me and watched his back as he turned west and walked toward Sheridan Square. Jane was getting jewelry for Christmas from the Bleeker Street antique shop, as usual. Christmas, anniversary and birthday—it was always the same—Jane got something from Owen's Antiques.

Seven

When I got back to the office, I found Kerry and Max in the bathroom. "Well this is cozy." I said as I shrugged out of my jacket.

Kerry turned around, revealing Max, who had the start of a shiner on his left eye.

"Oh my stars, what happened to you?" I asked as I crowded into the bathroom with them to get a closer look at his eye.

"A guy named Carlos, that's what," Kerry offered.

"Okay, okay, show's over, thank you very much." Max started herding us out of the bathroom, clutching a cold cloth to his injured eye.

"Carlos?" I asked as I tucked my scarf into the arm of my jacket.

"He's a mechanic," Kerry tattled as she headed back to the outer office.

"Oh right, the guy with the Englishwoman's car. The car that would take an hour and a half to find?" I flopped down on his visitor's chair and dangled my legs over the arm.

"Shut up," Max growled softly as he settled in behind his desk.

"What happened?"

"Well I told you last night what a maggot this slimeball is. So this morning, I found the SOB and went to get our client's car. You wouldn't believe the operation he has. He's got a garage full of high-priced antique cars that he says he's working on—Jags, Volvos, T-Birds, even a '60 Chrysler New Yorker that has a record player in the dashboard.''

Cars not being one of my things, I didn't have a clue what a Chrysler New Yorker was, but I nodded knowingly and made a noncommittal sound of appreciation.

''So like I said, I caught up with him this morning and he tells me that our client *sold* him the car. Sold him the car: well I know for a fact that she didn't, so I ask for the papers. He tells me that unless I have a warrant, he won't show me shit.''

''And then he popped you in the eye.''

''No.'' Max removed the cloth, and I was reminded of the RCA dog from the forties. ''Then he told me to get the fuck out of his garage.''

''I see. *Then* he popped you in the eye.''

''No. Then I grabbed him by the shirt, threw him up against a sweet '59 Buick, and asked him once again, very nicely, if maybe he didn't want to reconsider and get me out of his hair because I wasn't about to disappear, and I could make his life miserable.''

''Then he popped you in the eye?''

''Then he *tried* to pop me in the eye. But you know me . . .''

''Oh yes, Mr. Testosterone.'' I clutched my hands under my chin and batted my eyelashes.

''That's right. Son of a bitch didn't know what hit him.'' Max got up and went back into the bathroom, where he said over the running water, ''I, however, didn't know that there was a gorilla working for the maggot who feels protective toward his boss—or cousin—I should say. Next thing I know, I'm off the ground and halfway across the room.''

''Two against one?''

''That's right.'' Max came back with the cloth over his eye again.

''I hate that.''

''Me too. I was, however, able to get what I went there for.''

"How?" I asked, not knowing if I really wanted to know the answer.

"After the gorilla beaned me, I found out he had a glass jaw, which I took advantage of, naturally."

"Naturally."

"When Carlos didn't have someone else there to protect him, it didn't take much to persuade him to give me what I wanted."

I got up and grabbed my jacket. "So, congratulations. Another case closed by CSI. Bravo."

Max's silence hit me by the time I got to my office door.

"Another case closed?" I asked.

Max sighed. "He told me that the car is in Queens. I'm headed out in a minute to check it out."

"I see. Well"—I smiled and sang softly—"The run, run, run, run the run-around. Good luck." With that I ducked into my office, eager to take what Gil had given me on the Longs and start the ball rolling.

Kerry had started to gather information on Wallace Long. So far everything she had I basically knew. I placed another call to Peter's girlfriend, Nancy Albus, and met with frustration again. How could a person living in the twentieth century not have an answering machine?

Next I called the two men who had found Peter's body. I left a message for one of the men, Donald Kessler, and actually got through to Lawrence Novack, who agreed to meet me at five-thirty in the Village.

Next I put in a call to Wallace and Louise Long. What the hell? I figured the worst that could happen was that I wouldn't be able to get through.

On the seventh ring someone picked up the receiver.

"Hullo?" It was a woman's voice.

"Hello, is Louise there?" I decided the direct, familiar route would probably get me farther in the door than anything else.

"Who is this?" The voice was cautious and the words slightly slurred.

"My name is Sydney Sloane."

There was a long pause during which I could practically hear the woman thinking "Who the hell is Sydney Sloane?" which was fine with me. I waited patiently. She exhaled as if she had been holding her breath.

Finally she said, "I don't know you."

"I'm a private investigator, Mrs. Long. Someone's hired me to look into your son's death." Honesty is, after all, the best policy, and I assumed this would catch her attention. "I was hoping you and I could meet this afternoon."

"Who hired you?" she asked softly.

"Vanessa."

"Vanessa?" She sounded confused. "Who's Vanessa?"

Now it was my turn to be confused. I knew that Vanessa had changed her last name to Stephens, but I had assumed she'd kept her given name. I dodged her question and asked Louise if she could give me half an hour of her time. After a long pause, she agreed to meet me at her hotel room. She didn't want to be seen in public.

Max offered to come with me, but Louise was skittish enough as it was. The last thing I wanted was to scare her off. I grabbed my bag and coat, borrowed a token from Kerry, and took off, surprised that I was feeling the familiar low rumblings of anticipation that hits whenever I start a new puzzle.

As I rode down to the hotel it kept nagging at me that Vanessa knew it was Peter in the *Times* article. She was estranged from the family, no one—not even the police—knew she was involved with him, so how could she have known it was Peter at the pier? Brendan Mayer might have called her—after all, she had given me his number—but the uncertainty had me feeling like I'd stepped barefoot on a bee. I called Kerry from the hotel lobby and told her to get everything she could on Vanessa Stephens. I suggested she start with our files, which had her work address and number, the bank account on which her check was drawn, and her home number and address.

"Oh, and Kerry?"

"Yeah?"

"Would you try and get me an appointment with Clifford Bartholomew for tomorrow?"

"Clifford Bartholomew? The radio dickhead?"

"That's right."

"He's going to be impossible," she whined.

"Well, you'll never know if you don't try, and I need you to try."

When I hung up she was complaining, but not whining. Progress.

It was easy to peg Louise Long as a drinker. I mean a Drinker. It wasn't her cheeks, which were as red as berries without the aid of Clinique or Lancôme. It wasn't the tired, sad, watery look of her eyes. It wasn't even the broken capillaries on her once-shapely nose.

No, it was the fact that if I had a match, she could have become a blowtorch the minute she opened her mouth.

I had been knocking on her hotel door for close to five minutes before she answered. I was about to return to the lobby and call up when I finally heard a tired voice from behind the door ask, "Yes. Who is it?"

"Mrs. Long? It's Sydney Sloane. I just spoke with you on the phone."

Once she opened it, she held on to the door.

"Hello," I said, ignoring the fact that she was having some difficulty focusing. "Thanks for taking the time to see me. May I come in?"

She squinted at me and nodded slowly, moving a fraction of an inch to let me pass.

The suite was lush and smelled stale. I glanced around and was struck by how untouched it looked. Two enormous bouquets of flowers were sitting on a table with their cellophane wrappers still intact and the card inserts unopened. There wasn't a thing out of place: nothing to indicate that the rooms were occupied. No newspapers half-read on the coffee table, no shoes or scarves or coats scattered about, no briefcases or purses left on a chair or table. Nothing. I sank into the plush rose-colored carpeting and walked into the room.

Louise Long closed the door quietly behind me,

slipped the chain into the additional lock, and turned with effort to face me.

"You'll have to excuse me, it's been a difficult few days." She was wearing a black, long-sleeved dress with a high collar. Her silver hair was pulled into a French twist. A glance at her answered one question—there was no doubt she was Vanessa Stephens's mother. Apart from the age and ravages from obviously years of drinking, the two women looked so much alike it was eerie. She motioned to the sofa. "Won't you have a seat?"

"Thank you." I chose to sit on a knockoff of a Chippendale chair instead of the couch. "I'm terribly sorry about your son, Mrs. Long."

She waved her hands gently in front of her as if to say, "I can't handle that right now."

"As I said on the phone, I've been hired to investigate Peter's death."

Louise Long took a seat on the sofa and crossed her shapely legs. A tumbler of a clear liquid sat on the coffee table between us. I suspected it was neither water or seltzer. "Peter was all I had," she said softly.

Proclamations like that make me nervous. How could one person be all that someone has?

"Your daughter has hired me to find out what happened to Peter. For some reason, she thinks he never could or would have committed suicide."

"Paula?" She looked startled. "Have you seen Paula? Where is she?"

"She's here in New York. But she uses the name Vanessa now."

"Vanessa." She nodded knowingly. "Of course. She had an imaginary friend named Vanessa when she was little. Why hasn't she called me?" Louise Long leaned forward clasping her hands to her chest.

"I don't know."

"How is she?" She was on the edge of her seat now, her face pinched with expectation.

"She's fine." I reassured her, wondering what it must be like to be in her shoes. One child having run away, severing all ties; the other dead. I couldn't help but think of my own parents and how much I missed them.

"But," I continued, "she's convinced that Peter didn't kill himself."

"How could she say that? She hasn't seen Peter since she left." Louise Long rubbed the palms of her graceful hands together and added, "she didn't know Peter. He was only a child when she left."

"Apparently they kept in touch."

Louise flinched. "How? How come I didn't know? Why didn't she contact me?" Anger flashed in her eyes but was quickly replaced with the pain that I suspected kept her drinking.

I shook my head. "I'm sorry, I don't know." As a private investigator, it's never easy to question family members when they've lost someone so close to them, but to get to the truth, you have no choice. "I know this is a hard time for you," I started gently, "but if I could just ask you a few questions, to get an idea of who Peter was, it would help enormously. After all, who knew him better than you?" Manipulative, but effective and, probably true.

"No one. Peter and I were good friends. I know most boys shut their mothers out after a certain age, but Peter and I were always chums. Which is why—this just came as such a shock." She took a sip from her drink and wiped the bottom of the glass with a dainty handkerchief before setting it back on the coffee table.

"So you agree with Vanessa—Paula—that it is unlikely Peter would have killed himself?"

"I don't know what to think." She shut her eyes and sighed.

"When did you last see Peter?"

"Saturday. He stopped by here and we had a late breakfast together. He and his father had had a falling out the night before." She offered without my prompting. I said nothing. "Peter had gone with us to a fund-raising event Friday night. He left before it was over. That distressed Wallace."

"Did they argue?"

"Oh no, there were too many people around. But we knew that when they had a moment alone, there would be a reckoning of sorts."

''They fought a lot?''

''We don't fight, Miss Sloane. We have disagreements. We avoid scenes at all costs.'' The sharpness in her tone reflected clearly her feelings about their mannered life.

''So, you and Peter had breakfast. Then what?''

''He knew I was lonely, so he insisted on taking me sight-seeing.'' She straightened her back and said, ''He was so sensitive. Always concerned about my well-being.''

I nodded.

''I knew Peter had other plans, but he made a phone call, and when he came back he said that he was mine for the whole afternoon.'' Louise smiled sadly at the recollection.

''What time was that?''

''Around ten, ten-thirty.''

''Do you know who he called?'' I asked.

''No, I don't. I always respected Peter's privacy. I didn't want to make the same mistakes with him that Wal . . . that *we* had made with Paula.''

I knew that there would be a hotel log of all calls made. Getting it, however, would require some doing.

''So you didn't hear with whom he spoke or what was said?''

''No.'' She picked up her drink in both hands, and added haltingly, ''But I did hear him raise his voice once during the call.''

''Did you hear what he said?''

She ran a finger along her lower lip and hesitated. ''I'm not sure.''

''What did you *think* he said? It could be important, Mrs. Long.''

She took a deep breath. ''He said 'Fuck you, I know what I'm doing.' At least that's what I think he said. I could be wrong. As I said, he was in the other room at the time.''

We both knew that that was exactly what Peter had said and that Mrs. Long probably heard a lot more, but I wasn't going to push it. Not too much.

"Was that all you heard?"

She swallowed and nodded emphatically. "Yes. That was all."

"And then you spent the day together?"

"Yes. We walked along Fifth Avenue from Rockefeller Center to the park, stopping in a few stores, and then we actually took a ride through the park in a horse-drawn carriage. I've always wanted to do that. Have you ever done that?"

"Yes. It's fun, isn't it?"

"Oh yes. Absolutely lovely, like a Currier and Ives drawing. It was cold, but they throw a blanket over your legs and then it started to snow when we were ending the ride so Peter had the driver take us all the way back to the hotel in the carriage. It was wonderful." She started to bring the glass to her lips, then changed her mind and put the glass back on the table.

"What time did you get back to the hotel?" I asked.

"About three, three-thirty. I was tired by then and wanted to nap. We had another dinner engagement that night. Peter left me here, and that was the last time I saw my boy. He opened the door, put the key to the room in my purse, kissed my forehead, and told me to have a good nap."

"Did you expect him to be at the dinner that night?"

She sighed. "I knew he wasn't going to be there. He had never liked 'family portrait events' as he called them. He *said* he'd see us later that night, but I knew better. I know my boy. He never had any intention of showing up at the dinner."

"Why was Peter here with you and Wallace?"

"To lend support to his father's campaign."

"Yet he didn't participate in any of the events?"

"I believe he left one early and chose not to attend one." Her voice had an edge of defensiveness to it. "I'm sure that Peter would have been at the other events had he—" She stopped short, unable to finish the sentence.

I looked away as Louise Long struggled with her pain. After several moments I continued. "Tell me about him."

"Oh, Peter was special." She opened her eyes and

stared at the wall-to-wall carpeting. "He was an idyllic baby, always slept through the night, hardly ever cried. He was the happiest baby you ever saw. And cute—oh my, people would stop me on the street just to look at him. Everyone said he should have been a model. Even when he was older. He was tall, strong, he looked a lot like his father. Do you know Wallace?"

"No, I'm afraid I don't. Do you have a picture of Peter?"

"Of course I do." She seemed to lighten as she talked about her youngest child. "Let me get it for you." She took her drink with her into the bedroom, and when she came back, the tumbler had been replenished. She handed me a framed five-by-seven photograph of Peter.

I could feel her pride as she studied me looking at the picture. She wasn't kidding when she said he had model good looks. Peter Long was nothing short of magnificent. A dark-haired young Adonis. In the photograph, he and his mother were laughing. His muscular arm was draped easily over her shoulders, and they were both leaning forward, caught in the middle of a hearty laugh. His features were almost too perfect: a square jaw, even white teeth, wavy brown hair that fell over his left eye, deep brown eyes with thick dark lashes I would have killed for. The picture was obviously taken in the summer, and they were on or near the water. He wore an opened work shirt, and his unblemished skin was tanned to a deep golden brown. Louise was hidden behind wide sunglasses that made her look like a bug. Her face was shadowed by the brim of her huge straw hat, but it was clear that the photographer had caught them in a moment of utter delight. I couldn't help but smile as I looked at the two of them.

"You're right. He was a handsome man."

"Boy." She corrected me. "He was just a baby." She reached out for the picture. "My baby."

"Did your husband take that picture?"

She didn't seem to hear me at first, she was so engaged in the picture. "Wallace? Oh no, this was taken this past summer out on a lake near where we live. Wallace hates water. He can't swim. But Peter, he loves to swim.'' She put the picture on the coffee table facing us so that she could glance over and look at it as we spoke. ''No, Brendan Mayer took that picture. He and Peter were good friends. Best friends. They've known each other since grammar school. They spent part of the summer together last year.''

''I'm surprised at how muscular he looks in that picture. Vanessa said he wasn't much of a jock.''

Louise bristled. ''I don't know what *Paula* thinks she does or doesn't know, but Peter was very much a *man.*'' She reached for her drink.

''She never questioned his manhood, Mrs. Long. She just thought that there was some friction between your husband and Peter because—''

She cut me off. ''Wallace loved Peter. The man is torn apart by what's happened. He and Peter were like this.'' She held up her right hand and crossed her middle and index fingers to illustrate the point.

''Was Peter happy?'' I changed the direction.

''Peter was twenty, Miss Sloane. It's a difficult age.''

''Is it?''

''Certainly. Children are just being faced with adulthood. It's a painful transition. But yes, in answer to your question, I think Peter was happy. He was popular at school. He had a wide range of friends. He was smart, funny, and as you can see, quite handsome.''

''And he had a girlfriend?''

Louise seemed unsettled with this one. ''He was seeing someone, but I don't know that I would call her his girlfriend. He was a very social boy; everyone wanted to be his friend.''

''You realize the picture you're painting is not that of a boy who would kill himself. Tell me, Mrs. Long, do you know if Peter had a problem with drugs?''

''Absolutely not!'' The silence that followed was loaded. We had both heard her response, and we both knew that—if it was true—it only strengthened Vanessa's assertion that her brother wouldn't have killed himself with heroin, of all things. And if it wasn't true—for her response had been a little quick on the uptake—it was clear that she could have been hiding something.

Either way, we both sat uneasy for the next few seconds.

"Mrs. Long, Peter's dead. Either by his own hand or someone else's. Knowing how much you loved him, I can only imagine you would want to know why this happened as much as Vanessa does. Will you help me?"

Louise slowly reached for her drink and clasped it on her lap between her hands. Without a sound she started crying. She didn't attempt to hide or wipe away her tears. Before she could catch her breath to answer we heard a key fit into the lock of the hallway door. The door pushed open but was stopped by the chain.

"Goddammit, Libby, open the fucking door." A deeply male voice with a Southern accent, assaulted us both.

Louise called out, "Coming." She then took a long drink from her glass, placed the glass under the sofa and wiped her cheeks as she moved quickly, though somewhat unsteadily toward the door.

The voice on the other side of the door muttered something I couldn't catch. Louise closed the door, unlatched it, and opened it again. In walked Wallace Long with two other men.

Wallace was a large man with a barrel chest, dark thinning hair, and steel gray eyes. When he walked into a room he took possession of it without needing to say a word. It was easy to see where Peter got his good looks.

"What the hell are you doing putting a chain on the door?" His irritation was palpable, making the room feel heavy and confining. Louise reached up to kiss him, but he brushed right past her. The two men followed his steps into the room. They both saw me before Wallace did. But then, judging from their size and stance, they were trained to see things quickly. When the taller, lanky companion glanced at me, his gaunt, pale face remained expressionless. The third man was built like a football player, big, thick, and muscular. He had short hair and smiled when we made eye contact.

Wallace stopped when he saw me. "Who's this?" He asked the room at large.

"Sydney Sloane," I answered for myself.

"And you are?" He leveled his gaze at me. I could see how a child would be intimidated by the force of this man. I, however, wasn't.

I reached into my bag and pulled out a business card. "I've been hired to look into your son's death, Mr. Long." I walked across the room and handed him my card.

He loosened his tie and glanced at the card. "Is that so? And who, may I ask, hired you to do this?" He slipped my card into his jacket pocket.

"Your daughter."

He pushed his shoulders back and glared down at me. "I don't have a daughter." He said evenly.

"Oh, Wallace," Louise murmured sadly behind Wallace's companions.

"We've been through this before Libby, and I don't want to do it now." He shrugged out of his jacket and tossed it carelessly on the back of a chair. "Look, Sloane is it?"

I nodded.

"As far as I'm concerned, I don't have a daughter. Now I don't know what her little game is in getting you involved in all of this, but our pain is a private thing."

"Not so private, it is, Mr. Long? Or doesn't Mr. Bartholomew's show count?"

He blinked once, maintaining a solid poker face. "Quite honestly, what my wife and I are going through right now is hard enough without that little girl trying to complicate things. Do you understand?"

"No, not really." I met his gaze. "Your son is dead, Mr. Long. Your daughter—whether you acknowledge her or not—doesn't think he killed himself and has hired my company to investigate. I would think you'd welcome someone trying to find out exactly what happened to him. Certainly you have questions. Even if your son *did* kill himself, don't you want to know why?"

"What makes you think I don't know why?"

There was something about the way he spoke that made the short hairs on the back of my neck stand on end.

I smiled. "If you do know, sir, I wish you'd tell me.

The faster I get the answers, the sooner I can close this case.''

''He was miserable. It's as simple as that. Some people can handle this world, and some people can't. Pete was a good kid, but he didn't have much of a backbone.''

We heard the bedroom door slam before any of us seemed to notice that Louise had left the room. Her sobs could be heard through the closed door.

''I hope you're happy, Miss Sloane.'' Wallace motioned toward the bedroom door, implying that I was somehow at fault for Louise's departure. ''Lyle, see this young woman out, would you?''

''Mr. Long,'' I said to his back as he headed to the bedroom. He stopped and sighed.

''Yes?'' He said without turning around.

''You and your wife have just described two very different people. I find that curious.''

His shoulders eased down as he turned to face me. ''My wife has a different view of everything. She's not a well woman. Now if you'll excuse me.''

''One more thing, sir. I understand you've received several death threats during the last few months.''

He turned and glared at me.

''Do you think there's a possibility that the threats could be somehow connected to your son's death?''

''I think, miss, that you are trying my patience.'' One glance at the boys let us all know that my meeting with Wallace Long had come to an end. He closed the bedroom door behind him, and the three of us looked a little like the guests who wouldn't leave.

''Hi.'' I said to Frick and Frack. ''My name's Sydney. You are?'' I went to get my coat and bag.

''Lyle,'' said the football player, moving toward me with the awkwardness of a teenager. He held out his hand, which I shook. He had big, bearlike paws for hands. Manicured paws.

The tall, quiet guy nodded a silent command at Lyle, and walked past me to the sofa.

Lyle held out his hands in a helpless gesture and said, ''I'll be happy to see you to the lobby.''

I turned to get my jacket and found the mute holding it in an outstretched hand.

"Thanks," I said as I took it from him. "I'm sorry, I didn't catch your name."

"I didn't toss it." He smirked.

"Ooh, quick repartee. I like that in a man. It's so . . . Neanderthal." I started toward the door. "Thanks anyway, Lyle, but I think I can find the lobby all by myself."

"Oh, it's no trouble." He was already holding the door open for me.

At the elevator he tried to help me on with my jacket. I assured him I'd been putting on my coat all by myself for the last several months and I was getting pretty good at it. To busy himself, he pressed the elevator button a couple of times.

"So, Lyle, have you worked for Wallace long?"

He looked confused. "Well, sure, I work for him now."

It took me a few seconds before I understood. "No, not Wallace Long, I meant have you worked for him a long time."

He chuckled and looked down at his size-twelve feet. Italian leather shoes with delicate tassels. Not what I would have imagined for him.

"I've only been with Mr. Long about three or four months now. Art's been with him a long time." He paused and pressed the elevator button again. "Art came across pretty rude back there, but people expect that of guys in our line of work. He's not such a bad guy."

"What is your line of work?"

"Security. Art's more like a confidant, too, but me, I'm just there to look tough and scare people away."

"What lead you to this business?" I asked. Bodybuilder. Cop. Bouncer. Construction worker. It could have been anything.

"I was a teacher." He said this almost wistfully. "I was actually a gym teacher at Peter's high school."

The elevator dinged twice for down. There were two men in business suits discussing hockey when we entered. They both smiled at me, glanced at Lyle, and returned to their conversation. Lyle pressed the already lit lobby button, hooked his hands behind his back, and watched the numbers light as we descended.

Safely in the lobby I said, ''Well, thanks for the ride.''

''Hey, Sydney.'' He put his hand on my right arm and shrugged. ''I have some free time right now. Can I buy you a drink or a coffee or something?''

I looked at my watch. It was four-fifteen, which gave me an hour or so before my meeting with Lawrence Novack. Here was a guy who knew Peter and liked to talk. Never look a gift horse in the mouth is my motto. ''Sure,'' I said, and let Lyle lead the way to one of the four lobby bars.

Eight

We settled into a booth and Lyle excused himself. "I just want Art to know where I am," he said as he backed into a waitress with a full tray of glasses, obviously accustomed to avoiding collisions with out-of-towners. She gracefully dodged a mess and tersely assured Lyle that it was, "No big deal."

When he returned, his face was slightly flushed.

"Is everything all right?" I asked, noticing for the first time that his eyes were dark brown and soulful. I hadn't dated men in years, and had no desire to now, but Lyle fit the physical description of my ideal—a big old teddy bear.

"Everything's fine, it's just that Art can be a pain sometimes. He didn't think it was *wise* for me to have a drink with you." He motioned for the waitress.

"And?" I prompted him.

"And Art doesn't make my decisions for me." He smiled slightly and asked what would be my pleasure.

"A gin and tonic, please."

"Tanqueray? Bombay? Beefeater's? Gordon's?" The waitress ran off my list of options. I went with the Tanqueray and was surprised when Lyle ordered an Absolut Citron on the rocks with a twist.

"Don't you have to work tonight?" I asked.

"Yeah, but it takes more than one drink to slow me down. In case you didn't notice, I'm a big guy. I can handle just about anything.'' He looked uncomfortable, but handsome in his powder blue shirt, red tie, and navy suit. As if reading my mind, he loosened his tie and undid the collar button, exposing a tuft of dark, thick chest hair. ''So, tell me about yourself. How does a good-looking woman like yourself become a private investigator?''

''Oh just lucky, I guess.'' I reached for the bowl of goldfish crackers and popped a few in my mouth. ''What *I* want to know is how do you go from teaching to the protection service? It seems like a big jump.''

He nodded. ''It was. Mr. Long had asked me to work for him a year earlier, but I turned him down. The money was appealing, but it would have taken up way too much of my time. Then he asked me again a few months ago.''

''Why you?'' I asked.

Lyle smiled and nodded. ''I asked myself the same thing when he first approached me to work for him.'' He laced his fingers together, turned his hands palm out, and popped his knuckles. ''Peter and I had a good rapport when he was a student, so I figure his father wanted to thank me in his own way. Besides, look at me; I look like I eat nails for breakfast.

''But also, my life had changed and I guess he thought—and rightly so—that I would be more amenable to the schedule that this job presented. Obviously he also thought I would be good for the job.'' Lyle took his hands off the table to give the waitress room to place our drinks. ''Thank you.'' He said politely. When she left he held up his glass and toasted, ''To meeting you.''

I held up my glass without clinking his and asked him to go on.

He fished the twist out of his drink and popped it into his mouth. ''Where was I?'' he asked.

''You were telling me how you got the job with Long.''

''Ah, that's right. Well, I didn't know anything about security, but he said Art would teach me everything I needed to know. Now when they had approached me earlier, I—'' He stopped and looked sheepishly across the table at me. He laughed. "Christ Almighty, it sounds like someone wound me up and the spring broke. I'm sorry. I don't mean to run off at the mouth like this." He shook his head and clutched his drink tightly in his hands.

"No, please don't apologize. It's great." The last thing I wanted was for him to clam up now. Besides, there was something appealing about his openness.

He stirred his drink with his index finger. "Marjorie, my wife, was worried that I could get hurt being a bodyguard, that's one of the reasons why I didn't take the job in the first place. We were expecting our first baby then, and I figured even if the money was three times more than I was making—which it was—it wasn't worth the time it would take up. I mean, I wanted to be a part of her pregnancy." His eyes got darker as he paused and took a sip from the glass dwarfed in his hand.

"How does Marjorie feel now that you're working for Long?" I asked.

He shook his head slowly. "Something went wrong. I came home from school one afternoon and found Marge on the bathroom floor. She had hemorrhaged and bled to death. The baby died, too." He took a deep breath and stared into his drink.

"I'm so sorry."

"I think all of this with Peter has, I don't know, maybe stirred up old feelings. At the time, I didn't know what hit me. I took a leave from teaching and just stared at the walls, if you know what I mean. Anyway, Mr. Long got wind of my situation and asked me again if I wanted to work for him. I thought what the hell? If I was lucky I might get killed in the line of duty. As it turns out, it's an easy gig. Boring, if anything."

We drank in silence for a moment. Then I said, "Peter's death must have come as a shock to you."

Lyle seemed not to hear me at first. I was about to repeat myself when I realized that he was trying not to cry. Of course, if he had been Peter's teacher in school, the boy's death would hit him hard.

"I hate death," he told his Absolut Citron. Then he

looked up at me and said, "Peter was a good kid, he really was."

"Would you have been aware if he was doing drugs?"

He shrugged. "I don't think he was, but then anything's possible. The way I see it is, he could have been upset about something, didn't know what the hell he was doing, bought some smack and ODed by accident. I *do* think it was an accident. Your medical examiner's office even said it was an accident."

"Unless they have absolute proof of either suicide or murder, they call any drug overdose accidental."

"Is that true?" he asked, genuinely curious.

"Yes."

"Huh. I didn't know that."

"Even if he was upset, why heroin?" I asked. "Why not go to the hotel bar and get drunk or get some grass or cocaine?"

"I don't know." Lyle looked me straight in the eyes and seemed to be weighing his thoughts carefully. "The reason Art didn't want me to have a drink with you was because he thought you'd try to pick my brain about Peter." He stopped. We both knew it was my game plan, so I saw no reason to respond. "The fact is, I liked Peter. A lot. I don't know why he killed himself, but out of respect for him, I think we should know. Because of that, I'll do whatever I can to help you. All I ask is that you be honest with me in return, you got that?"

"Yes."

"Okay. Now what do you want to know?"

"Was it a happy family?"

"I don't think anyone can say what goes on in someone else's home, but I knew Peter since he was a sophomore in high school. He was a nice kid, not a competitive athlete, but a good, solid swimmer. He told me he liked to swim because it was a solo activity. Apparently he didn't like to have to depend on other people because, as he put it, people disappoint you. An interesting concept for a kid if you ask me, and not one you would expect from a particularly happy one at that."

"What about his mother? I understand they were quite close."

"Oh yeah, he was devoted to his mother. Just take this trip. My guess is Mr. Long had his wife ask Peter to take time away from school and join them here for the week. His mother's going through hell with this. I can just imagine the guilt." His voice was thick with emotion.

"What school did he go to?" I asked, trying to keep him focused.

"He was enrolled at a local community college." Lyle finished his drink and motioned to the waitress for another round, though I was barely halfway through mine. "Peter didn't want to go to college," he said.

"Really? What did he want?" I asked, nibbling on a fresh handful of goldfish. I had, single-handedly, gone through half a bowl of crackers.

"He wanted to be a sailor."

"Like in the navy?" I asked, half-joking.

He nodded. "He was always into boats. That's how his parents got him to agree to college. They bought him a boat when he was in high school."

"High school?" I couldn't hide my surprise.

"Well, people who can afford it buy their kids cars when they're sixteen or seventeen, why not a boat?"

"At sixteen a kid's not stable enough for that sort of responsibility."

"Maybe you weren't, and *I* certainly wasn't, but Peter was pretty remarkable about his boat." He took a deep breath. "Wallace gave Peter the sailboat, but it meant he had to agree to finish college and join his father's business for two years."

"And he agreed to that?"

"The water was the one place where the kid could feel free. What would you have done?"

"I don't know," I said. "A year left of high school?" I asked.

"Three years."

"I would have finished school without the boat, then joined the navy."

"No way. A month takes forever to a kid. Three years

would have seemed like an eternity. I would have opted for the boat."

"Not me."

"That's 'cause you're a girl." Lyle smiled. "She's a beaut, too. His dad's no fool, he knew the perfect bait to dangle. And he caught Peter at that awkward age, when a kid's just starting to rebel, but wants things, big things. Hell, Peter would have probably sold his soul for that boat."

"Maybe he did." I thought about Vanessa's assessment of the same scenario. I let the waitress take my drink and started on the fresh one.

"Personally—and this is strictly between you and me—but I think one of the reasons why Peter struck the deal was because his father hates the water. Peter loved the water, I mean *loved* it. That's why when I heard they found him at the pier, I wasn't surprised. If he did kill himself, he'd do it by the water." The sadness in his eyes and voice wasn't something conjured up for my benefit. Clearly Lyle had been deeply affected by Peter Long's death. He looked away.

"Was Peter gay?" I asked, and explained that the pier where he had been found was a well-known pickup spot for gay men.

"I don't think so. But now wait a minute, these guys hang out on the pier and do it? How could they? It was freezing that night." Lyle's uncomfortable laugh was low and surprisingly sexy. Again he ate the lemon peel from his drink.

"You'd be surprised." I fished the lime out of my drink and squeezed it into the glass. During the next fifteen minutes, the picture Lyle drew of Peter wasn't one of a boy who would kill himself, nor of one who had created a list of enemies over the years. He also gave me an insight into Wallace Long as a man who created the illusion of tension and danger around him to enhance his self-importance. During the few months that Lyle had worked for Wallace Long, there had been no occasion where Lyle had ever felt truly needed.

"What about Brendan Mayer?" I asked as he paid the check.

"What about him? He was Peter's friend." Lyle told the waitress to keep the change.

"What's he doing now? I understand he lives here."

"Oh yeah, Brendan was out of Texas in a flash. As soon as he graduated he came here. I heard he's taking acting lessons. He's another good-looking kid. And he loves to bullshit, so who knows, he might have a chance at a career in the movies."

"Did they see each other while Peter was here?" I stood up and reached for my jacket.

"I don't know. I suppose they would. It wouldn't seem right for him not to." He gently took my jacket from me.

"As Mr. Long's security, don't you guys keep tabs on everyone?"

"Not Peter. The Mr. and Mrs., but Peter insisted on being left alone. Mr. Long respected that."

I let him help me on with my jacket. "Lyle, do you know why Long didn't use the security that the New York police suggested when you first got here?"

"He was livid that the New York police department wasn't going to do it. He said if he had to get his own security, he didn't need these wussie-assed pansies to give him a list." Lyle chuckled. "He was mad, all right."

"But he didn't get extra security?"

"Nope."

"So he's a man who's willing to cut off his nose to spite his face?"

Lyle shrugged.

"Doesn't anyone think it's odd that Wallace has been threatened several times and then his son dies?"

"The general consensus is that Peter killed himself."

"I understand that, but don't you think the two *could* be connected?"

He considered this as we walked through the busy lobby, weaving between groups of people visiting New York for business or pleasure, from Texas, like Lyle, or France, like the man who was gesturing wildly with a smelly dark cigarette.

"I don't know, Sydney, maybe you're right. There's

no proof that they're *not* connected, right? So, I tell you what, I'll talk to Art about it. If Mr. Long will listen to anyone, it's Art."

"One last thing."

"What's that?"

"Peter made a phone call from his parents' room on Saturday morning. It was between ten and ten-thirty. Seeing as how you're a member of Long's staff, it would be easier for you to find out who he called. Would you do that?"

He scanned the lobby before shrugging. "Sure. Why not? The hotel staff is great here. I'm sure they'd be willing to help me."

"Good. Here's my card. If you could call me when you have it . . ."

"No problem." He took the card.

Once outside the cold air felt like an embrace. I took a deep breath and thanked him for the drinks.

"Sydney?" He stopped me as I had turned to go. He shoved his hands in his pants pockets and said, "Seeing as though we're going to be working together—in a way—I was wondering, well, I have tomorrow night off and I was thinking we both have to eat. Maybe I could take you out for dinner. I mean, I don't really know New York, and this is the one night I'll have some time. What do you say? That way I can tell you in person what I get on this phone-call thing."

"Sure," I said without thinking. "You have my card. Call me tomorrow afternoon and we'll set a place."

He nodded and backed up, bumping into a uniformed doorman. "Oops, sorry." He turned back to me, "Well, good night."

It felt like midnight though it wasn't yet five o'clock. Not wanting to face more Christmas shoppers I took a taxi from the hotel to the Village. It took longer than the subway, but it was oh so reassuring to have Diop Thiop, a driver from Senegal, behind the wheel on the icy streets. Oy. A hot bath and a good book. That's what I needed. But that's not what I was going to get. Not yet, anyway.

Nine

My five-thirty meeting was with Lawrence Novack, one of the men who'd found Peter. He worked as a computer graphic artist in the Village, and we'd arranged to meet at a coffeehouse in Sheridan Square.

Coffeehouses have cropped up in New York like kudzu in the South. Where we once would go to a coffee shop for a perfectly fine cup of joe, we now have to decide between Colombian, Italian, French, and what-have-you roasts, decaf, half and half, espressos, steamed milk, lattes, mocha lattes, cappuccinos, iced or not. It's enough to make your eyes roll around in your head.

"I'll have a coffee, please." I gave my order to a young woman who was wearing about eight times too much makeup, but it went well with the nose ring.

"That's it?" She sounded disappointed.

"That's it."

"Light decaf cappuccino for me." Lawrence Novack winked at the waitress as he placed his order. I couldn't tell if his good looks were compliments of Mother Nature or Mattel, but his face was a work of art. The rest of him wasn't bad either; tanned (in December, so I assumed it came from a tanning salon), jet-black hair, chiseled features, and a body that was the stuff manly cologne ads are made of.

The waitress smiled goo-goo-eyed at Lawrence and

backed away from the table. ''Light decaf cap? Cool. I'll be right back.''

''So.'' Lawrence pulled out a pack of Dunhill lights and offered me one.

''No thanks.'' Light decaf, light smokes, he was just a light kind of guy.

''Mind if I do?''

''No, go ahead.'' I watched as he slipped the filtered tip between his lips and brought the gold lighter up, flicked the end, and voilà—smoke. He inhaled deeply, shut his eyes, and exhaled. His shoulders eased down, and he tipped his head back, releasing a cloud of smoke and apparently all the tension in his entire body. Not only did he make smoking look like the most sensual, enjoyable pleasure a person could possibly experience, he made it look downright healthy.

''That's better,'' he said when he opened his eyes. ''I don't smoke at work, not that I can't, but I'm the only one there who does, so I try to keep the environment clean for the others there.''

''Very chivalrous.''

''Yeah, right,'' he said, self-mockingly. ''So, you want to know about the other night, right?''

''That's right.''

''Well, I don't know what I can tell you. We went out to the pier—''

''You and?''

He flicked the ashes of his cigarette into a small glass ashtray and squinted. He exhaled the smoke with a hiss. ''Quite honestly, I don't even know the guy's name. Dan or Doug, something like that. I was pretty bombed at that point.''

''Why did you go out to the pier?''

He looked at me as if I were either a space alien or a Mormon. ''Forgive me, but you look like a pretty savvy lady. Why do you *think* we went out to the pier?'' He leveled his hypnotic eyes at me and brought the cigarette back to his mouth.

''I know why people go to the pier, Lawrence—''

''Larry.''

''Larry. But I can't imagine pulling down my pants

with a windchill factor of twenty below. Not even if I'd been celibate for eight years.''

The waitress sashayed up to the table, dropped my coffee in front of me, and then carefully put the light decaf cap in front of Larry. There were two shakers left on her tray. ''I didn't know if you wanted cinnamon or chocolate, so I brought both.''

''Then I'll use both. Thanks.''

She melted, sprinkled his drink with both the cinnamon and chocolate, and then hurried back to the counter, where her fellow waitress was watching the exchange out of the corner of her eye. Poor kid. How could a girl who looks like that not know about a boy like this? It didn't make any sense.

We tended to our drinks in silence. Larry extinguished his cigarette, but not before lighting another from it.

''A man has needs,'' he said, picking up the conversation right where we had left off.

''No, no, no. I don't buy it. A guy like you doesn't have to go sneaking off to the pier in a snowstorm to get laid.'' I shook my head, dismissing his implausible suggestion. ''Look, the situation is this: it's quite possible that that boy was murdered, but as far as the police are concerned, it never happened. The case is closed. But you saw what he looked like, Larry.'' I hadn't, but I've seen heroin ODs before, and it's not a pretty picture. Theirs is not, as one might think, a serene death. Quick, maybe, but not clean. ''He was a kid. And I just can't let his death get swept under a rug because no one's willing to get involved. Or because they think their secrets are so precious. Believe me, anything you know just might make the difference in solving this thing, and I promise you—you have my word of honor—that anything you tell me will be strictly between us.''

He took a long drag off the cigarette and shook his head. He pushed back uncomfortably in his chair and sighed. ''Okay. Like I said, I was pretty fucked up that night. I was drinking and doing some other stuff, feeling absolutely no pain. So this guy and I start dancing, bullshitting, having a pretty good time, fooling around a little bit, and just when it starts to get hot he tells me he's got to go meet someone.''

''Did he say who?''

He shook his head. ''No. All he said was that the man had 'excellent coke' and that he wanted me to go with him. All he had to do was meet the man, pick it up, then I'd be his for the night. I figured what the hell? It's a Saturday night, I'm ready for some action, why not? So we leave the bar, and he starts walking across the street to the pier. I said, 'What are you, fucking nuts? It's cold out here.' Well the man wasn't without his persuasion, gets me good and excited, tells me it'll only take a second. So me, like a fucking dog in heat, I go following after him.'' He stopped, took a sip of his cappuccino, and wiped his mouth with his index finger. ''I was the first one to see him.''

''Peter?''

''Was that his name?''

''Yes.''

''Yeah, Peter. Anyway, this guy Doug—he didn't see him at first.''

''Don.''

''Whatever. As soon as we get to the pier he wants to fool around. At first I go along with it, but man it was cold out there and the sucker started playing a little rough. So I said to him, 'Look, who the hell are you meeting out here? I'm getting fucking cold.' He says, 'He'll be here in a minute.' That's when I saw—Peter?''

''Yes.''

''Well, really all I saw was this person sitting at the end of the pier. I mean, have you been to the pier?''

I had.

''Then you know how far it is from when you first enter. So, I point out there and this guy, Don, says, kind of surprised, 'Yeah, that must be him. Let's go.' Well it was too fucking cold not to move, so I went with him.'' Larry put out his second cigarette. ''When we first started walking toward him, I got to thinking maybe it wasn't a person after all. I mean, it could have been a bag of garbage—just a big, dark thing. But when we got close . . . it was awful. I've never seen anything like that in my whole life. Totally fucked me up. I've had nightmares ever since that night."

"Tell me what happened when you found Peter."

"Well, I threw up. Don"—he said the name with distaste—"just stood there looking at this guy like it was the most fascinating thing he ever saw. Then the asshole starts running."

"Where to?"

"That's what I wanted to know, not that there are many places you can run to at the end of a pier. Anyway, I wasn't about to be left with this dead guy, and I'm in better shape than Don, so I chase after him and tackle the asshole. Suddenly this schmuck isn't looking so good to me, you know what I mean? I mean, *he* lures *me* out there and then as soon as we find a dead body he takes off like a bat out of hell."

I envisioned Bob Hope and Willie Best in the movie *Ghost Breakers*. I also wondered what version of this I'd get from Donald Kessler.

"So I tackle him and start screaming. I mean, this was not what you would call a moment of calm. I'm screaming, 'Who the fuck was that?' and he's trying to get me off him, squawking that that's not the person he was meeting."

"So he actually *knew* who he was meeting."

This stopped him short. "What do you mean?"

"The way you said it before—that he was meeting a man with excellent coke—it sounded like it could have been a middleman, someone he didn't know."

"Jeez, I didn't even think about that. I *assumed* he knew who he was meeting, but now that you mention it, all he said was one of his pals arranged for him to get some 'excellent coke, man, simply superb.' Stupid fucker." Larry lit another Dunhill and polished off the cappuccino.

"So then what happened?"

"Then this dog turd motherfucker says, 'Look, why don't we just call it a night, okay?' " Larry bobbed his head several times with incredulity. "I'm like, what? You're just going to leave him out there? And he says it's none of our business!" Larry slapped the tabletop.

"Can you believe that? It's people like this stupid asshole who run the whole fucking world. That's why things are so fucked up. Nobody wants to get involved."

Our waitress, who had brushed her hair and applied yet another coat of lipstick, bringing to mind the art of Chinese lacquering, joined us. "You two okay?" She asked Larry. "'Nother decaf?"

"We're fine, thanks." Larry graced her with a quick smile.

"You sure? It's on the house."

"Yeah? Why?"

She giggled. She actually giggled. I was mesmerized that her face didn't crack when she did this. "Because we like you. Happy customers return." Oh barf.

"That's real nice of you." He turned to me. "Would you like something, Sydney?"

"Some more coffee, please."

"Un-huh." She flicked her hand in my direction. "And you?" She asked Larry with as close to a husky voice as she could achieve at age, what, nineteen?

"Nothing, thanks."

She finally took no for an answer and left us alone.

"So he wanted to leave Peter out there?" I prompted him.

"Yeah. He said he was afraid that the police would find out he was there to buy drugs. Jesus Christ, how stupid could I have been? If he was so sure it wasn't 'the man,' then why would he have been afraid the cops would find out about the coke? I can't believe I never made the connection."

"It happens." I watched the waitress fill customers' coffee cups, making it a point to avoid our table.

"The stupid asshole was only concerned about himself. The guy was a real piece of work."

"Why didn't you tell this to the police?"

Larry shook his head sadly. "I was afraid, too. Not about the drug bullshit, but because of the whole situation. I mean, there we are out on the pier in the middle of the coldest night of the year, two stupid faggots out to get laid. By then I was sober enough to be embarrassed. When we finally calmed down, we agreed before we called the cops that we'd tell them we were out to get some air after being in the bar, and we found the body. We'd let them draw their own conclusions—which we knew they would anyway—and that would be it."

"So you called the police?"

"Yeah."

"Where from?"

"A phone on the corner. He wanted to leave, just make like an anonymous call, but I insisted we stay there. I mean, hell, the poor schmuck was dead. In some way we'd been connected through his death, you know what I mean?" He chewed on his lower lip and slipped another Dunhill out of the pack. He tapped the filter tip against the tabletop.

"And that was it?" I asked.

"Yeah, that was it." He lit the cigarette and held his breath. His lungs were taking a beating. "After the police were finished with us, I went to another bar, where a friend of mine works. I just couldn't go home. I'm telling you, I'll never forget what I saw that night. It was awful."

"I know." I've seen death any number of times and have learned that it never gets easier. It's not one of those things that I could ever be cavalier about.

I paid for the coffees and Larry and I parted company at the Christopher Street subway station. By the time I reached the Eighty-sixth Street station, a chill had settled into my bones. I looked at my watch. It was almost seven, and I didn't have plans for the night other than a hot bath, a good book, order-in Chinese food, and sleep. If I made a right, I would be home in five minutes. If I made a left, I'd be at the office in five. I stood indecisively on the corner as the wind whipped around me. I started to my right. A hot bath. Then, halfway across Eighty-sixth Street I did an about-face. Peter Long had been dead three days, and I had a lot of work ahead of me. There would be plenty of time to soak.

Ten

I was ending the day the way I'd started: alone in the office. I love my office. It's a large room with windows facing north and east, which means I get a lot of light and a view of the sky. As you enter the room, my desk sits against the west wall, facing the room, and there's a sofa along the wall to the right of the door. A large philodendron sits between the sofa and the east-facing windows. The windows facing the north are filled with plants as well, but the eastern windows are my favorite part of the room—wonderfully large arched windows that have canvas drapes which I only use in the summer when the light is too direct and bright. My ex, Caryn, is an artist, and had painted the walls in a fresco style which makes you feel like you're somewhere in Italy.

I considered picking up some moo shu pork or broccoli in garlic sauce en route to the office, but decided that a Snickers bar could tide me over until I got home.

Kerry had left two telephone messages and two folders on my desk. One folder was for Wallace Long and the other was Vanessa's. One telephone message was from Brendan Mayer, the other from Gil.

Before I even took my jacket off I dialed Brendan's number. This time I nearly clicked my heels in the air when I got a real live person on the other end.

Brendan sounded younger than I could remember ever

having been. There was a long pause when I explained that I was calling with regard to Peter. "Brendan, are you there?"

"Yeah, sure. What about Peter?"

"Well," I hesitated, not knowing if he knew Peter was dead. If he didn't know, I wasn't about to break the news to him over the phone. "Is there any way I can see you tonight? We really need to talk."

"I have a couple of minutes right now."

"Great. Where do you live? I can be there—"

He cut me off. "No, I mean literally, a couple of minutes. I have plans for tonight."

"Then maybe we can get together later this evening?" I felt like an awkward teenager begging for a date.

"I'm not going to get home until late." He paused. "You can't talk about it on the phone?" He sounded justifiably wary.

"I'd prefer not to. If tonight's no good, then how about tomorrow morning?"

After ten minutes of negotiating, Brendan agreed to come to the office the next morning at ten, but not without first letting me know that he had a rehearsal right after our meeting and people would be expecting him. For whatever reason, this kid was afraid. The likelihood that his fear and Peter's death might be somehow connected did not elude me.

I read Gil's message: *Cause of death, acute heroin intoxication, pending further study. They need to quantify just how much was in his system.*

I got a glass of water from the cooler, unwrapped the Snickers bar, put my feet up on my desk, leaned back, and started perusing the material on Wallace. There were six articles Kerry had apparently copied on-line, three of which were interviews, two of them profiles (one business, one political) and one article written by Wallace regarding the computer industry and the direction he saw it heading.

In the next hour I learned more about Wallace Long than I needed. As I read I kept hoping to find something utterly fascinating about this man who had single-handedly created an empire built on developing computer components, but I didn't. From everything I read, Wallace Long was a driven workaholic who believed in America, apple pie, and Pat Robertson's ideology regarding family values. (This from a man whose children hate him and whose wife drinks to dull the reality of her life. No big surprise there.)

In the seventies—when personal computers were just a twinkle in the eyes of some now very wealthy nerds—Wallace jumped on the bandwagon and put all of his money into developing computer parts. Now he specializes in computer chips—essentially the brains of a computer—and supplies not only computer manufacturers, but a wide range of electronics companies as well. I wondered if any of Wally's contracts were connected to the government. That could make things a little sticky if he were running for office. Oddly enough there was nothing unfavorable written about him—at least not in the files Kerry had provided. That didn't make sense. Here's a big businessman running for office. Where was the dirt? I made a mental note to call Eddie Phillips, my friend who is a bullheaded but extraordinary photojournalist. If anyone could get the real scoop on Wallace Long, he could.

I tossed Wallace's file onto the desk and opened the file Kerry had started on Vanessa. I finished the Snickers before starting.

So far all I knew about Vanessa was that she got my name through Leslie, she used an alias, worked in real estate, and lived in Chelsea, which is the teens and lower twenties on the west side in New York City. Nouveau trendy. It was time to find out a little something about the woman who had hired me. The woman who had gotten my name through Leslie.

Just as I cracked open her file the phone rang. "CSI, can I help you?" I asked tucking the phone between my shoulder and chin.

Nothing.

"Hello." I sang the word into three syllables.

Heavy breathing.

"Un-huh, I'm sorry, the otolaryngologist isn't in now,

but I'll have him call you as soon as he can.'' I dropped the receiver into the cradle with a bang and went back to the file on Vanessa Stephens. In the back of my mind, though, I kept thinking it had been Tom Cullerson on the other end of the phone line. Was panting his way of extracting revenge?

Kerry learned that Vanessa had been at her current address for only a year. Before that she had an inexpensive studio apartment in a fourth-floor walk-up on the upper east side for three years, she was in midtown before that for two years, and the lower east side for the five years prior to that. For $1,500 a month she currently rented a six-hundred-square-foot one-bedroom apartment which didn't have a view but did have laundry facilities and a doorman. It's amazing what New Yorkers are willing to settle for just so they can live in Manhattan and not one of the other geographically undesirable boroughs. During the last six months Vanessa had changed her home phone to an unlisted number.

She had a driver's license—clean as a whistle—not even a parking violation, and her social security number had been issued in New York. She was single, had never been arrested, and had worked at Newcomb Levinson for the last four years, where she was listed as a commercial real estate broker.

When I finished her file, I called in a favor from a computer hacker friend I have dubbed the Wizard. I needed a quick line on Vanessa's financial situation, and my friend was just the woman to get it. If I were to track down the information myself, it would take at least a week. I told the Wizard that we had less than twenty-four hours. If the Longs were going to leave town within that time, I wanted to have as much information at my fingertips as I could get.

I input on our computer what information I had on Peter Long: all of the people I had spoken with, impressions of them, possible motives, relationships—everything was recorded and entered. It was close to eight-thirty by the time I finished, and I was tired and starving. I tried to call Nancy Albus again, let the phone ring thirty times on speaker phone, and finally called it a night. If I got up at six or seven the next morning and called her right away, it would be before dawn her time. She'd have to be there then, unless she was out of town, or sleeping elsewhere.

"The hell with it," I said out loud, and closed up shop for the night. I paused at the front door, debating whether I should try Donald Kessler again. When my stomach growled loudly, I decided to listen to it and call him after dinner.

Once home I ordered Chinese food and jumped into a hot shower. I needed to get warm, needed to unwind. But instead of relaxing in the shower, I could feel my anxieties start to vibrate. Normally I could let go of the outside world, but oddly enough, the Cullersons seemed to loom over me like toxic fumes. Was Tom lying in wait for me like Joyce said, or had she said it as a way to get me to agree to help her? Then there was Vanessa Stephens. For the first time in my life I questioned if I had made a walloping mistake by taking on a job. Maybe Max was right, maybe I was just trying to fix the things I'd botched with Debi Cullerson by taking Vanessa as a client. On top of all of that, there was the Long's bodyguard, Lyle. *I should cancel with him*, I thought as I stood under the normally soothing hot spray of water, *But he's right in the middle of where I need to be.* And again my mind shot back to Tom Cullerson. I could just call and confront him. After all, what kind of a threat could this guy actually pose? He was real good when it came to terrifying a child or beating his wife, but in the scheme of things, I knew Tom Cullerson couldn't hurt me. What I didn't know was that Tom Cullerson wasn't my only problem.

After dinner—orange beef and bean curd with vegetables—I fell into a blissful sleep on the sofa in front of the television while Doris Day, Gig Young, and Rock Hudson ricocheted their sexual energy all over the place. When I awoke, still cuddled under a blue comforter from the night before, a black-and-white Joan Crawford movie was playing. Joan was in a snit, eyes agog. It was seven-thirty in the morning and I had slept, uninterrupted, for close to ten hours. For the first time in weeks I felt refreshed and hopeful.

The radiators were clanking loudly as I went through the morning ritual of yoga, coffee, shower, and the *Times*. Instead of jeans I decided to wear an off-white silk shirt, black woolen slacks, a black cashmere jacket, and black boots. As I scanned the *Times* and indulged in my second English muffin with cream cheese and salt and pepper, I remembered I had meant to call Donald Kessler the night before. It was eight-fifteen, maybe too early, but better early than missing him.

A groggy voice responded. Donald, who apparently lived uptown and worked nights, reluctantly agreed to meet me at five at the West End Cafe, a Columbia University watering hole with good live music. I was looking forward to meeting this guy. I wanted to see if Lawrence Novack had leveled with me or lied. Instinct told me Lawrence was sincere, but I didn't feel as if I could trust my instincts much anymore.

Before I left for the day I checked my messages from the night before. There were two, and they were both from Leslie. I debated whether or not to return her calls and as I was halfway out the door changed my mind again, went back to the kitchen and dialed her number. Her machine picked up on the second ring.

"Leslie, it's Sydney. It's about eight-thir—"

"Sydney?" Her voice was thick with sleep.

"Good morning," I said softly.

"Good morning." She cooed like the old Leslie. Our early-morning phone calls have always been like a slow dance: a gentle, erotic awakening of the mind and body to the start of a new day.

I grabbed a sponge and started wiping down the already clean countertop next to the sink. Part of me was regretting having called. After all, I had insisted that we take a few days away from each other, but here I was calling her first thing the next morning. I reasoned that I was returning her call, knowing that she would have taken it personally if I hadn't, but the fact is, I missed her.

I listened as she stretched.

"That sounded good," I said moving the coffeemaker and wiping behind it.

"Mmmm, I miss you. I wish you were here right now."

"Is that right?"

"Yes. It is. What are you doing?" she asked.

"I'm just on my way to work."

"So early? How about having lunch with me? I found a new place you might like."

I wondered with whom she had found this new place and realized that doubt had eked its way into a place where there had once been complete trust. The effect was jarring.

"Actually I'm on a case right now so I don't know what my time will be today." There was no mistaking that I had just erected a high wall. I scrambled to create a doorway. Who knew? Maybe she had found this new restaurant with her mother or a friend or even her sister the psychologist. "I may be free for dinner tonight, but I have to keep it open."

There was a short pause. I knew we were both struggling. For me it felt a little like treading water when your limbs are numb with fatigue.

"I want to see you, Syd. I really do miss you," Leslie said.

"I miss you, too," I said, tossing the sponge back into the sink and checking the time. "Can I call you later, when I know my schedule?"

"I'm overseeing the installation of an apothecary cabinet in Mrs. Linshaw's new kitchen. I should be done by noon. Can I call you?"

"Sure." I paused, torn between wanting to get on with the day and not wanting to end the call. "So you're almost finished with Mrs. Linshaw?" As a budding interior decorator, Leslie has access to some of the richest, craziest people in New York.

"Well, no. She's so excited about the kitchen, now she wants me to do the guest room."

"Good for you."

"Yeah." She stretched again. "But the lady's a nut job. Yesterday she came in wearing a belly dancer's outfit, complete with bells. Not a pretty sight considering the shape she's in. You should have seen the carpenters: they nearly choked."

I had met Mrs. Linshaw, and the image Leslie conjured up wasn't one I wanted to stay with. "I have to go," I said softly.

"Sydney?"

"What?"

"I've been doing a lot of thinking."

"Yeah?"

"Yeah." She paused. "I think I've been pretty stupid. About us."

I nodded, but kept mute.

"You still there?" she asked. I assured her I was, but didn't know what to say.

"Just say you'll stay open to me," she said.

Again I nodded. "Okay."

"Thank you. Have a good one."

"You too. I'll talk to you later."

I picked up three bunches of tulips (one red, one pink, and one purple) on my way to work; one for each of our desks. If I wasn't careful, the next thing I knew, the Christmas spirit might sneak in and take hold of me.

When I got to the office, the top lock was unlatched. As I was the first one to arrive, and the last one to leave, I did a mental check, trying to recall if the night before when I had left in such a hurry, I'd only locked one lock, but it was a blur. I could have sworn I locked it, but then I remembered stopping to consider calling Donald Kessler.

First order of business was to put all the flowers in vases. Max got the purple tulips, off to the right side of his desk so you saw them first thing when you entered the room. Kerry got the pink tulips in a short round vase, dead center on her desk. The red tulips were for me. I put them on the left side of my desk, which you couldn't see so well when you first entered, but were beautiful from my vantage point. The messages on the answering machine could wait because the next thing to do was coffee.

"Good morning," I greeted Kerry cheerily as I measured out the coffee.

"What's wrong?" she asked as she took in the flowers on her desk and the smile on my face.

"Nothing. Why? Should there be?"

"Well you know, you seem a little perky, and it's not like perky's been your middle name lately. Besides, I was reading your horoscope on the way to work, and things don't look good for you because the sun is in conjunction—"

I don't much believe in horoscopes, but I was curiously defensive. Here I woke up on the right side of the bed and now she was going to tell me that every single Leo on the planet should beware. "Oh no you don't." I added the last scoop of coffee, snapped the filter casing shut, and flipped the switch to on. "I refuse to listen to that mumbo jumbo—"

"You're being totally absurd." Kerry hung her jacket on the coat rack and pulled off her mittens. "This astrologer, Patrick Walker? He's not like everyone else, he's *really* good."

"Right, and all the others are quacks. Look, I'm in a good mood, and no astrologer is going to take that away from me. Got it?" I asked, hearing my voice edge near sharpness.

Kerry paused as she slipped her scarf off and folded it neatly. "Okay," she said slowly as she turned and put the scarf on her desk. Then she turned back and said in a rush, "But I just have to say that your reaction alone gives credence to what I'm saying. That's it." She held up her hands in truce, "You think what you think and I think what I think and they don't have to be the same thing, right? Right. Thank you for the flowers, they're beautiful."

I stood there speechless. If I addressed the stupid horoscope nonsense, she would only think it validated her point of view. If I said nothing, I ran the risk of exploding. After several long seconds, I smiled, took a deep breath, and went into my office, where I placed another call to Nancy Albus in Texas. My tulips were in the wrong place. Too close to really appreciate.

Damn the woman. Where the hell was she? She was really beginning to piss me off. I'd be damned if I was going to let anyone spoil my good mood, and that was all there was to it. I hung up the phone, got up, walked to the office door, poked my head out and said to Kerry, "The smelly man who sells candy downstairs? Chances are, he's a Leo. And the imbecile who roller-skates up and down Broadway screaming anti-Semitic slogans—*he* could easily be a Leo. And Mitterand, and how about some old lady who's too poor and frail and alone to even get a decent meal in a day. All of these people *may* be Leos, but they cannot possibly share the same fate for the day. It is impossible." I nodded once, feeling oh so smug, but that much better. Right then the phone rang. Kerry opened her mouth to say something in response, looked at the ringing phone, sighed, and answered in her chirpiest voice, "CSI, can I help you?"

I returned to my desk feeling infinitely better. I was about to place a call to Eddie Phillips, photojournalist and all-around good guy, when the phone rang. Kerry was still on the first call, so I picked up this one.

"CSI, can I help you?"

"Sydney, please." The voice was low and soft, but there was no mistaking that it was a man on the other end of the line.

"Speaking."

"Bang, bang. You're dead."

Before I could say, "Tom, I know it's you, cut the crap," the line went dead. So, Tom Cullerson's revenge had begun. I sat there with the receiver in hand and looked up. Kerry was standing at the doorway.

"Two things." She said holding up two fingers.

"Yes?" I put the receiver back in its cradle and folded my hands in my lap.

"First, that was Bartholomew's secretary. You have a two o'clock appointment with him today."

"Excellent. Thank you." I reached for the tulips and got up. Sunlight was pouring through the large arched windows, and I decided they would look best sitting on the sill in the direct light.

"And two, Max left a message on the machine. He

won't be in till after eleven. He has a ten o'clock with Beverly Tiari's accountant.''

''Okay.'' Much better. The flowers seemed to perk up as soon as I put them in place.

''And third—''

''You said there were two things.'' I backed away from the windows, admiring God's handiwork. Flowers are an amazing thing if you think about it.

''I lied. Third, I think you're a jerk. You can think what you like, but if you asked Minnie, she'd tell you that this astrologer is incredible. Very accurate.''

My aunt Minnie's psychic prowess includes daily chats with the deceased and an occasional ability to predict things like a visit from a long-lost friend or where you left your keys.

''Minnie talks to dead people, not asteroids,'' I answered stubbornly as I settled back behind my desk.

''Minnie is a woman of great insight and vision.''

''That's true.'' I wondered what Minnie would have to say about Tom Cullerson. ''By the way,'' I changed the subject, ''you did a great job on the Long file. I appreciate it.''

''All in a day's work. Good move, the flowers look better there. Coffee's ready. Want some?''

''Yes please.''

Kerry wasn't out the door thirty seconds when suddenly I was in the middle of a blitzkrieg.

I didn't know what the hell happened, but it felt and sounded like the building had been bombed and was collapsing around me. One minute I was reaching for the phone, and then next thing I knew I was on the floor. *Old buildings collapse all the time*, I thought. *Or maybe it's an earthquake, that makes sense, everyone knows the westside is built along a fault.* I heard a scream, uncertain if it was Kerry or me. When I looked over I saw her standing in the doorway. I hollered at her to get back and slowly started crawling around the desk, trying to keep as low as I could. The explosion felt like it lasted for minutes, but the truth is, just as quickly as it had occurred, it was over. When I peered out from behind the desk I saw that one of the arched windows facing

Broadway was gone and the frame around it looked as if it had been chewed up by King Kong. Street noises along with the cold rushed into the office, but an eerie calm had fallen over the room.

I got up off my knees and stumbled backwards. I held out a trembling hand to keep Kerry back as I carefully neared the gaping hole. Glass shards covered the floor like a sparkling carpet all the way to my desk. The vase of tulips was gone, but little shreds of red from the petals speckled the floor and sill. In the distance I could hear the shouts and cries from the street below.

"Call the police," I said with a calm I didn't feel. I slowly neared the window, afraid that with each step that I took, another explosion would blow me into the next world. Glass shards crunched under my boots as I reached the windows and looked down to see if anyone had been hurt. On the street below about three dozen people had gathered and were stupidly peering up to see what had happened. Oddly, the street hadn't turned into chaos. Just a bunch of bewildered onlookers, their curiosity overwhelming the fact that they might be in danger. Fortunately, as far as I could see, no one was lying on the ground with a chunk of glass sticking out of their head. I reached down, picked a tulip petal out of the debris, and rolled it tightly between my thumb and index finger until it was nothing.

Eleven

Though the explosion had sounded like the earth caving in when it happened, the fire department said it was clear that whoever had planted the device did so to frighten more than damage. They had achieved both goals, but one more long-term than the other. Once the smoke had cleared my fear was quickly replaced with anger because the damage done to my beautiful office was devastating to me. True, only the one window on the left facing Broadway had been destroyed, but the frame was gone and the walls for two feet surrounding it were a mess. The window next to it was cracked and would also have to be replaced, but it remained in the frame. The look of old, weathered Italian walls was ruined, and I was both livid and saddened that the painstaking care with which my friend Caryn had painted the space could be erased in less than a second.

I was, however, alive. And, miraculously, without a scratch.

The fire department arrived less than five minutes after the blast. Directly on their heels were the police and, finally, Con Edison—to be certain that the explosion wasn't the result of a gas leak.

It wasn't.

Apparently a small, timed explosive had been puttied to the outer, lower edge of the window. After a thorough search, it was determined that there had been only one bomb planted in our offices. In the scheme of such things, it was a baby explosive, but the fire department, and police and bomb squads are particular about bombs in New York. My normally serene office was thrown into chaos as the pros went to work.

I answered the questions that the investigators posed, including giving them a roster of enemies made through work or personal life. The list was relatively short, considering our line of work. There were two names of recent run-ins (neither of whom I thought would be capable of a pea-shooting, let alone a bombing); there was a Middle Eastern man with a personal grudge against me; CSI provides security for the Hackle Corporation executives overseas (they make gas masks), and last, but not least, Tom Cullerson.

I told them about the lock having been tampered with, and I suggested that Cullerson would top my list for people to question. My own background search on him hadn't been in-depth enough to know if he had a knowledge of bombs or even breaking and entering, for that matter, but I did know he had done a stint in the army as a young man.

After that there was nothing I could do for them. Rather than watch helplessly from the sidelines, I took my papers, set up shop up at Max's desk and let Kerry flirt with the nice men in uniform—she's always been a sucker for a uniform. It was nearing ten-thirty and I was wondering if Brendan Mayer was going to be a no-show.

No question about it, the incident had frightened me. When I sat at Max's desk, I could feel my knees shaking.

I had been trying to focus on my work for about twenty minutes when I looked up and saw a young man standing in the doorway. He was close to six feet tall and wore black jeans, black motorcycle boots, a knee-length winter coat—obviously purchased at the Salvation Army—and a beret. Curly brown hair hung below the beret down to his shoulders, framing a round, fleshy face.

"Brendan?" I asked as I walked toward him. "I'm

Sydney Sloane. Come on in.'' I held out an opened hand and gently beckoned to him.

He didn't say a word. He stood, like a deer caught in the headlights, hypnotized. His soft lips, too small for his large face, seemed to be moving but no words came out.

''As you can see, we've had a little accident here.'' I succeeded at sounding light, but my stomach was as tight as a drum. Brave though I may be, I don't take kindly to the idea of someone trying to blast me out of my life.

''What happened?'' His eyes darted anxiously around Max's office, past the opened doorway into my office, where a crew was gathering evidence.

''An old client doesn't want to pay his bill.'' I smiled reassuringly as I closed the door between our offices. ''Come on, we'll be more comfortable in here. Okay?''

''Sure.'' Brendan looked around the room at the assortment of toys and books, the dart board and the Nerf basketball hoop hanging over the door. ''Cool,'' he said as he shoved his hands deeper into his pockets. He slowly chewed a wad of gum that was taking up 60 percent of his mouth cavity. ''Very cool.'' He nodded to the dart-ridden portrait of Oliver North.

''So,'' I said, moving the flowers back and perching on Max's desk, ''you know about Peter.'' It wasn't a question.

Brendan moved to the dart board and retrieved all six projectiles. He mumbled something in the affirmative and stepped back from the board. ''So, what really happened out there?'' He nodded to my office. ''That have anything to do with Peter?''

''No. Should it?''

He shrugged.

''Peter was your best friend, wasn't he?''

''Yeah. We grew up together. But I've been here a couple of years now, so we didn't see much of each other.''

''What does that mean?''

He shrugged again and tossed a dart. It missed the board and stuck into the wall. I don't know if it was the activity of having the darts in hand or the obvious police presence, but Brendan Mayer seemed more composed than when he first arrived.

"Brendan, I've been hired to investigate Peter's death. Is there anything you can tell me?"

"Who hired you?" The next dart hit Ollie's shirt collar.

"His sister."

This seemed to get his attention.

"Paulessa?" The play on her two names—Vanessa and Paula—seemed to please him.

"That's right."

He nodded and seemed to lose interest in the darts but kept tossing away. "All I know is Petie didn't kill himself."

"How do you know that?" I asked.

" 'Cause the last time I saw him—"

"Which was?" I asked.

"Friday night. He was kidding around, but he told me if he died, that was the reason why. I just thought he was fucking around, like always." He tossed another dart.

"*What* was the reason why?" Clearly I was missing something here.

"The piece of paper he gave me. It was like blueprints, I guess." Brendan looked at me suspiciously.

"He gave you blueprints? Of what?"

He sighed as if he was talking to a jackass. "How should I know? I'm an actor, not an architect." He blew a large bubble, glanced at me, and popped the gum. "How do I know Paulessa hired you?"

"You can call and ask her." I motioned to the telephone on Max's desk. He looked at the phone, then back at me. "I have her number if you want it." It was, I thought, a perfectly reasonable request on his part, but Brendan flipped his hand and shook his head.

"Nah, that's okay." The fourth dart hit Ollie in the cheek. "Yes," he hissed, congratulating himself on his athletic prowess.

"Tell me about these blueprints." I crossed my arms over my chest and tucked my fingers under my armpits.

The whole place was getting cold as a result of the gaping hole in my office.

He tossed the fifth dart. It bounced off the wall and landed on the floor, point down.

"Do you know what the blueprints are for? A boat? A house?"

"Not a clue."

"Where is it?"

He turned and smiled slowly. Then he tapped his temple with an index finger, "I got kidneys, lady. I hid it to protect myself. If Petie got *killed* cause of this thing—"

"You should have taken it to the police right away." I tried not to scold him, but it was impossible. He obviously knew from the start that Peter had been killed. Why hadn't he gone to the police right away with the information he had?

"I was afraid." He let his shoulders go slack as he tossed the last dart without any enthusiasm. He turned back to me without seeing that the dart had hit Ollie in the right eye.

"Afraid of whom? Of what?"

He shrugged.

"No, Brendan, that's not good enough. I can't help Peter anymore, but I can help you. You have to understand, I'm one of the good guys."

"Lady, I don't know you from shit. All I know is my good friend gives me these stupid pieces of paper, makes a joke about dying, and the next thing I know—he's dead. Then I get a call from you. How do I know *you're* not after those pieces of paper? Or what you would be willing to do to get them?" He scratched nervously under the beret, but kept it on his head. "You have the balls to ask me what I'm afraid of. Shit, man, I'm afraid of everything. Everyone. You think I want to wind up like Petie? I don't think so. All I know is he's dead, and I have the thing that probably killed him. I don't know who they're for or what they're for, but I got them and let me tell you something, I don't want them."

"So give them to me."

He chewed the wad of gum loudly and moped over

to the sofa, where he finally sat. He was all legs and knees.

"I don't have them."

"Where are they?"

"I mailed them to myself."

"When?"

"Monday. As soon as I heard about Petie."

"So you haven't gotten them yet?"

"No. They're in the mail."

I sighed. Given that it was the holiday season, it could be weeks before we saw the blueprints.

"I thought it was a pretty smart move," he murmured defensively.

"Can you tell me anything about the blueprint?"

"No. Like I said, I thought he was fucking around. I just shoved them in my pants pocket and forgot about them."

"Was it his only copy?"

He held up his hands. "I don't know."

"What can you tell me about them?"

He pressed his lips together and puffed out his cheeks.

"Were they the original prints he gave you?" I prompted him.

"No. It was a copy."

"Did he say he'd be back for it?"

"No."

"How big was it? One page? Two?"

"I dunno. Maybe five."

"Okay, so tell me about the last time you saw Peter."

He took a deep breath. "It was Friday night. Saturday morning. He had gone to some sort of fund-raiser with his parents, and he was wired. He came over around eleven o'clock Friday, and we sat in my living room bullshitting for a couple of hours. Then at around one in the morning we decided to go to the Village. Petie didn't know the city, so I decided to give the man a tour."

"Where did you go?"

"Just places." He tried to avoid my gaze. "You know, bars, that sort of thing."

"Which bars?"

"I don't remember."

"Bullshit. Gay bars? Straight bars? After-hours clubs?"

"All of the above." He barked back at me. "What the hell difference does it make?"

"It could make a big difference. Did Peter meet anyone that night?"

"Yeah, sure. He was flirting his ass off. But he didn't go with anyone. I mean, he came home with me. Not that *we* did anything," he quickly added. "I mean, Petie and I were just friends. Good friends, but just friends. You know what I mean?"

"Did he go off with anyone that night?"

Brendan studied the palms of his huge hands. "Just for a minute. I didn't even see the guy. Petie was back before I even finished my drink."

"Did he know this person?"

Brendan exhaled a laugh. "If not before, after."

"So they just had sex together. It wasn't as if he had any previous knowledge of this particular person."

"Nah. Just a quick blow job." He tried to look defiant.

"And you didn't see this person?"

"No, I was talking to the bartender. The place was packed. It could have been anyone."

"Did Peter do drugs?"

"No way." He was emphatic.

"You're certain about this?"

"Absolutely." He shook his head. Speaking in affirmatives while shaking his head in the negative. I asked him again. "I'm telling you, he steered clear of drugs, even in high school when *everyone* was into *something*."

"Did he practice safe sex?"

"How the hell should I know? I didn't have sex with him. Besides, what difference does it make? It's not like he died from AIDS or anything." He popped his gum.

"The way I see it is if anyone has anonymous sex without protection, they have some sort of death wish. Now, this is a stretch, but if he had a death wish, as far as I'm concerned, he'd be a more likely candidate for playing Russian roulette with drugs. Imagine this: he has a fight with his folks, picks up some junkie at a bar, a little sex, fuck it, what's the big deal if he shoots up a little smack?''

Brendan was shaking his head. ''No way. Petie didn't kill himself. And if he did, it wouldn't be with drugs. Especially heroin. He hated needles. He practically passed out when he had to have a blood test for school.'' Brendan hiked himself out of his seat, found the waste-paper basket, and spit his gum into it. Hallelujah.

''What else happened that night?''

''Nothing. We got home about four in the morning, and there was a message on my machine from his father. Pissed as hell. Petie couldn't care less about what his old man thought, so he just passed out on the sofa, said he'd call him when he felt like it. We got up at about seven the next morning—because my roommate's a noisy fuck—and then Petie left. That was it.''

''So when did he give you this blueprint?''

''Maybe an hour after he got to my place Friday night. I forgot all about it until I heard about him being found at the pier.''

''How did you hear about it?''

''Our old gym coach from high school works for Mr. Long now. He called me. He didn't want me hearing it from a stranger or reading it in the papers. His name is Lyle Grubbs. Good man.''

''Grubbs,'' I repeated, wondering why Lyle didn't tell me that he had contacted Brendan. He had to know that I would have found him.

There was a knock at Max's door. ''Sydney.'' Kerry poked her head in the doorway. ''I'm sorry to bother you, but I thought you'd want to know that the police are done out here. I called the glass people, and they should be here in a few hours. I don't know that they'll be able to put in a window, but at least they'll get it boarded up for you. Okay?''

''You're the best.''

''I know.'' She winked at Brendan and shut the door.

''Brendan, you need to talk to the police. As far as they're concerned, the case is closed. What I'd like to do is set up a meeting for you to talk to them. I'll even go with you if that would make you more comfortable.''

''I don't know, man. Petie was like a brother, but I don't want to get mixed up in this shit.''

''The fact is, you already are. However, you have two good allies—the police and me. Now Peter's dead, there's nothing we can do to change that, but we can find out what really happened to him. To do that, we need your help. What do you say?''

Brendan chewed on his thumbnail for a good fifteen seconds before nodding. ''Okay.''

''Good.'' I dialed Gil's number. As always he sounded like he was in a rush when he picked up the phone, but I quickly told him what I had. He agreed to meet with Brendan at his office downtown.

''Can you go now?'' I asked Brendan. He shifted and heaved a sigh, but finally acquiesced. ''Do you have rehearsal?'' I asked, knowing what he had told me when he agreed to meet me in the first place.

''Oh, right. Screw it, I can miss that.'' He shrugged like it didn't matter, which confirmed my initial suspicion that there was no rehearsal. Having been a theater major once upon a time, I know actors live for rehearsals because rehearsals mean they're working on a project, and acting is, after all, their life's blood.

''Okay, Gil, he'll be there in half an hour.''

I gave Brendan Gil's name and address. ''Would you like me to go with you?'' I offered.

''Nah, that's okay.'' He sounded confident enough, but his body seemed to sag.

''You sure?'' I pushed. When he insisted he was fine, I pulled one of my cards out and said, ''I want you to keep my card on you until this is cleared up. If you think of anything or need anything, just call me, okay?'' I scribbled my home number on the back of the card and handed it to him. ''Anytime, day or night. You got that?'' He studied the card. ''There's no reason for you to be afraid, but it's always nice to know you have a friend.''

He shoved the card in his pants pocket as he stood. ''You think you'll find out what happened to Petie?''

"Absolutely." I walked him to the door and paused. "Brendan, do you know Vanessa?"

"I never met her, if that's what you mean. I mean, sure I know *about* her, I knew that she and Petie kept in touch with each other, but I never had a chance to meet her."

"Do you know if they saw each other?"

"You mean during this trip? I don't know. Maybe. I know for sure he was *planning* on seeing her either Saturday or Sunday, one of those days."

"Do you know if they saw one another in the last few years?"

"Yeah, they did. I know one time when they hooked up in Chicago. We went there for our senior trip in high school. The rents didn't know about it."

"Rents?" I asked.

"Parents," he explained with a sigh as if to say, "Get with it, lady."

"Cool," I said, wanting him to know I was totally with-it.

He stopped in the doorway and turned slowly. "You think I'm like in any danger or anything?" His light brown eyes looked almost sleepy as he looked down at me.

"No. But like I said, you'll feel a lot better after you talk to the police. Gil's a good man, you can trust him. Okay?"

He nodded once, repositioned his beret, and left just as Max was walking through the front door.

Twelve

"What are you doing here?" I asked Max from the doorway to his office. He was wearing an eye patch over his left eye, the one Carlos had popped him in but good.

"Funny thing, I work here." He was winded, no doubt from having taken the stairs two at a time. "Yes, indeed, I was walking down Broadway after an exhilarating meeting with Ms. Tiari's accountant when I happened upon a police barricade, and guess what I saw? A gaping hole where there was once a window. And in our offices. I want to know what happened. Are you two all right?"

"We're fine," I tried to assure him calmly.

"So says you. If anyone's interested in what I think—it sucks." Kerry was sitting behind her desk. "The idea that I need a safety belt at my own desk is not good. Not good at all."

"Was anyone hurt?" Max squeezed her shoulder.

"No," Kerry replied. "Unless you call having the shit scared out of you hurt."

"It was a small device meant more to scare than hurt," I quoted the police, but Max knows me well enough to see through my insouciance.

"And who might be responsible?" he asked as he started into my office.

I followed him. "It could be anyone, but my first thought was Tom Cullerson. I gave the police his name as likely candidate number one, along with a few other names. It's a long shot, but the Hackle Corporation might be somehow involved."

"A real long shot," Max grumbled as he examined the damage. "Well, it shouldn't be too hard to fix. Are you sure you're okay? Honestly."

"Honestly, it scared the hell out of me, but I'm fine." I held out my arms to prove the point. Oddly enough I'd gotten through the explosion without so much as a smudge on my clothes, let alone a scratch on my body.

He nodded once and started toward the door.

"Where are you going?" I asked. He was already halfway across the room.

"I'm going to show that son of a bitch Cullerson what it really means to be scared," he said without missing a step.

"Waitwaitwaitwaitwait." I turned the one word into one word as I chased after him and caught him by the arm when he was nearly at the front door.

"Wait for what, Sydney? For the police to talk to him? For him to try to blow you up again? For him to do more than scare you the next time?"

I took a deep breath and exhaled slowly, never once taking my hand off his arm. I knew that Max was angry because he was scared for me, because he loves me. But I was between a rock and a hard place; as much as I appreciated what was driving him, I was capable of taking care of myself. I didn't need a big burly guy to race in and butt heads with another guy for my sake. Or, did Max think I did?

"Can we please talk?" When I opened my mouth I was surprised at how even-tempered I sounded, considering the conflict that was raging inside me.

"There's nothing to say. The man obviously understands only one language." Max's eye darted from me to Kerry and back to me again.

"Is that right? And I suppose you're the only one who can speak it? Well, then, tell me something, Max, just where the hell are you going to find him?" If we both hadn't been caught up in our own anxiety, we would have been able to respond to the absolute absurdity of the situation. We stood directly in the crossroads between laughter and rage.

The flicker of recognition was in Max's eye for a moment before it just as quickly disappeared. He knew that I knew that he didn't know where in the world Tom Cullerson lived or worked. The Cullersons had come to us when Max was fully absorbed on another assignment. The most contact he had had with the psychotic couple were the accounts I'd reported nightly during my week and a half employment with them.

The tendons in his neck strained and released several times. He said nothing. I released his arm, turned and stormed into my office, slamming the door behind me.

I was angry, not so much at Max as I was at myself. I knew Max was acting out of love—not because he thought I was incapable after the way I'd botched it with Debi Cullerson—but I was feeling overwhelmed with my own sense of ineptitude. There was no question that I felt accountable for Debi Cullerson's death, ergo, Tom Cullerson was my responsibility and mine alone.

I knew Max would follow, and he did.

"Just what the hell was that all about?" he asked with obvious restraint as he slammed the door behind him.

I was at the far end of the room, lifting a large spider plant off the window ledge. I needed to be busy, and with the window broken it was too cold in the room now for my plants. I decided to store them in Max's office for the time being.

"Why don't you tell me?" I asked as I carried the twenty-pound planter across the room. I was glad to have the hearty plant between us, concealing us from one another for the moment.

"Now what's *that* supposed to mean?" he yelled, as I passed him and went straight into his office. His voice followed closely behind me. "Oh fine, good, don't tell me what you're thinking. I'll just read your mind!"

If he had been able to read my mind, he would have discovered that at that precise moment I was thinking that Max and I were both acting out of fear. He was afraid for me, and I was trying desperately not to consider the looming possibility that I might have lost what it takes to do my job, to deal with such insanity. I set the planter on his window ledge and whirled around. ''Oh no you don't, cookie. Don't you go turning this around to be my problem.'' The anger was out before I could put a lid on it. Max and I don't fight often, but when we do it's with total abandon because we know that no matter what we'll be there for one another when the dust settles.

''Turning it around! Hey, this *is* your problem. That son of a bitch wasn't trying to scare me. Or do I need to remind you of that?'' His face was turning a dull shade of crimson.

''That's right, Max, Cullerson is *my* problem. Not yours.'' I positioned myself defiantly in front of him. ''But that's not what we're talking about. Just take a good look at what's happening here, because when you do you'll see that Cullerson didn't scare me, he made me mad, mad as hell, but he did scare you. And because of that you went off half-cocked, like some testosterone-hyped idiot complete with fists flailing thinking what? What, Max? That I'd be grateful because you're here to protect me? That I'm not capable of handling things anymore and what a relief it is to have the big man there to fight my battles? Well let me tell you something, as far as I see it, you just acted like a fool. A big old macho . . . zit!'' I pushed past him and went back into my office, where I made a beeline to the philodendron next to the sofa.

''What, if I may be so bold, is a macho zit?''

This was followed by a lengthy pause. I kept my back to Max and fluffed the philodendron.

''Does that mean a really manly pimple?'' Max pondered softly from the doorway dividing our offices. ''Or a stubborn one in the middle of your forehead that just won't go away?''

Something was bubbling up inside me, and I could feel it surfacing. Tears? Laughter? Laughter? Tears?

''I don't think I'm a macho zit. A horse's ass, maybe, but definitely not a macho zit.''

Laughter prevailed. I sank down onto the sofa and laughed until the tears started. By then Max was sitting beside me, continuing his monologue about the infinite possibilities of what a macho zit might be.

The room was freezing cold, and my fingertips were starting to numb. I handed him the philodendron and grabbed the three small African violets from my desk top.

Once we had silently transferred all the plants from my office to his, we closed the door to stave off the windchill factor and started over again.

"Cullerson has to be dealt with." Max pulled up the patch and gently rubbed his eyes. The shiner was as bad as it was going to get. Dark purple rimmed his bloodshot eye.

I nodded in agreement. "You know as well as I do that the police hate people who play with explosives, no matter how small. Cullerson's on the top of their priority list right now, and they want to chat with him as badly as . . ."

"A chat—" he said with disgust.

"I know, I know, but the fact is, men like Cullerson are cowards. If nothing else, knowing that the police are on him might make him suspend his activities *for a while*: no wait, hear me out." I stopped him before he could interrupt me. "Which only means that it would give us a little time, but right now that's just what I need. Look, I met Peter Long's best friend, and I'm convinced that someone killed that kid. Now, we've been hired to find out who and you know as well as I do if we don't act fast, we may never get the answer. I have to stay focused—"

"Right, *you* do, but we're partners, remember? If there are two problems and two of us, why don't we each take a problem and run with it? You deal with Long, and I'll deal with Cullerson." It was logical, simple, and direct. But for whatever reason, it wasn't that easy for me.

"You hit the nail on the head before, Max. Cullerson is my problem. Seriously, how would you feel if you were in my shoes?"

I let the question sit between us like a lead weight. We both knew that Max would respond the same way I was; Cullerson was a personal thing and someone I had to deal with alone.

Max sighed. "I hate this."

"Me too." I pinched a browning leaf off an African violet and balled it gently between my fingers. "Max, I promise you, if I need help with Cullerson, you'll be the first one I call, okay?"

He shook his head slowly.

"Look." I sighed. "I know you don't think I botched it with Debi Cullerson, but I do. For the first time in my career I really wonder if I'm doing the right thing. I mean, maybe Leslie's right. Maybe this line of work isn't for me anymore. I don't know. But I do know if I'm going to get any answers, I have to find them for myself. And don't forget, Tom Cullerson isn't the worst shithead I've dealt with."

"I know that Cullerson is a personal thing for you," Max said gently as he pulled the patch back down over his eye, "but the fact is, that son of a bitch might wind up killing one of us. Not just you—not that I'm diminishing anything here—but I believe from the bottom of my heart that you have to deal with him, and deal with him right now. I know you have a time crunch with Long, but honestly, I don't think you have the luxury of time with this fucker." He shifted his weight and shrugged.

There was nothing I could say. He was right. I knew I had to deal with Cullerson, and the longer I put it off, the more at risk I placed Kerry and Max.

When Max continued, he addressed the floor. "Sydney, I know what you're going through. I think we've all been there in some way or another, but the one thing I've learned after all these years is that I've never accomplished anything alone. We need friends and people to lean on. That doesn't mean you're less strong or less capable. It just means that you know how to take care of yourself." He nodded once, and added, "I just hope it doesn't kill you to learn that lesson."

"Me too."

"So, what do you want?" Max asked with resignation.

"I want to bring Debi Cullerson back to life."

"And?"

"I want to be the perfect weight without ever having to diet."

"And?"

I bent my head, put my face in my hands and massaged my forehead, temples, eyes, cheeks, lips, chin and finally my scalp. When I was done I felt like a puppy after a good belly rub. "I want you to go with me to my two o'clock interview with Clifford Bartholomew. That's one thing I'm not up for alone right now. What do you say?"

Max raised his one eyebrow not covered by the patch. "Are you telling me you need a macho zit to assist you with this Bartholomew?"

I laughed. "Yes, that's exactly what I'm telling you."

"You know me," he drawled, "When my testosterone's in hyperdrive, well, little lady, I can chew the butt end off a tank and spit it out into little bullets. You know what I mean? So, I suppose a man like this Bartholomew would be like a Sara Lee chocolate cake with vanilla icing to a man in my state, huh?"

"Let's hope so."

"The game plan?"

I glanced at my watch. It was already nearing twelve-thirty, and I was surprisingly hungry for a woman whose stomach had recently been tied in knots.

"Bartholomew's office is in the fifties. How about some lunch first?"

"Carnegie Deli! You know what I always say." Max's smile was beguiling. "In times of stress, one should always eat a sandwich bigger than their head. Let's go." He was up and into his jacket before I could blink.

Kerry wasn't thrilled about being left alone in the office, but agreed to stay there until the cleaning crew and glass workers had done their thing. Then she could take the rest of the day off.

"By the way," I said, as Max and I headed to the subway. "I like the eye patch. Very Hathaway." I was referring to the shirt ads with the dashing models wearing Hathaway shirts and eye patches.

"I thought it would be more effective with Tiari's accountant than looking like the RCA dog. It was leftover from Halloween last year."

"I remember." A car backfired, and I jumped like I'd been shot in the side.

"Nervous?" Max asked calmly, not missing a step.

"Me? Nervous? What's to be nervous about?" I said, linking my arm through his and drawing closer. "The only thing that would make this day complete is a subway fire."

"Bite your tongue." Max laughed as he held out a token for me. "I have a date tonight with Marcy, and I'm not about to miss it because you're jinxed."

Jinxed? Did Max think I was jinxed? Nah, he was just kidding. I dropped the token into the slot and pushed through the turnstile, following close behind him. Maybe I was jinxed. Maybe my Karma with Debi Cullerson was going to haunt me until I paid my debt. Maybe everything that was happening was happening as a result of powers outside of . . . no. If I kept thinking like this, the next thing I knew I'd be reading horoscopes, chanting like the Nichiren Buddhists in front of a gahanza, or, worse, calling up the dead with Minnie, asking for their help and advice.

"Where are you?" Max nudged me as we sat side by side on the Broadway train headed to Columbus Circle.

"New York City," I answered. Coming through the subway car was a man in rags singing at the top of his lungs. He smelled like he hadn't bathed in a year and as he passed us he stuck an outstretched palm in our faces. "Where else?" I said as I dropped a quarter into his callused hand. "Where else?"

Thirteen

The radio station where Clifford Bartholomew worked was on the twenty-eighth floor of a midtown office building.

The receptionist, who was sitting under the station's logo at a curved desk with a telephone board that looked like it was the control panel for a DC-10, held up an index finger and told us she'd be with us in a minute. Fifteen calls later she apologized and asked, "Can I help you?" Another call came in and she put them on hold.

We told her we had an appointment with Clifford Bartholomew, and she nodded. "Down the hallway on the right, third door on the left. He's on air, but there's a room where you can wait for him." Without waiting for a response, she was back on the phones.

The waiting room for Clifford Bartholomew had a window so you could watch the DJs perform. He wore a headset and was leaning back into a black leather swivel chair. We couldn't hear what he was saying, but I liked the idea of being able to watch the man without having to hear him. I'd never actually heard Bartholomew, but apparently he had become one of the biggest names in the business, inciting callers from around the country to follow his myopic lead regarding politics, consumerism, and everything else under the sun about which he had an opinion—which covered just about everything. That an ultraconservative egotistical misogynist bigot could rally such support was a sign of our times, one that both disturbed and fascinated me.

Bartholomew was gesticulating with both hands over his head. He was facing a control room which was to our left, so we studied him in profile. The best word to describe him was crisp. His white shirt was without a wrinkle, his blue-and-white-striped tie was still knotted neatly at the collar, his fringe of pure white hair was trimmed and looked as if he had combed it not a second before our arrival. When he wasn't gesturing wildly, his fingers were tucked into the waistband of his dark slacks under the Gucci belt. He was not what I would call a good-looking man, but that could have been because I knew he supported the NRA, antiabortionists, and Pat Robertson; those sort of politics always color a person's looks for me. His face was ruddy and a little puffy, his blue eyes seemed to be sunken in their sockets, and his nose was both wide and upturned.

"Not a pleasant-looking man if you ask me." Max turned away from the viewing window and picked up the copy of *Vanity Fair* someone had left behind. "Snouts are cute on pigs, but people? I don't think so." He threw his jacket on one chair and took a seat on the sofa. "With the kind of money he has, you'd think he'd have a nose job."

"Why? He's a disc jockey. It's not like he has a television talk show."

"These guys do personal appearances all the time."

"What for?"

"I don't know. They cut the ribbons at openings for malls and bowling alleys, those sort of things."

"I thought soap opera stars did that."

"They do. It's the same mentality, but different audiences."

"How do you know so much about this?"

"You'd be surprised at what I know."

"We should call Kerry." I peered through the glass and saw that Bartholomew was still talking. Just then I caught someone in the control booth waving to me. I looked behind me and realized the only other person they could be waving at was Max. I tentatively waved back. She nodded and beckoned me to come to her. Well, there was only one door to the room, so I turned and went back through the door we had entered, which led out into the hallway.

The woman was hurrying toward me. ''Hi, I'm Clifford's assistant, Nan, and he had to take on Michael Lennan's show, which he's doing now, because Michael was in a car accident. You *are* here to see Clifford, aren't you?'' She took a breath, and I nodded. ''Good. Well, Michael's going to be fine, but Clifford's running a little late, and he wanted you to know he hasn't forgotten about you. Michael's show's only an hour, so you won't have to wait much longer. Can I get you something to drink while you're waiting for him?'' Already she was backstepping to where she had come from.

''No, that's okay, I'll just wait in there.''

''Okay. Good.'' She turned and started jogging up the hallway.

''Wait!'' I called out. ''Where can I make a local call?''

''In the waiting room. Just dial nine first.''

Max was sprawled out on the sofa by the time I returned. I threw his coat over his legs and took the only other seat in the room. I dialed the office. Kerry picked up immediately.

''Finally,'' she said when she heard my voice.

''Are you okay?'' I asked, afraid that something had happened after we left.

''I have the willies like you wouldn't believe. You know I thought I was okay when you guys left, but do you have any ideas how many unidentifiable sounds come from this building?''

''Take a deep breath.'' I tried to calm her.

''Is she all right?'' Max asked, kicking up into a sitting position.

''She's fine,'' I said, motioning for him to lie back down.

''She's not fine,'' Kerry countered. ''The phone hasn't stopped ringing since you left. You ready?''

I fished a pen and spiral pad of paper out of my bag. ''Okay. Go.''

"First of all, Leslie's number is 555-0098. She'll only be there till three-thirty, so you should call her before then. Someone named Lyle called regarding dinner tonight. He'll have to call you back because he won't be at any definite number all afternoon. He said seven-thirty would be good for him. Vanessa Stephens called again. Not a very pleasant woman, if you ask me, which shouldn't surprise me because women that attractive always seem to have a bug up their butts."

I didn't remind her that she was, in fact, one of those attractive women, and she didn't seem to have a bug up anything.

"Sydney, if you don't swear to call her as soon as we get off the phone, I'm leaving, which means you won't have anyone here when the window people come." She paused. "You still with me?" she asked.

"I am."

"What happened to your two o'clock with Bartholomew?"

"He's running late. Next."

"Gil called. He wanted to know what happened to Brendan."

"Excuse me?"

Kerry sighed. "Let's see, he said, and I quote, 'Where the hell is the kid? I don't have all day.' "

"Where the hell is he?" I asked rhetorically.

"How the heck should I know? Anyway, the ever-patient Gilbert Jackson said he couldn't wait all day. Let's see what else we have . . ." She went through the next eight messages, commenting on each of the callers. "Also, Minnie called."

"When?"

"About three minutes ago."

"What did she say?"

"Call her when you have a chance."

"Where?"

"Home, I guess."

"Okay. If Lyle calls again tell him I'll meet him at seven-thirty at . . . where can we go for dinner?"

"Bouley?" Kerry suggested one of New York's best restaurants.

"I don't think so."

"Petrossian?" Again with the hundred-dollar dinners.

"No, how about The Gingerman?" Just across the street from Lincoln Center, the restaurant is quieter than most others around it.

"Okay. And what about Leslie?" Kerry asked.

"Never you mind about Leslie, thank you."

Max glanced over the top of his magazine when I got off the phone.

"What about Leslie?" He asked.

"Why is everyone so concerned about me and Leslie?" I asked as I dialed Vanessa Stephens's number.

"Because we love you and we want you to be happy. Leslie makes you happy. Usually." He dismissed me as he returned to his magazine.

Vanessa wasn't in, so I left a message on her voice mail—which is only a fancy-schmantz word for answering machine—and then I dialed Gil's number. The line was busy so, my next call was to Leslie. She answered on the second ring.

"Hey there, it's me." I said.

"Hey, you. No, Mike, put that under the piece. Under it!" She called out instructions to a worker, and I could hear that she was having a hard day. In the past I would soothe her with words of support and love and insist that I pamper her come evening. Which I always did. A bottle of champagne or wine. A light dinner and, for dessert, a massage. If the thought was crossing my mind, I had to assume that it might be crossing hers as well.

"I have bad news," I said.

"Oh goody." She sighed.

"I can't see you tonight. I have a business thing."

There was a prolonged pause. "A business *thing*? You know, most people have business dinners or business meetings, but you—you have a business thing." She paused again, and I wasn't sure as to how to respond. I was fighting defensiveness when she added, "Which we all know *could* be just about anything."

I took a deep breath and let the relief sink in.

"And after your dinner thing, are you busy?" she

asked. I could hear the tension in her voice, the tightness that masks insecurity.

"I'll tell you what." I paused, not knowing exactly what I was going to say.

"What?"

"Will you have dinner with me tomorrow night and then perhaps we could go out dancing or whatever?" Having heard my words, I realized how formal I sounded, and how right it felt. There was an arm's-length distance between us that needed to be respected, which is an odd thing considering the intimacy we normally share.

"You're asking me out on an official date?"

"I am."

"With dancing or whatever?"

"That's right. I'm feeling better able to compete with the legions of women vying for your attentions."

"Is that so?"

"Yes."

"And what has brought about this change?"

"I don't know. Desire, maybe."

"Well, I know what I desire. Mike, are you *blind*, for God's sake!" She covered the mouthpiece and had a quick argument with one of the guys she does regular installations with. "Look, I've got to go. This is driving me crazy. I'll see you tomorrow."

"Okay."

"Oh, and Sydney?"

"Yeah."

"Just for the record, I think I'd prefer whatever over dancing, okay?"

"Okay." When I hung up the receiver I was keenly aware that Max had put down the magazine and was listening to my call.

He smiled and patted his hands together. "I've been rooting for the two of you to kiss and make up."

"I wish I knew what the hell I was doing. She's never going to like what I do for a living." I dialed Gil's number again.

"And you're crazy about decorating?"

"Shit. He's never on the phone this long."

"Who?"

"Gil."

"What's wrong with Gil?"

"He was supposed to meet with Brendan." I dialed Brendan's number, but after two rings a machine picked up. "Brendan, it's Sydney. Are you there?" I waited. "Okay, it's about two-thirty, and I'm in a meeting, but I'll call you as soon as I can. If you're not going to be home, leave a number with my secretary where I can reach you."

"So he stood Gil up? I'm not surprised. The kid's a flake." He sat up.

"Really? And just how did you come to that conclusion? You didn't even meet him." Over lunch I had told Max what I had learned from Brendan. It didn't elude either of us that they use blueprints in manufacturing computers.

"I saw him. That was enough. Trust my male instincts. Guys know guys."

Fortunately before I could respond the door to the waiting room burst open. Clifford Bartholomew's assistant, Nan, poked her head in and said, "Ms. Sloane? You want to come with me?" She looked like a taller, slimmer version of Dot from the Little Lotta comic books I'd read as a kid. It was as we were getting our coats that she saw Max. "Excuse me, who're you waiting for?" she asked abruptly.

Max gave her his sexy guy smile and poked a thumb in my direction.

"You're together?" She looked as if she had to go to the bathroom, jiggling her body weight from one foot to the other while she hung on to the doorknob for dear life.

"Yes, we are," I answered for him.

She sighed. "Okay. Let's go. I'll show you to his office now." We followed her as she dashed through the corridors like a busy little drone bee.

"Tell me, Sydney, is this girl hyperactive or am I suddenly in a time warp?" Max said, as we—not wanting to jog—stayed a good ten paces behind Nan. At the end of the hallway, she pointed to a door, told us to make ourselves comfortable, and hurried off.

Clifford Bartholomew had a corner office which, with the stacks of files and papers lining the floors, reminded me of an attorney's chamber. It was bright, cluttered, and uncomfortable. While his ostentatious ebony desk took up most of the room, there was a single visitor's chair across from his desk and then, across the room, there was a well-worn leather sofa hidden under newspapers, magazines, and other periodicals.

Less than a minute after we arrived, Bartholomew came barreling through the door.

"Sydney?" He stretched his hand to Max and smiled expansively. "Good to meet you. Sorry I had to keep you waiting, but you know how it is."

Max shook the hand offered, and said, "I'm Max Cabe. This is my associate Sydney Sloane. Sydney, Clifford Bartholomew."

Clifford turned and extended his hand to me. "Sorry about that, dear. No doubt you have that problem all the time."

I smiled. "That's okay, hon." I assumed if his assistant knew I was a woman, he knew as well. Let the games begin.

We leveled a gaze at one another, summing up our opponent's strengths and weaknesses. Then Clifford cut it off and took a seat behind his desk. "Sit down, sit down," he suggested. "Might as well take a load off, right?"

I took the seat across from his desk and Max perched on the windowsill.

"Now, what can I do for you?" He leaned back into his chair and crossed his arms over his chest.

"We're investigating the death of Peter Long—"

He cut me off. "And just who hired you?" Bartholomew oozed enough arrogance to turn the simple query into an accusation.

"A family member."

"Yes, but which one?" He squinted at me like I had suddenly grown a second head.

I started to say, "I don't think it's necessary," but again I was cut off.

"Well I do, Miss Sloane. I happen to think it's very *necessary*." Clearly he was attacking me, but what, I wondered, for? I glanced at Max, who was obviously amused by this.

I studied Bartholomew. There was no way a man like this could conceal his hubris. Nothing could ever disguise how enamored Clifford Bartholomew was with Clifford Bartholomew. He watched me watching him. He arched his left eyebrow and smiled with the right half of his mouth. Undoubtedly he believed this was a cunning look, the sneer of a savvy man when, in fact, it made him look only mildly retarded.

"Mr. Bartholomew, you know perfectly well who hired me." I crossed my legs and eased my shoulders. His nod was almost imperceptible. "So why even question that?"

His broad smile was a cold, ugly thing. "To see just how forthright you would be, my dear." He nodded, and in a flash his smile was gone. "Now then, what can I do for you?" He studied his desk top like a kid in a candy store wondering whether to pick the licorice or the jawbreakers. *Yes, Cliffy, I understand; you're a very busy man.*

"How well did you know Peter?"

"Fairly well."

"Is there anything you can tell me about him—from your own perspective—that might paint a clearer picture of him?"

Bartholomew eyed the papers on his desk and slid a folder out from under a short stack. "Peter was my best friend's son. He's dead, and I believe that he killed himself. Perhaps accidentally, but by his own hand nonetheless. Now, your little investigation is only making things more painful for Wallace and his good wife Louise. To assist you in this is only to give credence to something I believe to be completely and utterly bogus."

"Were you aware that several threats have been made on Mr. Long's life?"

Bartholomew looked up from the folder. His face was flat for the first time during this meeting. "Yes, I was."

"Doesn't that mean something?"

"The threats, I believe, were launched at Wallace, not Peter."

"What better way to hurt someone than killing a loved one? Killing Wallace Long would have been one thing, but his son—now that's quite another matter. That's sure to get attention."

"It's an interesting hypothesis, but unfounded and therefore invalid." He tossed the folder back onto the desk. "Look, Peter was a nice boy. I can't say as I knew him intimately—as I said I was friends with his parents, not him—but I will say that he was a moody kid who made it clear that he thought he was better than his father. It's always broken Wallace's heart that he and Peter didn't have a better relationship."

"So Wallace and Peter didn't get along?"

His eyes jerked up. "Oh no, I'm not saying that, not saying that at all. Men have different relationships from women. That may be something a young girl such as yourself can't understand." Bartholomew turned to Max. "Isn't that right?"

"Oh, I don't know. As I understand it, the father and son didn't get along." In the direct light, with his left eye hidden behind the patch and his salt-and-pepper hair catching the light, Max looked striking. "I think that's all Sydney is trying to establish."

Bartholomew gave Max a smile that was meant to chill. Max looked past Bartholomew, out at the view.

"Why do you think Peter killed himself?" I asked.

"Because he wasn't important enough for anyone to want him dead." Again he plastered a smarmy smile on his face. "Or did you mean *why* did he kill himself? If that's what you meant, I wouldn't have a clue."

"Did you see Peter during this trip, Mr. Bartholomew?" I asked.

He shook his head. "No, no I didn't. We were at the same dinner party Friday night, but Peter left early."

"So you didn't see him there?"

"Well, I saw him from across the room, but I didn't see him to speak to him."

"I see. And you two didn't talk all evening, not even to say hello?"

"That's right. I was running a little late, so by the time I arrived, everyone was seated."

"Can you tell me how he appeared that night? Was he anxious or unhappy?"

"He seemed fine. Wallace and Louise raised their children to be socially adept. Good breeding."

"Did you see him leave?"

My line of questioning seemed to be boring the important Mr. Bartholomew. He took a deep breath and yawned. "Perhaps I did, I don't really remember."

"If you could try to remember, sir. It was, after all, the last time you were to see him alive."

He stared at the papers on his desk and pushed his lower lip out. After several seconds he finally said, "Now that I think of it, I did see him leave. He had been sitting next to his mother at the dais and just before dessert was cleared, Peter stood to leave. It was apparent that his parents didn't want him to go, but they weren't about to make a scene. He left, and for the show of it, all was well, but I can tell you every single one of us sitting in that room knew what bad form it was and our hearts went out to Wallace and Libby."

"You said before that the Longs had taught their children to be socially adept. Does that mean you know their daughter?"

"Paula?" He looked as if he was passing the sanitation works on the West Side Highway. "No, I've never had the pleasure. But I know all about her. She sounds like a spoiled little ingrate who, from what I can tell"—he looked directly into my eyes—"is just out to cause as much heartbreak and trouble for her parents as she possibly can."

"I suppose Wallace has told you all about her?"

He laughed sharply. "Hardly, my dear. He won't have a thing to do with her."

"I thought that they were in contact with one another," I lied, wondering where it would lead.

"Is that what she told you? Well she lied. He wanted nothing to do with her."

"I see." I continued to play the dumb broad because, as much as I hated it, I figured it was the easiest way to get him to open up. "It must have been *Louise* who kept in touch with her."

His laugh sounded like a tire going flat. "Libby didn't know anything. She was devastated when Paula disappeared. Wallace didn't want her to have to go through that again and again, so he made a point to protect her from Paula. He's known where she's been the whole time, but he never told Libby. You know as well as I do how easy it is to trace someone. Everyone leaves a paper trail. And with his kind of money, Wallace could find a pin at the bottom of the ocean."

"So they were never in touch with Paula?" I asked, somewhat incredulous.

"That's right."

"Then how did you know all about Paula, if neither Wallace or Louise talked about her?"

This seemed to throw him a little. He looked at me, then away from me, and exhaled an uncomfortable sigh, meant to be a laugh. When he looked at me again his cheeks were slightly flushed. He offered me the sort of smile that a clergyman might bestow on the misguided. "Naturally Wallace and I spoke about his family. Perhaps not at length, but one doesn't need a dissertation to get the gist of the situation. Besides, whatever has been said in confidence between Wallace and me is none of your business." His facade of mellowness couldn't hide that fact that I had just tripped onto something that made him touchy.

"I'm not asking you to betray confidences, Mr. Bartholomew. But your best friend's son is dead, and I believe it was neither an accident nor a suicide. That leaves one option. I intend to find out who killed him, and why."

"Well, goody for you." He leaned back in his chair and tucked his hands into his waistband. He looked like a seal swimming belly up.

"I understand that the Longs wanted to keep their

son's death out of the papers, away from general scrutiny. Is that right?"

"It's an impossible thing to keep from the public, Miss Sloane."

"Yes, I agree. Is that why *you* decided to make it public?"

"It wasn't *my* decision, if that's what you're getting at."

"Yes, sir, that is what I'm getting at. So if it wasn't your decision, whose was it?"

"Every radio station has certain policies. Decisions of that nature are never made by one person."

"Really? That's interesting. And who makes these decisions?"

Clifford pushed his lips into an unattractive pout and sucked them back in. "I don't see how this line of questioning can get you anywhere. And I'm much too busy a man to waste my time." He bestowed on me another deeply insincere smile.

Despite his dismissal, I stayed with it. "I would imagine, given your status at this station, that the ultimate decision to make Peter's death public, would be yours. Am I mistaken?"

"I don't know what you're driving at."

"Why did you air Peter's death when the Longs had wanted to keep it private?"

Neither of us moved a muscle. We stared at one another until it became uncomfortable. He pulled his glance away first, and said, in a voice dripping with camaraderie, "You know how the press is. If they were to get their hands on this, they would have torn Wallace apart. Wallace is my friend, but I'm also a staunch supporter of his political aspirations. Something like this could ruin him forever. So yes, in answer to your question, it's true, I convinced him that if *we* were the ones to make it public, he would be more likely to have the support of the community."

"Rather than their suspicion," I concluded for him.

He spread his hands open. "Public hangings have always been popular."

"I see."

"No, my dear, I don't think you do." Clifford leaned back into his chair and bounced gently back and forth. "It may sound cold to a young woman such as yourself, but one thing has nothing to do with the other. We're talking politics here, and that boy's death had nothing to do with his good father's run for office. As I see it, we made a wise decision. So you and all your liberal friends can cast whatever judgments you like, but the fact remains the same. Wallace Long is a noble man who would be an asset representing the people of his home state. His son's untimely death should not interrupt the otherwise natural course of events."

"How fortunate for Mr. Long to have a loyal and focused friend, such as yourself."

Clifford nodded humbly.

"Tell me, Mr. Bartholomew, during this trip have you been responsible for all of Mr. Long's fund-raising events?"

"Why do you ask?"

I shrugged. "I'm curious that a candidate who is running for local office would go out of state to raise funds. Mr. Long is running for the office of governor, isn't he?"

Bartholemew poked his tongue against the inside of his right cheek as he considered my line of questioning. Finally he sighed and explained, "There are loyal party members across the country, Miss Sloane, who like to support worthy candidates, regardless of the office they seek."

"I suppose that's true. Have you hosted Mr. Long's fund-raising effort here?"

"I don't see that as a matter of relevance, young lady. Not that I have anything to hide, mind you, but my life is not being questioned here, is it?" He smiled.

I smiled back at him. "Not yet." Without missing a beat I said, "Do you know much about Mr. Long's business?"

"Some. Why?"

"Nothing, really. It's just that some blueprints have come to our attention . . ." I let it hang there, waiting to see how he would respond.

He paused and shrugged. "I'm afraid I can't help you with that. Wallace and I don't often talk about business. Politics—you betcha, but business?" He shook his head.

"You should know that we have no intention to hurt Mr. Long, either politically or personally," I explained. "But his son is dead. I would think his parents would want the truth, if only to better understand his death. Quite honestly, Mr. Bartholomew, I could use all the help I can get. Is there anything you can tell me—no matter how insignificant you think it might be—that could help?"

He stared at me and nodded. "Yes. You shouldn't wear black. It washes you out." He had the good grace not to smile with his final insult.

I nodded once and stood to leave. "Mr. Bartholomew, there's something else I think you should know."

"What's that, dear?" The smile returned. I could see Max moving to the door.

"There's something hanging from your left nostril, sweetheart." His hand shot up to his nose and I could hear him sputtering as Max and I left without another word. Ah, assholes, every now and then it feels good to beat one at his own game.

Fourteen

By the time we left Bartholomew it was nearing three-thirty. Max had found the Englishwoman's car the day before, but it was undrivable. He had promised to retrieve it for her that afternoon and deliver it to an "honest garage" in the city—which I suggested was probably one of them there oxymorons. We considered my joining him and afterward the two of us interviewing Donald Kessler at five, but given the traffic and Carlos's scorecard, I didn't have much faith that Max's venture back to Queens would bring him back before seven.

I went back to the office. Not knowing what to expect, I was what you might call a little overly cautious. Before I unlocked the door, I took out my gun, a Walther compact, but I didn't need it. The glass workers had been there and boarded up the windows with plywood, which made the room as dark as a cave. It didn't help that it was after three in the afternoon and the middle of winter and the sky was already beginning to turn to night. Just what I needed to lift my spirits after my tête-à-tête with the charmer Bartholomew.

Bartholomew. God, what a putz. The more I thought about him, the angrier I got, not just with him, but the whole system. It seems that more and more, the people our society set up as hero figures turn out to be turds. I mean, I knew going into it Bartholomew was a jerk, but who knew he would care more about his own agenda than a young boy's death? Though my father raised me to believe that good guys finish first (Mom was the family pragmatist and never committed herself to such a sweeping statement), the older I got, the less I trusted Dad's altruism. Hell, it was his adherence to this very school of thought that got him killed.

I banged around CSI, turning on every single light in the place. Not until all the lights were on did I put the gun back into my bag. The gun. I remembered the Colt .38 that had belonged to my father, the one I keep hidden in my desk. I checked to make sure it was still there. It was. As I held the gun I wondered how Dad would have dealt with Bartholomew. I knew, though, that Dad would have been met not with contempt and belligerence, but respect and equality.

There was one phone message on my desk: *Lyle. 7:30. Gingerman. Okay.*

"It's not easy being a woman, Sinda." My aunt Sophie's voice echoed in the empty office.

"It's not easy being a *person*, Sophie. What are you teaching the child?" As I put the .38 back into the bottom drawer of my desk I could hear my father's words trail Sophie's.

"You were both right," I announced to the pink tulips Kerry had taken from her desk and set on mine.

I pushed aside the ghosts and reached for the phone. If Bartholomew wanted to be an asshole, that was his business. I had bigger problems than that self-important, ego-inflated bag of wind.

Eddie Phillips: if anyone could help me now, he could. I wanted to know why the press had steered clear of digging into Wallace Long's personal and political life, and Eddie was just the one who could find out.

As a freelance photojournalist, Eddie's home is his office. He's lived at his small one bedroom in Hell's Kitchen for the better part of twenty years and doesn't mind that in an area of serious gentrification, his tenement apartment building has gone untouched. But for that matter—his apartment's gone untouched, as well. To the best of my knowledge his apartment hadn't been painted—or thoroughly cleaned—in the whole time he's lived there. I crossed my fingers as the line rang, once, twice, four times. On the fifth ring, it was picked up, and I heard the receiver hit several hard surfaces before there was a moment of silence. Then, I listened as someone mumbled a string of swear words as he fished the receiver back up over the same hard surfaces it had hit on the way down. Another pause. A sigh. And finally, "Hello." Gruff and gravelly-voiced, there was no mistaking Eddie's inflection.

"Good morrrning, Eddie." I tried to imitate Topo Gigio, the little mouse from the Ed Sullivan Show. I checked my watch for accuracy. Okay, so I was off by more than three hours.

"Sloane? What the hell do you want?"

"I'm fine, thanks. And you?" I answered cheerily.

"I've got a hangover, a cold, *and*, if I didn't know better I'd swear I was PMS. I lost four rolls of film that I shot in Bosnia last week, I broke my little toe in a very stupid way last night, and a woman I wanted to date told me she'd rather have herpes than join me for even a cup of coffee. So now, how do you think I am, detective?"

"I know the perfect place for you to work off your frustration."

"I've already told you, I don't exercise." I had tried in the past to get Eddie interested in boxing, but he'd have none of it. He has always maintained that exercise is overrated and too damned time-consuming.

"No, Ed, this is mental gymnastics. Hear me out. You know Wallace Long?"

"What do you think I am, stupid?" he answered, cranky as a toddler without a nap.

"How come the press doesn't go after him?"

There was a short pause. "Who cares?"

"I do," I answered.

"No, no, no," he grumbled irritably. "I mean, really, who cares? The man's got money, power, and has convinced the people he's a choirboy. He's boring to the press." He sneezed loudly into the phone.

"Gesundheit."

"Right. So that's it?" He blew his nose.

"Well, no. I think there's more to it. He's big business, and he's running for office. I'd say those two elements combined are enough to stimulate curiosity, wouldn't you? I mean, I was thinking, he's got this computer company and he's running for office. Maybe he even has a contract with the government. That's possible, isn't it? That would hardly be ethical, would it? Don't you think people would want to know something like that?''

Eddie was losing patience with me. I could hear him scratching his beard, which, rumor had it, had begun to grow out of control. ''First of all, *if* that were the case, it would be public already. Secondly, the man creates jobs, Sydney. Very important, especially given our economy. On top of that, in his home state he's practically created a town where there was nothing, which means lots o' jobs, which makes him Santa Claus, which means that he wields a lot of power.

''Now—'' He did a verbal shift and cleared his throat. ''People love to ass-kiss money. Trust me, if you have enough money, you can get away with anything. Just look at the news for the last few years, and you tell me how many boys with bucks have gotten away with rape and murder, literally.'' He took a deep breath and, as if explaining to a child, continued. ''Lemme ask you, who gets free drinks at bars? Guys like me or Sylvester I-think-I'll-lift-my-face-again Stallone? I'll give you a clue. It ain't me. And why, you might ask, is that? I'll tell you why. People won't admit it, but in the back of their minds, they hope with all their heart that rich people will ultimately share their goodies.

''For example, in business, a restaurateur gives Mr. Moneybags a free bottle of wine, thinking that Mr. Money will reward him handsomely—either by writing him into the will or sending all his friends in for the best food in town, but it's bullshit, 'cause, you see, I could be sitting at the next table—a local who's likely to come in anywhere from three to five times a week and bring with me one or two people each time I go there whereas Mr. Money may or may not return, that's not the point. The point is—''

I cut him off here. ''The point is you want a freebie.''

"Yes, I do, goddammit, but *that's* not the point. The point is, there are a zillion fucking schmucks out there who really do believe if they kiss ass, they'll be kissed back. But it doesn't work that way, or when it does, it's very rare.

"So, if Mr. Long is good friends with Joe Blow Willow, editor in chief of the local ethical press—or even a friend to a client whose advertising keeps the presses rolling—you tell me, who's gonna dig into Mr. Long's laundry and keep their job? Now you're talking courage, my dear. A rare and wonderful commodity that most people sadly lack. And in a no-win situation like this, you can't blame 'em. One gung ho journalist goes after the big guns and gets shot down. The only difference he or she winds up making is to themselves because suddenly they don't have a paycheck, but hey, they stood up for something they believed in. And to some exceptional people, that's actually worth more than money.

"Now, this isn't to say that bringing down a hotshot can't—and hasn't—been done. It's done all the time. It's also failed much of the time, but the point is, you better be damned sure before you start fucking with the big boys because they'll have your ass in a sling before you can say oops. Have I answered your question?"

"I have no idea."

He blew his nose again.

"And what if Wallace Long's son was murdered?" I asked.

"What do you mean, what if? Was he or wasn't he?"

"That's still to be determined." My talk with Brendan had convinced me that Peter was murdered, but I had no proof, and without proof, my convictions meant nothing.

"Yeah, well, as I understand it, the kid killed himself. It happens. And it only makes Long more sympathetic to the people." How fortunate that I caught Eddie in such a good mood.

"Just hear me out, okay?" I gave him the background on the Longs—Peter, Vanessa, and Bartholomew. It took close to fifteen minutes to detail everything for him, but he let me get through the whole thing without an interruption.

"So, what do you want from me?" he asked when I had finished my abbreviated history of the last few days.

"A few things. First, I want to find out why the press is leaving him alone—"

"His son just died. Give the press a little credit," Eddie said sarcastically. Unafraid to record death on film, Eddie still draws the line at the sensationalizing human tragedy, the very stuff that sells papers. "My guess is Long's clean; otherwise, he would have had bad press by now, but go on." He let out a sneeze that made me want to wipe my hand that was holding the receiver.

"Bless you. And Clifford Bartholomew—"

"I love Clifford, Sydney."

"Clifford is a pig. Can you have the library at one of your magazines dig up everything they can on him?"

"What for?"

"I just came from a meeting with Mr. Bartholomew, and if he's not hiding something, I'll eat a can of worms. He and Wallace are best friends—which doesn't mean anything, I know—but there's something here that's not kosher. Besides"—I knew I could be honest with my old friend—"he's a cretin. I don't think I'd mind making his life a little miserable."

Eddie agreed to help. Not out of the goodness of his heart but because he wanted to vent his anger somewhere. And because I promised to make him a homemade dinner of roasted duckling with cranberry-orange relish, Brussels sprouts with chestnuts, and garlic-mashed potatoes. He even made me set a date before he'd hang up. I marked the date on my calendar and knew I wouldn't cancel because Eddie likes to eat almost as much as I do.

After we rang off, I called Vanessa Stephens again. This was getting as ridiculous as trying to contact Nancy Albus, whom I also tried with no luck. I left a message on Vanessa's machine, and after not getting through to Texas, I tried calling Gil, who had left for the day. I dialed Brendan's number—which by now I knew by heart. Another machine. Where the hell was everyone?

I was beginning to feel like Burgess Meredith in the episode of the *Twilight Zone* where he was the last man on the face of the earth.

For all I knew Brendan and Gil had connected two minutes after Gil spoke with Kerry. In this city, public transportation—which is great—can sometimes be frustrating. Brendan could have gotten caught between stations on the subway and hooked up with Gil later. I couldn't worry about that now.

Now I had an appointment at the West End Cafe. I double locked, and double checked the office door before leaving. I was looking forward to my five o'clock with Donald Kessler. I wasn't, however, looking forward to my dinner with Lyle Grubbs, the man who said he wanted to help and then withheld information. Nope. I wasn't looking forward to that at all.

Donald Kessler was sitting at a booth with half a mug of beer when I arrived. He had told me he would be wearing a cowboy hat, and he was.

"Donald?" I asked as I approached.

He looked up and eyed me in a way reserved for ill-mannered straight men and teenagers. Ogling, they used to call it.

"Sydney?" He sounded surprised.

"That's right."

"So you're what a lady dick looks like." He offered me his hand.

"I'm a private investigator, not a police officer." I explained as I took his hand. Just the way he shook hands made me feel yucky. But then, I didn't know if this was instinct on my part or if I had been swayed by Larry Novack's story—which, for all I knew was nothing more than a fabrication. Christ, I wouldn't be able to live with myself much longer like this. *If you feel it, trust it*, I told myself as I went to the bar after our introductions and got myself a club soda and him another pint of John Courage.

Once the drinks were squared away I thanked him for taking the time to meet with me.

"My pleasure," he said, touching an index finger to

the brim of his well-worn hat. Oh yeah, urban cowboy. Yahoo. Next I was expecting him to call me ma'am and spit tobacco juice into a corner.

"I just need to ask you a few questions about the other night . . ."

"There's not much I can tell you."

"That may be, but I'd still like to go over what happened. You and a friend found the body?"

Donald made a sour face and shifted uncomfortably. He draped his arm over the back of the booth and hiked his knee up onto the upholstered seat. "I wouldn't call him a *friend.*"

"Then what would you call him?" I fished the lime out of my drink and squeezed it into the soda.

"I'd call him a gay boy." His eyes sparkled as he winked conspiratorially at me.

Okay, I was stumped.

"And you, Mr. Kessler? If I'm not mistaken you met . . . you met Gary at a bar near the pier, is that correct?" Maybe it was the recent bombing, but I was feeling extremely cautious, and if he didn't remember it, I didn't want to use Larry Novack's name with Kessler.

He sighed. "Well now, I *did* meet him at a local bar—"

"A gay bar," I said, to make sure we were walking on the same road.

He ran his tongue along his upper teeth and reached for his beer. "I didn't know what kind of bar it was when I first got there. After I had a couple of drinks the place started to fill up, and I realized just what kind of establishment it was." He shifted his gaze to the bar while he drank a third of his pint. For all I knew the gay scene was new for Donald Kessler and he was having a hard time coming to terms with it. Clearly his troubles with it went deeper than being in a closet. Whatever it was, it was unmistakable that this forty-some-odd-year-old cowpoke had a big problem with his homosexuality.

"No big deal," I said casually, "I'm just trying to establish that you left the bar with this other gentleman and together you discovered a body at the pier, is that correct?''

Donald Kessler's eyes pulled into two little slits. ''That's right. We both found the body.''

''What time was that?''

He shrugged. '''Round one, maybe.''

''Can you tell me how you found the body and what happened afterward?''

Kessler took a deep breath and pushed his shoulders and head back. ''Sure, no problem. This guy I met at the bar, this Gary? well initially I thought that he came into the place like I did—you know it being a mistake and all—but we're bullshitting and he tells me he has some weed and asks if I want to smoke. Naturally I said yeah, after all, I'm a product of the sixties. I mean I was at Kent State when the shit hit the fan.'' He nodded proudly, as if expecting me to say, ''Oh wow, man, far out. That must have been really intense.'' When I didn't, he continued. ''So, I followed him outside and one thing I remember is that it was cold. I mean, really cold.''

I nodded.

''You have to understand, I was pretty bombed by that point, so if it's a little sketchy, that's why, but I remember as soon as we got outside I told him to light up. Instead he starts walking across the street. In the direction of the water.'' Kessler reached into his shirt pocket and pulled out a bag of Drum tobacco and a packet of rolling papers. ''Want one?'' he asked as he laid out a paper and pinched fresh tobacco from the pouch.

''No thanks.'' I studied his face as he rolled a cigarette with one hand. It wasn't hard to see what Larry Novack had been attracted to—the rugged good looks, the relaxed tough-guy style, the deep-set, almost cold eyes, and the impression of being dangerous, which I didn't think was threatening so much as being off-kilter, like a spring wound too tightly.

''So he started toward the pier, not you?''

''Yeah, that's right.''

''And what did you do?''

''Like I said I was pretty bombed, I wanted to get a

buzz from some weed, so I followed him.'' I expected Kessler to light his cigarette with a flint-tipped match struck against the thumbnail, but instead he pulled a neon green Bic lighter from his pocket and used that. ''It was dark, but we could see that there was someone at the end of the pier. He wanted to see who would be so stupid as to sit out there on a night like that.'' He picked a piece of tobacco off his tongue and exhaled smoke through his nose, looking not unlike Ferdinand, the cartoon bull. ''I don't mind telling you it scared the shit out of us. I've never seen anything like it.'' He polished off the beer and wiped his mouth with the back of his hand.

''What happened when you found the body?''

''We went to a phone on the street and called the police.''

''That's it?''

''Yeah, that's it. What else should there be? It's not like we wanted to hang out with a corpse in the freezing cold or anything.'' He dropped the cigarette into a black plastic ashtray.

''So let me get this straight. Around one o'clock on Saturday morning you and Gary left The Eighth Ball—which is the name of the bar, in case you didn't know—you left the bar to go outside and smoke a joint. However, when you got outside, instead of lighting up, Gary started across the street to the pier.'' I glanced at him and he nodded as if bored, but following. ''After you walked to the end of the pier and found the body, you walked back to the street where you called the police. Is that about right, Mr. Kessler?''

He rubbed the side of his nose. ''Yeah. I'd say that sums it up pretty good. Like I told you, there isn't much to tell.''

''Did you know the young man who died?''

His eyes snapped to attention. ''What are you driving at?''

''I'm not driving at anything.''

''Do the police know you're nosing around in this?'' He wiped his wide, veined hand along the tabletop.

''Yes. Do you have a problem with my questions?''

"No. But I have a problem with being parched. Is this going to take much longer? 'Cause if it is, I'll get another beer."

"Twenty minutes?"

"I'll be right back." He swaggered to the bar and came back with another pint of the dark ale. When he was seated, I asked him again if he knew Peter.

"I already told the police. I didn't know him. Hell, I barely looked at him."

I figured the shortest distance between two points was a straight line. "Gary said that you didn't want to call the police."

"Gary's a faggot." He knocked back half of his beer.

"What's that supposed to mean?"

He snorted a nasty laugh and explained, "It means that you can't trust him. It means that he's a liar. Everyone knows faggots are liars. Liars and cowards."

"Really? Should the police think you're a liar then?"

Donald's face froze, and I could see that I had made a judgment error regarding this guy. His eyes caught mine and held them in place long enough for me to see that Donald Kessler was, in fact, a very dangerous man. I held my breath as we stared one another down. Finally he moved his right hand to his hat, which he lifted ever so slightly, allowing just enough space so his left hand could slick back his sandy, graying hair.

"Are *you* suggesting I'm a faggot?" he asked ominously.

"I'm not suggesting anything. I don't care what you are. I'm only trying to find out what happened to this young man—"

"If he was out at the pier, he probably got what he deserved." He prepared to roll a fresh cigarette.

"What's that mean?"

He frowned as he leveled off the tobacco with his index finger. "Look, you seem like a decent person, so I'm going to level with you. I know it looked bad for me the other night being at that bar, and I know the police probably think I'm a frigging faggot, but the truth is, I hate faggots. As far as I'm concerned, all those buttfuckers, if you'll pardon the expression, should be either locked up or injected with the AIDS virus, because it was them who brought the fucking disease here in the first place. I'm sorry to tell you this because the little dead boy may have been a friend of yours, but if that kid was on the pier looking for action, as far as I'm concerned he got the action he deserved.'' By now Donald's eyes were glassed over. I guess three pints of beer in under forty minutes will do that to you.

I felt dirty sitting at the same table with him. I nodded once and gathered my coat and left. I didn't even break my step when he yelled out, ''Truth's hard to swallow, but it is what it is.''

Fifteen

Once I was out on the sidewalk with the fresh air as a balm, I realized I could no more leave that evil man with the last word than I could change a carburetor. I was damned if I was going to suffer through two Bartholomews in the same day without some satisfaction. I walked back into the bar, ordered a pitcher of Courage, and went back to where Donald was sitting.

"I was hoping you'd come back," he said with a slow, easy smile.

"Oh, I had to," I said as sweet as molasses, placing the pitcher on the edge of the table.

"Did you?"

"Yeah. It was what you said about the truth." I reached into my bag and wrapped my hand around my Walther.

"The one and only thing I learned from my father," he said like a true cowpoke.

"Is that right?"

"Yep."

"Well, you know, Donald, your father was right, the truth is what it is, and in truth, you're a liar." He shifted, but he didn't move. "You went down to The Eighth Ball for a reason, and my guess is it wasn't to get laid or even for the drugs you promised Gary." Donald white-knuckled the side of the table and looked ready to pounce. "I wouldn't try anything if I were you." I nodded to my right hand and showed him the gun I had leveled at him. "I know how to use it, and I will.

"Now, Saturday night you wanted to bolt after you found that boy because you have a secret, don't you? A big old nasty secret you'd rather the police not know. It has nothing to do with the kid at the end of the pier, but it has everything to do with you and why you like to visit boys' bars." From the look on his face I'd just hit pay dirt. "The truth is, Kessler, just because *you're* a liar and a coward it doesn't mean all gay men are."

Kessler was squinting up at me. He released his hold of the table and leaned back. "What are you saying, Sloane?" He crossed his arms over his chest.

"I'm saying it's going to get a lot more difficult for you to hurt anyone in the future."

"Really? You got a faggot brother who's going to stop me?" he asked, amused with himself.

I released the gun and closed my bag. "Baby, the faggots I know could pulverize you." I turned to go and came back around. "*Ach*, silly me, I forgot. Drinks are on me." With that, I took the pitcher, poured the contents on his cowboy hat, and left quickly without turning back.

When I hit the sidewalk I ran to the street and hailed a cab. I didn't know if Donald Kessler was behind me, and I didn't want to find out. I gave the driver the address of The Gingerman restaurant and then sneaked a glance out the rear window. The street was crowded, but there was no sign of Kessler. I leaned back and shut my eyes. I was exhausted, and the last thing I wanted was to entertain some yokel from Texas.

Lyle was waiting for me when I arrived. He was dressed casually and well into his first drink, which looked to be vodka on the rocks, same as the night before.

"You look nice," he said as he pulled out a barstool.

I smiled and glanced down at what I was wearing. Black and ivory—the same outfit Clifford Bartholomew had said washed me out. So much for his fashion sense. I suggested we get a table. Lyle seemed like a nice enough guy, but the fact is I was tired, cranky, hungry, and more than a little pissed off at him for not having told me that he had spoken to Brendan.

"So," I said when we were seated and handed menus. "You spoke with Brendan the other day."

He sipped his drink and nodded. "I did. I thought he should hear about Peter from a mutual friend."

"Why didn't you tell me that?"

He shrugged. "As I recall, I gave you a lot of information that day. You know what they say about gluttony. Besides, I knew if you were any good at what you do, you'd find out soon enough." He put his glass on the table and twisted the glass around, drying its bottom on the white tablecloth. "Just for the record, I asked you out for dinner, not an inquisition."

"If I recall correctly, you said you would be willing to help me find out what happened to Peter."

"I did. And I meant it."

"Withholding information—for whatever reason—does me no good."

We summed each other up in a long moment of silence. Finally Lyle took a deep breath and said, "You're right. And I'm sorry. I did call Brendan. I didn't tell Mr. or Mrs. Long, and I didn't tell you. But you have to understand something, Sydney. I like these kids. Maybe I understand them a little better than others because I was a part of their scene for a while, or maybe it's because I'm just a big kid at heart, but the fact is, they deserve a little privacy, too." He paused while the waiter placed a glass of Chianti in front of me. "I'll make you a deal." He held up his glass as if to toast. "You can ask me anything you want, anything at all concerning Peter, and I'll tell you what I know. But when you're finished, we put your work aside and we just talk. Just get to know one another. Is it a deal?"

Having dealt with Cullerson, Bartholomew, and Kessler in one day had me trusting men about as much as an ant should trust an aardvark, but Lyle seemed different from the others.

"It's a deal." We clinked glasses, and I started working. "First of all, did you get anything on the phone call Peter made Saturday?"

"Oh, yeah, here." He pulled a piece of paper from his jacket pocket and handed it to me. It was a local number that I was familiar with. I slipped it in my pocket and thanked him.

"Did you call it?" I asked.

"What? That number?" He seemed oddly surprised.

"Of course the number. Weren't you curious?"

I was delighted to see him blush. "Well, yeah, as a matter of fact I did call."

"And?" I asked.

"I got the answering machine. It's the home of a woman named Vanessa."

I nodded. "Peter was carrying blueprints. Apparently he gave Brendan a copy of them and told him if he died, that was the reason why."

"Are you serious?"

"Brendan didn't tell you that when you spoke?"

"Not a word."

"Do you know anything about blueprints?"

"No. Are you sure Peter wasn't kidding?"

"That's what Brendan thought at first, but then Peter died. How would you feel if you were in his shoes?"

"Scared."

"Me too."

"Let me see them." Lyle pulled a pair of reading glasses from his jacket pocket.

"I don't have them."

"Where are they?"

"That's one of the sixty-five-thousand-dollar questions." I sipped the wine. "Mr. Long uses blueprints in manufacturing computers, doesn't he?"

"I would think so, but I don't have anything to do with his business. I'm just hired to protect the man."

"Did Peter work at his father's company? Would he have had access to blueprints?"

Lyle shook his head. "He didn't work with Mr. Long, but I don't know if he had access to blueprints or not. For all I know Mr. Long keeps that stuff at home. I know he has a safe in his office at home, and no one has the combination except Mr. Long."

"Mrs. Long?"

This seemed to stump Lyle. He exhaled a faint laugh and leaned back in his chair, a man comfortable no matter where he was. "Funny thing about Mrs. Long. You just never seem to consider her. It's like she kind of disappears into the background."

"Funny thing. So, tell me about the family."

During the next forty-five minutes I learned that Wallace and Louise Long hadn't shared a bedroom for the last seven years—like about four hundred other couples I know. I figure that's half the fun of having a live-in partner—you get to cuddle every night.

Louise drank—big surprise. Peter dated a series of nice girls, but none of whom he was serious about. His current girlfriend, Nancy Albus, was older than him, which had caused Louise some concern, but had pleased Wallace because Nancy worked for Long.

"What do you mean by that?" I asked.

"Mr. Long wanted Peter to join him in the business. Christ, he bribed the kid to do it. When Peter started dating Nancy, Mr. Long was thrilled. He figured the relationship wouldn't last—because of their age difference—but Nancy might turn Peter on to computers."

"How much older than Peter is Nancy?"

"Mmm, I think she's thirty-four, which would make her fourteen years older than him."

"Did you ever see them together?"

"Sure."

"And?"

Lyle shrugged. "And they seemed to be, I don't know, maybe mismatched is the word. Nancy's real serious, and Peter wasn't. Hell, he was in college, and she's a systems engineer at one of the hottest computer companies in the world. She has a lot of responsibility at LongTec."

"So what was the attraction?"

"How should I know?" Lyle laughed. "People are attracted to people for different reasons. I will say, though, Nancy's what they call a technogeek, which always made me wonder about the two of them. I mean, Peter was a handsome kid, he could have had anyone. Nancy's this simple woman who only seemed to care about her work. Until she met Peter, I guess. It was obvious that she was head over heels in love with him. Who wouldn't be? He was a great kid."

"I've been trying to reach her for the last two days. There's never an answer."

"That's because she's a workaholic, I'm telling you. You should try her at LongTec; she's there most of the time."

He gave me the number for the company and we moved on, Lyle continuing the overall picture for me.

Peter was charismatic, very much aware of his own influence over others, yet still surprisingly insecure. During the last several months, however, he had seemed to be growing stronger, more confident, less afraid of his father.

Lyle's partner, Art, had worked for Wallace for at least fifteen years, starting back when he worked as Long's executive assistant at LongTec. Art was easily impressed with power, and tried to act as if he had far more than he actually did.

Lyle knew that Peter had left the dinner early the night before he died, and he knew from Brendan that the two of them had spent that time together. The family hadn't made a scene, but it was evident that Peter was going to do what Peter wanted, and nothing his father said or did would dissuade him. Lyle knew how chagrined Wallace had been, but Lyle was glad to see the boy standing up for himself. "Hell, all he wanted to do was go out for a night with his old friend and get bombed. Why not?"

Lyle didn't know how Peter had spent his Saturday night. The Longs had gone to a cocktail party and then had dinner with Long's friend, Clifford Bartholomew, on Saturday evening, but he didn't know what Peter had done.

I listened as Lyle talked about the Longs and the sadness he felt for their disjointed family unit. The more he talked, the more I genuinely liked him. Before I knew it we were talking about our own lives.

"I know people at home would think I'm crazy if I told them this, but I've been talking to someone for the last four months. I think it's helping." Lyle reached across the table with his fork and took a taste of my mango sorbet.

"A therapist?"

"Yeah. I needed help after Marjorie died. People at home think you're screwy if you tell them that you're seeing a shrink. I haven't told anyone."

"No one?" I asked, somewhat amazed. I'd been in therapy and remembered coming home and telling Caryn everything I'd learned from one particular session or another.

"Well, actually, I did tell Marjorie's sister, Susan. She's different, though. She's a lot like Marge. Susan doesn't pass judgment, she just listens, then tells you what she thinks. And she's really supportive about the therapy because she thinks I should be getting on with my life now."

"It sounds like you have a good friend in her."

"Oh, yeah, I do. She's great. She's like my best friend. We used to teach together, which is how I met Marge in the first place. Through Susan. She still teaches at the same school. English." His eyes lit up for the first time during the evening.

"You know, Lyle, the best relationships I've seen are built from friendships. I think a lot of couples break up because the two people never were or never could be friends."

"Yeah, or they grow apart. I know a few couples who married right out of high school and after twenty years they just can't relate anymore."

"Mmhm. But it sounds like you have a good friendship here."

"I do." He paused and his cheeks colored. "Wait a minute, you mean, *Susan*?"

"Why not? It sounds like you both care about each other, know each other, have a lot in common. Why does that sound so weird?"

He paused before murmuring, ''We're sister and brother-in-law, that's why. Do you have any idea what people would think?''

''It doesn't matter what people think.''

''Right, it's easy to *say* it doesn't, but you know as well as I do that it *does*.''

''No. It really doesn't. All that matters between two people is what *they* think. Does Susan feel the same way about you?''

''I don't know.'' By now his wide cheeks were beet red, but he didn't change the subject or make a joke. ''Look, we love each other, but like best friends, that's it. You don't understand about these small towns—everyone's got something to say about everyone else.''

''Sure I do. Look, Lyle, I'm gay. I know what it's like to have other people thinking they can pass judgment over my life. But the fact is—''

''You're *gay*?'' He practically shouted. Fortunately this is New York and most people act pretty blasé about these sorts of things—even if they're not.

''Well, now that you've told everyone in the restaurant . . .'' There were only three other occupied tables in the large space and clearly none of them were taking an interest in our conversation.

''I'm sorry. I'm just stunned. You don't look gay.''

I gave him a pained expression in response.

''Okay, okay, what do you expect, I'm from Texas.''

''Tell me, what do gays look like in Texas?''

''I don't know. I don't think there are any.''

With that we both burst into laughter. When our laughter died down, he got serious.

''You know, the truth is, I have thought about Susan. I didn't mean to, but one night I had this dream about her, you know? And it got me thinking.''

''And?''

''And I got depressed as hell.'' He bent his coffee spoon in half. ''You see, I really do love Marge. I miss her like hell, and I'd do anything if I could just see her again. Everyone tells me I'm a young man, and I should start dating again, and they're right, I know they're right, but it feels like I'm being . . . unfaithful, you know? It's bad enough thinking about being with *any* woman, but then to have it be her sister . . . it just seems so wrong. And what would Susan think? Maybe she'd think that I'm substituting her for Marge. And worst of all, what if that *is* what I'm doing?" He looked like a puppy in a cage at a Bide-a-Wee.

"I like you, Lyle. You think and you feel. Two characteristics you don't often see in a man."

We finished dinner and lingered over a cognac. When we left, Lyle insisted on walking me home. It was cold, but the chill in the air was refreshing rather than biting. It didn't feel like we'd just walked a mile. When we reached my corner I stopped and put out my hand. "You're a good man, Lyle. It was really nice meeting you."

He clasped my hand warmly between his and smiled. "If you're ever in Texas, look me up, okay?"

"I promise." Despite his protests, I assured him I would be fine walking the half block to my apartment. He gave me a peck on the cheek and said good-bye.

West End Avenue is a wide, residential street that is home to majestic apartment buildings. It is also surprisingly quiet for an avenue in New York. On a winter night like this, when the streets are covered with snow and the boughs of the trees look silvery against the streetlights, it's easy to transport yourself back in time and get a feeling of what New York was like when life was simpler, safer.

As I turned to go into the walkway of my building I thought I heard someone say my name. Thinking it was Lyle, I turned, but before I could get all the way around, I was grabbed from behind by the shoulders. Whoever it was was taller than me and had some powerful arms. He clamped down on my shoulders so hard that my knees practically buckled. I twisted around and saw two legs in dark slacks. He was also wearing construction boots with plaid laces. I bent my right elbow and hauled it back as hard as I could, but I missed my mark. The man behind me was dragging me out of the light from the walkway into the shadows. He was also tightening his grip around my neck to the point where I could barely breathe, let alone call out for help.

The feeling of helplessness kicked me into fifth gear. As I struggled to pull away from him, I raised my left arm and slammed it back as hard as I could. I knew from the sound that I had made contact with his nose, and I prayed that it hurt like hell because the move had wrenched my shoulder. It didn't, however, make him loosen his grasp. All it did was make him stop dragging me and while we were stopped I brought my foot down on his with everything I had in me.

Big deal. The man was wearing construction boots. He kneed me in the back of my thigh, causing the leg to cramp, and shook me like I was a little rag doll, which is exactly what I was beginning to feel like.

I let my body go limp, hoping this would create a deadweight for him. I didn't know where the hell he thought he was taking me, or what he wanted to do with me when he got me there, but I sure as hell wasn't going to make it easy for him. Sharp pains were shooting down through my shoulder into my back, and I still couldn't call out, but I hoped that someone on the avenue would see this and do something noble. Most people think New Yorkers don't get involved, but they're wrong.

I tensed my body again, this time trying to pull him over me, but it was impossible. I was in an awkward, unworkable position, and my shoulder was nearly worthless. When he called me a bitch I could smell the liquor on his breath.

We were in the shadows on West End, just below Mrs. Klee's first-floor apartment. Mrs. Klee is a sweet old lady who's gone blind and deaf with age, so I knew she wouldn't hear the commotion just outside her window. He was moving us toward Ninety-first Street, which would be deserted at that time of night. I was getting light-headed from lack of oxygen, when suddenly the body behind me shifted upward. All I could see were his feet. He held on to me as he was lifted off the ground. I snapped away from his hold and fell to the icy sidewalk.

I could hear the scuffle behind me, but by the time I

was able to get my bearings, Lyle was kneeling beside me.

"Are you all right?" He gently cupped my face in his hands.

I wanted to say, "yeah, I'm fine, no big deal," but the words wouldn't come. Though the man was gone, I could still feel his hands pressing against my throat.

"Where is he?" I finally asked, feeling my heinie turning numb from the cold, but unable to move.

"He ran off. I didn't want to leave you." Lyle moved his hands to my arms and said, "Come on, let me help you upstairs."

I didn't resist.

Feeling angry and foolish, I let Lyle help me into the apartment. Once we were inside I offered him a cup of decaf for his troubles. He took me up on the offer, but insisted on making the coffee for us while I sat at the kitchen table and iced my shoulder.

"Who the hell was that?" he asked as he made himself at home in my kitchen, measuring out coffee, locating cups and spoons, sugar and milk.

"I don't know. I couldn't see him." I felt like an ass. "Did you get a good look at him?" I asked.

"He was white, about six feet, average build, wearing a torn green down jacket, black ski mask, and boots. He wasn't wearing any gloves. No jewelry that I could see." He stared at me and looked sad. "I'm sorry I didn't chase him, but I was so concerned about you."

"So was I. Thanks." I rubbed my shoulder. It seemed that the ice pack was helping. As far as I could tell, it wasn't Kessler. Kessler was taller, thinner, and his drink of choice seemed to be beer, not hard liquor. The more I thought about it, the more I was convinced that it had been Tom Cullerson. I had only myself to blame, and I knew it.

"Nice town you live in."

"Oh yeah. I'd rather live in Texas, where postal workers go crazy every other month and shoot everyone at the local McDonald's."

We took the coffee into the den, a room that had once

been my sister's bedroom, and Lyle lit a fire in the fireplace.

"Good coffee," I said as I stretched out on the sofa, leaving plenty of room for him at the other end. If I thought about it, it might have seemed odd being so completely comfortable with this man whom I had met less than forty-eight hours earlier, but it just felt natural, as if we'd been doing this for years. Lyle was a good egg.

"*Ach*, coffee's nothing. You should taste my pot roast."

"So you cook?"

"Oh yeah, and bake and sew. My mother believed a man should be able to take care of himself just like a woman."

"Smart lady, your mom."

"My dad hated it. Said she was going to turn me into a sissy." He eyed me. "A *faggot* is what he actually said."

"Oh of course, faggot. Now there's a good universal slur."

An hour later we were still chatting away, only now Lyle had my feet in his hands and was masterfully massaging the cares and troubles out of my entire body via my tootsies. I was in heaven. I told Lyle about Tom Cullerson and all that had happened during the last two weeks. He listened quietly, letting me get through the story, and my self-doubts, without interruption. It deeply disturbed me that I hadn't been able to fend off the attack on my own.

"He took you from behind, Sydney. There was no way you could have fought him off by yourself."

Whether Lyle was right or not, I didn't know, and I didn't care. All I knew was that everywhere I was turning I was butting heads and losing. Deep down inside I could feel the stirrings of anger, but it was distant, like the Metro North train whistle you can hear in the dead of night on West End Avenue.

Lyle suggested we call the police.

"Tomorrow. I promise," I said sleepily. Right then,

at that very moment, I felt safe and warm and soft and I didn't want to lose the sensation.

Lyle continued massaging my feet. I didn't know what time it was, and it didn't seem to matter. I was, for the first time in weeks, genuinely relaxed, and it felt wonderful. I closed my eyes and leaned my head back on the pillows behind me.

"You look content," Lyle said.

I managed a low groan. "I am. I needed that, thanks."

"You're welcome." His strong fingers worked their way up past my foot and just above the ankle. "You know, it's a shame."

"What is?" I asked feeling far away from time and space.

"That you're gay and I'm still in love with my wife." He studied my feet as he massaged the lower part of my leg.

I don't know why, but the movie *Tea and Sympathy* popped into my head. The maternal, yet oh so sexy Deborah Kerr turning to a young, confused, John Kerr and whispering, "When you speak about this in the future . . ."

I studied Lyle. No doubt about it, the man had sex appeal. What attracts me to men is the complete antithesis of what draws me to women. Thank God. For example, I particularly liked the way his chest hairs popped out from his shirt collar, something I would find absolutely frightening with a woman. And his big, muscular arms, his flat, solid chest, the squareness of his jawline and the dark, coarse hairs that covered it. Before I knew what I was doing, I sat up, moved across the great divide of the sofa, and kissed him.

It had been years since I had kissed a man. His breath was warm and the roughness of his beard not nearly as pleasant as the softness of a woman, but still not without its own appeal. What the hell was I doing?

He pulled me gently to him and kissed me so that I felt it through my whole body. He hadn't been with a woman in over a year and it was obvious that he had missed the closeness. I felt small and feminine in his arms. His tongue ventured cautiously into my mouth and before I knew it, Lyle and I were lying on the sofa making out like a couple of hormone-hyped teenagers.

The last time I had necked on the sofa like this I was a junior in high school and my date, Bobby Larson, was two years older than me and very much the man about town. Despite his bragging, I never did become a notch on Bobby's belt, as much as I wanted to. On the one night when it might have happened, my father came home unexpectedly, caught us in a wrinkled state, and offered to escort Bobby home.

''Does this mean I'm a lesbian?'' Lyle whispered as he gently ran his fingers along the back of my neck and nibbled at my ear.

''Oh God, I hope so,'' I said, knowing that a part of me was dead serious because it would make things easier in the light of day. We twisted and turned, our lips never losing contact, and now I was on top of him. His mouth tasted sweet and his lips were surprisingly soft.

At first it just felt delicious. Lyle wanted me, and I needed to be wanted. But the more we kissed, the more crowded the sofa became. Suddenly there was Bobby Larson, and all the men I'd ever been with. Shutting my eyes and blocking them out was one thing, but when Leslie entered my head, all activity came to a grinding halt. Despite the fact that she was out playing the field, she was still the woman of my dreams, and no matter how curious Lyle made me, or how willing he was to make my every dream come true, I couldn't follow through with it.

''I can't.'' I sighed and pulled away from his strong embrace.

He didn't resist. Instead he let his arms flop to his sides and watched with the patience of Job as I sat up, perched myself on the far arm of the sofa, and combed my hair with my fingers. After several minutes he sat up, leaned his back against the other arm of the sofa, and stretched his legs out the length of the couch. His eyes never left me.

''Are you okay?'' he asked softly, his voice cracking at first.

I nodded nebulously. "I thought I could. I can't. I'm sorry."

"It's okay." He took a couple of deep breaths, and added, "Can I ask you a question?"

"Yes."

"Is it because I'm a man?"

I couldn't help but smile at the bewildered look on his face. "No, Lyle. It's because you're not Leslie. She may be a pain in the neck, but she's mine. I can't do this to her."

"You know, you're the first woman I've kissed since Marjorie." He hiked up his trousers and bent his knees.

"How was it?"

"Fabulous." The twinkle in his eye was priceless and made me want to pick up where we had left off, but the moment had passed. Instead, Lyle and I spent the rest of the night sitting on the sofa, drinking coffee, and talking about the women we have loved. At some point I must have fallen asleep in his arms because I awoke with a start, cuddled up against his side. It wasn't bad, but it wasn't Leslie.

Sixteen

Lyle had to be back at the hotel by eight. At the front door he gave me a bear hug, and said, "I'll never forget last night, Sydney. Thank you."

"It *was* fun. But Lyle?"

"Yeah?"

"Make me one promise."

"Anything."

"Tell Susan how you feel. It's not worth losing something special because of what other people think."

"I promise." He slowly put on his overcoat, looking pensive and tired. Before he left he held me at arm's length, and said, "I needed last night. You're a very special woman. Leslie's lucky."

"I'll be sure and tell her you said that. Now, get the hell out of here so I can get some sleep."

The apartment was cold, and I was wide-awake, so instead of climbing into bed, I decided to take a shower. I needed to think, and the shower is always a good place for me to do that. However, the water was only tepid, and every time I started to think, all I thought about was Leslie and Lyle and how I had spent my evening. A short shower, good. I didn't need to think anyway. I turned off my mind along with the shower, and by the time I got out of the bathroom, the heat was slowly working its way into the radiators, and the phone was ringing.

"Sydney? It's me." Max sounded surprisingly chipper considering the early hour.

"Hello, you. What are you doing up so early?"

"Spent the night with Marcy. She's on an early shift, so I got up with her." I keep waiting for Max to come to his senses and marry Marcy, one of New York's Finest, but he tried marriage once before and swears he has an allergy to matrimony. "Want some breakfast?" he asked.

"Sure. Where?"

"Your place, where else? I'll bring the fixings."

Twenty minutes later Max was in my kitchen slicing bagels, and I was making coffee. His eye patch was gone, and though the eye was bloodshot, the bruise around it was fading nicely. However, between the time that I'd last seen him, at three o'clock the day before, and now, he'd had his hair cut. It looked as if the barber had used a Boy Scout knife in lieu of scissors.

"Nice do," I said as I turned on the coffeemaker.

"New barber. You know me, a sucker for a pretty face."

"A new barber? Where? Creedmore?" I asked, referring to the psychiatric hospital in Queens.

"Okay, okay. Marcy ribbed me enough about this last night. I don't need it from you, too."

"Seriously, where'd you get it done?" I poured Max an orange juice and me a glass of apple juice.

"Queens," he said casually as he put three bagels into the toaster oven and started unwrapping the smoked salmon.

"Queens? I thought your barber was in the Village."

"I don't want to talk about it," he muttered as he put the salmon on a plate.

I put the orange juice in front of him and tried to repress an enormous grin. Queens. When I last saw him he was headed to Queens to pick up his client's Volvo.

"This haircut couldn't somehow be connected to the Englishwoman's Volvo, could it? I handed him a fat, red tomato to slice.

"Maybe." Max diced an onion and nodded. His ears were turning red.

"Okay, go on. What happened with Carlos and the car?"

Max cleared his throat and unwrapped the cream cheese. "The car is at a garage."

"Carlos's garage?" I could feel laughter bubbling inside me as I pulled out the plates and silverware.

"No. A garage in Brooklyn."

"An honest garage?"

By now Max was at the table with the sum total of breakfast before him. He started slathering cream cheese onto a bagel half and piling it high with salmon, tomato, and onions. "I don't believe I want to discuss this with you, Sydney," he said primly.

"You only make it more intriguing this way, Max. I mean, this hair . . ."

"Why don't you tell me about Donald Kessler." He was obviously going to steer clear of the Carlos story—which was just as well. I knew I'd get the scoop later.

"Scary guy."

"How so?"

"I'm going to have Gil run a check on him. He's a real sicko. Totally self-hating. He seems like the type to go to gay bars, pick up someone, and then beat the shit out of him, or worse."

"Did he shine any light on Peter Long?"

"No. I don't think there's any connection there. I do think, however, that it was a lucky thing for Larry Novack that they found Peter. Otherwise, that could have been *him* at the end of the pier."

"Wow." He reached for his second bagel. "How did Kessler respond to your meeting?"

I drank my coffee and hesitated, wondering if I should confess to Max how badly I'd ended my meeting with Kessler. Finally, I took a deep breath and told him what had happened, starting with the cowboy posturing and ending with the beer chaser.

"Jesus Christ, Sydney, what's wrong with you? We don't have enough problems right now?" He tossed his napkin on his empty plate and got up. "You want more coffee?" he asked irritably.

"Yes, please." There was nothing I could say because I knew Max was right. So I changed the subject. "I've got the Wizard working on getting the financial scoop on Vanessa Stephens. She should have something for me today."

"When did you give her the job?" Max asked as he pulled the milk out of the refrigerator.

"Yesterday."

"Right. If you get anything before next week, I'll be amazed." He came back to the table with the coffeepot.

"Be ye of little faith."

"Hey, I just deposited the woman's check. You know I want her to have a clean bill of health." As he said that, the doorbell rang.

"Leslie," Max predicted.

I got up and checked myself in the hallway mirror, convinced that Max was right, that it was Leslie. She had keys to my place, but considering the way things had been between us, it made sense that she wouldn't buzz to be let in downstairs but would ring the front door. I looked good. I didn't look at all like a woman who had just been up for the last several hours necking with a man for the first time in years.

But it wasn't Leslie.

It was a detective team from the Ninth Precinct.

Detectives Julia Lee, an attractive Asian woman with hennaed hair, and Ned Gould, who looked remarkably like beam-me-up-Scottie from *Star Trek*, introduced themselves and held out their IDs.

Detective Lee seemed to be their spokeswoman. "We're sorry to bother you so early, but we tried your office and no one was there."

"That's reassuring, since we're here." I asked them in and led them to the living room. No one sat.

"Is this about the office?" I asked, thinking that they had found evidence linking Tom Cullerson to the explosion. But that didn't make sense because they came from a precinct halfway across town.

They looked at one another.

"No. It's not." Detective Lee wore a gray woolen

overcoat that hung loosely on her small frame.

Max joined us. "Hello." He nodded to the two officers.

"This is my business partner, Max Cabe." I introduced the two detectives to Max, who offered them coffee.

Detective Gould looked tempted, but refrained when his partner got to the point of their visit.

"You're a private investigator?" She asked me.

"That's correct."

"I hate to start your day like this, but we need you to identify a body, Ms. Sloane."

"Whose?" I asked, stupidly.

"We don't know, that's why we need you. Your card was the only thing found on the deceased."

"Of course." I murmured as I felt my stomach pitch. "Have a seat. I'll get ready. Are you sure you wouldn't like some coffee?"

Both detectives accepted the second offer for caffeine. Max led them into the kitchen while I went to the back of the apartment to put on makeup and finish dressing.

"So who is it?" Max asked from the bathroom doorway while I finished applying blush.

"I don't know. My first thought's Brendan Mayer. I gave him a card yesterday, and it had my home number on the back." My second thought, which I didn't share with Max, was Lyle, to whom I had also given an identical card. The thought that something might have happened to Lyle had my stomach in knots.

"I'm going with you." Max said as I slipped a red-and-green ski sweater over my thermal tee shirt. "Very Christmas." Max pointed at the top.

"Ho, ho, ho," I said flatly.

The four of us drove to the morgue in silence. I watched the city streets dulled by the haze of winter gray, feeling a low-grade panic settle inside me. The last time I had been to the morgue was over eleven years earlier, when I was asked to identify my father's body.

Once inside the First Avenue building, Detective Lee escorted me past the reception area into a viewing room.

I studied the floor as I followed Detective Lee and

tried to take a deep breath, tried not to think that it might well be Lyle on a gurney in one of their vaults, awaiting identification.

Max and Detective Gould waited in the reception area while Detective Lee and I went into a private room just off the main entrance. Three worn gray sofas lined the walls. Two matching armchairs sat in the middle of the small room. There were three windows situated high in the exterior wall and one six-foot window that comprised the far interior wall. Behind this window was a metal plate that could be elevated with a flick of a switch. I knew that behind this window was a lift that went to the basement, where autopsies are performed and bodies are kept in individual refrigerated vaults.

"Have a seat, would you please." Detective Lee left me alone. I knew she was getting a picture of the deceased, which was how I would be asked to identify the body. Eleven years had done much to improve the system. Then I was brought to the basement and asked to identify my father as he lay dead on a gurney. It had been archaic and painful. Since 1989 much has been done to make things easier for the people closest to the deceased.

With irritation I paced the room and thought, *They could have brought me the picture and saved us all time.* I was upset because I wanted it not to be Lyle, or Brendan. I didn't want to be here identifying anyone.

When Julia Lee returned, she handed me a Polaroid picture. I looked down at the photo in my hand. It was a headshot of Brendan, who looked like he was sleeping, with a sheet pulled up to his chest.

"Can you identify this man?" Detective Lee asked respectfully.

"Yes." I swallowed, relieved that it wasn't my friend, Lyle. "His name is Brendan Mayer." I was surprised that Brendan's skin had an almost red hue to it. I asked why that was, but instead of an answer Detective Lee asked again if I was sure it was Brendan. I was.

"This is never easy," she said softly.

"No. It's not." My mouth was parched and my stomach felt hollow. I was glad I'd not eaten breakfast with Max.

"May I see the body?" I asked, knowing that it was only a short lift ride away.

"I'm afraid not." She looked apologetic. "Only family members have that privilege. It's the rules." Of course I knew that, but I was curious about the red tint to his skin, and it was clear that she wasn't about to answer my questions. I followed her back out into the hallway, where Max and Detective Gould were looking like a set of bookends, each with a newspaper spread in hand.

"Brendan?" Max asked as we came out.

I nodded.

"I'm going to have to ask you some questions," Detective Lee said to me, but glanced at Max.

"You all right?" Max asked, touching my arm.

"I'm fine."

"Okay. I'll be at the office when you're done," Max said as we walked to the exit.

"I'm waiting to hear from Eddie Phillips. If he calls, will you get the information from him?" I pulled up my collar against the cold and dug into my pockets for my gloves.

"Will do." Max walked to the curb as we started to the detective's car on Thirty-eighth Street.

"By the way," Max called out from the street as he tried to hail a northbound taxi. "You do anything yet regarding Cullerson?" His gloved hand was suspended in the air, pulling his coat sleeve up, exposing his arm to the cold.

"What's that?" I called out against the traffic, though we both knew perfectly well that I had heard him.

Max looked at me, nodded once, and let out an ear-piercing whistle for a taxi on the far side of the avenue. It did the trick, nearly causing a livery station wagon to skid into the back end of the short-stopping cab.

Without another word, Max jumped into the backseat of the cab and sped off. I turned and followed Detectives Lee and Gould, who had already rounded the corner.

I was less than two hours into the day, and clearly it

was going to be a rough one. I climbed into the backseat of their car and let out a huge sigh.

Detective Gould, who was at the wheel, looked at me in the rearview mirror and nodded, "I know whatcha mean. Shitty way to start the holidays. Here, maybe a little music'll help." With that he switched on the car radio, but instead of music he tuned into a talk show. "Oh yeah, this is just what you need." He said with enthusiasm. "This guy'll take your mind off everything, believe me."

Detective Lee groaned in the passenger seat. "Jeez, Ned, the man's a jerk."

"That's what makes him so great!"

Ned Gould was right about one thing. The radio show definitely took my mind off everything, but then, how often does a woman have a radio talk show devoted to herself?

Seventeen

The coffee at the police station was stale, but it was also warm, and I needed something warm. Detectives Lee and Gould arranged for us to talk in a small office away from the maddening crowd. I was preoccupied when we first settled into the ten-foot-by-ten-foot office crammed with a desk, file cabinet, and three chairs, but that could only be expected. After all, I had just experienced my first Clifford Bartholomew show and the subject matter had been privacy. His focus had been on a PI, "who shall remain unnamed, but whose initials happen to be the same as Hitler's secret police," with great legs—but questionable talent—who had been hired by the liberal lefties in the Democratic party to undermine the venerable Wallace Long when he's down.

Why Bartholomew felt compelled to bash me on the radio was a mystery to me. But a good defense is a strong offense, and I was curious just what he had to defend.

However, before I could deal with him, I had some questions to answer for the police. Unlike some other private investigators, I work well with the police. Maybe that's because I spent seven years on the force myself before starting CSI with Max. Or maybe it's because I trust the old adage that "many hands make light work." Whatever, I just don't see them as adversaries or the enemy. So when they asked me about my relationship with Brendan, I explained that I was working on a case in which his best friend had died. I didn't tell them that his best friend had been Peter Long and that Peter Long was Wallace Long's only son. I explained that when I last saw Brendan, he was on his way to see Gilbert Jackson and gave them Gil's number for confirmation. I asked Julia Lee what the circumstances were surrounding Brendan's death.

She and Ned Gould shared a glance, but then they told me that Brendan had been discovered at around midnight near Thompson Square Park on the lower eastside, in a stolen car with the motor running. An autopsy was yet to be performed, but it looked like he had killed himself. Carbon-monoxide poisoning; that at least explained the red hue to his skin.

"If Brendan killed himself, I'll eat your desk." When I crossed my legs I noticed that the salt and sand used to make the streets walkable were eating away at my boots. Damn.

"You said yourself you only met him briefly. Maybe the boy was unstable. Maybe the loss of his friend pushed him over the edge. It happens." She removed her left clip-on earring and rubbed the lobe.

"It does, but that's not what happened here." The longer it takes to solve a murder, the less information you have to work with. Though I had no proof, I had no doubts that Peter Long and his childhood friend, Brendan Mayer, had been murdered. If I could get the police department to work with me, we had a chance of solving this before somebody else got killed. I hadn't known Peter, but I did know Brendan, and I knew he was too young to die. And for what? What was it that was so damned important it was worth killing this innocent kid for? Again I saw Debi Cullerson in my mind's eye, sitting on a curb in San Francisco, her belly holding a new life resting on her lap.

Debi had laughed when I told her there was always hope. "Lady, hope is just another four-letter word for bullshit." She then fanned her maternity top over her stomach and shook her head. "I've looked the devil in the eye, and I know one thing for sure. You can't fight 'em. What's that old saying? You can run, but you can't hide? It's true. Just look at you. You found me."

"But I'm not the devil."

"Nope. Just his innocent messenger. Got a cigarette?"

"Sydney?" Detective Lee's voice brought me back to the moment. "Are you all right?"

I nodded. "Look, maybe we can help each other." I then told Julia and Ned the details about Peter Long, the blueprints, and how, as far as I knew, Brendan had never made it to his appointment with Gil. Maybe I wasn't responsible for any of these kids' deaths, and certainly there was nothing I could do for Debi at this point, but I was determined to find out what happened to Peter and Brendan.

Detective Lee listened without interrupting me. When I finished she nodded. "You say he mailed the blueprints to himself?"

"Yes."

"Did he get them?"

I shrugged. "As far as I know, he didn't have them yesterday morning."

"That was what? Eleven o'clock?"

"That's right."

"I appreciate your candor. I also think that about wraps it up here. Chances are you'll be hearing from us again." Detective Lee knew as well as I did that procedure would prevent them from including me in the investigation, but the two of us clicked. It was unspoken, but agreed, that we would help one another as best as we could.

"I hope so. I want to solve this just as much as you do," I said as I got into my jacket.

"Hey, Sydney," Ned called out as I was leaving. "By any chance was that you Bartholomew was talking about today?"

I answered with nothing more than a smile.

"Way to go, star." He nodded his approval.

Imagine that? I thought as I hailed a cab. *One run-in with this buffoon and I'm an overnight celebrity.*

Celebrity status like that, however, is not what I

wanted or needed. I figured Bartholomew could grandstand all he wanted. The more hot air he exhaled, the more I learned. As we passed within a block of the Long's hotel, I was tempted to have the driver drop me off, but I knew Max was waiting for me at the office. And as much as I didn't want to deal with it, I knew that Tom Cullerson had to be stopped, and he had to be stopped now. In order to do that I needed Max's help.

When I got to work Max had Beverly Tiari in his office, and Kerry was on the phone. I popped my head in and told Max I was back. Beverly, (who each time I saw her looked more and more like a nearsighted mole), squinted up and nodded a quick hello when I greeted her.

I made a beeline to my desk and plucked the telephone receiver up as I tossed my jacket on one of the canvas chairs. By now I knew Vanessa Stephens's work number by heart. It was time she and I had a little chat. Much to my surprise, she actually picked up when I was transferred through to her line.

"I've been trying to reach you." Her voice had an edge to it.

"And I've been trying to reach you. Have you gotten my messages?"

"Maybe one or two."

"No, it was four." I keep a log in a spiral notebook as to the calls I make regarding a case and what the upshot is of each call. Besides, as far as I'm concerned, one or two messages is usually more than enough. But I was impatient to talk with Vanessa, and I didn't want to do it over the phone. The more I thought about her, and the more I learned about her, the more questions I had. Something wasn't right here, and I wanted to find out just what the hell it was. "Vanessa, do you know anything about a set of blueprints that Peter might have been carrying with him to New York?"

"Blueprints?"

"Yes."

"What kind of blueprints?"

I decided to see what she had to offer. "That's just

it, I don't know. I thought you might have an idea, seeing as you two were so close."

"I don't understand. What have you found?"

"Nothing in hand, just hearsay and rumors."

Her end of the line was quiet.

"Vanessa, are you there?"

"I don't know anything about blueprints."

"Nothing at all? He never mentioned anything about plans for a new boat, or a house, or maybe an apartment?"

"Nooo," she drew out the word. "Oh wait," she said with a verbal finger snap. "I'm not sure, but my father's business might have something to do with blueprints." She cleared her throat away from the phone. "Why?"

"Did Peter work for your father?" Just then Max poked his head in the doorway. I held up my hand and mimed, five minutes.

"No. He was still a student."

"I see. So then he wouldn't have had access to your father's papers, or would he?"

"I wouldn't know," she said cautiously. Now why would she need to be cautious with me? After all, she had hired me, hadn't she?

What I really wanted to know was how Vanessa knew it was Peter on the pier, but it was a question I could only ask her in person. I had to see her reaction.

"Well, who knows, I'm sure it doesn't have anything to do with this," I said reassuringly. "However, I do think it's important that we get together. Do you have time today?" Not wanting her to start questioning me on the phone, I pressed on.

"Um, yeah." She hesitated.

"Where and when?" I asked. "If you like, I can meet you at your apartment." More than wanting to make it easy for her, I was curious how our client lived.

"I'd rather meet you at a restaurant, if that's all right. I moved in recently, and the place still isn't quite ready for company."

"That's fine." Personally I don't consider a year-old move recent, but I was willing to give her the benefit of the doubt. I'm the kind of person who moves and three days later it looks like I've lived there for months—even years. I hate clutter. I hate living out of boxes.

"Do you know Claire's on Twentieth and Seventh?" she asked.

"I do. I'll meet you there. Does six o'clock give you enough time to get home from work?"

"Aahh." She thought about this for a good ten seconds. When she finally said, "Yeah, that should be fine," it sounded like she was totally absorbed elsewhere. "But I have several questions," she started.

"Good, that's good. Write them down, and we'll go over it later when I see you." Before she could say "Uh," I was off the line.

I buzzed Kerry and told her if Vanessa Stephens called, I wasn't in. Then I dialed Gil's number. He picked up on the third ring.

"Gil, it's Sydney."

"You mean the communist?" He laughed. I wondered how many people I knew would have listened to the Clifford Bartholomew show and been able to connect the dots. "If I'm not mistaken, this Bartholomew character was talking about you today."

"The man's an ass."

"He's worse than that. But when you're stuck in holiday traffic, it's entertaining. That *was* you he was talking about, wasn't it?"

"How did you guess?"

"The legs."

"Ha, ha. Well, at least it wasn't the detecting skills."

"Well, the legs *and* your initials. Very subtle. Did you know that he compared you to the infamous SS? I won't go into the details, but essentially he said you had more in common with the organization than just letters."

"Just for the record, he never saw my legs."

It should probably have bothered me that this pompous ass was slandering me on the airwaves, but oddly enough it didn't. I think more than anything I was pleased that I had irritated him the day before more than he had irritated me. "Listen, what happened with Brendan yesterday?" I asked.

"Who the hell knows?"

"He never showed?"

"Not unless he's the invisible man."

"He's dead."

"Oh Jeez. When?"

"They found him in a stolen car at Thompson Square Park at around midnight. Looks like carbon-monoxide poisoning."

"Accident?"

"Nope."

"Suicide?"

"I don't think so."

"You think it's connected to the Long kid."

"Absolutely." I paused. "You should expect a call from two detectives from the Ninth Precinct." I gave him their names. "Tell me something, if they reopen the Long case, will his parents be required to stay in town?" I asked.

"Normally, yeah. But seeing as how he's such a muckety-muck, I don't think they'd ask him to stay. Besides, they really ought to be able to bury their son in peace." He had a point. "Well, I got a pile of shit on my desk," Gil said, ever eloquent. "Lemme know if you need anything. In the meantime, be careful."

"Yes, Gil," I said in my best schoolgirl voice.

"What?" He said suspiciously after a two-second beat.

"What do you mean, what?" I asked innocently.

"I know you, kid. 'Yes, Gil,' " he mimicked me in an unflattering falsetto. "That means you need something. What is it?" He sighed with the resignation of a man who knows his fate.

"Well, there is one other thing. I met Donald Kessler last night."

"Kessler, Kessler," he repeated.

"One of the guys who found Peter," I reminded him. "I think you should run a check on this guy. There's something very wrong there."

"Sydney." Gil's voice turned dangerously sweet on me. "Need I remind you that you're a private investigator? This, in case you forgot, is precisely what you do for a living."

"I know, that's why I called you. Just for your edification, the way us private investigators work is to call our contacts and get their help. *You*, you should be thrilled to know, are my favorite contact. Isn't that nice?"

"Mm-hm." He grunted into the mouthpiece. "I'm tickled down to my toes. So what's the problem with this guy?"

"I don't know how many cases are still open on gay bashing, but if this yo-yo isn't responsible for *some* of them, I'll hand in my license."

"Tell me what you got."

I gave him an in-depth review of my meeting with Kessler, leaving out the last five minutes. When I was finished, he thought it stank as much as I did, and he promised to run a check on him, personally. It couldn't have been in better hands.

I had Bartholomew on the brain when Max came into my office and planted himself on the sofa. Obviously Bartholomew was hiding something because of his radio attack. But what?

"Did Eddie call?" I asked Max before he could even put his feet up on the coffee table. He shook his head. "Did you notice how touchy Bartholomew got yesterday when I asked how he knew so much about Vanessa? That's one of the things Eddie's checking out. Maybe he can find out what contact Clifford and Vanessa had with each other during the last few years."

"Like maybe old Cliffy's screwing his best friend's daughter?" He had the eye patch in hand and was whirling it around an index finger.

"Maybe. Or maybe they had business dealings together. Or they were friends. Or . . ."

"Or something. Right. Now about this Cullerson . . ."

"I know," I said shortly. "But first, did you hear that Bartholomew was bashing me on the radio today?"

"No you don't, Sloane. We're going to deal with Cullerson whether you want to or not."

"I—"

"No, I want you to listen to me. I've been thinking about this, and I don't want to hear that it's *your* business because nothing is just yours when it comes to work.'' He cut me off with a no-nonsense tone I knew well. I said nothing. ''Your personal life is one thing. What you choose to do with or without Leslie is your concern and yours alone. How and when you pay your bills, that's your business. But when some stupid asshole is trying to fuck with my partner, it becomes my business as well. Do you understand? I've been thinking about our talk yesterday, and this isn't about my not trusting that you're capable of handling a situation. This comes down to acting smart and acting stupid. *I* know you can do anything—even if you don't—but you know as well as I do that schmucks like Cullerson are dangerous, especially when they're not stopped right at the start. Now''—he took his feet off the table and planted them firmly on the floor—''we are going to deal with this putz together, and we are going to do it today. Okay?''

I nodded. The fact is, I didn't want to deal with Cullerson alone. I knew from our encounter the night before that I wasn't quite up to facing all the bogeymen by myself. It was good to know I had Max by my side.

Max continued. ''Just so you know, I made a few calls and found out that the police did talk to Cullerson regarding the explosion here yesterday. He has an alibi for the time of the bombing, but the thing was on a timer, so that doesn't mean squat. His alibi for the night before? He was home watching television.''

''Can he prove it?'' I asked.

''Apparently his wife confirmed it.''

''Big surprise.''

''The police don't like Cullerson, though, and they plan on keeping an eye on him.''

As far as I could tell, whichever officer was ''keeping an eye on'' Cullerson had blurred vision, considering my run-in with him the night before.

''I also talked to one of Gil's associates. The police are setting up a sting for Joyce Cullerson. The guy may be a maggot, but the police still frown on contract murder. Go figure.''

I didn't know how I felt about Joyce Cullerson getting hoist by her own petard. How could I feel about a woman who didn't have the guts to stop the abuse, to pick up herself and her daughter and leave it, but suddenly found the energy to seek out a contract killing? *Screw her*, I thought as I listened to Max detail all that he had learned regarding Tom and Joyce Cullerson's happy little life together. Who knew? Maybe she'd be better off in jail for a few years than living with the abuse. Frankly, I didn't care.

Max got up and started to his office.

"Max?" If I was going to tell him about Cullerson's attack the night before, now was the time.

"Yeah?" He hung on to the doorframe and swung back into my office.

"About Cullerson?"

"Yeah."

"Someone tried to attack me last night."

Max let his arms fall to his sides. "Cullerson?"

"I think so." I folded the telephone message from Lyle the day before into an airplane as I spoke. "Nothing happened, but, well, I just feel like there's too much coming at me at one time."

"Sydney, you have to know when to lean. Trust me, I'm here for you. Okay?"

I nodded, and said, "Let me just make sure he's at work." Max left to get his jacket.

On the rare occasion when Max and I actually work together, it's a formidable team. As I reached for the phone to track down Cullerson, I felt more confident. *Okay, Cullerson*, I thought as I found his work number. *You may be nuts, but you got Max and me angry. You don't have a chance, shithead.*

Eighteen

Tom Cullerson sold pianos in the fifties on the west side, a quick subway ride from our offices. In less than fifteen minutes we were walking from Columbus Circle, east on Fifty-seventh Street, three blocks from Tom's place of employment. Max had put the eye patch back on.

"You know, I think I like it," I said as we passed Cafe Europa, a trendy restaurant with great sandwiches that I'd discovered one rainy day with Leslie.

"What?" Max glanced at me with his right eye. I was intentionally walking on his right side.

"The patch. Very distinguished." I neglected to mention that his new haircut, however, countered the effect.

"I thought Tommy would like it."

"So," I said, after we elbowed our way through a group of tourists en route to either La Bat Bar, the Hardrock Cafe, Planet Hollywood, or the Warner Brothers Store on Fifth Avenue where a larger-than-life Superman personally escorts the elevator between floors. "Any ideas how to handle Cullerson?"

Max shook his head. "Men like him ought to have their nuts tied in a knot and rammed down their throats."

I nodded, put my arm through his, and squeezed. I love Max for hating men like Cullerson. Max and my father, Nathan, had always had a lot in common. I'd actually met Max through my father. Dad and Max had known one another professionally and, given that the two of them were so much alike, they had become fast friends. It wasn't until after Dad died that Max approached me about starting a business together. It was close to eleven years, but seemed like a lifetime ago. We turned south on Seventh Avenue.

"Have you ever met him?" Max asked as we were hit by an onslaught of holiday shoppers from a tour bus, their arms loaded with dreck from overpriced midtown shops.

"Cullerson? Yeah, when they first hired us, I met with both Joyce and Tom."

"And?" He asked.

"And they *seemed* like a normal couple who had their fair share of problems. I mean, history has taught us that children don't up and leave for no reason at all, right?"

"Right."

"It was clear that he was the dominant one in the relationship, though if he said twelve words during the meeting, it was a lot. I remember he bit his nails the whole time we were together. It was kind of gross." I put my hand on his arm and stopped him. "But, you'll get a chance to meet him soon enough. We're here."

"He works here?" Max nodded to a storefront window where a miniature black baby grand sat with a halogen spot on the tiny keys. Above the door a curved metal sign with bold red letters read: **PIANOS Bought & Sold**.

When we entered it was as if all light from the street was extinguished and we were suddenly transported back in time. I envisioned Max with muttonchops and me in a corset and bustle. The walls were covered with dark paneling, a low tin ceiling was painted black, and brass lamps with green glass shades were scattered throughout the small piano emporium—one atop each piano as well as the salesmen's desks at the back of the store. Standing halogen lamps in two corners of the small space cast most of the light in the oddly inviting store.

Despite the darkness, I could see Tom Cullerson sitting at a desk in the back of the store. He wore a wrinkled white shirt with the sleeves rolled up to his elbows as he hunched over a paper, which he scribbled on with a stubby pencil.

As we approached him a young woman in a calico jumper and red turtleneck practically pounced on us and asked if she could be of assistance. Commission sales is tough. Before we could continue toward Tom, we had to promise Mindy we'd call her if we saw anything that caught our eye.

Cullerson looked up and saw us when we were ten feet away from his desk. He recognized me, jumped up, and bolted through a heavy mahogany door at the back of the shop. Max and I were right behind him.

The door led to a shabby lunchroom, which was also a storage and cloak room. At least twenty brown file boxes were stacked along the wall to the right as you entered, partially hidden behind a freestanding coat rack. The far left corner of the room was the kitchen, which consisted of a minirefrigerator, on which sat a microwave and a coffeemaker, and beside that a small sink filled with coffee mugs. There was a card table with four wonky metal chairs and a yellowed poster thumbtacked to the wall touting a Carnegie Hall piano concert several years earlier. A barred door in the back obviously led to a backyard—there are no alleys in New York—and another door, to our left, presumably opened to the bathroom.

Max ran to the back door and I went to the other door, which was, in fact, a bathroom. It was dirty, but fortunately empty. I dashed back through the lunchroom and went outside, where I found Max, who had Tom by the legs and was pulling him down off a seven-foot-high concrete wall that encircled what I assume was a cemented backyard.

I watched as Cullerson, who clung to the top of the wall, kicked at Max like a fish flopping out of water. Max grabbed hold of Cullerson's belt and yanked him off the wall. The two of them went down into sooty snow and, like a cowpuncher on a stopwatch, Max had Cullerson hog-tied in under six seconds. Max sat on

Cullerson's chest, his left hand clutching Tom's shirt, and his right hand poised to punch him in the face.

I came up from behind the two and told Max to stop.

Max paused, his fist in midair. ''Give me one good reason.'' he said, winded more from his rage than the physical exertion.

''Because we want to talk to Mr. Cullerson. If you break his jaw—right now—that will make it difficult.''

Cullerson had to be uncomfortable. He was lying in the snow wearing only his shirt, woolen slacks, and, of course, Max, who was a good fifty pounds heavier than he. He was also wearing the same pair of shitkickers with plaid laces that he had worn the night before when he had paid me a surprise visit.

''Get off me, you son of a bitch,'' Tom sputtered as he lamely kicked his legs.

Max leaned down onto Cullerson, grabbed his collar in both hands, and raised Cullerson's head two inches off the ground. They were nose-to-nose when Max growled, ''That's Mr. Son of a bitch to you, do you understand, boy?''

Cullerson's face was red, and I didn't think it had much to do with the cold. Again he struggled to be free of Max's hold, but it was clear that Max was in control. After several seconds, Cullerson let his body go limp. ''Would you please get off me?'' he said through clenched teeth.

Max didn't budge. ''We're going to have a talk, the three of us, and you're going to be on your best behavior, do you understand?''

When Cullerson didn't respond, Max repeated the question.

''Yes! Fine! Just get the fuck off me.''

I stood in the doorway, feeling the cold, knowing how uncomfortable Cullerson had to be with half of his body drenched from the freezing snow.

Max never released his hold on Cullerson. When they were both standing, he held Tom by the back of his hair and shirt. Cullerson was a mess. The filthy snow had soiled his entire backside, and his shirt had torn in the front when he tried to scale the wall.

"Shall we talk inside or out here?" I asked.

"You're going to be in a lot of trouble for this," Cullerson spit in response.

"Is that so?" I asked innocently. "Well, you know what they say about glass houses. Now, do you want to talk out here, or inside. Either way, I don't care, but we're not going anywhere until we come to some sort of an agreement, do you understand, Tom?"

He took several deep breaths.

"Okay, we'll talk out here."

I tucked my hands into my jacket pockets and asked him why he ran when he saw us.

"Because you're crazy. My daughter's dead because of you and instead of leaving us alone, you come back and harass us."

"Is that so? And how have I harassed you?"

"Do you have any idea how bad it looks for me to have the police come here?"

"That's what you get when you try to kill people," I reminded him.

"I didn't try to kill anyone. I leave that to people like you."

"Tell me something," I said calmly. "Just what did you say to Debi when you called my hotel room?" We both knew that the Cullersons had agreed not to call, but Tom did, and that call had obviously spurred Debi's decision to kill herself.

"She was *my* daughter. I don't need permission from some goddamned outsider to talk to her!"

"You pushed her off that building just as surely as if you were on the roof with her, and you know it. What did you tell her, Tom? That you wanted her to come home so you could continue your sick relationship? God, it makes me nauseous knowing what you did to her." Just the sight of him made my stomach turn. I looked down at our feet, dark and wet against the slushy snow. Finally I asked, "How could you? She was your daughter. You were someone she was supposed to be able to trust."

"That's right, she was *my* daughter, and she knew she *could* trust me. But people like you—" Before he could finish his sentence, Max threw him against the cold, hard wall. Tom didn't have a chance to catch his breath before Max had him by the collar and seat of his pants again.

"I know, people like me spoil all the fun for trash like you, don't we? Now I'll ask you again, why did you run, Tom?"

"I don't have to tell you anything." He struggled against Max's embarrassing hold.

"People only run when they're scared. You scared, Tom? Because if you weren't before, you should be now," Max hissed softly.

"God, I hate you," Cullerson said to me.

"It doesn't matter how you and I feel about each other," I said, keeping my anger in check. "You want to blame me for Debi's death, and I know you belong behind bars. That's not going to change, but—"

Before I could finish the sentence, he hauled back with his right elbow and caught Max unexpectedly in the ribs. In that fraction of a second when Max was taken off guard, Cullerson was able to break free from Max's hold. Instead of trying to run away, he dived for me. I was able to sidestep him, and he hit the ground. When he turned on his side I kicked him as hard as I could in the small of his back, which sent him sprawling flat on his stomach. He tried to push himself up, but before he could I stepped on his right hand with my left foot. As I applied pressure I could feel his hand give under my boot.

"Stop it! You're breaking my hand!" His voice cracked.

"I don't frighten easily, Tom, and you sure as hell can't bully me." I moved my foot from his hand to his face. His body twitched in frustration, but he didn't try to get up. By now Max was up and standing behind me. My hands were drawn up into fists, and I resisted the urge to bring my boot smashing down on Cullerson's head.

"You'll never lay another hand on me, Cullerson."

He went to grab my foot, but I only had to press down harder to discourage him.

"You so much as come near me again—"

"Next time—" He slobbered.

I cut him off by removing my foot and bringing it full force into his side. He rolled onto his back and clutched his side in pain. "There won't be a next time. You may be an asshole, Tom, but you're not stupid. The police know you're stalking me, they know what you did to my office, and they know what you did to Debi. And believe me, they don't take kindly to pedophiles and little men who play with explosives. So let's just call an end to it."

Cullerson was sitting up now, looking like he'd been run over by a truck. "I'll have you arrested for this." He struggled to get to his feet and staggered backwards once he was up.

"Good. Do that. Let's deal with this in a courtroom. But until then, I don't want to see you again." I looked up at Max and knew that if he could, he'd single-handedly defend all women and children against men like Cullerson. But he couldn't. And I wasn't about to let him start here. I tugged at his sleeve. "Come on, Max. Let's go. It's beginning to stink out here."

We left Cullerson in the cold, his body sagging in defeat. He wasn't a man accustomed to people fighting back. *Too bad*, I thought, as we walked through the lunchroom and back into the salesroom.

Mindy, the eager salesperson, approached us again as we were leaving, offering us her card if we should have any questions regarding their wide selection of pianos.

Once we were back out on the street, I was shaking with anger.

"I have a feeling that made a difference," Max said as we passed a Korean fruit market. Poinsettias and miniature pine trees complete with pint-sized Christmas ornaments crowded the sidewalk in front of the store.

"I hope so." I needed to believe our confrontation with Tom Cullerson hadn't been an exercise in futility.

"Man, is he a piece of work, or what?" Max took off the eye patch and replaced it with a pair of sunglasses.

"Have you ever met anyone more vile?"

Max draped his arm over my shoulders, and asked, "You okay?"

"No. You?"

"No." We walked in silence to the end of the block. "Life isn't always pretty, Sydney."

"Good adage, Maxo. Got any more?" I was on the lookout for a public phone that wasn't broken or being used.

"Sure. Let a smile be your umbrella. It's always darkest before the storm. Every cloud has a silver lining. Wait a minute," he said as we crossed the street. "Do you think all proverbs are based on meteorology?"

"Maybe, but you know haste makes waste, and I have a zillion things to do before I meet Vanessa Stephens. Got a quarter I can borrow?" We had already passed nine phones with waiting lines.

"Are you going back to the office?" He fished the change from his pocket and gave me four quarters, two dimes, and a nickel.

"I'm not sure. You?" Two blocks and still not an available phone in sight.

"No. I've got to go downtown. I've got some work to do for Tiari. It should take a couple of hours." He sounded bored, and, from previous dealings with Beverly, he could expect to feel that way for the duration of his investigation.

"That reminds me, what really happened with the Englishwoman's car?" I found a pay phone where I promptly lost Max's small change in an attempt to reach Kerry.

"The garage was locked up when I got there."

"No!" I simulated shock.

"Don't be such a wiseass. I got them to open it up and our happy client now has her car, which won't run." He directed me to the three phone stalls in front of the Coliseum Bookstore, where there were two people waiting on line.

"We'll be here forever," I complained.

"No, *we* won't, but you might. I have to get downtown. When will you be back at the office?" A woman using one of the phones put another coin in the slot and turned a deaf ear to the man's objections on line behind her.

I held up my hands in a "who knows" gesture. "Maybe twenty minutes, maybe a few hours. All I know for sure is that I have a six o'clock with our client, Ms. Stephens."

Before Max took off, we each agreed to check in at the office by four.

When he left I went in search of another phone and found one in the lobby of a large office building. My first call was to Louise Long. I figured since I was less than five blocks away from her hotel and still had questions regarding Peter, why not make things easier for myself.

Louise answered on the first ring.

"Mrs. Long, it's Sydney Sloane. How are you today?" I knew it had to be hard for this woman. Her favorite child was dead, her daughter was in the city and hadn't contacted her despite Peter's death, her husband was the big man on campus, and she lived her life in the shadows. I supposed the tumbler of vodka or gin or whatever it was she drank made the darkness less oppressive.

"Sydney?" She sounded far away and small.

"Yes."

"My baby's dead." She whimpered. I hate phones. From the sound of her voice all I could imagine was that Louise Long was in a fetal position, alone, a mess, and frightened. My heart felt like it was clenching in my chest.

"Louise? Is anyone there with you?" I asked gently.

"What?"

"Are you alone?" I repeated.

"All alone." There was an eerie quality to her voice, something that made me fear for her. Imagination or not, Louise Long sounded like she was slipping off the deep end.

"Listen to me, Louise. Can you hear me?"

"Yes." So small, so faint.

"I'm coming to see you, okay? I'll be there in ten

minutes, all right?'' I felt the adrenaline race through my veins. ''Louise?''

''Yes.''

''Let me in when I get there, okay?''

''Okay.'' The line went dead.

''Shit,'' I hissed as I frantically dug through my pockets for the quarters Max had given me. I dialed Aunt Minnie's number and prayed she would be there. I nearly let out a yelp for joy when she picked up the phone.

''Min, it's me. I need your help. I want you to meet me in midtown as soon as you can.'' I gave her the hotel name and room number. ''I can't explain anything right now, but please, please hurry.'' I practically threw the receiver back into the cradle and raced out of the lobby, back into the street.

Max was right, you had to know when to lean on friends. I knew Louise Long needed help, and Minnie, who's done volunteer work at a local hospital for the last twenty-five years, was just the woman for the job.

I just prayed we got to Louise before she did something stupid.

Nineteen

Thirteen minutes later I was knocking on the door to 2007. There was no answer. I tried the doorknob, thinking that maybe she'd left it open for me. No such luck. As I was about to leave and get the manager to let me in, Minnie got off the elevator. She looked like an angel of mercy in her red coat, silk scarf, and mink hat.

"What is it?" she asked as she pulled off her gloves. I gave her a quick synopsis and said, "She didn't sound right, Min. Something's wrong, I just know it. I'm going to go get the manager to let us in."

Minnie looked up the hallway and patted my arm. "Wait just one minute, I'll be right back." She then approached a young maid who was pushing her cart outside a room three doors down.

"Yoo-hoo." Minnie called out to the young Philippine woman. "My dear, I'm so sorry to disturb you, but, silly me, I left my key with my husband and I, well, I *must* get into the room. My bladder's not what it used to be if you know what I mean. Would you be so kind?" She gently laid her hand on the woman's arm and postured herself in such a way that would lead one to think an accident was imminent.

Never having witnessed Minnie operate in such a way, I watched with fascination as the young woman nodded sympathetically and quickly let us into room 2007.

"Thank you so much." Minnie offered her a few dollars, which she refused.

"My grandma uses Depends," the maid whispered to me as we started into the room. "They're good. No more messes."

"Thanks." I smiled before closing the door between us.

Minnie was already in the bedroom kneeling beside Louise, who was lying on the floor wearing a terry robe, one slipper, and a long white nightie.

"Get a cold washcloth," Minnie ordered, as I entered the room. "It's all right, dear, you're going to be just fine," she cooed to Louise, who was moaning softly. "Just fine. That's right."

Minnie wiped Louise's face tenderly with the cloth and told me to order coffee, toast, and juice from room service. I did as she bade and then went through the medicine cabinet to see what, if any, pills Louise had taken. The cabinet was sparsely filled with the usual assortment of over-the-counter drugs; Advil, aspirins, Excedrin PM, pills for leg cramping, but no prescription drugs. Not a one. Her collapse was apparently a combination of alcohol, depression, and exhaustion.

Louise started crying when she felt Minnie's arms around her. She reached up, wrapped her arms around my aunt, and let the floodgates open.

I stood in the bathroom doorway and waited until Louise's cries subsided. Then, together, Minnie and I got Louise into the bathroom, where again, Minnie took over. By the time room service had arrived, Louise was sitting up in bed, looking pale, drawn, and fragile, but a fat lot better than she had when we'd first arrived.

"Here, dear, take a sip of this." Minnie held up a glass of orange juice. Louise held up her hand in refusal, but Minnie was persistent. "It will make you feel better, I promise. And you need to be strong now."

"I want to die," Louise mumbled as she let Minnie raise the glass to her parched lips.

"It only feels that way right now." Minnie motioned for me to get the coffee. "But tomorrow, or the day after, or even the day after that, you'll wake up, look outside your window, and thank God you're alive."

"It feels like I've been dead for years." Louise looked around the darkened room. Little light filtered past the still-drawn shades and drapes.

"Here." Minnie put the juice glass on the nightstand and reached for the coffee cup. How do you like your coffee?" She motioned for me to open the shades. I complied happily. I have never liked dark bedrooms.

"Black, please." Louise reached for the coffee and tried to steady her hands before taking a first sip. I opened the drapes, then the shades. "Oh my God, close the drapes."

"We need a little light in here," Minnie countermanded strongly.

"I don't want anyone to see me like this."

"Oh that's fine," Minnie said, ignoring Louise's objections with a wave of her hand. "You're a beautiful woman, Louise. You shouldn't ever want to hide."

"Where's Mr. Long?" I asked from the far side of the room as I drew open the last set of heavy drapes.

"Wallace has business," she said with acrimony.

"More fund-raising?" I asked, against Minnie's silent disapproval.

"I don't know." Louise's hands and voice were steadying and she finished the coffee. "May I have more, please?" she asked Minnie.

"Certainly. And how about a little toast?" Minnie held the cup out to me.

I brought over the pot of coffee along with the plate of toast. Two slices of dry toast for four dollars. Amazing what hotels can get away with. One lousy egg would have set the Longs back seven dollars and fifty cents.

"Mrs. Long, about our conversation yesterday . . ."

"I'm not supposed to talk to you anymore, Miss Sloane." Louise rested back onto the four pillows behind her and shook her head. "Wallace says you're a pest."

"What do you think?" I asked Louise, who was nibbling halfheartedly at a piece of toast.

" 'No one's asking you to think, Louise.' No one cares what I think," she mumbled as she tossed the dry toast back onto the plate.

"I care," I said.

Louise gave me a long hard look and then turned to Minnie. She reached out a frail, yet elegant hand to Minnie and squeezed it. "I'm terribly grateful to the both of you. I don't know what happened . . . I just . . ."

"Sshhh," Minnie hushed. "People shouldn't have to get through pain alone."

I thought of Max's words the day before; "I've never accomplished anything alone. We need friends and people to lean on. I just hope it doesn't kill you to learn that." And now here I was hoping Louise Long wouldn't die trying to learn the same lesson from a different point of reference. But was it so different? We both had to reach within to reach outside of ourselves. I had asked Max to help with Cullerson and now Minnie was at the hotel with me. It hadn't been so difficult to reach out to my two friends, and it made things infinitely easier, not to have to shoulder the burden all alone. I couldn't imagine the burden of knowing a child of mine was dead, possibly murdered, and not knowing the truth.

"Mrs. Long, I believe your son was murdered, but I need help proving it. I need your help. Please."

Minnie flashed me a look that could have killed, but I had to trust my instincts. This might be the only time I could get some answers from Louise. Wrong or right, I couldn't let the moment pass.

"What can I do?" she moaned.

"You said that when you saw Peter on Saturday he made a phone call."

"That's right."

"Did you hear more of his conversation than 'I know what I'm doing'?"

"No," she said faintly. I didn't believe her.

"Tell me, Mrs. Long, you have a safe at your home, is that right?"

She looked bewildered. "Yes."

"Can you tell me what's in that safe?"

She looked at Minnie in confusion. Minnie reached out, took her hand, and said, "Sydney knows what she's doing, dear, you must trust her."

"We keep stocks and bonds in there, our passports,

family documents like birth certificates, the deed to the house, jewelry, and cash—not a lot—but Wallace always likes to have cash on hand.''

''Do you know if Mr. Long keeps any business documents in that safe?''

She shook her head. ''No. Everything related to work he keeps in a safe at his office.''

''You're certain of that?''

''Yes, I believe so.''

''Is there anything your husband might keep in the safe at home that might be related to his campaign?''

''No. As I said, everything related to work is kept at his office. Besides, what would Wallace have to hide with regard to his campaign?'

I couldn't answer that.

''Mrs. Long, do you know the combination to the safe at home?''

''Of course I do,'' she answered slightly indignant, which meant she was feeling stronger.

''And what about the safe in the office? Do you know the combination for that?''

''No. But Wallace has a copy of that combination in our safe at home, should anything happen to him.''

''And do you remember the last time you personally opened the safe at home?''

''Before we came to New York. There was some jewelry I wanted to take. Why? Is it missing? I put it in the hotel safe when we arrived.''

''No, I'm sure it's still there. Do you know if Peter knew the combination to either safe?''

''Peter?'' She looked from me to Minnie and back to me. ''I don't think so. No. There was no need for Peter to know the combinations. There was nothing in the safes that could have been of interest to him.''

''Not even his passport or birth certificate?''

''If he ever needed that, his father or I would have gotten it out for him. But why on earth would he need either of those documents?''

''I don't know that he did. I'm just trying to get an overall picture.'' I perched myself on the wide windowsill, where heat was gently rising from an encased radiator. "When you opened the safe to get your jewelry, was Peter with you?"

Louise gave this some thought. Finally she said, "No. He wasn't." But her voice was flat.

"What?" I asked.

Minnie squeezed Louise's hand and nodded silent encouragement.

"A month, maybe a month and a half before we came here, I was working at home when Peter surprised me with a visit during the middle of the day." She turned to Minnie and explained, "He liked to do that, come over and take me to lunch or out for a walk, he was always so kind and considerate that way."

Minnie smiled and took the cold coffee from Louise, which she set on the nightstand.

"What happened that day?" I asked, not wanting to lose momentum.

"As I said I was working at home. I was paying bills, which I always do in the office, which is, of course, where the safe is."

"Was the safe open?"

Louise squinted as if trying to see into the recent past. Finally she nodded slowly. "Yes. Yes it was. You see, I only pay the bills once a month and I keep the household checkbook in the safe, as well. It's not necessary, but it's something I've always done."

"Can you recall if Peter looked in the safe while he was there?"

She took a deep breath and held up her graceful hands. "I don't know. I can't imagine why he would, but—" She paused. "Now let me think. He was in very high spirits that day as I recall. He flopped down on the armchair across from me and told me to wrap it up because he was starving. He was always starving. That boy could eat like there was no tomorrow and never put on an ounce. I teased him about that. I used to tell him one day he was going to wake up and be a hundred pounds heavier, just like that overnight." She stopped and studied her hands, neatly flattening the sheets over her.

"And what happened?" I asked gently.

"I told him I had three more checks to write before

I could go anywhere and that he would just have to be patient.'' She smiled to herself. ''Patience was not one of Peter's strong suits. He's just like his father that way. Anyway, he groaned and said he needed something, anything. I told him there was a fresh pot of coffee in the kitchen.''

''And did he go to the kitchen then?'' I asked.

''No. He didn't. I got him the coffee.'' She smiled uneasily at me, as if in apology. ''I'm one of those awful mothers who tend to wait on their children, but then, he was also my best friend.''

''So Peter was left alone in the office while you went to the kitchen to get his coffee?''

''Well, yes, but it didn't take more than a minute, and he was in the same place I'd left him. I'm afraid I don't know what you're getting at, Ms. Sloane.''

''Mrs. Long, do you have any dealings whatsoever with your husband's business?''

This seemed to take her out of left field. ''No,'' she said clearly. ''In all honesty computers don't interest me. Wallace has tried to get me to convert the household expenses to computer, but I prefer pencil and paper. I'm old-fashioned that way. Naturally we have a computer in the house, but I never touch it.'' She took a deep breath, relaxed back into the pillows, and closed her eyes. Minnie and I watched her, not knowing if she were asleep or what. Finally she opened her eyes, and said, ''I'm sorry. I'm afraid I've not been getting much rest.''

''Just one more thing, if that's all right,'' I asked. She nodded, and I said, ''Were you aware that there had been threats on Wallace's life?''

''Oh yes.''

''I take it this was cause for concern?''

''Well, certainly we were concerned. Initially Wallace thought it was a prankster. Art—do you know Art?'' she asked, referring to Wallace's other bodyguard.

''We've met.''

''Well, Art had the local police run some tests on it, and he came to the conclusion that there was nothing to be concerned about, but he's a cautious man—thank God—and after we received several more threats, he suggested that Wallace get another bodyguard for extra security. An ounce of precaution, you know. That's when Wallace hired Lyle.'' Louise again turned to Minnie, and said, ''Lyle was Peter's teacher in high school. Poor man lost his wife in childbirth, I believe.''

''What a shame,'' Minnie said softly.

''I'm surprised that no one took these threats more seriously,'' I said aloud more to myself than anyone else.

''Apparently you have to expect these things in politics. That's what Art said, and he knows his business.''

''How?'' I asked.

''I beg your pardon?''

''Do you know how Art knows his business? I thought he was initially Wallace's assistant at LongTec.'' I had assumed, when Lyle told me that, that Art's area of expertise was computers and business. I hadn't given it much thought, if any.

''He was. If I'm not mistaken, Art came to Wallace as a computer security person. But, as I said before, I don't get involved in Wallace's work. It's all too much for me to fathom.''

''One last thing, Mrs. Long. Did Peter endorse your husband's political aspirations?''

''I don't think that's any of your goddamned business.'' Wallace's voice came from the bedroom doorway and shattered what calm the three of us had found. ''Now I thought I told you to leave us alone, young lady. And Libby, I specifically asked you not to talk to her.'' He tried valiantly to keep his tone amiable.

''Why?'' I asked.

''Excuse me?'' He cocked his head to the side as if he were hard of hearing.

''Why didn't you want Mrs. Long to talk to me?''

''Because you're upsetting my wife, little girl, and I don't think that's necessary after what she's already been through. Besides, I don't think I have to answer to a snotnose like you.'' He glanced at Minnie and nodded. ''Forgive my language, ma'am. And you are?'' He bent in Minnie's direction.

''I'm a friend of Louise's. You must be Wallace.''

She stood and extended her hand. ''It's a pleasure to meet you. I've heard so much about you.'' The charm was oozing from her every pore.

''Is that right? And how do you know this fine woman, Libby?'' He took Minnie's hand between both of his and smiled tensely at his wife.

''I was alone, Wallace. This has all just been too hard for me—''

''Well I'm here now, Libby. So let's just ask your nice friend to say good-bye, shall we?'' Wallace was amazing. He could actually smile with his lips and no other part of his face. It was both fascinating and scary at the same time. He held out his right hand, showing Minnie the door. ''Libby needs time to rest, Miss . . . ?''

''Minnie, will do.''

''Minnie. Well then, Minnie, why don't you and Miss Sloane leave at the same time. My wife and I would like to be alone.'' He towered over Minnie like a vulture over its prey.

Minnie pushed herself to her full five feet nothing and stood firm. ''Your wife has been left alone quite enough, if you ask me.''

''I didn't. Good-bye.'' He gently put his left hand on Minnie's right shoulder with hopes, no doubt, that she would leave gracefully. He didn't know Minnie.

''Get your hand off me, Wallace. I will leave when Louise asks me to and not a moment before.''

''What did you say?'' He was flabbergasted, which made two of us. I nearly let out a laugh, but knew that we were on the brink of something volatile, and I didn't need any more bombs that week.

''You heard me. When Louise asks, I'll leave. In the meantime your wife needs a friend, and I plan on being here for her. I wonder what the papers would say about a man like you were he to deny his wife solace in a time of need.'' Minnie looked up into Wallace's eyes and didn't back down for an instant.

Way to go Minnie, I thought as I watched David face Goliath. For a moment it felt like all the oxygen had been sucked out of the room.

Wallace turned to me, red-faced and ready to blow.

"I suggest that you and I have a little talk in the other room. Now!" With that he shot out of the room like a bullet.

I gathered my jacket and purse and went to Louise. "You know, Minnie's a good woman to have as a friend." Louise looked stunned. "You should take her up on her offer." I paused. "If there's anything I can do for you, let me know." I pressed my card into her hand and left.

Wallace was pacing the outer room when I joined him. I noticed that his faithful bodyguards, Art and Carney, were conspicuously absent.

"Where's Mutt and Jeff?" I asked as I slipped into my jacket.

"Who *is* that woman?" he asked through clenched teeth.

I shrugged. "She was right, though. Your wife not only needs friends, Mr. Long, she needs help."

"Understand this and understand it fast, missy. I don't need you telling me how to live my life, you got that?"

"Yes, sir." I refrained from saluting.

"And when I told you to stay out of my business, I wasn't fooling. I meant it."

"Yes, sir."

"Now I want you to leave, and, when you do, don't ever bother me again, you got that?"

"Yes. But let me ask you one quick question before I go, okay?"

"What is it?" he asked impatiently.

"Why didn't you take the death threats seriously?"

He took a deep breath and shook his head. "I did take them seriously, I still do. But there's only so much you can do to protect yourself. I have done what I can. In this world you have to take chances if you want to get anywhere. Art and Lyle are both capable men, but if someone wants to kill me, they'll find a way. I can't be constantly looking over my shoulder, afraid of every shadow. But"—he held up his right hand as if taking an oath—"I do not believe, as I understand you do, that the threats and my son's death are connected."

''How can you be so sure?'' I asked, genuinely curious.

''I can't, but if someone killed Pete, they would have made it very quite clear that it *was* murder because they would have wanted to scare me. It wouldn't make sense for them to conceal their message.''

''His death didn't scare you?''

Wallace let his shoulders sag for a fraction of a second. He caught himself and pulled back up to his picture perfect posture. ''You said one quick question.''

''Well, there was one other thing.''

When he didn't toss me out on my keister, I forged on ahead. ''You use blueprints in your line of work, is that correct?''

''What?'' He was clearly annoyed at the unexpected query.

''You make computers, right?''

''I manufacture components for computers.''

I followed him into the entryway. ''Well, in manufacturing these components, do you use blueprints?''

''Now what do you think?''

''I think you do.'' I zipped my jacket.

''Why?'' He held the door open for me.

''I'll try not to bother you again, Mr. Long.''

Twenty

It was nearly three by the time I got back to the office carrying a bag from the local Burger King. When I arrived, Kerry was running lines with a scene partner for her acting class, which is a practice both Max and I have gotten used to at work. Since I was going to be there for the rest of the day, I told her she could leave. This delighted them both, and I wondered if Kerry was doing more than acting scenes with this partner. He was cute—and he knew it—which made him automatically not my kind of guy, but then, men and their attractiveness was a whole kettle of fish I didn't even want to think about. And I hadn't. I had all but forgotten my tryst with Lyle the night before. Foremost on my mind at that moment was food. I'd not eaten since dinner with Lyle the night before, and I was so ravenous my head was starting to pound. I started in on the fries before I even opened my office door.

To my joy the glass workers had come and gone during my absence. At least I had a window in my office instead of plywood, and I could have my cheeseburger and fries while watching the street below. As I unwrapped the burger, I considered all that had happened since I'd last eaten. Cullerson's late-night visit. Lyle. Identifying Brendan. Bartholomew's caustic radio attack. Cullerson again. The fright with Louise Long. I was exhausted just thinking about it, which reminded me that I was running on zero sleep. Oddly enough I wasn't the least bit tired. Adrenaline is good.

When I finished lunch, I called the Wizard, my computer friend whom I had called the day before and, contrary to Max's pessimism, she was able to supply the information I had asked for. Oh, Vanessa, this was going to be an interesting client meeting.

I switched on the computer, ready to key in what I'd gathered on the Longs, when the phone rang.

It was Gil saying he was running a more extensive check on Donald Kessler, but he didn't go into detail. "Just thought you'd want to know. If I come up with anything interesting, you'll be the first one I call, okay?"

Gil wouldn't be taking a more thorough look into Kessler if he didn't think there was a pile of dirt hidden under the rug.

I remembered that Lyle had given me Nancy Albus's work number the night before. I dialed Peter's girlfriend and was finally able to reach her. She already knew about Peter's death—apparently everyone at the company did—and when I explained who I was and that a member of the family (not specifying who), had hired me to look into his death, she was relieved to have someone to talk with.

We were on the phone about twenty minutes (sixteen during which she cried almost incoherently), but those four clear minutes were illuminating.

When I got off the phone with Nancy, I called to leave a message for Minnie and thank her for her help. I knew if I called now, she wouldn't be there and I could just leave a message, which is, after all, the whole purpose behind the invention of answering machines. It enables us to leave messages while never having to actually connect with the other person. A godsend, as I see it. "Hello, I'm thinking about you. Good-bye." Boom, a three-second message instead of having to spend thirty minutes on the phone. I was floored when Minnie answered.

"You're home." Deductive reasoning. It's what I do for a living.

"What? Did you call just to leave a message? I know

people who do that, you know. They call when they know the other person isn't going to be there, so they can just leave a message and not have to talk. I hate that. I have a friend in California who does that all the time. She thinks she'll just leave me a message and then we can talk on my dime. Is that what you just did?"

"No." Guilt was written all over my face, but fortunately we're not quite at the Jetson stage of telecommunication with videos.

"My dear, I never knew how exciting your job is."

"That's right, Min. Never a dull moment in this here detecting business."

"Well, you know, I was thinking on my way home that you could probably use someone like me more often, don't you think? Who would suspect a sweet old lady of being an undercover agent?"

"No one. Not even me. But you were wonderful today. Louise needed someone just like you, as did I, so thank you."

"Oh, tish tosh, it was my pleasure."

"So what happened after I left?"

"Well, that nasty man Wallace came back into the bedroom and asked me to leave again. I told him not yet and would he please leave Louise and me alone for a moment."

"Way to go, Min. What did he do?"

"He left. I think he's afraid of women who look like me. And he was clearly raised to respect his elders. Anyway, Louise and I are going to have breakfast and then go to church tomorrow morning."

"*You* in a church?" Minnie and I share a profound distrust for any formalized religion.

"I know." She sighed. "But if this poor woman can get some consolation from that, who am I to stop her? Besides, I like her. She's got guts."

"Does she?" I asked, wondering if it was guts that press people into the shadows.

"Yes, she does. Her husband's a brute, she lost her daughter's trust, and now her son is dead. And yet she's still here."

"If I hadn't called—"

"If you hadn't called, she would have awakened on the floor when her husband came home to pick her up. Remember, Sydney, she didn't have to answer the phone, did she? She was, in her way, reaching out. Give the woman a little credit, would you?"

"Did she tell you anything more about her son?"

"Such a loss for her. They seemed to have had a unique relationship, didn't they?"

"Yes. Did she tell you anything?"

"No. Not really. I didn't stay much longer than you."

"Did she tell you when they're going home?" I slipped on my reading glasses, cradled the receiver between my shoulder and chin, and started typing.

"Tomorrow evening."

"Oh?"

"That's how we started talking about church. She told me one of the hardest things for her this week is that she'd not been able to go to church and pray for Peter. Why people think they need a church to pray, I don't understand, but obviously they believe they have a more direct line that way. Anyway, I told her that was ridiculous when we had about eight thousand churches right here in Manhattan. Maybe more. I think it's more. What do you think?"

"I think there's probably eight thousand on Fifth Avenue alone."

"You could be right. Anyway, she said she wouldn't be able to talk to her pastor *in person* until Saturday—apparently they've *spoken*, but it's just not the same as being face-to-face—which, again, I don't understand, but that's how some people are. So I asked her, 'Why Saturday?' and she said, 'Because we don't go home until late tomorrow, and by the time I get home the church will be closed,' which is *another thing* that bothers me, the thought that people think they have to wait for the appointed hours to get spiritual comfort, but don't get me started on that." She took a deep breath which gave me a split-second window to ask, "Did she tell you why they're leaving tomorrow night and not during the day?"

"Nope. When she said that I suggested we meet in

the morning and go to church together, which just perked her up right away. There's only one problem."

"Let me guess. Which church?"

"Precisely. I mean I didn't even ask her which denomination she is. Do you think that matters?"

"Well, I think you'll be safe if you don't take her to a synagogue or a Buddhist temple." Who knew? My mother was Jewish and wanted my brother and sister and me to have some understanding of religion, so she sent us off to Sunday school until we were confirmed. My father was a firm believer in a strong spiritual center, which—as far as he was concerned—didn't have a thing to do with formalized religion. After nine years of hiding the alarm clocks every Saturday night in hopes of missing Sunday school, I hardly felt qualified to answer her query, but I tried. "Personally I like the Little Church Around the Corner. It's sweet, don't you think?" The church, which isn't far from where Minnie lives, is noted as being a church for actors. Why, I don't know, but it's in the thirties on the east side and it has a country-church feel to it.

"What kind of church is it?" she asked.

"A cute one. She'll love it."

Minnie promised to call after their outing, and I returned to the computer screen. It was hard to concentrate. All I could think of was my six o'clock meeting with Vanessa.

I had input a good two-thirds of the Long information when the phone rang again. I was tempted to switch on the answering machine.

"CSI." I said shortly.

"Sydney? It's Leslie."

Leslie! Shit! I had completely forgotten about our date for dinner and whatever.

"Hi. How are you?" I said with more enthusiasm than the question warranted.

"Okay." She sighed. "It's been a crazy day. I'm looking forward to tonight."

There was a short pause as I tried to calculate when I could see her.

"Sydney, you do remember we're getting together tonight, don't you?"

"Of course I do," I said with a laugh.

"You forgot," She accused me accurately.

To lie or not to lie, that was the question. There are moments when defensiveness doesn't do a smidgen of good, and this was one of those times. After close to a year of intimacy, Leslie knew me well enough to know when I was hedging and when I wasn't.

"It's not that I forgot, it's just been a full day." I debated whether to tell her about identifying Brendan or having participated in beating up a pedophile or having been witness to a woman's descent into grave depression and realized that since she hates what I do so much, it was prudent to keep my mouth shut. "I also have a six o'clock meeting downtown. Can we get together later?"

"What time?"

"Eight?" It seemed like a perfectly reasonable time for dinner. Why, even a play was titled such. That's what time people in New York eat dinner if they don't have kids, and aren't octogenarians or hypoglycemic.

She sighed, and I wanted to say, "Well *excuuuse* me. As much as you may hate it, I have a job." But I didn't. Instead I waited. And waited. And waited.

"Leslie? You still there?" I asked, though I could hear her breathing on the other end of the line.

"Yes, I'm still here. I'm thinking."

"What about?"

"I was wondering why you forgot about our dinner date. What that means."

"It doesn't mean anything. And besides, I didn't forget."

"Did too."

"Can we talk about this tonight over dinner, or are you going to punish me?" Testy, testy. I let my shoulders relax, and said, "Look, I don't want to fight anymore. I was looking forward to seeing you, but it's been one of those action-packed days, you know?"

"No, I don't know." Ice wouldn't have melted in her mouth.

There was nothing I could say, and I was too tired to go racing in circles chasing my tail.

"That's just it, Sydney, when you say it was an action-packed day it could mean anything from a shoot-out in a subway tunnel to God knows what."

"Oh go on. You make me sound like Kojak." I said this facetiously, but the truth was, I liked the idea that my life wasn't predictable and boring. I liked the notion that from day to day I never knew what to expect. I know at least twenty people who complain constantly about the day-to-day routines that they're stuck in, the proverbial rut they call life. It felt good to be confronted about my life choices and want to defend them instead of meekly wondering if Leslie wasn't right. She wasn't right.

"You are like Kojak." She was definitely softening.

"Would you like to have dinner with me tonight?" I decided to ignore the comparison between me and Telly Savalas.

"Yes." Pouting, but hanging in there. There was hope.

"Okay. Why don't we go to the Lone Dove?" Our friend Maurice owns the quaint little restaurant in the Village, and as far as I'm concerned it has the best food in town. But more than that, the atmosphere is perfect on a cold winter's night. It's romantic and comforting at the same time.

"All right. Eight o'clock?" she asked suspiciously.

Knowing that I was skating on thin ice, I refrained from making it a half hour later. "Eight o'clock. I'll see you then."

When we got off the phone I felt uncomfortable, like suddenly my clothes were too tight. I was shocked, too, to see that it was already close to five. I turned off the computer and took half an hour before leaving to prepare myself for my meeting with Vanessa Stephens.

Just as I was getting ready to leave, the phone rang. Thinking it might be Vanessa, I answered at Kerry's desk, wearing my jacket and gloves.

"Sydney? It's Lyle." He sounded muffled, as if he was talking into a tissue.

"Lyle. How are you?"

"I have news about Brendan."

"Oh, God, Lyle, I should have called you. I'm so sorry. How did you find out?"

"I called him to see how he was doing, you know, after Peter and all, and his roommate told me. You knew?"

"I identified the body."

"You? Why you?"

"It's a long story."

"I have time."

"But I don't. I understand you're leaving tomorrow."

"Yeah. Can't say that I'm not looking forward to it."

"When do you leave?"

"Mr. Bartholomew's throwing a final cocktail party-fund-raiser, and then it's home sweet home."

"Clifford Bartholomew's throwing a party?"

"Yeah."

"But don't the Longs want to get home?"

"I'm sure they do, but Mr. Long has said from the beginning that he's committed to the people, and he'll see it through. It's a lot harder on her. But you know that, don't you?"

"You'd think their 'best friend' would sympathize and cancel the party so they could get home."

"I don't know. Apparently this particular gathering could bring in more backing than all the others combined."

"Really? Where is it?"

"At Bartholomew's house."

"Is that in the city?" I asked, pulling off my gloves and reaching for a pen.

"Yes." Clearly he knew what was coming next. Much to my surprise, he gave me the address when I asked for it.

"Planning on crashing the party, Ms. Sloane?"

"Only to see you, Lyle." If he had been there I might have batted my eyelashes in self-mockery, but instead I wondered aloud, "You'd think Bartholomew would be able to get that backing without Long's actual presence, wouldn't you? Doesn't he have that kind of sway over his friends and fans? I mean, if Long was my friend, I'd want them to get home and deal with their pain instead of having to put on a happy face.'' Having lost both of my parents, I couldn't see how anyone could rise above their pain and be social within days of their child's death.

Lyle sighed and said, ''I don't know, and I don't care. As far as I'm concerned the only good thing about New York was you.'' Now it was *his* turn to bat his eyelashes. Oh, ain't flirtation fun?

''Do I detect an unhappy camper among the ranks?''

Lyle's laughter suited him—it was a low rumbling sound that seemed to come from deep within. He promised to keep in touch (I didn't), and we ended the call with enough time for me to get to my six o'clock meeting with Vanessa.

I was looking forward to this meeting. I wanted to see again the woman who had hired me three days earlier, a woman who apparently had a lot more to hide than just her real name. No more phones, just one-on-one with a simple thing called the truth.

Twenty-one

Except for the restaurant workers and three men at the bar, Claire's was virtually empty when I arrived. I was given a table by the window, where I spent the next fifteen minutes watching the bundled masses hurry up and down Seventh Avenue.

I should have ordered a piña colada, given that the restaurant has the look and feel of Key West, but I opted for a pot of Mandarin Orange tea instead.

When Vanessa finally arrived, she offered apologies and ordered a Manhattan up with a twist. She carried with her a purse and a heavy, bulging, briefcase.

"What a day. I'm trying to work out the final arrangements for this big commercial space on Madison Avenue—six thousand square feet of prime rental—but everyone wants to nitpick the deal to death. You'd think with that kind of money, these people wouldn't try to Jew you down, but they do. Christ, it's infuriating."

"Jew you down?" I asked.

"Yeah. It means—"

"I know what it means, Vanessa. I find it offensive."

"You're not . . . you're not Jewish, are you?" I watched as her eyes grew large, realizing her faux pas.

"That's not the point."

"Well, I'm sorry if I offended you." She blinked a smile at the waiter, as he placed the drink in front of her. "It's been a difficult day, that's all I'm saying."

I sipped my tea as she shrugged off her coat, draped it over the back of her chair, leaned her briefcase against her chair, and put her purse on the table beside her. I was curious to see where Vanessa would take the conversation, left to her own devices, so I kept my mouth shut and waited.

"So." She let her shoulders drop after a long sip of the Manhattan. "We should talk."

"Yes. We should." I leaned back and crossed my legs. I wanted to be comfortable for this.

"What have you learned so far?" She propped her elbows up on the table and leaned forward. This was a different Vanessa Stephens than the one who had hired me, or so I thought, and I wondered was it me or her? Had the information I'd learned about her changed her in my eyes or had this nervous, controlling woman actually been the one I'd met three days ago? The one who had hired me to look into her brother's death.

"I met Brendan Mayer yesterday."

"You did? Good. Was he able to help with Pete?"

"He might have. But he's dead."

This bit of information took her completely by surprise. "Dead?" she said softly. The color washed from her face, but she didn't move a muscle.

"That's right."

"But how? Why?" She slowly drew herself back into her chair and reached for her drink.

"I thought you might be able to help me figure that out."

"Me? I barely even knew him. I mean, of course I knew all *about* him from Pete, but he and I never had contact with one another."

"I think, Vanessa, that it's time you were honest with me."

"I *am* being honest," she said, plaintively at first, and then added, defensively, "What's that supposed to mean?"

"It means that the more I look into this mess, the more I learn about *you*. The more I learn about you, the less I find I can trust you. Now, you can either come clean with me, or I can keep on digging and digging until I piece this whole thing together all by myself—''

''Need I remind you, Ms. Sloane, that I am your client?''

''No.''

''Then why is it you obviously feel compelled to investigate me, rather than my brother's death?''

''Well, Vanessa, it's like this''—I uncrossed my legs and poured a fresh cup of tea—''I do believe the two are connected.''

Her mouth twitched, but she said nothing. Her eyes scanned my face, then shifted toward the street, where a bag man had stopped to relieve himself at the curb. She closed her eyes and shook her head.

''How did you know it was your brother in the paper?'' I asked, while her eyes were still shut.

She opened her eyes and looked warily at me. ''What are you talking about?''

''The *Times* never listed a name. Your brother was written up as a John Doe, and yet you knew it was Peter. How did you know that?''

She looked uneasy and said nothing.

''Who told you, Vanessa? Was it Bartholomew?''

She said nothing, her face remained impassive.

''Did Clifford Bartholomew tell you that Peter had been found at the pier?''

''No,'' she mumbled. ''I don't know Clifford Bartholomew.'' She seemed to get smaller as she sat there. It was as if she was fading before my very eyes.

''Is that so?'' I asked with only the slightest hint of sarcasm. ''Okay, then if you won't tell me how you knew it was Peter, perhaps you'll answer this. Why was it you thought Peter had been murdered?''

''I told you. He wasn't the kind of person who would kill himself.''

''Accidents happen.'' I countered.

''He never touched drugs. Look, why are you questioning me on this?'' She clenched her jaw and balled her hands into two delicate little fists.

''I've already told you, but let me make it clearer.

You know a lot more than you've told me and by withholding vital information, it only makes you look bad, real bad."

"Information." She spit out the word. "What kind of information? I have been absolutely forthright with you."

"Is that so? Well then, shall we start with the blueprints?" I watched her carefully.

"I already told you on the phone earlier, I don't know anything about blueprints." She bit her lower lip and reached for the nearly empty Manhattan glass.

I took a deep breath and shook my head. "No, of course not. I forgot, you don't know anything. Ms. Stephens, I promise you I *will* find out what happened to Peter. And when I do I'll share everything I have with the police, who can then look into your role in this whole thing. And I hope, with everything inside me, that when the truth does surface, you'll get exactly what's coming to you." I pushed the teacup away from me and went to move my chair back.

"No, wait." She thrust out her hand as if to stop me. "Please, wait." She looked sheepishly around the restaurant and motioned to the waiter for another drink. "You're right. Maybe I do know a little more than I told you, but it's not because I've done anything wrong. I just didn't think it was necessary."

I gave her a look of disbelief and continued reaching for my jacket.

"I had nothing to do with Pete's death, I swear. I loved my brother. He was my best friend."

"That may be, but you knew Peter was murdered not because he would never kill himself, but because of something else. What was it, Vanessa? Was it the blueprints you had him steal from your father?"

"I don't know what you're talking about."

"Bullshit." I pulled my jacket off the back of my chair and leaned into the table. "You know, Vanessa, when you first came to my office I wasn't going to take your case, but Leslie recommended you, and you seemed to be sincere. I believed you really wanted to know what happened to your brother, and I respected that.

"I don't know what your game is, but during the last few days I've discovered I don't have time for liars and cowards. Life's too short to waste on people who are afraid to stand up for what they believe in, and, lady, that seems to sum you up." I stood up, and, as I pulled on my warm leather jacket, I said, "I don't know what you're hiding, but believe me, I'm going to find out what it is." With that I jammed my fists into my pockets and started toward the door.

Vanessa called out my name, but I ignored her. I could feel the anger and frustration that had been building up inside me bubbling just below the surface, and I wasn't about to make a public display of my rage.

I was three tables away from her when I felt my head being yanked back. Vanessa had grabbed a fistful of my hair and was yelling, "You can't leave!" I saw the three men at the bar turn, slack-jawed, as I was pulled back. It was so unexpected that I lost my footing and fell back, my knees buckling under me. In the split second that it took for me to hit the ground I had recovered enough to free my hands from my pockets and I squeezed Vanessa's wrist between my hands, pulling her down with me. Unfortunately, she fell forward, landing on top of me like a ton of bricks. My head was smooshed under her stomach, and I could hear her muffled cry, "You . . . can't . . . go!"

Of course I couldn't go. I was trapped under her like a cub beneath a walrus. I pushed her hard and she finally rolled off to the side, her skirt hiked up to her *pupick*, as Tina would say. I struggled to get to my knees and saw the waiter rushing to us from across the room, his face reflecting amusement more than concern. I could just hear him telling the boys about the catfight that started his evening.

Vanessa flailed at me, trying to grab my jacket again, but this time I was ready and slapped her across the face. It didn't stop her, though. She caught the front of my hair as I pulled away and again she pulled me down. She was fighting like she was on PCP or

CRACK, with superhuman strength, legs kicking, arms grabbing, all the while crying.

I had thought when I had my hair cut for my thirty-ninth birthday that I would be rid of people yanking at it, but I was wrong. Vanessa tangled her fingers in my hair and hung on for dear life, tugging my head to the right, then to the left, and back again. I was able to get onto my knees, but she kept pulling my head, forcing me down to her. Chairs had fallen around us, place settings went flying as she kicked out, hitting table bases with her feet, and my scalp was beginning to feel raw. I drew back my arm and caught her with a solid right, once in the abdomen. It was all I needed to free myself from her hold. I saw threads of my hair interlaced in her fingers as she went to hold her stomach.

So much for public displays of rage.

I was breathing hard, and she was crying, still muttering over and over, "Don't go. You can't leave me alone."

I got my bearings and saw the waiter's shoes behind Vanessa's head. When I looked up he had his hands on his hips, and said, "Really tacky, girls." He shook his head. "This is a restaurant, not a mud hole." The trio at the bar seemed to think that was amusing and applauded the referee.

I struggled to get to my feet.

"Sister, she's got it baaaad for you." The voice came from the bar behind me, and the accompanying chuckles were like little pinpricks in my back. I grabbed my bag from under a table where it had fallen and looked down at Vanessa, whose tear-stained face was pleading up at me.

"Please. I need help. I'm scared," she whimpered.

"I'm afraid you'll have to leave." A prissy voice crackled in my ear. I turned and saw the host who had led me to the table when I'd first arrived. "Both of you." He looked from me to the door and twitched his chin twice, as if to say "Go, go."

I hiked my bag onto my shoulder and sighed. Vanessa pulled her skirt down and let the waiter help her up. Her nylons were torn, under her eyes her black mascara was streaked like raindrops on a window, and her right cheek, where I had slapped her, was sporting a faint red welt. She was a mess, and I wondered if I looked quite as pretty for my date with Leslie.

"I can't help you," I said firmly.

"Please. I swear I'll tell you anything you want to know." She pushed back her own tangled mess of hair and was able, at that moment, to look proud and confident. It was amazing. "You're the only one who can help me. Please. I don't want to be next."

"As long as you lie to me, I can't help you."

"I'll tell you anything you want to know, I promise."

"Everything," I said.

She nodded. "Everything."

"Okay, girls, kiss and make up, I've got a business to run." The host with the Marilyn Monroe voice fluttered his hands in the direction of the exit.

The waiter had gathered Vanessa's briefcase, bag, and coat from the table and stood holding them out to her. The bartender handed the host our check, and I told Vanessa I'd wait for her outside.

The air was crisp as I stepped out onto the street. The back of my head still felt as if it was being pulled, my knee stung from hitting the ground, and my shoulder still ached slightly from my run-in the night before with Cullerson. I had a feeling this was how roller-derby skaters felt at the end of a race.

Vanessa was just paces behind me. "I'm sorry," she murmured as she ran a palm under her eyes in a futile attempt to clean herself up.

"You should be." I nodded uptown. "I suggest we finish this conversation at your apartment."

She hesitated, but only for an instant. We walked the next few blocks in silence.

The apartment building was an old prewar structure with a doorman who was probably on duty when the place was erected. Neither Vanessa nor I spoke until we were in her apartment with the door closed behind us.

As soon as I stepped into the place it was clear that

Vanessa Stephens had lied yet again. Big surprise. The apartment she had said wasn't fit for company was gorgeous. It looked like a page out of *House Beautiful*. What struck me most was the artwork. Original paintings by luminaries such as Haring, Warhol, and even a charcoal on paper by de Kooning were scattered casually throughout the apartment like pearls washed up in the tide, left half-buried in the sand. I studied the paintings while Vanessa excused herself and went to wash her face. A small fortune covered this woman's walls, and I understood better the Wizard's three-year financial update on Vanessa.

What the Wizard had discovered was that until a year and a half ago, Vanessa had been living like most happy Americans, beyond her means but not prohibitively so. However, a year and a half ago, Vanessa started spending money, real money. And apparently for close to a year she had the wherewithal to finance the hefty spending. But just as suddenly as it had started, it stopped. She had now, across the board, way overextended herself financially. There wasn't an area of her life where she wasn't in debt, including being five months behind with the rent.

"Would you like a drink?" Vanessa asked when she returned, scrubbed and changed into jeans and a sweater.

"No. Thank you."

She went to a cabinet under the windows that faced another building and pulled out a bottle of bourbon and a bottle of vermouth.

"Quite a collection you have here," I said, as she fixed herself a drink. I was standing in front of a dark, but inviting painting of a lone house on a hill.

"That's by a new artist, Janice Libby. Haunting, isn't it?"

"Yes. And yet beautiful. You know, if you sold even one of these paintings, you could pay off your debts."

She stopped mixing her Manhattan but never turned around.

"Just how much do you know?" she asked, keeping her back to me.

"Let's assume I know nothing. Why don't you just tell me everything."

Twenty-two

"I don't know where to start." Vanessa sank down cross-legged into a plush armchair and balanced her drink on her knee.

"Who told you Peter was dead?" I was sitting across the coffee table from her in an identical chair feeling a little like Lily Tomlin's character Edith Ann.

"I don't know," she said softly before taking a sip from her drink. I wondered if the adage, like mother like daughter would hold true for Vanessa, and she would wade through the rest of her life with a bottle in one hand and a glass in the other.

"Vanessa, I don't have time to coax things out of you. Now, who told you?"

"That's just it, I have no idea. I got a call early Sunday morning. I was sleeping, and there was a man on the other end of the line. I was in a fog, so I didn't understand him at first."

"What did he say?" I asked, peering at her over my kneecaps.

"He said, 'Your brother died last night at the pier. You could be next.' " She rubbed the palm of her left hand along the arm of the chair. "It wasn't until I read the article in the paper that I knew it was true." She glanced up at me and confessed, "All right, I guess I knew it was true from the moment I got the call."

"Who was it?"

She shrugged.

"Who *could* it have been?"

She took a deep breath before answering. "I got involved in . . . something a while ago." She cleared her throat and stared into her drink. "I guess I thought it was him."

"Go on," I said, when she withdrew into silence.

"I met a man a while ago and we . . ." She exhaled as if the recollection itself was burdensome. "We got together. I met him through some real estate people I know who knew him through a deal that fell through. His name is Nicholas Bernstein, but he goes by Nicky Beena," she explained. Why a grown man would choose to call himself Nicky Beena was beyond me. I nodded for her to continue. "Anyway, Nicky and I hit it off right away. Or rather—if I'm being completely honest—I went after Nicky because he had money. I was tired of struggling to make ends meet, and Nicky had money to burn. He wasn't bad-looking, I mean he took very good care of himself, and he knew how to dress. All in all, I reasoned that I could have done a lot worse. For a while it was great. He would take me to the best restaurants, fly us to Las Vegas for a weekend of gambling and shows, a trip to France, jewelry, everything. I wasn't in love with him—I could have never been in love with him, he was boorish and cruel—but I was willing to put up with that for the *things* I got in return." She paused and took a long drink from her Manhattan.

"As you can see, I like nice things." She glanced around the room affectionately, taking in all the accoutrements that seemed to define Vanessa Stephens. "Nicky gave me that." She pointed to the de Kooning. "It was the first extravagant present he gave me. He got it at an auction." Her eyes barely grazed the squiggly-lined nude. "I may be a little like my mother in the fact that I have quite an addictive nature. Not to booze or drugs, but money and things. I had no idea—until I met Nicky—that I was like that. It's funny, isn't it, the way we learn about ourselves? Anyway, I learned a lot with Nicky. He may have been a barbarian in some ways, but he was one hell of a teacher, and he knew the real thing, whether it was art or jewelry, music, cognac, whatever.

"He was the one who convinced me to move here. He hated coming to my old apartment. He told me the only way to grow was to stretch yourself, which always made me want to laugh, but the concept was good—to push yourself to the limit."

"Can you tell me anything about him? Age? Address? Line of work?"

Vanessa paused and gave this some thought before she shook her head and sighed. "Amazing, isn't it? He wouldn't tell me his age, though from the shape he was in, I'd have to guess around fifty. He lived somewhere in Queens, or so he said, but I never went there, so I don't know if it's true. As far as what he did for a living." She shrugged. "He never told me. Every time I asked, he said, 'Baby, even I don't know what I do.' And then he'd laugh like it was the funniest joke he ever heard. Frightening, isn't it? That I would sleep with a man and know absolutely nothing about him?"

I made a noncommittal noise and suggested she continue. Having just spent the night with a man I knew nothing about—other than what he told me—I was in no position to pass judgment.

"Well, he loved auctions. Any kind. Art. Antiques. Estates were his favorite because they had everything. And of course, being with him I started to learn more and more about art and to cultivate my own tastes. I also know a good deal when I see one, and I hate to pass up a bargain. I remember the first time I got so carried away at an auction that *I* started bidding. Before I knew it, I was the proud owner of that." She glanced up at the Keith Haring on the wall over the sofa. "I could barely sit in my chair I was so excited. It was exhilarating. My heart was beating, my palms were sweating, my skin was like pins and needles. It was great."

Personally I thought it sounded like flu symptoms, but I kept my observation to myself.

"Then it hit me. I didn't have the money to pay for it anymore than I could fly to the moon. Which, of course, placed me in an awkward situation. Nicky was well-known there, and the last thing I wanted was to make him look like a fool. He would have killed me.''

I glanced at my watch, willing her to hurry. At the rate she was telling this story I was lucky if I'd see Leslie by next week.

''To make a long story short, Nicky loaned me the money.''

Wow, maybe I had inherited Minnie's psychic abilities. I willed her to accelerate to the night Peter was killed.

''When we got home and I put it up, it was a rush like I'd never known before. I can't really explain it.''

''Don't try,'' I said as gently as I could. *Let's go, let's go, let's go.*

''The next auction—''

''Vanessa, could you please get to the point? We're talking about Peter.''

''I am. You want to know who told me, and I'm trying to tell you.''

''Unfortunately, I have a time crunch here and I need answers before next Thursday. Are you trying to tell me that you think Nicky Beena killed Peter?''

''He might have.'' She plucked an invisible hair off her sweater.

''Let me see if I can quickly sum up where you were headed. The longer you were involved with Nicky, the more money you spent. You maxed out on your credit cards and you borrowed more and more from Mr. Beena. Is that about right?''

''Basically, yes.'' She looked overwhelmed as she lifted her glass to her lips and drained the drink.

''And then your relationship—for whatever reason—ended. That was what, about five or six months ago?''

''Six. How did you know?''

''That's when you stopped paying your rent.''

Her jaw dropped. ''How did you know that?''

I ignored her question and kept the ball rolling. ''Did Nicky threaten you?''

She lowered her eyes and nodded.

''How much do you owe him?''

She rested her empty glass on the arm of the chair

and ran her fingers through her hair. "Close to a hundred thousand dollars."

"And I take it that's what brings us to Peter stealing your father's blueprints."

"Yes." Her voice was barely audible.

"Let's start there," I suggested, looking casually around the apartment for a telephone. The Lone Dove restaurant was only a quick ride away, but at seven-fifteen it didn't look as if I'd be on time for my date and whatever with Leslie.

"When we broke up in July, Nicky said he was going to give me a Christmas present: I had until the twenty-fifth of December to pay him back without interest. After that, he said, he'd have to teach me a lesson." She exhaled a bilious laugh. "I'm a bright woman, but I believed all along he was going to ask me to marry him. I never would have gotten so in debt to him if I thought I had to pay him back. I did find out—after the fact—that I wasn't the first woman Nicky screwed over. Apparently this is his history with women."

"Peter," I reminded her.

"I was scared. I told Pete right away about the trouble I'd gotten myself in—"

"You told him or wrote to him?" I asked, wanting absolute clarity.

"Told him. Despite Wallace's insistence that Pete live at home during college—because it was in the same town and Father's too controlling to bear the thought of his son being out of his sight—our mother intervened and last year Pete was allowed to move into his own place. Obviously that gave us a lot more freedom to have contact with one another. When I called Pete, he told me it was too bad we couldn't hit up the old man because he has a chip that's going to blow the market away."

"A computer chip."

"That's right."

"Like a Pentium?" I asked.

She made a vague gesture. "This chip is going to make Pentium obsolete. It's worth a fortune. Do you know anything about the computer industry?"

Now it was my turn to act vague. I nodded slightly. The fact is I'm still trying to figure out how radios work, so computers are totally beyond my grasp. Over dinner once, the Wizard tried to explain how computers work with regard to the binary system, which was enough to have my eyes rolling around in their sockets by the end of the evening. On, off. Yes, no. One, zero. Who cares?

"Let's just put it this way; if you can get your hands on a bundle of chips, you can make a bundle in return. Most chips don't have serial numbers, so you can't even trace them. They're small, which makes them easy to carry around, and they're legal to own. On top of that, the demand for them just keeps growing and growing.

"Obviously I wasn't about to ask the Longs for a loan, but I needed money, and I needed it fast. Believe me, the artwork here wouldn't come near satisfying what I owe Nicky, and besides, I've become attached to them all.

"So, after I talked to Pete, I started thinking. If I could make the right contacts, and Pete could get his hands on the chip design without Wallace knowing, we stood to make millions of dollars. I mean *millions*."

"So you figured, the hell with stealing, let's say a box of chips, which someone might have noticed was missing. You decided instead to go right to the source."

"That's right. We could copy the blueprints, find the highest bidder, deliver the goods and walk away with a briefcase or a Swiss account filled with enough security for the two of us. If things had gone as planned, no one would have been the wiser. I know what you're thinking, but I was doing it as much to free Pete from Wallace as I was to pay back Nicky."

"So why do you think Nicky killed Peter?" I was confused. "Nicky said you had until Christmas. Why would he kill Peter two weeks before then? For that matter, why kill Peter at all—especially if he was your direct line to paying Nicky back? Besides, did he even know about Peter?"

"He knew about Peter." She climbed out of her chair and returned to the bar for a fresh drink. "Nicky called me at Thanksgiving and asked if I had the money yet. I told him I'd have it. But he has contacts like you wouldn't believe. He knew I had about eight cents in my account and that business was dead for me. He told me—'' She stopped as she poured Old Grand-Dad into her glass.

''What?'' I asked.

''He told me there would be no extensions, and it would be a shame to rearrange such a pretty face.''

''Which only substantiates that Nicky has it in for *you*, not your brother.'' I rubbed the furrow that was deepening between my eyebrows. ''So now we're back to who killed your brother and who called you Sunday morning with the news. Did anyone know what you and Peter were up to?''

She shook her head decisively. ''No. No one.''

''Not even Nancy Albus?'' I asked with incredulity. Nancy was, after all, the woman who had actually been by Peter's side when he lifted the blueprints from his father's safe. Not knowing what actual document he was looking for, Peter had needed Nancy's help. After a date where they had been drinking rather heavily, Peter asked Nancy to show him her office. As they both had security clearance, getting into the factory late at night hadn't been a problem. She showed him her office, and while they were there, Peter wanted to make love. ''We were drunk and silly that night. Of course I'd make love with him in my office, even though it was dangerous, I mean a security guard could have come by at any minute. But you know how it is, that just made it more of a turn-on.'' She had cried on the phone to me earlier.

Naturally, Nancy went along with it. But the hotter it got, the more Peter wanted to make love in his father's office. It terrified Nancy, but she wanted to please Peter, so she followed him into her employer's office. There Peter drew out the seduction. He took a bottle of wine from his father's private collection, and they quietly continued to drink and make love. They kept the lights off, but there was enough illumination from the parking-lot lamps that they could see everything they needed. ''By this point we were both bombed, and the next thing I know, Petie's got his father's safe opened and he's pulling out stuff and asking me, 'What's this? What's that?' By now I'm in a panic, and I don't care about making love. I made him shut the damned thing.'' Which he did, but evidently not before getting what he had come for. He then made love to her, right there, on the carpet, in his father's office.

''Nancy Albus didn't know anything,'' Vanessa insisted.

''Nancy Albus knows that Peter took the blueprints from your father's safe.''

''She does not!'' Vanessa sloshed the Manhattan on her hand when she turned to face me.

''And how do you know that?'' I asked calmly.

''Pete told me. She was drunk. She didn't see him take anything.''

''The woman was in love, not stupid. She knew what your brother was up to.''

''Did she tell you that he stole them?'' Vanessa stood behind the big armchair and looked like a schoolteacher demanding to know who hit her in the head with a spitball.

''No. Of course she didn't, she was trying to protect him.'' From my call with Nancy, it was, in fact, clear, that she was clueless to the actual theft. I moved on. ''Could your father have known about the theft?''

''Pete didn't *steal* the blueprints.'' She sighed as she slid back into her chair.

''Don't waste my time.''

''He *borrowed* them.''

''Oh, right, he borrowed them. Well then, could Wallace have known the blueprints had been borrowed?''

''I don't think so. No. Pete was extremely careful. He copied the blueprints before leaving the company that night and put them back where he found them before they left.''

''And he didn't think Nancy *knew* this?''

''Pete said she had gotten sick and had to go to the ladies' room. Apparently Wallace's secretary has a copy machine right in his outer office. He copied them while she was in the bathroom. By the time she came out, Pete was finished and waiting for her.''

"You would think for a million-dollar heist, you and Peter would have been a bit more cautious."

"He did just fine," Vanessa said defensively.

"Not fine enough," I said evenly. "Did he tell you if they encountered security while they were there?"

"Sure they did. First when they got there, then again when Pete was waiting for Nancy while she was in the bathroom."

"How many guards do they have there at night?"

"Two or three." She shrugged. "I'm not there. Pete took care of all that. Look, he felt confident that no one knew what had happened that night."

"And what was your role?" I asked.

She wet her lips and took a deep breath. "Let's just put it this way—there are several Korean businessmen who know that to make a fortune, you have to spend a fortune."

"Is that so? And when are you supposed to trade goodies?"

She scratched her forehead. "Next week," she mumbled. "But I suppose by next week I'll either be dead or wish I was."

"Where are the blueprints now?" I asked.

Vanessa looked stunned. "I thought you had them."

"No."

"Oh God. I was counting on you to have them."

"No."

"That means they're still out there." She seemed to go through a series of internal readjustments before she finally asked, "Do you at least know where they are?"

"I know where one set is."

"*One* set? I don't understand." She squeezed her glass until I thought it might crack.

"Your brother gave a copy of the blueprints to Brendan and told him if he died, that was why." I let the words fall between us with a thud. "I can only imagine that the set of blueprints Peter planned to give you are somewhere he thought to be safe. I don't yet know where that is."

I didn't stay much longer. I was already late for Leslie

and knew that I had gotten from Vanessa all that she had to give.

"So, Sydney, am I still your client?" she asked as she walked me to the door.

"I have no intention of finding those blueprints just so you can steal from your father," I guaranteed her.

"No. I still want you to find out who killed Pete."

"We don't usually work pro bono," I said as I wrapped my scarf around my neck. I knew the retainer check that Max had deposited earlier in the week would be bouncing back any day now.

"I'm good for it," she said as she hung on to the opened door.

"Right." I stepped past her into the hallway. "And I can swallow fire." At the elevator I looked back at Vanessa, who was still hanging on to the door. "Don't worry, Vanessa, we'll find out who killed Peter and Brendan. I think you have other things to worry about." The elevator door opened, and I stepped in, without waiting to hear her mumbled response.

Twenty-three

By the time I arrived, the Lone Dove was crowded, and Leslie was into her second glass of red wine. Maurice, the owner of the restaurant—whose girth is matched only by the size of his heart—dwarfed the stool he was sitting on beside her. He was facing the entrance, and from the look on his face when he saw me, I knew that I was in a peck of trouble.

"Hi there." I said, fabricating cheer. If I had my way, I would have forfeited the intimate dinner with Leslie and paid a visit to Mr. and Mrs. Long. As it was, I was itching to get to a phone to call Max and find out what—if anything—he knew about Nicky Beena. Instincts told me that Nicky Beena didn't have beans to do with Peter Long's death, but it's always nice to have an updated scorecard on all the players.

"You're late," Leslie said, without turning to greet me.

"I apologize. But this is New York City; fifteen minutes is only to be expected. Hey, Maurice, how are you?" I embraced the big bear as he slid off the stool and offered me his seat.

"It's Christmas, Sydney. I hate Christmas."

"Well, you could have fooled me. The place looks great." Fresh pine garland threaded with white lights was strung along the brick wall and white branches were hanging from fishing line above the bar, also laced with white lights and velvet tartan bows. Huge poinsettias lined the windowsills. ''Really, Maurice, it's beautiful.''

''I can *dreckorate* for any occasion. It doesn't mean I like it.'' He stood between Leslie and me like St. Nick and motioned for the bartender. ''Sydney would like?''

''A glass of red wine, please.''

The bartender took a glass from under the counter, flipped it in the air, and caught on the descent, the stem between his index and middle fingers. ''Voilà.'' He said with a Midwestern accent.

''Don't do that, Scott.'' Maurice sighed. ''Do you have any idea how many glasses and tons of ice I've lost with his stupid antics?'' he asked us.

Scott winked at me. ''Not a one yet, boss, but I'm working on it.'' He placed the glass on a cocktail napkin in front of me and smiled. ''Merry Christmas,'' he practically sang.

''Remind me to fire him,'' Maurice mumbled as he left us to greet newcomers at the door.

''So.'' I studied Leslie, who had still not looked me once in the eyes. ''I'm sorry I'm late. It couldn't be avoided.''

She waved her hand lethargically, as if shooing away a gnat or a fly.

''I don't know what that means,'' I said, capping my own irritation.

''It means I should expect that from you by now. It means it's okay. I'm still here, aren't I?''

''Well you're still *sitting* here, but I don't know how present you are.''

''Look, I don't want to fight,'' she said, but it seemed crystal clear to me that that was precisely what she had in mind.

''Neither do I.'' I locked my jaw and took a sip of wine through clenched teeth. After four more sips I was ready to break the silence that was just about to consume us whole. ''Okay, may I make a suggestion?'' I turned to face her and rested my elbow on the bar. I waited for an acknowledgment of some sort. When she finally took a deep breath, exhaled, and nodded once, I continued. ''You're mad at me for any number of reasons and I'm just as mad at you. Now we can leave here and go fight someplace in private, we can leave here and go in separate directions, or we can take a deep breath, have a great dinner, and hope that by dessert we'll be mellow enough to talk openly and honestly in private when we leave here."

"So you're saying we can't talk about it over dinner?" It was a challenge, not a question.

"We can try. It's just that things seem to be so volatile between us lately."

We watched one another carefully, and I was entranced by the transformation she went through without uttering a single word. I could almost see the conversation going on inside her head, but she sat there staring at me, holding on to her glass of wine. Finally she said, "You're right. It has been volatile."

Just then Maurice joined us and said, "Ladies, I have a table by the fireplace just for you and a bottle of Perrier Jouet—on the house—which is chilled to perfection. If you'll just follow me." He lifted our wineglasses off the bar and gracefully disappeared into the second room of the restaurant.

I stopped Leslie with a gentle touch on her shoulder. "You know, just because the honeymoon's over, doesn't mean we have to make ourselves miserable. I love and I like you, and if we're not going to be lovers anymore, I'd still want to be friends."

"Do you want to be lovers?" Her black hair was pulled back into a loose ponytail, and her blue eyes shone with uncertainty.

Two weeks earlier the answer would have been a resounding YES, but as I stood there, staring into her magnificent, huge eyes, I paused. "Let's have dinner," I said softly, and kissed her forehead. She reached out, grazed my hand with hers, and followed me into the other room, where Maurice was patiently holding out a chair at a table for three in front of the fireplace.

There are times in our lives when work supersedes our everyday routines and relationships. By the time we were finished with dinner—Leslie had scallops with glazed garlic and champagne sauce, and I had roasted loin of pork with a prune-and-apricot compote—it dawned on me that I had lost myself in work recently, and only I could change the tide. It was easier to hate myself for having fudged the investigation with Debi Cullerson than to take responsibility for what was happening in my own life with Leslie. She was concerned about me and my knee-jerk response was to push her away. By the time the waitress cleared our dessert plate, which we had scraped clean of chocolate bread pudding we had shared, both of us were feeling more relaxed.

We left Maurice scolding the bartender, Scott, who had just broken a glass in the icemaker. Our taxi driver got on the Westside Highway and made it uptown in no time at all. It's a novelty to find a cab driver in New York who knows the city *and* knows how to drive. Leslie and I sat back, held hands, and let our chauffeur lead the way. I don't know when I fell asleep, but Leslie shrugged her shoulder to waken me in front of my building. I wiped the drool from the corner of my mouth and yawned.

I let her pay for the taxi and I slid over the backseat, out of the car, following her lead.

She held my hand as we crossed the street. "You went out like a light," she said, slipping her arm through mine. "All of a sudden you were snoring."

Snoring. The thought of sleep was irresistible. It had been too long since I'd actually experienced that magical, mystical dream state, and I knew there was no way I could rouse myself to meet Leslie even halfway that night—despite the three cups of coffee I had had at dinner.

I fumbled around for my apartment keys. By the time I found them, Leslie had taken hers out and was letting us into the lobby where Mrs. Jensen—one of our more colorful tenants—was protecting our building from evildoers with one of those water guns that shoots up to twelve feet away. She stood in the center of the lobby wearing her housedress, sneakers, and a cunning disguise—a pair of fake eyeglasses with nose and mustache attached. Where had she been the night before when I could have used her?

"Where do you think you're going, sister?" Mrs. Jensen asked as she squirted the front of Leslie's jacket with water.

"It's okay, she's with me, Mrs. Jensen," I called loudly so she could hear me.

"You? You used to be a good girl," she sneered at me.

"Oh I still am, Mrs. Jensen. Better than ever." I pushed the button for the elevator.

"Bullshit," Mrs. J. mumbled. "Someone took my yo-yo, and the doorman told me it was you!" She aimed her water rifle in my direction.

We have doormen from six in the morning until ten at night and I doubted that either of them would have told Mrs. Jensen that I had stolen her yo-yo.

"Nope. Wasn't me." I smiled as I opened the elevator door. "See you later, Mrs. Jensen." As I turned to get into the elevator, I was hit in the back of the head with a blast of water. This seemed to amuse Mrs. Jensen, because we could hear her cackling even after the elevator door was closed, and we were ascending.

I had recovered from my taxi nap enough to open the door to the apartment without assistance. Leslie led the way. Without pause and without stopping to turn on any lights, she moved through the space as if it were her own. She removed her clothes as she glided through the darkness, me following far enough behind to enjoy the casual way in which she disrobed. First the gloves, each of which she slid into a coat pocket. Then her coat, which slipped easily off her shoulders, onto her arm and then dragged along the floor while she unwound her scarf. The scarf was then inserted into the sleeve of her coat and the coat was finally draped on a doorknob.

Despite our rocky start, dinner had been surprisingly easy and flirtatious. Leslie had even toasted, with our first glass of champagne, "To growth and love, no matter how painful it all is."

At the bedroom door she slipped her black cowl-necked sweater over her head and tossed it on the armchair. She stood at the foot of the bed wearing only a black silk camisole, a sexy bra, a black woolen skirt with a slit down the front that clasped on the side, black leggings and lace-up boots. I leaned against the doorframe, mesmerized, still wearing my gloves, scarf, and jacket.

Leslie turned to face me, unbuttoned her skirt and let it slip to the floor. She then sat on the edge of the bed, where she took her time unlacing her boots, glancing up at me from time to time and finally freeing her feet. It was quite a show. She said nothing, and yet her eyes were speaking volumes.

I stifled a yawn and let it bounce from my chest down to my stomach.

When Leslie sat on the edge of the bed wearing nothing more concealing than a smile, she held out her arms to me. I joined her at the foot of the bed, too tired to even unzip my jacket. She took the same care and time undressing me, as she had taken with herself. I stood passively before her, caught between wanting to lose myself in sleep and wanting to find the intimacy we had recently sidestepped.

When I was as bare as she, I let her pull me on top of her. Soft. Warm. The fluidity of two bodies who know one another's rhythms so well that a single touch can cause shocks of desire to course through the body from head to toe and back up again.

This was no stranger. Not like the night before when I had found comfort with a man whose body was as foreign to me as beef tenderloin is to a Hindu. Her body was soft, curvaceous, firm, sleek, and mine. It was a body I knew well, and adored. A body I knew how to please. I straddled her, and, with my hands, my mouth, and my tongue, I made love with her until we were both spent and I fell into a blissful sleep, snuggled contentedly between her legs.

Twenty-four

The alarm clock read 6:33 when I first opened my eyes. Six and a half undisturbed hours of sleep, and I felt like a new woman. I turned on my right side and faced Leslie's back. I reached over her and drew her closer to me. She was warm and the scent of her—of her perfume and the faint trace of our lovemaking—drew me back to her like a magnet. Though half-asleep, she inched back into me and without even a second's hesitation we began the morning with a fresh start, exploring one another as if for the first time, playfully, passionately, and with total abandon.

When we awoke for the second time it was nearing nine, and though I felt the pressure of valuable time slipping away from me, I was just as equally lulled into the laziness of lingering in Leslie's arms for ten minutes more.

"So," she said, taking a deep breath. I watched her flat, smooth stomach rise and fall as she inhaled.

"So I like starting the day that way, how about you?" When I breathed in, all I could smell was Leslie. It was wonderful—comforting and exciting at the same time.

"I've missed that." She ran her hand through my hair and pressed me closer to her.

"I think we'd be fools not to try and work through the hard stuff, Lez. What we have is good—"

"But not as good as what you had with Caryn," she cut me off.

"Excuse me?" This came out of left field, and I had to look up to see if she was serious. She was. "I've never compared you and Caryn. That would be ridiculous."

"It would be impossible not to. You two were together for a long time. I'm the first serious relationship you've had since she left for Ireland. Of course you would make a comparison. I'm younger, less predictable—"

"Is this what's really been bothering you?" Though I'd never even considered it before, the idea that she was jealous of what I'd had with Caryn was like a bell ringing loud and clear.

"A little. I mean, it's true, I don't like what you do for a living because I can't protect you." She put a finger over my mouth. "Wait, just let me say what I have to say and get it off my chest."

"And such a lovely chest."

"Stop it. Now, you have no idea what it's like to be on the other side of your life. I knew when we got involved what your work entailed, or at least I thought I did, but I didn't, really. And it's true, for the most part, it's a pretty harmless job. But those times when it's not, those times when you come back to me broken and lost—like with this trip to California—I don't have any way to make you feel better."

"But that's life, Leslie. You can't be all things to me all the time, it just doesn't work that way. There are times in our lives when no one can make us feel better. It just has to come from within."

"I don't know that I agree with that. But I do know you pull farther and farther away from me—"

"Because you push harder and harder—"

"Maybe, but I can't sit back and do nothing. Because I love you. I thought, okay, I'll go out, see other people, maybe this relationship isn't all that I think it is, but I couldn't stand it. I don't want to be with anyone else, Sydney. If I've learned anything this week, it's that. I want to be with you. I want to live with you."

Live with me? She could have bowled me over with a feather after that one. It was, without a doubt, the last thing I expected to come out of her mouth. I looked at the bumps our feet made in the blankets and said nothing.

There are advantages and disadvantages to both sides of the coin. I like being alone just as much as I enjoy sharing life with a partner. I linked my fingers through Leslie's before I found my voice again.

"I don't know if I'm ready for that. Especially after these last few weeks."

"What does that mean?" she asked, pulling the sheets up over both of us.

"It means I can't jump into anything." I glanced at the clock. Already it was six minutes after nine and I was getting anxious about the Longs. I wanted to catch them both before they went out.

"After close to a year I wouldn't call it jumping," she observed.

"Okay, here's a question for you." I sat up and crossed my legs into a lotus position. "What would you say if I told you I had an essential business call to make right now?"

"What are you talking about?" She pushed her hair out of her eyes and frowned.

"I have to make an important call. If I don't make the call now, I may never reach these people, and it could make the difference between ending the case I'm working on right now or not." I glanced at the phone. My bag was by the side of the bed where I had let it fall the night before.

Leslie sighed and slumped down into the bed linens.

"See? You take it personally. If I lived alone, I wouldn't have to worry about hurting your feelings." I stretched out along the length of the king-size bed, reached for my bag, and retrieved my spiral notebook. "And I do worry about your feelings. But the fact is, when I'm on a job—especially a job like this—I don't have the time or the room in my head to worry about hurting your feelings. Not because I don't care, but because I am so focused on what I'm doing. For example, right now I'm committed to finding out what happened to this kid, so I figure, and maybe wrongly so, that our relationship—which is healthy and strong—can wait an hour or a day while I deal with his death. I don't know if that's fair to do to you. I like to think it wouldn't bother me, but honestly, I don't know how I'd respond if I was on the receiving end.'' I reached for the phone. ''I do know, however, that if I don't make this call right now, I may blame the two of us for blowing something I've worked too damned hard on to let slip away.'' I dialed the number for the Longs' hotel and gave the operator their room number. It rang fifteen times before I hung up without being reconnected to the operator. Leslie lay there the whole time, running her hand up and down the length of my leg.

''Missed them?'' she asked sympathetically.

''Yes.'' I could feel the irritability surfacing. It was ten after nine and if I missed them by ten minutes, I knew it was a lot. Damn.

''Well, you can either blame us and hate what we did this morning, or you can get up, take a shower, have some breakfast, and then get on with it.'' By the time she finished her sentence, she was at the bathroom door. ''I'm willing to share the shower with you, provided you don't hog.'' With that she disappeared into the bathroom without another word.

I shook my head as I followed the sound of the shower being turned on.

After a quick shower and an abbreviated breakfast, Leslie and I went our own directions, planning to reconnect at the end of the day. At ten-thirty, I was the last one into the office. Kerry jumped up as soon as I walked in.

''Where the hell have you been?'' She practically barked.

''Home. Why?'' I poured myself the dregs from the coffeepot and started into my office.

''I was trying to call you.''

''Well, I was there until ten minutes ago. What's up?'' I hung up my jacket, scarf, and sweater and looked sadly at the office. Sunshine was pouring into all four windows, but the damage done by Cullerson was made only more conspicuous in the bright light. I made a mental note to ask Leslie to find someone who could patch it back to new. After all, she is a decorator: if anyone could find an artist to fit the bill, surely she could.

"The police were here. They had a long talk with Max. I'm not sure, but I think they don't think Mr. Cullerson did that." She nodded to the windows. "I think you're also in trouble because of some meeting you had with Mr. Cullerson?" She looked confused, but held her notepad in her hand and kept pacing back and forth in front of my desk.

"Is Max here?" I asked.

"Yeah, but he's got Beverly Tiari in his office. That's another thing."

"What?"

"She came in while Max was talking to the police, and she went ballistic." The smile on Kerry's face was irrepressible.

"What?" I asked, knowing that she had some good scoop on Ms. Tiari.

Kerry perched on my desk, leaned closer to me, and whispered, "Beverly has a major crush on Max. That's why she hired him in the first place. She came in here crying, burst into his office while he was talking to the police, and she starts screaming, 'I can't do this anymore. My therapist says I have to tell you the truth!' And then she throws herself at him, and tells him that ever since she met him she's been head over heels in love with him."

The two of us were like schoolgirls. "Then what?" I asked, grinning like a fool.

"Then the police explained that they were conducting an investigation and asked her to leave, but she refused."

"No."

"Yes. I swear to God. She told them they'd just have to come back later because she wasn't sure what she would do to herself if she had to go through this all over again."

"And they left?"

Kerry nodded, as amazed as I was at their acquiescence.

"How long has she been in there?"

"Ten, maybe fifteen minutes."

"So what's going on?" I tiptoed to the door that separates our offices and strained to hear something, anything.

Kerry shook her head. "You can't hear a thing. I tried. I even used a glass." With that she burst into laughter.

I shook my head and went back to my desk, remembering that the Longs were leaving that day, and I had a lot of work ahead of me.

"Okay, so do you know why the police don't think it was Cullerson?"

"No."

"What else?"

"Vanessa Stephens called to make an appointment with you today."

"You didn't make one, did you?"

"Well, I didn't want to, but she said you saw her last night and agreed to get together today, so I made one for three-thirty. No good?"

"No good."

"She sounds awful."

"She should. I want you to—"

"You also got a call from a Detective Lee. Julia Lee. She said to tell you she got the mail, and you'd know what that meant."

"Excellent. Did she leave a number?"

"Yeah." She handed me a piece of paper with Detective Lee's number and the best times to reach her. "Also, Eddie Phillips called. God, is that man slime or what?"

"I've told you before, he's a very nice guy and a brilliant photographer. He just has a crush on you and no social skills, that's all."

"Barforama. Anyway, he called and told me to tell you 'No go on Wallace, but he has an interesting tidbit on his hero.' " She stopped reading his message and asked, "You know what he's talking about?"

I nodded. Eddie's hero was Clifford Bartholomew, and I was curious to know what he had. "Is he home?" I asked.

"He said if his phone rings more than twenty times, give up and call back later." She made a sour face. "Just talking to him on the phone gives me the creeps."

"He does it for effect," I reminded her again.

"Right. Special effects. Anyway, last thing. I knew you'd be bummed out about the windows, so I called and got a few names of painters who might be able to fix the walls. I've already set up three appointments for today to get estimates."

"You're fantastic."

"I know. I should get a raise."

"So should I. Listen, I want you to get anything you can on a man named Bernstein, Nicholas Bernstein. He also goes by the name Nicky Beena."

"Nicky Beena?" She smiled.

"The only thing I know is that he *may*, and that's a big question mark, have connections with the mob and he likes auctions, that's a definite. My guess is you should start with the auction houses."

"That's it?"

"Yep."

"Age? Address? Anything?"

"Nada. Maybe he's in his fifties, but that's it. I'll make a few calls, too, and see what I can come up with."

"Okay."

When I picked up the receiver to call the Longs again, Kerry went back out to her office and closed the door behind her. Again there was no answer at the hotel. Then I remembered that Minnie was taking Louise to church this morning. Playing a long shot, I called the Little Church Around the Corner, hoping Minnie had taken my advice and gone there.

A machine answered at the church giving the hours when the church was open for business. I slammed down the receiver after sitting though the five-minute message which never allowed me to connect with a real being, let alone a higher one.

As I was getting ready to return Julia Lee's call, Max came bursting into my office looking like he'd just seen a ghost. He stood in the doorway, staring at me, speechless, then crossed to the sofa where he flopped himself down lengthwise.

"Oh, oh they're—going to the chapel and they're—gonna get maaarried," I sang softly as I peered at him over the rim of my reading glasses.

"It's not funny." He covered his eyes with his arm and moaned.

"Sure it is."

"No, it isn't. It's pathetic."

"Max, women fall in love with you every day. Christ, just look at you." I followed my own advice and studied my old friend. It was true, Max is an exceptionally handsome man, and a man who generally knows how to treat people right. "Seriously, you have rugged good looks, a full head of salt-and-pepper hair, a sense of style, and you keep yourself in shape. Aside from that you're a great cook, an avid reader of women's fiction, and one of the best detectives in the business. I mean, if it wasn't for that stupid black eye and totally rad haircut, I'd even call you a hunk."

"You have no idea what I just went through. That woman practically disrobed in my office just now."

The thought of Beverly in the buff made my stomach pitch. "Well, hey, that's happened before in your office, as I recall."

"This is different. This is really sad."

"Does this mean the investigation's off?"

"Ha. Ha. Not funny. She said I led her on."

"Max, the woman was bound to turn on you. It had to happen. Just look at how paranoid she is. Christ, you've had to investigate three of her past boyfriends. She's bonkers. You can't take this so personally."

"Do you have any idea how embarrassing it was when she stormed into my office and threw herself at me in front of those officers?"

"No, but I can imagine. Speaking of which—"

"No, you can't imagine. And by the way, where the hell were you?"

"I was at home. With Leslie. What did the police have to say?"

"They said they're satisfied that Tom Cullerson couldn't have been responsible for the bombing."

"What convinced them?"

"Everything. They said that whoever did this knew what they were doing. It might have been a simple device, but it had a sophisticated timer. They had to know how to break and enter undetected, set it in just the right place so as to do the most damage but the least harm. After investigating Cullerson, they just don't think he's capable of it. Besides, he has an airtight alibi for the night before."

"I don't call two days much of an investigation. So who do they suspect?"

He shrugged. "They don't know. They were hoping we could provide some answers." He shook his head.

"Kerry said that Cullerson complained about us."

"I guess he did. We didn't get that far because Beverly came in."

"Ah-ha! Saved by the ding-a-ling."

"Yeah, I guess you could say that." Max stood up and stretched. "I feel like I've already put in a full day. Unlike my partner's, my day started at six, when I went jogging with Marcy in the park." He nodded with self-satisfaction. I didn't bother to tell him that my day had started at six as well.

"I need a rest." He stretched.

"Well, get a nap in before six and then take out the old tux because you're gonna be my date tonight."

"Is that right?"

"That's right. You and I are going to crash a party tonight. Doesn't that sound like fun?"

"Scads. Whose party?"

"Cliffy's throwing a little moneygrubbing soiree for Wallace and then it's back to Texas for the Longs. I thought we could eat a little pâté, drink a little champagne, and solve a little murder all at the same time."

"So you think, what, that Bartholomew is responsible for the kid's death?"

"I don't know. I just know he died because of these blueprints." I told Max about my wrestling match with Vanessa the night before and updated him on her story.

"I knew that check was going to bounce. I felt it from the second I touched it," he said.

"That's okay, we can make it up by padding Beverly's bill."

"Touché." He smiled for the first time since joining me that morning. "Well, at least we made enough from the Englishwoman to buy a box of paper clips. Nice woman. Too bad Carlos ruined her car."

"I don't want to hear about it." I stuck my fingers in my ears and hummed. "Oh, by the way, do you happen to know Vanessa's friend, Nicholas Bernstein or Nicky Beena?"

He scratched his chin and thought about it. "Nope. Seems like a name you'd remember, though, doesn't it?"

"Seems like a name you'd change." I fished Bartholomew's address out of my bag and wrote it down on a separate piece of paper for Max. "Here. Clifford's address. I know you'll be the belle of the ball."

Max glanced at the address. "Mm-hm, Grammercy Park, nice, very nice. And how did you get this, if I may be so bold?"

"Long's bodyguard, Lyle."

"Oh yeah, that's right, you two had dinner the other night. How was it? You get chummy with the insider?"

"He's a very nice man, actually."

"Un-huh. Did he *get* as much information from you as he gave?"

"I'd say it was a two-way street."

"Oh I hate those."

"Oh you do not. Go home and take a nap."

"I can't. I promised I'd go to the precinct and deal with Cullerson's complaint against us."

"Thank you, Maxy."

"And what do you have planned for the day?"

"Well, I thought I'd get a manicure, facial, pedicure,

you know, the works for this party tonight, and then maybe I'd buy a Norma Kamali dress that will hide my Walther. What do you think?"

"I think you're nuts." He sauntered to the door. "Anna Sui's more your style."

I let out a laugh. "You even know fashion! And you wonder why Beverly threw herself at your feet, silly man."

"What time is this party tonight?"

"Six, six-thirty."

"Shall I pick you up or meet you there?"

"Let's go together. I'll need help walking in heels in this weather."

"Okay. I'll pick you up at six. That way we can be fashionably late."

"Un-huh. Good luck with the police. Oh! If, for some reason they decide to lock you up, leave a message on my machine so I can get another date for tonight."

"Yeah, yeah, yeah." With that he went into his office, and I called Julia Lee, the detective who had Brendan's mail. She wasn't in, so I left a message. Julia had the blueprints Peter gave Brendan, which meant the copy of prints he had intended to give to Vanessa were still floating around somewhere. I knew Vanessa didn't have them, so it was safe to assume whoever killed Peter had the big prize. I took out a piece of paper and wrote up a list of possibilities, starting with the entire Long family—Papa Long figuring prominently at the top of the list—and working my way down from the sublime to the ridiculous, including Nicky Beena and the unknown Korean buyer.

By the time I was finished with the list my stomach was growling so loudly I could barely hear myself think.

"I'm getting lunch," I announced to Kerry. "You hungry?"

"I'm starving. But I'm dieting." She glanced at her watch. "No wonder I'm hungry, it's after one."

"Really?" I looked at my own watch, amazed that so much time had passed. "Well, I'm going out foraging for food. What'll it be?"

She gave this a moment's thought and said, "A turkey

and Swiss on a roll with vinaigrette, lettuce, and tomatoes, but make sure they use fresh tomatoes and not those gross rotten ones.'' We shared a glance that let her know I'd be sure and tell that to the deli guy who barely spoke English. ''Oh, and a seltzer. And an apple or something.''

''Anything else?'' I asked knowing that this was the kind of dieting that all the naturally thin women I know practice. They talk about dieting, use the Stairmaster at the gym—a torture device if ever there was one—and never have to do anything more vigorous than skipping a dessert once a month.

''Oh, what the hell? I'll take a brownie, too. I'm craving chocolate. The diet can wait a day.''

''Absolutely.''

I left with visions of a corned beef sandwich with American cheese on rye floating in my brain. Bag of chips, ginger ale, a little lettuce on the sandwich because I needed my veggies. Mmmm good.

So engrossed was I in my food fantasy that I wasn't even aware that my name was being called until I felt a hand on my shoulder. I spun around, ready to strike out, when I saw Lyle's surprised face staring back at me.

''Whoa, tiger.'' He held his hands up in surrender. ''Feeling a little skittish today?'' He smiled shyly and nodded in greeting.

''Christ, Lyle, don't you know not to scare a person like that?''

''Like what? I've been chasing after you for the last block and a half. Where are you?''

''Here, no thanks to you. You nearly scared me right out of my own body.''

''That would have been a real shame.'' He winked. *Yuck.*

I eyed him suspiciously. ''What are you doing here?'' Admittedly my ego was creeping up on me, and I feared that I had myself a new suitor in this Southern gentleman. Not a thing I fancied.

''Mr. Long sent me over to fetch you. He wants to talk to you.''

''And he couldn't call me?''

Lyle shrugged. "Hey, I'm just following orders."

"Well, I have to eat first. I'm starving."

"Me too." He broke into a bad-boy grin and draped his arm around my shoulder. "What do you say we play hooky and have a little lunch together. I just passed a nice place down the road."

"I thought you were hired to jump when Mr. Long made the suggestion."

"I was. But hell, when you weren't in your office, and you weren't at home, I just had to patiently wait for your arrival." This seemed to please him.

"Well, hang on, I have to get lunch for my secretary."

"Very egalitarian of you."

"I'm an eglatary kind of gal." I slipped out from under his arm and found myself checking the streets for Leslie sightings. The last thing I needed was to meet up with her while I was with him. Not that I had done anything to be ashamed of, but things often seem different in the daylight than at night.

I got Kerry her big-girl lunch and left Lyle waiting for me on the sidewalk while I ran upstairs to drop it off. When I walked in she was talking to a young man with shoulder-length hair and a Salvador Dalí mustache.

"Oh Sydney, this is Frank, one of the artists I was telling you about. Frank, this is Sydney: it's her office that needs the work done."

Frank lounged in the guest chair, hiding behind his Foster Grants. He repositioned himself and looked up at me over the rim of his glasses.

"Frank has a studio in SoHo, but he sometimes paints apartments to bring in extra cash, right Frank?"

I think he nodded, but it was such an abbreviated gesture, I couldn't be sure.

"And does Frank know how to speak for himself, or is he a mute?" I asked, putting her lunch sack on her desk.

"Forceful. I like that in a woman." He bobbed his head up and down, looking dumber by the moment.

I bobbed my head in Kerry's direction. "Dense. I expect that in a man."

Frank seemed to like my slur and horse-laughed his appreciation, which only endeared him to me. I couldn't help but smile back at him.

"I have an unexpected meeting with Long, so I may not be back before you leave," I told Kerry as I raced back out the door. "You canceled Vanessa, right?"

"Yes, but—"

"Gotta go. Leave any messages for me on my machine at home. Bye." With that I was out of there like a flash. It was not Lyle that I was rushing for, but lunch. Just the word made me salivate. Lunch. Lunch. Lunch.

Lyle led me to the worst restaurant on Broadway, and I led him over to Amsterdam Avenue, where a whole new crop of restaurants have braved the neighborhood to open their doors to the hungry moneyed people on the upper west side. Amsterdam was for years considered forbidden terrain, peopled by the great unwashed and illegal immigrants. Fact is, it's always been a real neighborhood avenue, where more people speak Spanish than English. Now it's joined the ranks of Columbus Avenue and become totally trendy. Go figure.

Popovers Restaurant was once a tiny hole in the wall when Amsterdam was verboten, but it's grown with the neighborhood. Stuffed teddy bears are scattered throughout the restaurant, and the ladies who lunch love to lunch amid the bears. Me, I wanted as much food as I could get as fast as possible.

Lyle looked only somewhat out of place. I asked for a table in the back of the restaurant rather than a window booth, again with Leslie in mind. *Oh ye sinners, repent!*

"What's good?" Lyle asked as he stuffed himself between the table and the booth seat.

We both ordered sandwiches and coffee and I got us a popover to tide us over before our meal arrived.

"So what does Mr. Long want?" I asked after I'd inhaled half of the popover slathered in strawberry butter and felt mildly civilized.

"I'm telling you, I don't know. I'm just the messenger boy. I was hoping we could talk about something other than Mr. Long.'' He poured milk into his coffee and stirred it too hard, causing the coffee to slosh over the side of the cup and puddle in the saucer. ''I think you make me nervous.''

''I do, do I?''

''I think so,'' he said this to his saucer as he poured the coffee back into his cup.

''Well, there's no need to be nervous. I don't bite.''

The look we shared was enough to make us both blush. I was grateful when the waitress arrived with our chicken sandwiches and pasta salad. Lyle refused to talk about Long over lunch and wanted instead to talk about me and my life. He was especially curious about Leslie, but as I had insisted the night before, talking in detail about my life with her seemed like a violation of her, so I brushed it aside. We wound up talking about our childhoods, which was okay by me. I was ready to empty my mind of the present for the present. We ended the meal with a blueberry cobbler that we shared, and finally I was ready to meet the great, omnipotent Oz once again.

Whatever Wallace Long had in his little mind, I wanted to know.

Twenty-five

When Lyle read off Clifford Bartholomew's Grammercy Park address to the cabby, I was tempted to bolt, but I didn't. More than anything, I was curious not only as to why Wallace Long suddenly wanted to meet with me after he'd been so dead set against me before, but why at Bartholomew's home and not his own hotel suite. It didn't make sense, but then, so far not much in this case had.

"So, Lyle, do you know where we're going?" I asked casually, taking in the sights as the driver took a circuitous route downtown. We had entered the park on Ninetieth Street and were headed uptown. I figured it wasn't my dime, and I could use the time to digest lunch.

"Mr. Bartholomew's house." He pointed to a gaggle of cross-country skiers making their way through the patches of snow in the park. "Amazing how you people get by here."

"Amazing." Suddenly a voice screamed loudly in my head, *DON'T TRUST THIS MAN, YOU MORON!* The calm part of me responded quietly, *Don't be ridiculous. You know this man. He's a good man. He's not a jerk. YOU'RE ONLY SAYING THAT BECAUSE YOU SLEPT WITH HIM. GOOD GOD, WHAT'S WRONG WITH YOU?* Okay, now I was giving myself a headache. "Oh shut up."

"Excuse me?" Lyle looked surprised from his side of the taxi.

"Sorry?" I asked.

"Did you say shut up?" he seemed genuinely hurt.

"No. I don't think so."

"Yeah, you did, lady. I heard you." Our driver nodded vigorously.

I glanced at the name on his license, and said, "Martin Belzerf, you should know I work for the taxi commission." I flashed my detective's license at him and put it back in my pocket. "Your name and license number have been recorded and you'll be hearing from us within the next two weeks."

"Huh?" His eyes worked between the road and the rearview mirror, trying to catch my reflection. "Wha' for?"

"Fare gouging, a meter that's been tampered with, taking advantage of a passenger by putting extra miles on the meter. Your destination's Grammercy, yet you head to Harlem. Doesn't look good for you, Mr. Belzerf. Not good at all."

It was satisfying enough to see the panic in his bloodshot eyes, but I was tickled pink when he turned off the meter and said, "Oh my God, would you look at this? I had no idea I was heading in the wrong direction. An honest mistake. Look, the rest of the fare's on me."

Lyle was mystified. I asked Belzerf to close the plastic panel that separates driver from passengers, and said to Lyle, "You have to watch out for these guys."

"I guess so." He laughed. "New York." He shook his head.

"Like that never happens in Texas." New Yorkers are always getting a bum rap.

"Wouldn't know. I've never taken a taxi in Texas. I drive everywhere I go."

"Sounds like a country and western song, 'I Never Took A Taxi in Texas but I Fell in Love with a Cabby Named Pearl.' " Despite my rising concerns about my upcoming meeting, we had a good laugh. Nerves will do that to you.

When Martin-the-taxi-gouger left us in front of Bartholomew's town house I looked toward the corner of the block for a pay phone.

"Is something wrong?" Lyle asked, touching my arm gently.

"I just remembered something I forgot to tell my partner. There's a pay phone over there: let me just make a quick call."

"Don't be silly. I'm sure Mr. Bartholomew won't mind if you use his phone. Come on." He took my hand and started toward the front stoop. "Hell, it's not like you're calling Outer Mongolia."

"Oh, I don't know, it is near Amsterdam Avenue," I mumbled, which made Lyle laugh again.

"I swear, you're the funniest woman I've ever had the honor to know."

We were halfway up the steps and I saw a lace curtain flutter from a front window. *RUN, ASSHOLE, RUN!* There was that voice again, banging away in the back of my head. *Don't be ridiculous. Neither Bartholomew nor Long would be stupid enough to do anything. Especially here.*

The door opened before we reached the last step, though there was no one in the doorway to welcome us. I looked at Lyle, who smiled reassuringly at me. Who wouldn't trust a face like his? It was warm and tender and kind.

I followed Lyle into the house. The first thing I saw in the foyer was a magnificent bouquet of roses sitting atop an antique side table. It took a little while to adjust to the lack of light, but I saw soon enough that the man who had opened the door was neither Long nor Bartholomew. It was Art, Long's trusty bodyguard and humorless sidekick.

"Hey, Art." Lyle greeted his friend.

"Lyle," Art remained poker-faced. He kept one hand in his jacket pocket and stared at me without so much as a nod in my direction. "What took you so long?" he asked with a calm I didn't trust.

"Sydney was with a client when I got there," Lyle lied easily as he locked the door behind us and looked past Art into the front room. "Where's Mr. Long?" he asked.

"He'll be here any minute now. You kept me waiting close to two hours." The accusation was left untouched. He stepped back a foot and raised an eyebrow. "Ms. Sloane, won't you have a seat?"

I stood in the archway between the foyer and the living room without budging. "I have a busy schedule, Mr.?" I still didn't know Art's last name.

"Art is good enough," he assured me.

"Well, it's not for me. Your last name, please?"

I could feel the friction between Art and me like an electrical current.

"Oh for God's sake, Art." Lyle said from the sofa he had settled onto. "His name's Arthur Grants."

"Shut up, Lyle," Art said calmly, but not before I caught his surname.

"What's with you, man?" Lyle asked, obviously surprised at his friend's behavior.

"Ms. Sloane?" Again Art motioned for me to come full into the room. This time I listened to the voice in my head and stayed put.

"Come on in, Sydney. You might as well take a load off until Mr. Long gets here," Lyle tried to coax me.

"But Mr. Long's not coming, is he, Art?" I assessed the possibility of getting out the door before Arthur Grants could stop me. I was three feet from the front door, but it had been bolted behind Lyle, and if I followed my instincts closely (that little voice I had been ignoring for the better part of the last hour), I knew Art had a gun in the hand he hid in his jacket pocket.

"Don't be silly." Lyle dismissed the idea with a laugh. "Why else would he have had me come and get you?"

"Did he?" I asked, never taking my eyes off Art. He was tall—about six-two—and lanky, but I had a hunch that under his suit what little he had was all muscle.

"Sure he did." Lyle's voice softened, as if he wasn't telling the absolute truth.

"Did he? Or did Art tell you Mr. Long wanted to see me?" In my bag was my Walther, but there was no way

I could get to it at that moment. I had to be patient and careful. Clearly the ball was in Art's court, whether as a henchman for Long or not, and I had to play by his rules for the time being.

I took Lyle's silence as an answer.

Apparently, so did Art. I watched him change tactics midstream.

"I saw you holding Ms. Sloane's hand on the steps, Lyle." He paused as if this was somehow significant. I was reminded of the boys in sixth grade who taunted Howie Golden when he kissed me at his birthday party. Kids can be so cruel. I had a feeling that Arthur Grants hadn't matured much beyond that emotionally. He was just bigger, and he had a gun. Which made him dangerous.

"Yeah? So? There's ice on the steps." Lyle sounded just as defensive as Howie when the boys had taunted him.

"So I wonder how far Miss Sloane has gone to win your trust and confidence. Or should I say confidences?" Art's jaw twitched. Was he getting nervous? And if he was, why was he?

"What's that supposed to mean?" Lyle asked with more than an edge to his voice. He was leaning forward now, but he was still sitting, which left Art in the position of power. It was like watching a little brother preparing to confront his older brother. "Oh yeah?" "Yeah." "Oh yeah?" "Yeah." "Oh yeah, well, make me."

"It means, Lyle, that a woman like Sydney has been trained to get what she wants, however she can. Isn't that right, Ms. Sloane?"

"Oh please, Art, let's not stand on formalities. You don't have to call me Ms. Sloane. You can just call me Mata Hari."

"Funny. Very funny," he said, without the hint of a smile.

"Yes, well, I'd love to stay and entertain you some more, but I have an appointment with the police commissioner and his lovely wife, June." I took a step backwards and wasn't surprised when Art pulled the gun from his pocket. It was a .45 with a silencer attachment. Big gun for a big guy.

I don't know if Lyle could see it from where he was, but the fact that he was still sitting didn't cheer me.

Art inclined his head ever so slightly and said quietly, "Perhaps you'd like to reconsider my offer. Why don't you just come in and we can have a little chat?"

"I thought it was Mr. Long who wanted to talk to me." I glanced over his shoulder and looked at Lyle.

"He's been delayed. He and Mrs. Long needed some time together. He asked me to look after this for him." I realized when he said this that Art never seemed to blink.

"Did you know about this, Lyle? Were you in on this with your pal here?" It was a calculated risk. If I could create a disturbance between the two of them, maybe I could get out of there before all hell broke loose. There was, of course, the possibility that Lyle was in on this with Art and Mr. Long and Clifford Bartholomew, in which case I was screwed.

"Look, Art," Lyle stood up slowly, "What the hell's going on here? You told me Mr. Long wanted to see Sydney."

"He did, Lyle." Art kept his back to Lyle, so I still couldn't tell if Lyle knew Art had a gun in his hand. "As I said, he's been delayed, and I was asked to take his place."

"Why didn't you say that when we got here? Why did you lie?" I asked. "And why do you need a gun to keep me here?"

"A gun?" Lyle asked, moving around the coffee table. *Some bodyguard he must be,* I thought.

Art moved his left foot back, opening himself up to both Lyle and me and told Lyle to stay where he was. "I don't want to have to hurt your friend, Lyle. But the fact is, she's been working against Mr. Long, and now it's time that came to an end. Ms. Sloane, I'll ask you this last time to join us."

I had no doubts that Art would use the gun whether he had to or not, so I held my bag closer to my side and moved past him.

From where I had been standing in the foyer I couldn't get the full impact of Clifford Bartholomew's town house, but once I was in the living room it was clear that he had paid beaucoup bucks to have the place gutted and decorated. The living room opened up to a second-floor landing, and I was amazed at how light and airy the place felt. I was also surprised at Clifford's predilection for statuary. Big, heavy pieces—basically male nudes—were scattered throughout the two-story area. I don't know what I had expected—maybe big neon beer logos flashing on the walls—but in a way, I suppose this ostentatious display of wealth was Cliffy's way of going gaudy.

"Art, what the hell's going on?" Lyle stood in the center of the room, and though he was talking to Art, he looked at me, his face awash with confusion.

"Sit down." Art ignored Lyle and pointed his gun at me. This time I complied, choosing to perch myself on the only straight-backed chair in the room, a Parsons chair painted gold with flecks of silver. "Unfortunately because you took so long getting here, I'll have to accelerate things, but I'm sure you won't mind, will you?"

I shrugged. "No. Like I said, the commissioner—"

"Shut up." He raised his voice for the first time. Touchy, touchy. Arthur was getting anxious. I glanced at my watch. It was a quarter to three and I began to understand his concern. I had a friend in the catering business once who had explained to me how they work their magic. If Clifford was throwing a bash that evening, and the guests were due at six, the caterers would have to get there at least two hours ahead of time to set things up. That only gave Art an hour to bother me, kill me, and dispose of my body. And he couldn't do it right there because the guests would be sure to see the nasty bloodstains on Clifford's designer furniture and rugs.

Lyle stood there like a big, stupid lug, his hands hanging limp at his sides. I don't know what I expected he would do, maybe knock out Art, tie him up, and call the police—that would have been nice, but he just stood there.

"I don't know what you want, Art," I said evenly. "But if you wanted to ask me a few questions, there are easier ways to win friends and influence people."

"I don't need to fuck you to get answers."

If he had slapped me in the face, I wouldn't have been as stunned. I looked at Lyle and felt betrayal turn into stone-cold hatred. Lyle looked away from me and shook his head.

"What do you want?" I asked coldly.

"You know what I want."

The fact is, I didn't have a clue as to what Art could want from me, and I told him so. Before he could shed light on it, the phone rang, having the same effect as an electric prod. Lyle and I jumped at the sound of the ringing. Art chewed his lower lip and moved carefully to the phone, which was by the front windows. He turned up the volume on the answering machine and we all waited breathlessly until the machine kicked in and we could hear the voice on the other end of the line. It was Bartholomew. "Nan? Nan, are you there? Goddammit, pick up the phone." Pause. Sigh. "Okay, I hope you get there in time for the liquor store delivery. The caterer should have enough space in the refrigerator for the food, but you should tell them to chill the wine outside in the snow in the backyard and remind them that I don't want anyone near my office, okay? Also, do you have the papers on McDonald? I can't find them anywhere. Call me." He sounded on the phone as he did in person, self-important and inflated. I didn't think, however, that he had a clue that the three stooges were sitting in his living room.

Clearly the call had an impact on Art. I wondered if Art really could be using Clifford's house without his knowledge and, if so, how could he have gotten in? And then there was the big questions mark—Was Art acting alone or in concert with Wallace and Clifford?

Art used the muzzle of the gun to part the curtains as he glanced out onto the street, no doubt watching for

Nan. You could practically see the gears working in his head.

"Art, just tell me what you want to know. I don't have anything to hide."

"Is that so?" He looked amused. "Then where are they?"

"Who?" I asked, baffled.

"Who?" He exhaled. "The blueprints, Sydney. You want to play the dumb blonde, fine by me, but I will get those blueprints by the end of our little meeting or—"

"Sydney has the blueprints?" Lyle interrupted.

"No, Sydney does not have the blueprints," I answered for myself. "You knew about them?" I asked Lyle.

"Just what *you* told me." He frowned. "What are these blueprints, anyway?" he asked the room in general.

"They're gold," Art whispered, and nodded to Lyle. "That's why Sydney kissed up to you, Lyle. She wanted to get her hands on those blueprints because she knew if she had them, she could make an easy fortune. Isn't that right, Sydney?"

Now it was Lyle's turn to look betrayed. He glared at me with the same hatred I was feeling for him. I vowed at that moment, if I lived through this, I would never flirt with a man again. They're too much damned trouble.

Art crossed over to me and pressed the gun to my temple. "We're going to have to finish this conversation elsewhere," he informed us. "Lyle, get my briefcase." He ordered his good little foot soldier. He then wrapped his enormous hand around my upper arm and yanked me up from the chair. "Come on." He was a deceptively powerful man. I let him steer me toward the back of the house, into the kitchen, a big room with sliding doors that led out to a decked backyard. At one point I struggled to see behind me, to see if Lyle was just following the orders of this mental case or if he had had an original thought and decided that a gun pointed at my head denoted trouble.

Art tapped my head with the gun and said, "Uhuhuh,'' but not before I could see, to my dismay, that Lyle was nothing more than a big old stupid lamb, following blindly behind us, his cohort's briefcase in tow.

There was an internal door next to the sliding doors that led to the basement. Art ordered me to open it.

I've never been keen on basements. They're musty, cold, dark, and usually home to a variety of bugs who know better than to venture into the actual living quarters of their hosts.

The stairs were carpeted with gray industrial stuff that resembled soft Astroturf, and bright lights flooded the staircase, which thrilled me. Art squished beside me, keeping his gun pressed to my head, as we inched our way down the stairs.

The door at the foot of the stairs opened into a basement like I'd never seen before. It was dark, but it was gorgeous. A large mahogany table with four matching chairs were the first things you saw as you entered the room. It was cool, but not cold. The wall dividing the room in half, just beyond the table, was wine, a veritable wall of wine. The walls were paneled, the floor was wall-to-wall carpeting, two big armchairs separated by a big ottoman were placed along the wall to the left, and a structure resembling a sauna sat along the opposite wall. The same care had been giving to the subground space as had been afforded the rest of the house. I felt safe that this was, indeed, a bug-free environment. I could at least rest easy about that.

Art pushed me down onto a chair and ordered Lyle to place his briefcase on the table. Which he did. My hero.

''What are you going to do?'' Lyle asked, sounding a lot calmer than the situation warranted.

''I'm going to get some answers, that's all. You know as well as I do the pain the Longs have suffered, Lyle. They're good people. Now, I want you to go upstairs, turn off the lights, shut the door to the basement, and join us back here. I promise, this won't take long, and I won't hurt your friend.''

When Lyle nodded, I said, ''You really are a scumball, Lyle.''

Without responding, he went to go about his appointed chores, leaving me alone with the affable Mr. Grants. When he was gone Art positioned himself to my right and pushed the gun against the side of my mouth. "I don't like you, but you know that, don't you?"

It would have been hard answering with a .45 in my mouth, so I said nothing.

"Now I understand you have the blueprints, and I want them back. And I want them back now."

I pulled my head slightly away from the gun and said, "Why do you think I have the blueprints?"

He laughed. Oh good, he did have a sense of humor after all. "I spoke with Brendan's roommate. He told me that a woman, a detective, came by and took Brendan's mail yesterday. That would be you."

"No, it wouldn't. It would be a detective with the Ninth Precinct."

Art pulled back his hand, and as I moved to the left to avoid his hit, he surprised me by cuffing the left side of my head. One of his fingers caught me in the eye, the nail scratching my eyeball.

"That's not the answer I wanted Ms. Sloane."

"Obviously. However, it's the truth." I touched the side of my eye to check for blood. There was none. I could hear Lyle's footsteps on the floorboards above us. "Look," I tried to reason with him, "I understand your loyalty to Mr. Long, but I don't have the blueprints. That's the truth. Detective Julia Lee at the Ninth Precinct has them. All you have to do is call and ask her, she'll tell you."

"Is that so?"

"Yes."

He moved in front of me and perched himself on the table, dangling his right leg while keeping his left foot planted firmly on the ground. "Okay, I want you to tell me everything you know. You have five minutes."

"All right." I put my bag in my lap, hoping that somehow I'd be able to get inside it and at least get my gun should he go bonkers and decide to shoot me mid-sentence.

"As you know, I was hired by Vanessa Stephens to find out who killed Peter."

"Translated to the truth means that you were hired by Paula Long to retrieve the blueprints that her weaselly little brother stole from their father."

We both turned as Lyle came back down the stairs. I was half-hoping that he would have found his courage along with the coat he had left upstairs, but I was wrong again.

"Everything secured?" Art asked.

Lyle nodded.

"Okay." He looked at me. "We're just getting a little lesson in honesty here, Lyle. Pull up a chair, this should be interesting. Ms. Sloane will answer a few questions, and I will translate it into the truth. Continue."

"Vanessa did hire me to find out who killed Peter."

"That means Mr. Long's daughter hired Sydney to get the blueprints Peter stole from his father."

I sighed.

"Oh, I am sorry, I'm distressing you, aren't I? Okay, and did you find Peter's killer?" He squinted.

"I guess so." I squinted back up at him. "You know, if you hadn't contrived this stupid kidnapping, I probably never would have figured it out," I lied.

"Kidnapping? Is that what you'd call this?" Art's spirits were improving by the second.

"I'd say so. Which, by the way, Lyle, makes you an accomplice." I tossed this over my shoulder to where I assumed he was standing.

"And who did kill Peter?" he asked almost brightly.

"You did, Art. No doubt you did it because Mr. Long asked you to, but it's all the same in the eyes of the law, isn't it?" I glanced around the room, looking for something—anything—that could help me get the hell out of here. There were no windows that I could see from where I sat. No stairs that led to the great outdoors.

"Very interesting hypothesis. Now why would I want to kill Peter?"

"Because he stole the blueprints for a new chip that

LongTec had recently designed, and he planned to sell it to the highest bidder.''

''Which, in fact means, Lyle, that Ms. Sloane here killed Peter when she found him. She realized the money she could make from the blueprints and she got greedy. She knew that if she had the plans, she could take them to the highest bidder and neither Peter nor his slut of a sister could fight her because they were all doing something very much against the law. But Peter did fight you, so you killed him and made it look like suicide. Mr. Long's last remaining progeny wouldn't have the guts or the wherewithal to get the very thing she'd hired you to find, so you'd be in the clear. Isn't that right, Ms. Sloane?''

''No.''

''I want those blueprints.''

''I told you Detective Julia Lee at the Ninth Precinct has them. Call her. She'll tell you.'' I knew Julia only had the second copy of the blueprints, but it was clear that Art believed this was the only set in existence.

''You're a liar.'' He barked at me before bringing his fist full up into my jaw. He hit me so hard I went flying to the floor, tipping the chair over with me.

''Hey!'' Lyle called out as he rushed to help me up. ''Cut it out, Art. There's no need to hurt her.''

I pulled away from Lyle's helping hand.

''Touching. Very touching.'' Art was still half-seated on the tabletop.

''There's nothing touching about it,'' Lyle spit. ''Look, if she killed Peter, we should take her to the police and be done with it.''

''Yeah, Art. Take me to the police.'' My jaw felt like it was on fire.

''Sit down,'' Art said as he reached for his briefcase with his free hand.

Lyle had righted my chair and was standing behind it with his hand on the back of it. I kicked the chair back onto the floor.

''Suit yourself.'' Art motioned for Lyle to right the chair again, which he did. ''You have an enviable imagination, haven't you?'' Art seemed impressed.

"No. I learned the truth. I'm good at what I do." I had gotten up from the floor and was standing awkwardly between Lyle and the door to freedom.

"Not good enough, I'm afraid." He snapped open the briefcase and pulled out a thick roll of duct tape. He held out the roll of adhesive to Lyle, and said, "Lyle, would you be so good as to cover Ms. Sloane's mouth. After all, it is a part of her anatomy I'm sure you're familiar with."

I could feel my face flush, not from embarrassment, but from anger. Damn Lyle. I should have known it—he was nothing but a good old boy from Texas coming back to the old corral and bragging about fictitious conquests.

I saw Lyle's hand reach past me to get the tape from Art. I couldn't believe he was actually going to do it. It was now or never. I grabbed the tape, hurled it at Art's head, and bolted for the staircase.

I made it to the third step before I felt a heavy hand grab me by the collar and pull me back. I was angry and stunned to see it was Lyle who had me and not Art.

Lyle whispered, "Don't," in my ear as he pulled me back into the basement to face Art, who was smiling. It was the same smile I'd seen on my brother's face before he'd torture worms on West End Avenue after a rainstorm. A little boy delighting in the power of causing something smaller than him pain. "They don't feel," my brother, David, used to say before squishing the worm under his thumb. "See. Didn't feel a thing."

I struggled against Lyle's hold, but it was an act of futility. He was bigger and stronger than me, plain and simple.

Art held out the tape to Lyle again.

"Art, I won't help you until you at least call the police to see if this Detective Lee really does have the blueprints."

Won't help him! What was he, totally deluded? As far as I could tell, he was helping him just fine.

Art studied Lyle, who had me in one hand and the tape in the other. Finally he nodded. "Okay, you want me to prove your girlfriend wrong. I will. What's the number?'' he asked as he moved to the phone on the table by the armchairs.

''I don't know it. You have to call information.'' I had the number in my bag, but so far he hadn't seemed interested in my purse, which meant I still had a chance of getting ahold of my Walther. As long as he had overlooked my bag so far, I wasn't about to bring attention to it.

Art got the number of the precinct, but, as luck would have it, Julia and her partner Ned Gould were out of the office.

''No. No message.'' Art dropped the receiver back into the cradle and said to Lyle, ''If we let her go now, she'll take off with the blueprints—or maybe even the money she's made from the sale of those blueprints—and we'll never see her again. I have a suggestion, Lyle.''

It was as if I wasn't even there.

''Any minute now, Mr. Bartholomew's assistant and a houseful of caterers will be here. After that, a hundred guests will arrive, along with Mr. and Mrs. Long. I suggest we make Ms. Sloane as comfortable as possible and return to her after the festivities are over. That way, you'll be relieved when Mr. Long is at the helm, and I won't have to seem the bad guy. How's that?''

Lyle thought about this, his breathing getting harder the more he thought.

''Oh goody, then you can just kill me as soon as it's over, isn't that right, Art? By then it'll be night, and no one will be around to see or hear anything. Except maybe your boss and his best friend.''

Art ignored me and cocked his head, waiting for Lyle's response.

''Okay,'' Lyle finally agreed. He took a deep breath and started to lead me back to the table and chairs.

''No,'' Art said. ''Over there.'' He motioned with his gun beyond the wine wall. ''Behind there.''

We all heard the floorboards above us creak at the same time. I let out a scream, but Lyle clasped his hand over my mouth before I could get out more than a peep.

Art was on me in a flash. He rammed the gun into my neck and promised to kill me if I so much as breathed. By the time he was done with his threat, Lyle had pulled off a four-inch piece of the tape and pressed it over my mouth. He was gentle, but it still hurt my jaw where Art had punched me before. Unsatisfied with his work, Art pushed his big hand across my mouth and pressed the tape more securely in place. Then he grabbed me by the back of my hair and shoved me past the wine. There must have been two hundred bottles of wine dividing the room, and behind it was an area of about ten feet long by fifteen feet wide. Two two-foot-round columns, probably the building supports, were about four feet from each wall. The rest of the space had been turned into a minigym, complete with rowing machine, stationary bike, free weights, and television. From the newness of the machinery and the shape of Bartholomew, I figured this setup was either a good intention or for show.

Art slammed me faceup against one of the columns and ordered Lyle to get the rope from his attaché case. He had me pinned against the support until Lyle returned.

Lyle stood there with the rope in hand, and said, "Art, don't tie her up. Look, why don't I stay down here with her until the party's over? I'll make sure she doesn't go anywhere."

Art continued pressing against me. "I wish I could, Lyle, but think about it. How could we explain your absence to the Longs? You know he likes to have the two of us on hand at these functions. No. I think tying her up is the only way to handle this. Trust me, Lyle. I've never lied to you before, have I?"

If my mouth hadn't been out of commission I would have pointed out to Lyle that if Long was aware of Art's activities, he'd okay Lyle's absence, probably even welcome it, which proved that Long didn't know and Art, in fact, had been lying to his good friend all along.

My bag was still hanging from my shoulder. I squeezed it under my arm, hoping that Art would just tie me and it up together, but of course, he didn't. He took my bag with one hand, held his gun to my head with the other, and had Lyle secure my feet and body to the post while he rifled through my bag. He pulled out the Walther and dropped the bag to the floor. "Nice, very nice." He admired my gun before he slipped it into his jacket pocket. My blood was boiling. When Lyle was about to finish tying my hands Art stopped him.

"You know, Lyle, I've changed my mind. You were right, you really should stay with Ms. Sloane." Before he even finished his sentence, Art brought the butt of his gun down on the back of Lyle's head. Just the sound of it made me flinch.

"Sorry, Lyle," he said to the motionless heap at his feet. Art then put down the gun, heaved Lyle up—a feat which impressed even me—leaned Lyle against my support beam and, with the ends of the rope around me, tied Lyle's hands with mine. "There, nice and cozy." When Art was finished, Lyle slumped back to the ground, pulling my arms as far as they would go. Not a very comfortable position. We looked like a dance team in the final hour of a 1930s marathon.

"You see, Ms. Sloane, Lyle's tragic flaw is that he's too nice a guy. You understand I couldn't leave him here with you like that. We both know he would have let you go, don't we?" He looked at Lyle and shook his head.

I wished I was as confident about that as he was.

"Well now, if you'll excuse me." Art grabbed his gun, slicked back his hair, and flattened his tie back into his jacket. "I shall return. In the meantime, have fun with your boyfriend."

I listened as he closed his briefcase and opened the basement door. He switched off the lights, which threw us into total darkness. A second later he turned the lights back on and chuckled, "Only kidding." The door was closed, and he was gone.

Well, this was a fine mess I'd gotten myself into. If I had listened to my instincts, I could have avoided this predicament. If I had followed my hunch and jumped out of the taxi, I could have lived the rest of my days with knuckles that didn't drag on the floor. But no. There I was, tied to a post with a deadweight who was stretching my arms out of their sockets. A fine mess, indeed.

A buzzer rang, and within minutes there were footsteps and voices floating from above. The caterers had arrived.

Twenty-six

By the time Lyle showed any signs of waking I had managed to peel the duct tape halfway off my mouth. Slowly and methodically I had rubbed my face against the pillar, scraping the tape against the post while I used my tongue to push my skin, and therefore the end of the tape, closer to the all but useless flat surface. I was, however, making headway.

Lyle moaned. And then his weight shifted.

"Stop it." I said, but it sounded more like "Schtpt" because each time he moved, he pulled me closer to the post—as if that was possible—and by this point my face was smooched against the column. With each and every movement he made, I hated Lyle Grubbs more and more.

He smacked his lips, as if awakening from an afternoon nap on the sofa. I furiously worked the post, trying to free myself of the gag before he came to. The possibility that I wouldn't see the end of the day was all too real, but there was one thing I was determined about; if nothing else, this son of a bitch was going to get a piece of my mind before I died.

I pressed my face firmly against the post, attaching the gooey side of the tape against the hard surface, and then I snapped my head back as far and as fast as I could.

Oh my God. To think that women actually pay people

to do this to them on a regular basis. The pain from having the hair on my upper lip removed by the roots was nothing compared to my joy when I opened my eyes and saw that nasty piece of tape dangling from the freshly painted post.

Lyle let out another groan, only this time sounding like he was actually coming to life.

"Lyle! Wake up, you asshole." I would have kicked him had my feet been free, but tied as I was, I felt like a mummy in a sarcophagus. A desperately hot mummy, at that. I was still wearing my leather jacket, and I was schvitzing.

He groaned again.

"Oof. Christ. Lyle! Lyle, I am not kidding. Wake up." I struggled to move, but with him pulling at the other end of the rope, I was stuck. By now my hands were turning numb.

"Ooooh, God." He started to touch the back of his head and soon realized that his hands were tied. "What the . . . ?"

"Would you please get up and stop wasting time."

He sighed deeply and shook his head. Not a good move for a man whose just been beaned, but I figured this was something he could learn on his own. Apparently he did. "Oh my God. What happened?" He looked up and tried to focus.

I stared at him until it was clear that he knew who he was, knew who I was, and understood the fine situation he'd gotten us both into.

"Are you satisfied now, you big mouth?"

He opened and closed his eyes several times before asking, "Who did this?"

"Well, golly, let me guess. It wasn't me, so that leaves you or your good friend Mr. Integrity. Come to your own conclusion, you lying sack of shit."

"Hey, wait a minute." He rocked backwards and then forward to move onto his knees.

"No! No! No! Don't do that! What are you, blind?" I grabbed his hands, barely feeling my own, and shook them as hard as I could. "We're connected, see?" The thought did not thrill me.

''Oh.'' He studied our hands bound together with the rough rope. ''He did a good job.''

''I don't believe you. Look,'' I sighed, trying to keep my temper in check. ''If you would kindly get up without ripping my arms any farther from their sockets, I'd appreciate it. Gently, gently.''

He reached up, taking the stress off my arms, leaned against the post, and managed to rise up from both knees to one knee until finally he was standing. If I wasn't so angry at him, I might have had sympathy because it had to hurt like hell, but I was, so I didn't.

''You have some nerve, Lyle Grubbs. Just what did you tell that slimy bastard about the other night?'' Why I was so concerned about my virtue when we had more pressing things on hand, I can't say, but now I knew what Jenny Duggan, the eighth grade slut felt like when Ronny Kirshenbaum told all the guys he felt her up at the movies.

''I didn't tell him anything,'' his voice squeaked.

''Oh right, and they've got President Kennedy's brain in a jar.''

''They do?''

I stared at him. I had actually almost slept with this man. Amazing.

''Listen, Lyle, we have to get out of here. Your friend Art is crazy, and when he comes back, he's going to kill both of us. Do you understand?''

''I never told him about us.''

''I don't care. I just want to get the hell out of here. Now—''

''But you do care. And you should. Art and I share a room. He knew I never came back to the hotel that night. He knew I saw you for dinner. He drew his own conclusions. I never said a word to him.''

He was, if nothing else, sincere.

''Didn't you at least deny it?'' I asked quietly. Nothing makes a person feel cheaper than knowing an evening of intimacy for them was nothing more than a conquest to their partner. The thought that Lyle might have boasted about spending the night with a real live lesbian enraged me so because it hurt.

Lyle shrugged. "I figured if I denied it, he'd harp on it. So I didn't say anything."

Men approach the world very differently from women, which is probably why I prefer to be in relationships with women, but I realized I couldn't fault Lyle for not handling Art the way I might have, at least with regard to this.

"I'm sorry if I hurt you," he added.

"Thank you. Now, can we please get the hell out of here?"

"Sure. Let's see, hold still so I can get a better look at this." He examined Art's knots and whistled. "Wow, he was serious. Well listen"—he nodded to the floor behind me—"I used a slipknot down by your feet. See if you can wiggle your foot and loosen it a little."

I did as he suggested, but nothing was budging. "I can't believe you actually tied me up," I said.

"I tied you *loosely*." His left wrist was joined to my right and vice versa. He worked on the knot on my left wrist.

"Why on earth would you agree to tie me up in the first place?" I was getting angry again. *Concentrate*, I told myself. If I could get one boot off, I might be able to slip my foot out of the bottom half of my restraint, which could possibly loosen the rest of the rope. Already the rope was a little looser, what with Lyle standing up.

"Because I'm into bondage," he answered irritably. "Why do you think? I knew Art was lying because Mr. Long would never agree to anything like this, but I thought it was the only way to buy time for you. What? Would you have preferred he shot you?"

"If you hadn't gone along with it in the first place—"

"If I hadn't gone along with it—?" He stopped and took a deep breath. "Let's get this straight—when I was first sent to get you, I believed it was Mr. Long who had made the request. It's not unusual for Art to get orders from Mr. Long and pass them on to me. Now believe it or not—hold still." He tugged gently at his right wrist. "Hold this." He pointed to a section of rope. "Believe it or not, I was actually excited to see you again." He rolled his eyes heavenward. "But when we got here, I knew something was up. I didn't know what, but I had to listen to what he had to say. Hell, for all I knew Art was right about you. Maybe Mr. Long's daughter did hire you to get those blueprints. Maybe you were only nice to me to get information." He kept his head bowed as he worked on the knot, but he looked up at me like a kid with a bad report card.

"Do you really think I would be intimate with you to get information?" I asked softly.

He worked on the knot. I had my foot halfway out of my boot.

"You know what I mean."

I did. "I was intimate with you because I wanted to be, Lyle, not because I wanted anything from you. Except maybe to feel wanted." I paused. "Look, we may not live through this, so I'll tell you something. You knew I had been doubting myself lately, across the board; my work, my relationship, even trusting my instincts, everything. And then I met you. You were kind, you were strong . . . you were in therapy." I waited for him to acknowledge the joke. He didn't. "I'm kidding, but seriously, you were comforting—maybe that's what I really wanted—to be comforted. To be taken care of, you know? I guess I wanted to feel like a completely different person for just one night. I did with you. So I guess I owe you a thanks."

Lyle hadn't looked at me once during my True Confession, and I was beginning to feel like one of the characters from the comic books I'd read as a kid. Woman tied to a stake, danger imminent, breasts heaving, and a big hulk of a guy working furiously to save them as she spills her guts out.

Okay, so maybe my breasts weren't heaving, but the image was still there.

"I got my boot off! I got my boot off," I called out. It was an exciting moment.

"Good. Now try and wiggle your foot free." Lyle said. Believing he knew what he was talking about, I followed his directions and wiggled.

"My foot's stuck," I informed him.

"It can't be. Move it around. Get the boot out of there, it'll give you more room."

"Wonderful. Then my toes will be free."

"Sydney, this is no time to fool around. Do you have any idea what time it is?"

"No. What?"

He turned his wrist to look at his watch, causing me considerable discomfort. "It's five-thirty."

"Shit. No wonder my hands are numb. Do you realize you were out for over an hour?" Even I could hear the accusation in my voice. I kept trying to work my foot free, so I could miraculously untie his little slipknot with my nimble toes, but it was impossible.

"Just what did you do while I was knocked out?" he said with more than a little attitude.

"Well, I tried to do my nails, but I nixed the idea when I couldn't reach them. If you remember, Lyle, you gagged me." No wonder my mouth and chin felt raw. I had spent an hour rubbing my face against the post. That along with the punch Art had landed on my chin, I imagined I looked like just the woman Leslie wanted to greet at the end of the day. Leslie. We'd planned on getting together tonight.

"Wait a minute! My bag." I motioned to the bag lying in a heap on the floor, less than two feet away from us. "If you can reach it, I have a Swiss Army knife in there."

"Excellent." As his legs were free, I let him stretch, point, and drag. Once he snagged the purse and dragged it over to us, he went to bend down and pick it up.

"That hurts, Lyle," I said with my face sliding down against the pole.

"Sorry. Okay, you dip your shoulder and raise you hand, okay?"

After what felt like an eternity, Lyle was able to retrieve the knife from my bag and at six-fifteen a final cut set us free. Lyle untied his own hands first and then loosened the rope from around me so that it fell to the floor. I quickly followed the rope and slumped to the ground when my knees buckled out from under me.

"Are you all right?" Lyle stooped down to help me up.

"I'm fine, thank you." I slipped off my jacket and realized as I wiped the sweat from my brow, that I finally understood what my sister, Nora, was going through with menopause. "I want a drink."

All the while Lyle had been cutting us free, we had been listening to the steady flow of guests arriving upstairs. After I put my boot back on, I retrieved my bag, picked up a five-pound free weight and walked to the wine rack.

"Sydney, are you crazy?" Lyle asked as I studied the wines.

"Bordeaux or Burgundy?" I put my bag and the dumbbell on the table.

"I don't believe you."

"Come on, Lyle, Clifford owes us a good snort. Let's see . . . La Tache or, oh my yes, look at this, a Petrus Bordeaux, 1989. Very nice."

"Sydney, we don't have time to screw around drinking."

"Screw around, no, but a drink couldn't hurt." I pulled the Petrus from the rack and gently placed it on the table. "Lyle, I have no intention of going up there until the right moment. In the meantime, I deserve to be pampered a little."

"Oh really? And how do you know when the right moment will be?"

I pulled two wineglasses from the rack and set them on the mahogany table along with the wine. "A combination of instinct and timing, my friend. We don't want to go up there until we know there are enough guests to make it impossible for Art to do anything foolish and risk hurting Mr. Long's fund-raising." I walked away from the table in search of a bathroom, which I found just around the corner. I pointed to a corkscrew. "Will you open that? I'll be right out."

He nodded.

"Oh, and Lyle?"

He looked up, with the bottle in hand.

"Promise me you won't be going upstairs while I'm in here."

"Oh come on," he said offended. "You think you can't trust me?"

"Promise."

He sighed. "I promise for Christ's sake."

Lyle was still there when I came out. He had poured two glasses of wine and was nervously pacing around the table.

"I think the way we ought to handle this," he said as he circled the table, "is for me to go up and talk to Mr. Long personally while you stay down here."

"Oh, right, that sounds like a dandy idea." I shook my head. "I don't think so."

"I just don't think we should make a scene," he said. "Look, what if you wait in the kitchen and I go talk to Mr. Long alone. That way the Longs will be spared public—"

"What is with you?" I asked, only somewhat baffled by his fence-sitting skills.

"I like the Longs: they've been good to me." His hands twitched helplessly at his side, as if he was embarrassed by having these feelings.

"Here, Lyle, have a glass of wine." I handed him a glass of the Bordeaux and took the other for myself. "Here's to getting out of this alive."

"I'll drink to that," he said, then took a sip. One sip was enough to know that what we were drinking was a superb wine. "Wow," he said moving to the armchairs and ottoman. "This is really good."

"It should be. It probably set Cliffy back a couple hundred dollars." I sat at the table, put the glass down, and put my jacket back on, preparing for my imminent departure.

"Sydney. Answer me one question. *Did* the Long's daughter hire you to find those blueprints? Honestly."

"Honestly?" I moved back to the far end of the table. "I believe she hired me to find out what happened to her brother. No doubt the blueprints were in the back of her mind, but she never even told me about them. She—"

We both heard the upstairs door from the kitchen open at the same time. I positioned myself behind the basement door with the dumbbell in hand and watched as Lyle hurried to grab his wine and move away from the armchair, where anyone would see him as soon as they entered the basement.

He wasn't quite fast enough, though, and the door opened just as he was passing in front of it.

''Well, well, well.'' I heard Art's voice crackle. Though I couldn't see him, I assumed he had a gun, assumed he was alone. If Lyle hadn't been in the direct line of fire, I would have slammed the door against Art, but he was, so I waited. ''I'm impressed, Lyle. I must say, I didn't think you had it in you.'' The door moved open just slightly more and I braced myself to be hit with it full force. From where I stood, I could see Lyle, who was moving slowly to the table with his glass in hand.

''Art,'' Lyle said as if he was welcoming an old friend. ''Care for a glass of wine, you shithead?'' He sipped from his own glass. ''It's a hell of a lot better than the crap we're used to.'' I watched Lyle carefully.

''Where's your little girlfriend, Lyle?''

Lyle nodded behind him. ''I knocked her out. I told you she's not my girlfriend. And I don't appreciate being tied up. You don't need that gun, Art.'' Good. Lyle had said that for my benefit, which meant we were working together.

''Knocked her out? That doesn't sound like you, Lyle. Even if she isn't your girlfriend. And besides, was *that* glass of wine poured with me in mind? I don't think so.'' With that the door burst open and slammed me against the wall. I had been prepared for this and blocked it as best as I could with the left side of my body, but still it hit hard enough to knock the wind out of me. The next thing I knew, an arm was reaching around the door and grabbing for me. I smashed his wrist as hard as I could with the free weight. Lyle must have tackled Art because the door hit me a second time, whiplashing my head back into the wall. The free weight went flying out of my hand and across the room. I shoved back up against the door and slipped out from behind it.

Just as I stepped out from behind the door, Art pulled back and hit Lyle with a punch that I could practically feel myself. Lyle went reeling back and fell over the mahogany table, taking with him the bottle of Petrus. Such a waste.

Before Art could turn around I clipped him in the back of his knees with my right foot. His knees buckled and he went down to the floor, which was a better place for him to be in terms of equally matching the two of us. On our feet Art Grants could put me out in under ten seconds, but if he was on the ground and I could use my feet, I had a chance. I kicked out again and caught him in the side of his head. I had given it all I had but it was as if it were nothing more than a love tap. I saw him catch sight of the free weight at the right of the wine rack. There was no sight of his gun. It must have fallen when Lyle tackled him, but I couldn't see it anywhere.

Lyle. Lyle was moaning on the floor on the other side of the table.

Art grabbed my ankle and squeezed. It felt as if the bone would simply snap under the pressure of his fingers, but it didn't. He pulled me down. I hit the ground hard, but twisted so I would at least hit it on the fleshy part of my tush and not the base of the spine or my hip.

It still hurt. As Art pulled me down, he dragged me in front of him and leaned over me, as if to pin me down in a wrestling hold. There was no contest—Art was bigger and stronger than me. While he busied himself with immobilizing the bottom half of me, I grabbed a fistful of the front of his hair with my left hand and dug my fingers into his eye sockets with my right hand.

He did not respond well to this. It was like riding a mule post bee sting. Art came back with his elbow, and though I had enough time to see it coming, I didn't have enough time to dodge the blow to my ribs. When Art's elbow made contact with my ribs and I heard the faint sound of bone breaking I knew one thing—if I didn't fend this son of a bitch off, I was a dead woman. The last thing I could do was let him get on top of me. All he needed was one good shot at my head to put me out.

I rolled onto my side and kicked him everywhere I could as hard as I could. This way he would be so busy with my feet and legs he wouldn't have time to deal with the rest of me. With each kick I tried to move myself closer to the free weight. Every other blow or so caught him either in the face or the neck. Still he was able to get ahold of my left foot and was twisting it until I was about ready to holler uncle. I was four feet away from the dumbbell and stretching nearer to it, my fingers splayed as I inched closer and closer to it.

I was so focused on getting a weapon I didn't realize until too late that he had released his hold on me for a moment. During that second and a half he must have retrieved his gun and was pressing it hard into the back of my head.

"It's been fun, but it's over, Sloane." Art was out of breath, but not out of steam. He grabbed my hair, pulled my head back and then slammed my face back onto the carpeted floor. There is no such thing as soft Astroturf. I scraped my chin in the same place where he had punched me before, and it hurt like a son of a bitch. I was not going to be a pretty picture laid out in some funeral parlor.

"Say bye-bye to your friend, Lyle." Art pressed my face into the floor and pushed the gun muzzle into the base of my head. I held my breath, shut my eyes, and thought of Leslie. Then I heard the familiar click of the hammer hitting the firing pin.

Nothing. The silence that followed that metallic click was the most magnificent sound I've ever heard.

"Fuck." Art hissed. Before he could even inhale, let alone find out why he jammed, Lyle was on him like Lawrence Taylor on a quarterback. Being at the bottom of the mound was not a pleasant experience, but it was a fat lot better than the alternative. Lyle rolled Art off me and the two of them were locked in each others arms, each of them fighting to get possession of the gun. I crawled to where the free weight was, grabbed it, and scurried back to Art, who was on the bottom. I slammed his gun hand with the free weight and practically hollered for joy when he grimaced in pain and released the gun. Panting, I said, "It's over, asshole."

I was shaking. My entire body felt as if it was connected to an electrical current. I reached above Art's head and took his gun. The three of us were having trouble catching our breath, but with Lyle on top of Art, and Art's gun in my hand, I felt a little better.

Art was taller than Lyle, but Lyle had the bulk he needed to keep Art pinned to the ground without much effort.

"Go upstairs. Get help," Lyle wheezed.

"No. I'm not going to leave you alone with this son of a bitch."

"I'm fine, Sydney."

"Yeah, Sydney. Do what your boyfriend says." Art was having a little trouble talking with Lyle's big hand pressing his face into the floor.

"You know, Art. I just don't like you." I turned his gun around and tapped his head with the butt of it, knocking him out instantly. His body went limp under Lyle.

"Thank you," Lyle said to me as he eased off Art and put out his hand for Art's gun. "I'll take that. Why don't you go upstairs and get Mr. Long so we can settle this once and for all. I'll call the police. What's that officer's name?"

"Julia Lee." I gave him her number with Art's gun and paused. "I don't feel right leaving you alone."

"Sydney. I'm fine. Trust me." He examined Art's gun and looked up at me. "Now get out of here." He checked Art to make sure he was out and backed up to the telephone. "I just feel bad making you go up there alone."

"Believe me, our worst nightmare is right there," I said, pointing to Art. "Okay. I'll be right back. Oh wait—" I knelt beside Art and checked his pockets. The last thing Lyle needed was to turn around and find that Art had hidden another gun on him. As it was, I was thrilled to find my trusty old Walther still in his pocket. I put it in my pocket, tried to straighten my hair, and took a deep breath. With that I left Lyle, closed the basement door and climbed the eleven steps that led to the kitchen.

A roundish woman in blue jeans, spotted sweater, and soiled apron stood in front of a counter, placing bite-sized hors d'oeuvres on trays garnished with pine cones, flowers, and snow made from confectioner's sugar.

She barely glanced up at me when I first entered the room. Which was good. I knew from my visit to the bathroom that I looked like I'd blend in better at a wrestling match than a black-tie fund-raiser. My face was a color spectrum, splotched in varying degrees of red; the jaw from Art's punch was one shade of red, the lip-waxing was another: Art's finger in my eye had produced yet another tinge of red. God only knew what I looked like after this last go-round, but I knew I wasn't looking my prettiest when I entered that kitchen, brushing my hair back with one hand and holding the Walther in my jacket pocket with the other.

I nodded and smiled at the aproned woman, who smiled distractedly back at me.

I closed the door behind me and moved bravely through the kitchen into the crowd of well-dressed, well-mannered moneyed people. I was halfway through the dining room, turning down a tray of sushi, when a deafening crash came billowing up the stairs. The unmistakable sound of two hundred shattering bottles had the same impact as, I imagine, the air-raid sirens had in England during WW II, or, for that matter, being in my office two days earlier. The entire room became stilled, all movement and sound ceased in a fraction of a second. A woman with frizzy hair and orange lips in a white Dior suit froze, her hand dripping black soy sauce from the sushi. She stared at me with both uncertainty and excitement.

In less than three seconds—though it felt like minutes—Clifford Bartholomew huffed red-faced and swearing toward the origin of the sound. He passed me as he rushed through the crowd to the basement door, registered that it was me he had passed, and doubled back.

"*You!*" he screamed in my face. "What the hell are you doing here!"

Another horrible thunder of shattering glass came from below.

"Party crashing?" I asked as I tightened my fingers around the Walther. This time I wasn't going to be taken by surprise or taken advantage of. This time I was going to be ready.

Bartholomew's face turned more shades of red than mine as he spewed unintelligible things and finally turned and went to find out what had caused the sound, a sound for which I was clearly not responsible.

I hurried through the room, looking for Wallace Long, and found him in the living room, with his wife, deep in conversation with another couple, as if the noise from below hadn't yet reached them. Unlike the Louise Long I had met on two previous occasions, this one seemed poised, calm, and only somewhat removed. She clutched what looked like a vodka and tonic. The strain of the last week was evident, but not overwhelming as it had been each time I'd seen her.

Without waiting for an invitation, I joined their little foursome.

"Mr. Long, We need to talk."

"Is that so?"

"That's right." My back was to the back of the house, so when someone screamed, "My God, he's got a gun!" it was instinct that propelled me forward into the Longs, taking them both with me down to the ground.

Twenty-seven

I heard the familiar *thup* of a gun being fired with a silencer. By then I had both Mr. and Mrs. Long down on the ground with me, my Walther out of my pocket and ready to go. As I looked up protectively from my roost I saw total chaos. People were flying in every direction, trying to get out of the way but not knowing which way was out of the way. Under the balcony to the second-floor landing—maybe thirty feet away—two men were struggling. One had a gun.

"Get off me," Wallace snarled through gritted teeth.

"Shut up." I pushed Wallace back to the ground. As people ran for cover or fell to the ground in fear, the line of vision cleared and I could see the two men fighting were not Art and Lyle, but rather Art and Max. I didn't know where Lyle was and feared the worst.

I slowly stood, holding the gun firmly between both hands, never taking my eyes off Art.

"Stop it! Stop it!" A high-pitched scream cut through the confusion but didn't seem to make a difference. The voice continued to shriek, "My Rodin! My Rodin!" adding only another dimension to the already surrealistic scene of *When Republicans Go Bad*. It wasn't a pretty picture. I neared Max and Art and called out, "Drop it, Art!" When he didn't respond, I squeezed the trigger, pointing to the ceiling. Without the silencer, this gunshot had a different impact on the crowd.

The frizzy-haired women in the Dior suit fainted, several men bolted, and Art paused long enough to look at me, which gave Max just the time he needed to catch Art with a right to the jaw that knocked him out. It was at that precise moment Clifford Bartholomew went ballistic and came charging at me like a rhino in heat.

I tried to sidestep the oncoming Clifford, but it was impossible. I dropped the gun before he hit me full force. "My wine! My carpet! I'll kill you for this!" He screamed this as we rolled around on the ground; him pulling at my hair, my clothes, anything he could get his hands on. Finally we rolled in such a position that I could slap him. Hard. Someone had to, the man was out of control. I grabbed Clifford by his lapels and shook him. "Calm down. Calm down, it's all over."

When I got off him, I retrieved my gun and walked over to Max. His tuxedo jacket was torn, but he was otherwise unscathed. He had Art by the collar with one hand and Art's gun in his other hand.

"I thought I'd find you here," he said.

"How did you get in? I didn't see you when I came up."

"I told Bartholomew's people that I was with the caterer, then I told the caterer Mr. Bartholomew asked me to tend bar. You okay?"

"Better than I have been in a long time." I turned and joined Wallace and Louise Long. She was sitting on the same gold and silver chair I'd been in earlier, and he was fuming on his feet.

I held the Walther in my hand, which may be why people gave me such a wide berth. In the distance I could hear the police sirens getting closer.

"Your son was murdered," I said when I was standing directly in front of Louise. I was aware of a cold breeze coming in through the opened door and sweat trickling down the side of my face. "Tell me just how much of this you already know, so as not to waste my time."

"Now see here." Wallace Long indignantly drew himself up into his full six feet.

"No, you see here. Like it or not, you're in this up

to your eyeballs. Did you know the blueprints for your new computer chip were stolen, copied, and returned to your safe?'' From his reaction it was clear that this was something of which he was well aware.

"I see. And did you know who stole them?'' He looked blankly down at me. I couldn't tell whether he knew it was Peter who'd stolen the blueprints or not. "Arthur Grants killed Peter.'' From the way his face paled, it was safe to say that was something Wallace Long hadn't known.

After that bombshell, it was as if all the spunk had left him, and the big man took a seat at his wife's side on the edge of Bartholomew's coffee table. It was sad to see this rawhide kind of guy turn old before my very eyes.

"Why don't you start from the beginning, Ms. Sloane?'' He reached over and took Louise's hand in his as he prepared to listen to me without interruption. She was pale as she stared at the floor.

Softening the blows as best as I could, I explained to them how their son and daughter had plotted not so much against him, but more to save her life. She was frightened, and her brother had wanted to help her. It was stupid, it was wrong, but it was all they could think to do.

"Art found out about it. Only he can tell you how, but I suspect one of the night watchmen told him that Peter stole the papers. He's terribly loyal to you, as I'm sure you know, Mr. Long. If it were in his power, no one would hurt you—ever. Mind you, I'm speculating in part, but my guess is Art knew exactly what Peter planned to do and he figured he'd stop it in New York, where he could cover his tracks more easily. It doesn't make sense that he would kill Peter the *way* he did, considering that it would have certainly hurt you politically, but who knows what was going on in his head?

"Before Art killed Peter, Peter told him that he had given the blueprints to his friend, Brendan Mayer, which—in part—was true. Peter gave Brendan a *copy* of the blueprints, but not the copy he intended to sell. Peter probably thought by telling Art this he could placate him. He knew Art was on to him: however, he also knew Art was devoted to you and assumed *because* of that, Art would never hurt him. But he was wrong. He couldn't have known how far off the deep end Art had stumbled. In fact, by telling Art about the blueprints, all he did was sign Brendan's death warrant as well as his own.

"But now the hard part for Art was over; Peter was dead and his death was listed as accidental. Getting the blueprints from Brendan would be a breeze. However, Art hadn't considered that, upon hearing of Peter's death, Brendan would get rid of those blueprints as fast as he could.

"Art probably thought Peter's death would be enough to discourage your daughter from pursuing their initial scheme, and it might have been, but she threw a real cog in his wheels when she hired CSI to find out what happened to her brother.

"You see, more than anything, Art wanted those blueprints. This was his convoluted way of protecting you, which explains my presence here tonight. He had Lyle get me under the pretense of meeting with you, but when we got here, there was only Art." Louise continued to stare at the floor, while Wallace looked as if I'd stabbed him in the abdomen.

"Now, Art's purpose in bringing me here was twofold: he wanted the blueprints that he was convinced had fallen into my hands, but he also knew that I was getting closer to finding out what had actually happened to Peter *and* Brendan. He couldn't have that, which meant that he'd have to kill me, but before he could do that he *had* to have those prints. Unfortunately, I don't have them."

"Who does?" Wallace asked softly.

"I do," Louise said almost inaudibly as she gently squeezed his hand. This took us all by surprise. Still she stared at the floor. "When Peter and I spent Saturday afternoon together, he had made a phone call from our bedroom. I listened in on the extension. It's not something I would normally do, but he was so agitated, I was concerned. I didn't know with whom he was speaking, other than that it was a woman and they had plans to meet on Sunday morning, at which time he would give her what he had brought with him.'' Louise took a deep breath. I looked up to the doorway and saw Detectives Julia Lee and Ned Gould. I motioned for them to wait there. Ned was ready to bulldoze ahead, but Julia put out her hand and stopped him.

''When Peter died, I remembered the phone call and thought perhaps he was dealing drugs. When you went to identify him, dear, I went to his room in the hotel and went through it, finding only the blueprints. Though I have no active interest in my husband's business, I know enough to know Peter shouldn't have had those papers. So I took them. I knew I was being ridiculous, maybe even paranoid, but when you came to see us, Ms. Sloane, I was certain that that had something to do with Peter. I knew my son had been murdered.''

''Why didn't you say anything to me?'' Wallace was genuinely perplexed.

Louise let her hand go limp in his and studied his face. Finally she sighed. ''Quite honestly, I thought you were somehow involved in it, darling. You were so very much against Sydney investigating Peter's death, and I didn't understand why.''

''Why? Because I didn't want it to be any harder on you than it already was.'' There was no hiding the fact that Wallace Long was stunned. When his wife gave him a look of doubt, he added softly, ''And because I was ashamed. When Peter killed himself, he gave the world an opportunity to blame us.''

Before anything more could be said, Detectives Gould and Lee were standing in the middle of the room, flashing their badges for all to see. Three more police cars pulled up to the curb outside the house and Clifford Bartholomew's voice could be heard above everything else, screaming, ''Arrest that woman! Arrest that woman!'' as he followed Detective Gould from room to room, pushing his pudgy hands in my direction.

It took me about half an hour to tell Detective Lee what had happened, but by the time I was done, Art Grants had come to and a police officer was cuffing his hands behind his back and reading him his rights. I wanted to ask them to cuff him like a pretzel to Bartholomew's friggin' Rodin, or to Bartholomew, for that matter, but I didn't. Instead I went looking for Lyle, whom I found in the basement with a bump on his head the size of a golf ball.

"What happened?" he asked, not bothering to move from his prone position amid a sea of glass and wine, wine, wine.

"Arthur's been arrested for Peter's and Brendan's murders, Mrs. Long admitted to having the blueprints, and Bartholomew's miffed about his wine collection—" I looked around and found myself sympathizing with the misogynistic old poot. "Can't fault him on that. What did you guys *do* down here?" I asked with incredulity. Absolutely every single bottle of wine, every solitary glass—from the bulbous red wine goblets, to the snifters—was shattered around us. The wine walls were lying flat on their backs like little soldiers felled on the combat field.

"Dancing." He gave me a smart-ass response, but when he said it it sounded more like "Danthing," so I asked him to look at me and smile. Sure enough, his right front tooth was missing in action, which made him look a little more than goofy. I gave him a hand up and helped him upstairs as best as I could, considering that at least one of my ribs had clearly been broken by Art during our fight earlier. Once upstairs, I introduced him to Detectives Lee and Gould.

Several hours later Max and I were back from the police station and in my kitchen rummaging around for a decent meal. I thinly sliced some red onions and roasted red peppers, while Max tore up fresh basil and arugula, minced some garlic and chèvre, and mixed that all together with a little olive oil and balsamic vinegar. Max had already put on a pot of water to boil for pasta.

"You have to take it easy, like the nice doctor said. Now sit down," Max ordered as he sliced semolina bread.

"I'm fine," I said. Though I had felt and looked better physically in the past, I was in surprisingly high spirits.

After we had left the police station, Max and I made a stop at the hospital, where it was confirmed that Art had indeed broken my rib. I was told to take it easy and that the bruises on my face would just have to heal with time, along with my rib.

"I'm just amazed." Max had taken off his tux jacket and was working with his sleeves rolled up, an apron protecting his starched shirt.

"At what?" I asked, taking his advice and sitting at the dining table.

"Well, first that Long's kids would steal from their old man. He doesn't seem like such a bad guy." He tore some Boston lettuce and tossed it in a bowl.

I thought about Wallace Long and how he had looked at the police station—a sad, drawn man with the skill to run a multimillion-dollar enterprise, the stamina to run for office and yet a man who seemed—that evening—to be nothing more than a big old shell. It reminded me of my ex, Caryn, telling me about her father. Theirs had been a relationship that was both powerful and painful to her as a child. When she left home, she went for fifteen years without seeing him. They were reunited when she was a woman and she was stunned at discovering that her father—this towering figure in her past—was just a man, nothing more, nothing less.

"You know what they say about books and their covers. Think about it. We don't have a clue as to who Wallace Long really is. The way I see it, Vanessa thought her father never gave her the love and support she wanted. He had more than he needed financially, so she felt justified—as his offspring—to take what she needed."

"Do you think he would have given it to her had she just called him up and asked?" Max added watercress to the salad bowl.

"No," I said emphatically. "When I first met him he said he didn't *have* a daughter. You see, she deserted him, so he was determined to take it one step farther. Can you imagine—" Before I could finish the sentence the doorbell rang. Max volunteered to get it.

"Leslie," he said as he left the kitchen to get the intercom.

"Shit. Leslie." In all the chaos that had followed Bartholomew's, I had forgotten to call Leslie and cancel our tentative plans for that night. I lifted myself off the chair like a woman in her eighth month of pregnancy, and went to the phone in the kitchen. It might be Leslie at the door, but this way she'd at least have a message from me. I hit the first button for auto dial and listened with half an ear as Max called into the intercom, "Yes? Who is it?"

Leslie's machine picked up on the second ring. "Lez, it's me. I'm really sorry about tonight." I glanced at the wall clock and was shocked to see it was nearing ten. "And I'm sorry I'm calling so late, I really didn't know what time it was. But, you'll be glad to know this case is officially closed, and I'm feeling much better." I paused, hoping she would be screening her calls and pick up, and not in the elevator in my building. "Anyway, I'm home and chances are I'll be up pretty late. Give me a call." As I returned the receiver to the cradle, I remembered the moment Art Grants pulled the trigger. I shut my eyes and felt nausea wash over me for an instant and disappear. I had thought of Leslie when I believed I was going to die. Not Aunt Minnie or my sister Nora or my mother and father, or Caryn, but Leslie. As I turned back from the phone I saw Max, Wallace, and Louise standing at the doorway to the kitchen.

"I hope you don't mind this intrusion," Wallace said apologetically. Apologetically? Wallace?

"We've come at my insistence." Louise gestured to a chair at the table, and I invited them to sit.

"Can I get you anything?" I asked, ever the perfect hostess. On my way across the room, I switched off the pasta water and looked longingly at the salad.

"I could use a drink," Louise was the first to answer. Wallace admitted he, too, could use a shot of something, so Max fell back into his earlier role of bartender. When drinks had been poured all around, we sat at the table, and I asked the Longs how they were. They looked like hell.

Wallace scratched the side of his face with his index finger and sighed. "I'd say, without exception, this trip has been the lowest point in our lives." He paused and the room was painfully still. "It's not easy for a man like me to admit when he's made a mistake." He glanced at his wife, who nodded once as she brought the vodka and tonic to her lips. "It's not that I'm a bad man, you understand, but a bit myopic. I always thought if I gave my family the best, they'd be grateful. Louise here was, but the kids, I just never got it. I pushed them because—"

Louise put her hand gently on his and he stopped. "Right." He nodded at her silent advisement and took a hefty drink from his Dewar's on the rocks. "Anyway, I've been wrong about a lot of things lately. I was so caught up in wanting everything that it looks as if I've wound up with nothing." He flinched after saying this and took Louise's hand in his. "I'm sorry, I didn't mean it like that," he told her sincerely.

My epiphany that Wallace Long was just a man, and a potentially likable one at that, hit me like an ice cube down the back.

"I know. Go on." Louise let her hand sit dwarfed in his, and in that simple gesture I understood how easy it is to pass judgment over others' lives when we sit safely on the sidelines. As we were gathered around the table, it was suddenly quite clear that love had kept Wallace and Louise together for all these years. They understood one another in a way that no outsider ever could. Not Lyle, who had daily contact with them, or Vanessa, who had viewed them through a child's eyes, or me, who had presumed to know so much after barely a peek into their lives. I reached carefully for my own glass of red wine and sipped.

"So Louise and I want to know why Paula needed the money." The cut-through-the-bullshit-get-to-the-point Wallace Long I had grown accustomed to was back in the blink of an eye.

I explained the pickle their daughter had gotten herself into and ended by saying, "She has until Christmas to pay back the hundred thousand dollars.'' I left the implied ''Or else'' dangling.

No one spoke for the longest time. Our glasses were refilled by an attentive Max, but neither Wallace or Louise said boo. Louise then removed her hand from her husband's, opened her bag, and fished out a checkbook, which she slid over to him.

Wallace took a Mont Blanc fountain pen from his jacket pocket, opened the checkbook and started writing. As he did this, I asked Louise how Lyle was.

''He'll be fine. We sent him back to the hotel so he could rest. I don't think, though, that we'll be needing his services after we get home.''

''Really?'' I asked, surprised. ''Why's that?''

Louise changed the subject. ''Your aunt was very helpful, Sydney.''

''Oh, that's right. Were you able to go to church with her this morning?'' I asked, having forgotten they had spent the morning together.

''Yes. She's quite a woman, that Minnie. She has a good heart.''

''She's the best,'' Max said. I'm convinced if there wasn't over a thirty-year age difference, Max would marry Minnie.

''She's agreed to come and be our guest in Texas.''

''Is that right?'' I wasn't altogether surprised because Minnie has a way of making friends wherever she goes.

''Yes. She and her friend Enoch.'' She paused, glancing over as her husband signed his name to the check.

Enoch? Max and I shared a glance of utter confusion. Who the hell was Enoch?

Wallace folded the check in half and pushed it toward me. ''If you would do us a favor and give this to Paula. Tell her there are no strings. No need to call. We just wanted to make sure she was all right.'' The words seemed to come hard, but it didn't stop Wallace.

''Wouldn't you prefer to give this to her yourself?'' I asked.

Louise and Wallace shared a glance, which, to me, said yes loud and clear.

''Please, let me just arrange for the three of you to

get together before you leave. You're not still leaving tonight, are you?''

''We'll be leaving tomorrow morning. But I don't know.'' Wallace gave Louise a sidelong glance.

Louise shook her head. ''I think not. It's been a long time, and so much has happened. If you would just give that to her for us. We'll let time take care of the rest.''

I slid the check off the table and slipped it into my shirt pocket just as my stomach let loose a loud growl. With my stomach as empty as it was, the wine was going straight to my head. It was close to ten-thirty, and I invited the Longs to join us for a bite to eat.

''No, thank you.'' Louise demurred. ''Wallace.'' She said his name mildly and with needing no more than that to make her point, he said, ''Oh, right,'' and opened the checkbook once more.

''Both Louise and I are grateful for your persistence, Sydney, and we assume that if Paula paid you, it was by check and that check has already bounced. Is that accurate?''

Max told him it was too soon to know.

''In any case, please accept this as a token of our appreciation and, I will assume, full payment of any debt Paula may owe you.''

The check far exceeded our usual fee. I told him so and offered it back to him. Wallace closed the checkbook, gave it back to Louise, and said, ''Consider it a bonus for putting up with a pigheaded old man.'' When no one objected to his self-description, he stood up, polished off his drink, and held out his hand for his wife. ''It's time we were going,'' he said with finality.

After the Longs had gone and Max was back at the stove, I looked at the check they had written for Vanessa. It was twice what she needed to pay Nickie Beena back.

''Wow,'' I said softly as I passed it over to Max.

He whistled and wondered aloud if Wallace and Louise would be willing to adopt him.

''I doubt it, but I'd be willing to rent you out as a really slow chef. Are you almost done?'' I asked impatiently as I picked cucumber pieces from the salad bowl.

"You can't rush pasta," he said as he slapped my hand.

"You *can* rush pasta. Christ, it's only noodles."

"Which is why your pasta always crunches. Sit down." He handed me back Vanessa's check and waved me away from the stove.

"So, who's Enoch?" he asked, getting his gossip tone of voice.

"Beats me. Minnie always tells me about her new beaux, but she'd never mentioned this one." Seated again, I studied the Longs' check to CSI, allowing myself to revel in momentary greed. All was well with the world. With this check we were at least two months ahead of the financial game. The blueprints had been returned to Wallace. Art Grants was safely behind bars. And I didn't have to worry about cooking. *What more could a gal want?* I asked myself as I eased back gingerly into the chair.

The phone rang just as Max was pouring the pasta into a colander. Max answered and passed the phone to me.

"Leslie?" I asked.

He shook his head and hurried back to the pasta, no doubt as hungry as I.

"Hello," I said.

"Sydney?" The voice was faint, but distinctly feminine and vaguely familiar.

"Yes."

"I lost the number."

What the— "Joyce?" I asked hesitantly.

"Yes." We definitely did not have a good connection.

"Where are you?" I practically shouted into the mouthpiece.

"I don't know."

I held the phone out and looked at it. Part of me wanted to scream "Lady don't call me and play these stupid games," but the bigger part of me knew that I was probably the only person on the face of the earth she felt she could turn to.

"Joyce. Where are you? Are you at home?" I rose carefully from the chair and went to where Max was mixing the pasta with the arugula, basil, garlic, onion, red peppers, and chèvre.

"Home?" When she laughed it sounded like she had a mouthful of marbles.

"Yeah, are you home?"

"No. No home. I have nothing."

Two people in one night with nothing, but nothing was enough to give me heartburn. I scooped out a penne loaded with chèvre and basil and popped it in my mouth. Every move I made felt like a knife stabbing into my torso.

"Where are you?" I asked again.

"On the street." The sound of traffic behind her seemed to back her up on that.

"Where? Do you want me to meet you?" I asked halfheartedly.

"No."

"Help me out, Joyce."

It took several tries, but I finally got her to agree to come to my apartment. When I got off the phone Max had two plates loaded with pasta, salad, and garlic bread.

"We've got to chew fast. Joyce Cullerson's on her way over, and she doesn't sound good."

"Joyce Cullerson's husband has registered a complaint against us with the New York Police Department," he reminded me.

"I know. But this isn't Tom Cullerson, it's Joyce, and she doesn't sound good."

"Okay, okay, play Sister Mary Tess as long as you like. I'm telling you, this lady ain't about to be saved." He delivered this proclamation as he dug into his dinner.

"You've never met her." I said with a mouthful.

"Don't have to." He stuffed a forkful of Boston lettuce and penne into his mouth. Together we sounded like a couple of Neanderthals eating brontosaurus burgers. "The woman's trouble," he garbled.

"Yeah? Well she's our trouble now." I tried to spear a red pepper off his plate but the movement hurt too much. Max was right. Joyce Cullerson was trouble. I could feel it down to my toes.

It felt good to be back in touch with my instincts. Now, if I could only feel that something good was about to happen. But I didn't. And it wasn't.

Twenty-eight

By the time Joyce Cullerson arrived, Max and I had finished dinner and Leslie had called. Whether I wanted it or not, she was coming over to see me. It didn't matter that Max was there or that I was expecting Joyce at any minute. Leslie had to see me, and that's all there was to that.

Oh goody. Now she could see what I do for a living.

It was almost eleven when Joyce finally arrived. I knew how bad I looked, what with my face having been color-coded by Art and my posture more like Quasimodo's thanks to the broken rib, but I was nothing compared to Joyce. When I opened the door I was shocked to see that she was wearing only jeans, sneakers, and a sweater, and *that* looked like it had spent the last week and a half in a trash bin. She had her hands tucked protectively under her armpits and she pressed a scuffed black shoulder bag close to her side. Her clothes and face were covered with soot and her dirty hair seemed to be slicked to her head.

I had her come into the kitchen where, after taking one look at her, Max offered her something to eat.

''No.'' She glanced suspiciously around the room. ''Nothing.'' She seemed genuinely afraid of Max.

''Joyce, this is my partner, Max. Why don't you have a seat and tell us what happened.''

With her thin arms still wrapped protectively over her

chest she rocked back and forth. Plainly, this woman needed more than either Max or I could offer, and it wasn't a warm meal. She stood in the middle of the dining area, looking ready to flee at a moment's notice.

"Debi's dead." She uttered this so softly I wasn't sure she'd actually said it. Neither Max nor I responded. It was as if we were both waiting to see where she was headed.

"Debi's dead, and Tom blamed you." She turned her head slowly to her left, toward me, her dull brown eyes almost frighteningly devoid of life. It was scary, actually. She sounded like a waif, looked like a zombie, and yet had a dangerous edge to her that tripped off every single warning bell inside my head. I glanced at Max and could tell he was feeling the same thing.

"Perhaps you'd like a glass of water," he suggested, taking the opportunity to move to her right, therefore splitting us up and making it slightly more difficult for her to focus.

"No!" she screamed. That brought Max to a quick halt.

"Okay, okay." He held out his hands in an attempt to placate her. "We're not out to hurt you, Mrs. Cullerson. We're on your side."

"Is that so?" Her right eye twitched. "You told the police, didn't you?" She turned her accusation to me.

"About what?" I asked. The simple act of breathing hurt.

"About me wanting to hire you to kill Tom. You did, didn't you? You can tell me." She backed up to keep both Max and me in her line of vision.

"Yes. I did."

"Why?" She practically cried.

"I was trying to protect you."

"Like you tried to protect Debi?" Her eyes locked on to mine like a magnet. The dullness had all but evaporated, and madness took its place.

"There was no way I could protect Debi from Tom."

"Or me. Say it. Say it! That's what you're thinking, isn't it?"

"Joyce, you need help—"

"No, Sydney. I *needed* help, but you were too self-righteous to help me, weren't you?" She backed up again, and, when she unfolded her arms, she showed us that she was holding a .22—not a big gun, but an effective one if aimed properly. "I'm sorry. I didn't want things to get to this point." She waved the gun at Max and told him to move next to me, where she could see him. Joyce Cullerson was as uncomfortable holding the gun as we were having her aim it at us. I hate guns, especially ones being held by frightened, angry people who don't know anything about them.

For the second time in one night I was facing the very real possibility of being killed, and I didn't like it one bit. I'd been lucky with Art, but I wasn't so sure the Cosmic Joker would intercede on my behalf twice in one night.

"What do you want, Joyce?" I asked calmly.

"I want a lot of things. I want my daughter back, but I can't have her, can I?"

"No. You can't." I answered, fearing that by not answering I would incite her only more.

"I wanted Tom dead." She looked slyly through her curtain of greasy bangs.

"Did you get what you wanted?" I asked, knowing that no matter what, we had to keep her talking. Once the dialogue ceased, we ran the risk of her shooting.

She took a deep breath and straightened her back. "Yes. Yes, I did." The faint hint of a smile touched the corners of her mouth and disappeared.

"Did you kill Tom?" I asked, successfully masking my surprise.

She nodded once.

"Well, good for you," I said as if I was in her corner instead of backed into one by her .22. "How?" I asked, assuming she had shot him with the same gun she had aimed at us.

"Do you really want to know?"

"I do. Don't you, Max?"

"Absolutely. What'd you do, shoot him?" He put his hands in his pockets, which didn't sit well with Joyce.

"Keep your hands where I can see them." She fluttered the gun at us. Max eased his hands out of his pockets and showed her that he had nothing up his sleeve. "I didn't shoot him. This is his." She held up the gun, as if for show-and-tell, then pointed it back at us. "He was always threatening me with this. He was going to use this to kill you, Sydney. You should have listened to me. But you're so smart, aren't you? You just thought I was some dumb asshole who should be punished, didn't you? You thought I was responsible for Debi's death, but I wasn't. I tried to protect her. I tried. But against someone like Tom, you just can't win.

"He came home from work early yesterday, after you two beat him up." She allowed herself a smile. "I was thrilled when I saw him, but, of course, I couldn't let him know that. I did everything that was expected of me, but it wasn't enough. It never was. I bathed him, gave him clean clothes, poured his beer, but he was gone. He was mad at you and took it out on me. After he went to the police, he came home and gave me what he wanted to do to the two of you."

"I'm sorry," I said.

She shrugged. "It's not your fault. If you hadn't done that, he would have beaten me for some other reason. That's how it was. But last night, when I was falling to sleep, I knew it was the last time he'd lay a hand on me. When he came home from work tonight, I'd put some pills in his dinner. In less than twenty minutes after eating he fell asleep watching *America's Most Wanted.* I had bought some lighter fluid, a dozen cans. I emptied half of them all around his chair, on his pants, shirt, hair. The rest of it I squirted all over the apartment, in front of the doors and the windows. Then I went back to Tom and lit it." She grinned, tight-lipped, and nodded. "I sat there on the sofa, across from him and watched as he started to catch fire. It was wonderful."

Neither Max or I turned to one another, but I could feel him cringe. I'm sure he felt the same from me.

"He woke up when his pants were totally engulfed. You should have seen the look on his face. It was great. At first he was surprised, then he was scared, and then he got mad. I liked seeing him afraid. I was laughing.

He came at me and I just danced away from him holding a lighter up and lighting all the places where I'd sprayed the butane. I had his gun, but I didn't have to use it. He was rolling around on the floor, trying to put himself out, but he couldn't. By then it had just gone too far. I got out before the place went completely up in flames.''

She stopped and nodded.

''So now you want to kill us?'' I asked. ''Why?''

''Debi's dead,'' she said again. ''You blame me.''

''I don't blame you any more than I blame myself.'' I couldn't lie to her. She may have been mad, but she wasn't stupid.

''Everyone blames me. Me and Tom. And you. People blame you, too, you know. My mother does.''

''Joyce,'' I said, bidding for time, not knowing what to say. ''Is that why you gave Tom an alibi for bombing our offices? Because you wanted to even the score with me?''

''Tom didn't bomb your office,'' she sneered. ''He wouldn't know the first thing about that. He beat up women. Women and children. One child. Our child.'' She laughed derisively and rolled her shoulders. ''He honestly believed because she was his child, he and only he had the right to prepare her for womanhood.'' She held the gun firmly between her two hands, but tears rolled down her cheeks.

''Joyce, it'll be okay.'' I held out my hand to her for the gun.

''No it won't. Nothing will ever be okay again. My baby's dead. I killed my husband. And you're standing there telling me everything's going to be okay? I don't think so.''

It was as if we were all moving in slow motion. I saw Joyce move the gun away from us and slowly open her mouth into an O. She turned the gun and started to bend her elbow, bringing the gun up to her mouth.

I was a good ten feet away from her, with a table between us, but I threw myself across the room. I would be goddamned if another Cullerson was going to take her life in front of me.

I couldn't feel or hear a thing. It was just me and my

objective. I slid across the table. Joyce squeezed her eyes shut. I reached up and missed. She missed her mouth with the gun muzzle because her eyes were shut. She opened her eyes, saw me less than a foot away, tried to step back, and bumped smack into Leslie, who was standing there wide-eyed with surprise and a smile still frozen in place. I saw Max's strong arms reach out beyond mine and grab the gun before Joyce could scream, "*STOP*!"

I let my body go limp on the table. I was seized with a shooting pain from the broken rib that was so intense I was seeing stars. Everything that had been on the table was on the floor, along with Joyce, who had fallen to her knees when Max grabbed the gun. She clung to his legs and cried. I looked up and saw Leslie, flowers in one hand, a bottle of champagne in the other.

"Hi, honey," I said with a grimace. "Welcome to the wonderful world of detecting."

By one o'clock everyone, except for Leslie, was gone. Joyce had been carted off to a hospital for observation. The police knew where to reach me and didn't insist I come to the precinct. They even humored Mrs. Jensen, who tried to have me arrested for stealing her yo-yo. Max was the last to leave and suggested I take the next day off.

"Thanks, Max, it's Saturday," I said as he waited for the elevator.

"Really? Then take the next two days off." He kissed both Leslie and me good night and left us to find what little peace we could.

I ached. From head to toe I felt as if someone had run over me with a steamroller.

When I closed and locked the door, I turned and found that Leslie had vanished. I turned off the lights as I worked my way through the apartment and found her in the bathroom, running a tub of hot water. The room smelled like eucalyptus.

"You saved a woman's life tonight," I said as I watched her cap the bath oil.

"Don't be silly. It was an accident."

"So is ninety-eight percent of our lives."

"You think?" She dimmed the bathroom light, pulled a pack of matches off a shelf, and lit three candles.

I shrugged. She was beautiful. And she was confusing me.

"So, what's up?" I asked as she began to unbutton my shirt, the same shirt that held Vanessa Stephen's check for two hundred thousand dollars. "Wait." I held up my hand. "Wait just three seconds."

I hurried as best as I could into the bedroom and called Vanessa's number. After the third ring her answering machine kicked in. "Vanessa. It's Sydney." I told her to meet me at seven-thirty the next morning in the lobby of the midtown hotel where her parents were staying. I didn't tell her why. I didn't tell her that it was her parents' hotel. "Be there, Vanessa."

By the time I returned to the bath, Leslie was luxuriating in the suds in the candlelight.

"See, I'm beginning to understand a few things," she said with her eyes closed.

"Oh yeah? Like what?" I pulled down the toilet seat cover and sat. Reaching my boots wasn't going to be easy, but it would certainly keep me occupied for a day or two.

"Like, nothing I say or do is going to change what you do for a living."

"True."

"Like if it wasn't for your being a detective, I never would have met you in the first place." She opened one eye, saw me struggling to reach my boot, and shut her eye again.

"True." I pushed the heel of one boot with the toe of the other and, though it hurt like hell, it slipped off easily. Ah-ha. Self-sufficient woman conquers all obstacles. "What else?"

"Like I can let you make your choices about your life, and I can make mine. Like if you decide after I've taken the time to draw a hot bath for you that you have to make a phone call—screw it—I'll take the bath."

"Good for you." Two boots off. Unzipping my pants was easy enough, and though getting my top off was painful, I accomplished the task. At the end all that remained were my socks. I looked at my feet, looked at Leslie in the tub built for two and made an executive decision.

The water was perfect, Leslie made room for me, and my socks got clean in the bargain. Ah, life. Dontcha love it?

Twenty-nine

We awoke to the nasty sound of some asshole sitting on my doorbell. It was six in the morning, and though I had set the alarm for only half an hour later, I was enraged that someone had stolen those thirty precious minutes.

"Who is it?" I yelled into the intercom. It was Lyle, and I was suddenly confronted with a whole new set of difficulties.

I knew I had left Leslie in bed, buried under a sea of flannel sheets, blanket, and comforter, but I also knew Leslie required little sleep and curiosity might propel her out of bed. Thankfully, she was still in bed when I slipped in and out to get my robe.

"Who is it?" she asked sleepily, poking her nose out from under the warm covers.

"No one, darling, go back to sleep." I hurried through the room. Maybe, just maybe, she'd sleep through his unannounced visit and I'd never have to introduce the yin to the yang.

I eased myself into a terry robe and padded back barefoot to the front door. I couldn't be bothered with slippers. My feet were going to be the end of me thanks to this stupid rib.

"Sydney, I'm sorry to wake you, I know you're pissed, but I had to see you before I left." This was said from behind three dozen red roses. He peeked out and smiled shyly. "Hey, you look like shit." He laughed gap-toothed as he handed me the flowers.

"Hey, you should talk." I said as I took them and stepped to the side so he could come in. Aside from a bump on his forehead and the one missing tooth, he actually looked none the worse for the wear. I, on the other hand, probably looked like one of those lava lamps in varying blob shades of red.

"So, I wanted to see you before we left." He followed me into the kitchen, where I found a vase for the roses, filled it with water, and put the flowers in it, paper and all.

"I'm glad you did." It was true. I hadn't seen him since the police station the night before, and Louise Long's insinuation that he would be out of work back in Texas had bothered me. "I saw Wallace and Louise last night."

"After Bartholomew's?"

"Yeah. They stopped by." I gestured to the room at large. A lot had happened in this room the night before.

"He's decided to give up politics." Lyle put his hands in his overcoat pockets and nodded.

"Is that what Louise meant when she said they wouldn't be needing your services after this trip?"

He nodded again. "It's just as well. I want to go back to teaching anyway. This gives me all the reason I need."

I nodded. "So, that's good."

"Yeah. It's really good."

"Good."

He took a deep breath. "Listen, something's been bugging me. You know yesterday when you told me about . . . well, you know, the other night, about how you wanted to be a completely different person?"

I nodded.

"I just had to tell you, you don't *need* to be anyone else. Apart from Marjorie—my wife—you're just about the strongest, kindest, sexiest woman I've ever known. And I'm honored to call you my friend. And I'm sorry you had to go through all that bullshit yesterday. If I hadn't been so stupid—"

I held my finger up to my lips and stopped him. ''You saved my life yesterday, Lyle. I'm really very touched you came here today. And for the flowers. Thank you.''

He shrugged. ''You're welcome.''

''What time's your flight?''

''Eight-thirty.''

''So what time are you all leaving for the airport?''

''We have a limo picking us up at seven-fifteen.''

''Seven-fifteen? *Shitshitshit.*''

''What is it? What's wrong?'' This was asked by Leslie, who was standing the kitchen doorway. I didn't know how long she'd been there or how much she had heard. Oh swell, just what I needed. Okay, it was ten after six. On a normal day I could shower and be out of the apartment in twenty-five minutes, but because of my rib I should add another fifteen, which brought me to ten of seven. A fifteen-, twenty-minute taxi ride to the hotel—it would be enough time. Barely.

''I have to get ready. No, wait—you have to stall them, Lyle.''

''Who?'' He asked.

''The *Longs*. I'll be there at seven-fifteen, but you can't let them leave before I get there.''

''What are you talking about?'' he asked, looking at Leslie as if she could explain my erratic behavior.

I started toward the doorway. ''Oh. Leslie, Lyle, Lyle, Leslie.'' I introduced them as I scurried as quickly as I could to the shower. ''Don't let the Longs leave before I see them, Lyle. It's important. Really, *really* important,'' I called out from the hallway.

I called Vanessa as the water was working its way to hot and picked out my clothes at the same time. Only tops I could slip into, boots I could slide on, socks—damn.

''Vanessa, it's Sydney, pick up. Pick up goddammit.'' Much to my surprise, she did. ''You have to be at the hotel at seven-fifteen. Don't be late.'' I hung up without waiting to hear her response. Why I was rushing around to reunite these people instead of going back to sleep like a sensible person was something I didn't even want to think about, but I was pretty sure it had a lot to do with my mom and dad and the way they raised me.

When I got out of the shower Leslie was lying in bed, a cup of coffee in one hand and a book in the other.

"Are you deliberately testing me?" she asked.

"No. I know this doesn't look good but this client, Vanessa?—you know Vanessa, you told her to call us—anyway, she and her parents have been separated for the last zillion years. Her brother was killed during her parents' visit here, and now she's their only child, and I thought it would be nice if they had a little family reunion before they left. I know it sounds crazy, it even sounds intrusive when I stop and think about it, but I know if it was me and I hadn't seen my folks, I'd want someone to try to make us act like adults. Life's too short."

"For what?"

"Don't you miss your dad?" I asked her as I sat on the side of the bed and painstakingly worked my way into a pair of jeans.

"Of course I do. I just wonder if you're doing this for them or you."

"If it works, does it matter?"

"But what if it doesn't?"

She had a point. I slipped into a bra and was grateful when Leslie did me up in the back. When she was done she wrapped her warm arms around me and hugged me gently.

"I like what you're doing, Sydney. It may not work, but at least you care enough to try."

"Thanks. I needed that." I nuzzled her neck. "I know I've been a jerk these past few days, but I promise to make it up to you."

"Really. How?" She released me and burrowed back under the covers.

"Don't you worry, I'll come up with something."

"I'm sure you will."

Putting on makeup was a joke. When I studied my face in the mirror I saw exactly what Lyle meant when he said I looked like shit. A little base, a little eye shadow, mascara. Blush. Oh dear, that didn't help at all.

When I was ready to go I stood at the foot of the bed and asked Leslie, "Do I look as bad as I think I do?"

She put down her book and said, "Yes. You look like a horse stepped on your face. Wear sunglasses and a scarf. Maybe no one will notice."

"Right. I should just wear my Nixon mask."

"It would be an improvement."

"I'll be right back." I blew her a kiss.

"Mm-hm. Give Lyle my love." She said this to my back as I was almost to the door. I didn't miss a step but felt my chest constrict. I had actually left Leslie and Lyle alone with three dozen roses when I went in to take my shower. Oh boy.

I got to the hotel at 7:18. Wallace was at the cashier's window and Louise was slowly walking with Lyle through the lobby to the exit. Lyle seemed relieved when he saw me.

"Mrs. Long," I said, not removing my dark sunglasses.

"Sydney? What are you doing here?"

I searched the lobby for Vanessa and checked my watch.

"Well, there were just some, ah, questions I forgot to ask last night," I said, stalling.

"Oh?" She brought her hand to her chest and pressed it against the sable coat she was wearing.

"Well, I forgot to, um, ask you about," I cleared my throat, trying to come up with something to ask her about, and then it hit me. "Art. I forgot to ask you about Art."

"What about him?" Her voice turned cold, and she visibly stiffened.

Louise blinked at me. I kept my eye on the front doors. I was surprised at how many people were up and about at seven on a Saturday morning. Then again, these are tourists, and New York is a big city to see.

Wallace joined us. "Sydney." He tucked his wallet into his jacket pocket. "What are you doing here?" he asked me but kept his eyes on Louise.

"She wants to know about Art," Louise told him.

"What about him?" Wallace was less affected by the

mention of the man who had murdered their son than Louise was. Then again, they had been friends for a long time.

''Ah, well, we had . . . um, we had a bombing at our office, and the person we had thought was responsible wasn't. I was wondering if you knew if Art had any knowledge of such things.'' Damn Vanessa, where the hell was she?

Wallace nodded and pushed his lips out. ''Art was in the military for years before he went into computer security. I wouldn't be surprised if he knew something about it.'' He slipped his hand through Louise's arm and nodded to the door. ''We have a plane to catch.''

''Ah, yes, I know.'' I put my hand on his arm to stop him. ''But, just one thing more.'' I paused.

He sighed. ''Yes?''

I strained to think of something, anything to keep them from leaving before Vanessa got there. ''The, um, death threats.'' Now what the hell was I going to say?

A deep sadness washed over Wallace's face. He shared a look of resignation with Louise and took a deep breath.

''Go ahead, dear. Tell her.''

Tell her what? I had asked it only to delay them.

''We found out last night that Art and Clifford had devised the death threats as a way of getting public sympathy. It was a stupid idea, but apparently Art was adamant and Clifford thought it would bring attention to our campaign.''

''Jeez, you know a lot of dumb, loyal men, don't you?''

Wallace almost smiled in response. ''Now we really must be going. Our flight's at eight-thirty.''

''Please . . . just . . . one more thing.'' Now that I was thinking about Art, I had a hatful of questions. ''I know this is hard, but, if Art was so loyal to you, how could he have made Peter's death look like a heroin overdose?'' I struggled to find the words to ask a most indelicate question, but I was determined to keep them there until Vanessa arrived. ''Given your stance on crime and the nature of Peter's . . ." I paused. "It would only hurt your campaign, wouldn't it?"

"The frightening thing is, he sincerely thought it would *help* it." Wallace took a deep breath and stared into the lobby. When he exhaled I could literally feel his exhaustion. "I don't know what it says about me that I hadn't recognized Art's . . . I don't know what you call it, illness? before now, but the fact is he had a lot of us fooled. You would think that it would be easy to spot someone who's crazy, but . . ." He let the thought slip away as he shook his head. Wallace glanced at his watch and said sharply, "Art said that he thought Peter's death—the nature of his death—would make me a sympathetic figure, which would make me more appealing to the public. Cliff said that after Peter died, Art was convinced the voters would be confident that I would be tougher on crime because I had been directly affected by it. The scary thing is, Cliff bought it. We all did."

The pain reflected in the faces of both Wallace and Louise Long was enough to keep me still. Vanessa wasn't here, and it was her loss. I tagged along behind them with Lyle at my side.

"I like Leslie. She's beautiful," Lyle told me.

"You sound surprised." I said.

"I guess I am. I mean, you're beautiful, but I didn't think two beautiful women would both be—you know—"

"Lesbians, I believe the word is." I was mad at Vanessa and taking it out on poor old Lyle by being abrupt.

As we stepped out into the cold, a driver jumped out of a waiting limousine and ran to open the door for the Longs. It was 7:28.

We stood in a semicircle, each of us obviously uncomfortable in the awkwardness of the moment.

"Well," I said scanning the streets, "I suppose this is it."

Louise smiled wanly and let herself be helped into the backseat of the limo. Wallace turned and gruffly said, "Well, good-bye, Sydney. I wish you the best." With that said he followed Louise and let the limo driver close the door behind him. Lyle opened the passenger side of the front seat and turned to me. He opened his arms to give me a hug, but my rib was too tender.

"I can't. It hurts," I said. He looked confused. "My rib. Art broke it."

"Oh man, I'm so sorry."

"It's okay, believe me. I'm just glad his gun jammed." I was still trying to stall, though I had given up hope Vanessa would come through.

"Well, thanks for everything, Sydney. This has been a real education."

Wallace rapped on the car window to tell Lyle time was up.

Lyle kissed my cheek and got into the car.

The limo driver started the engine and they started to pull out just as a taxi pulled in behind them. Vanessa called out, "Sydney! Sydney!" through the open window.

I banged the trunk of the limo, causing myself considerable pain. But the car stopped and the back door opened.

"What is it?" a chagrined Wallace Long asked.

"Please, just wait half a second. There's someone here who wants to see you." By the time he was standing beside me, Vanessa was out of the taxi and walking toward us saying, "What is it?" in the same chagrined tone as her father.

And then they saw one another. I wasn't sure if they were both going to bolt in different directions, so I took a step back and decided to let nature take its course now.

"Dad?" She sounded small.

"Paula." He stood there, bigger than life, his breath coming out in puffs against the cold.

"Paula?" Louise's voice came out like a squeak from the back of the car.

Vanessa turned at the sound of her mother's voice, but stayed rooted to where she stood. "I'm so sorry," she finally whispered. "Can you ever forgive me?"

Wallace Long opened his arms and his daughter fell into his embrace. "We've all made mistakes. It's time to move on."

By now Louise was out of the car, tears streaming

down her reddened cheeks. "Paula?" She seemed to shrink away instead of moving closer. Wallace released his hold of her and turned so Louise and Vanessa could see one another.

"Mom."

Ultimately the three of them bundled into the backseat of the limo with every intention of making their flight back to Texas. I figured if the limo driver was worth beans, he'd be able to make it to Kennedy Airport with seconds to spare. I handed Vanessa the check her father had given me the night before and hailed a taxi myself, telling the driver to take me to Broadway and Eighty-first, where I went to Zabar's and bought breakfast and lunch for two.

Leslie was still in bed upon my return. I dropped off the groceries in the kitchen and carried a separate bag with me into the bedroom.

"Hi there," she said as she laid down her book.

"Hi." I stood at the doorway, taking in the scene. The light was edging past the buildings across the street, casting laser beams of light throughout the room. Leslie looked deliciously comfortable propped up in the king-size bed with a blue cotton blanket peeking out from under the white comforter. All the signs of our life together were scattered around the room, creating a sense of well-being and safety.

"Success?" she asked.

I nodded.

"I didn't doubt you for a minute."

"Is that so?"

"Yes. I'm a firm believer if your heart's in the right place, you'll always win."

"I like that concept."

"I thought you would. You have a good heart. Gil called," she informed me. From the tone of her voice I could tell she expected I would leave her again and go traipsing out into the cold.

"Yeah?" I didn't move.

"Yes. He said to tell you"—she reached for a notepad next to the bed and read—"you were right about Kesslet—"

"Kessler."

"Kessler. Who's Kessler?" she asked.

"A nasty man who likes to beat up gay boys."

"Oh. Okay. Anyway, he said you'd probably want to know that he's been brought in for questioning for some murder. He didn't go into it. He said you could call him, and he'd give you the scoop."

"Good." I moved slowly into the room.

"So, have you thought of a way to make it up to me?" she asked coquettishly, looking at the bag in my hand.

"I did."

"How?"

"Mmm, I thought a little breakfast in bed—"

"And?"

"And a nap."

She made a face.

"And then lunch in bed." I was at the foot of the bed, moving to the side where she slept.

"Sounds messy."

"And I bought you a little present." I handed her the bag and sat gingerly beside her.

"I love presents."

"I'll make a note of that."

She puffed up the pillows behind her, situated herself, opened the bag and looked inside. "I don't get it." She said looking up disappointed. "It's a whisk."

"Ah, but it's a wooden whisk."

"Yeah?"

"Remember what you said to me the other day about living together?"

"Yeah." She reached in and pulled out the whisk.

"Well, initially I thought if we had any sense, we *wooden whisk* it. Get it? Get it?"

She rolled her eyes and tried not to smile. "That's really queer."

"Good. So am I."

"Me too."

"One more thing we have in common." I took her hand and kissed it.

"So what do you do with a wooden whisk?" she

asked, holding it in her free hand and studying it with great intensity.

I shrugged. "I reckon we should live together until we figure it out, okay? We're bright women. I give us about a month before we know what to do with it."

"I don't know, Sydney," she said skeptically. "These are very complex utensils. This could take us a long time. Are you prepared for that?"

"Let's put it this way—I'm willing to try."